KINGDOM OF

SONGS AND

CURSES

By

PAGAN ALEXANDRIA

Copyright © 2022 Pagan Malcolm
Printed by P. S. Malcolm
Kingdom of Songs and Curses
Cover design by Bianca Bordianu
ISBN: 978-0-9756203-5-9
Second Edition (Published 2024)

This is a work of fiction. Names, characters, businesses, places, events and incidents are either the products of the author's imagination or used in a fictitious manner. Any resemblance to actual persons, living or dead, or actual events is purely coincidental.

Find out more about the author and upcoming books online on Instagram: @PaganAlexandriaCreative

For all the Leif fans out there.

PROLOGUE

In her visions, she saw four crowns.

One copper, one silver, one gold, and one bornite. A crown for each territory, for each ruler.

They were always there, in the back of her mind, haunting her. Singing to her. Reminding her of the one thing that kept her sane. But with each day that passed, she ignored these crowns that beckoned. She felt the most ancient bindings of the Undersea. Felt the ocean thrum in her veins. Felt the promise of an ancient sea witch caress her skin and a curse that still lingered in the cool waters.

She saw past and present and future. She saw all possibilities.

But she was bound to a curse of her own—bound to this ethereal body, to do its bidding, to lend her being to the ocean's many wills.

And so she remained, she obeyed, she made bindings and cast curses. And memories of a life she'd once lived dawdled just out of reach, *just* under the surface—only ever sparked solid by glimpses of those from her past. Of the girl from above who had finally found her again.

The Reigning Queen. The one that would save her...

If only she could master the fourth and final crown.

PART ONE

CHAPTER ONE

Kendra

My heart was thundering in my chest as I stared out into the ocean, waiting for Coral's head to appear in the violent thrashing waves she'd left in her wake.

But she never surfaced.

The longer I stared, the louder my heart seemed to grow. Beside me, Matt called out for her, and Melody was on her knees a few feet away, staring dejectedly at the ground. But minutes passed, and Coral still didn't resurface.

Before I knew what I was doing, I was moving, ignoring Matt's cry of alarm. My feet hit the cool water, and I used all my adrenaline to push through the thrashing ocean waves until I was far enough to dive. Salt water washed over my head as I plunged down toward the sandy floor, scanning the space around me, trying to catch sight of a body.

My heartbeat was like a crescendo in my ears now—the only thing grounding me in my desperation as I resurfaced for a gulp of air, then went under again to keep searching. But despite the rays of sunlight beaming into the clear water before me, I couldn't see her at all.

No... she's not gone.

I couldn't register the thought that a current had swept her out to sea. She *had* to be here somewhere. I resurfaced again to take another breath, blinking away the stinging saltwater from my eyes, but before I could dive again, a hand circled around my waist, tugging me back.

I turned, and Matt was wading beside me in the water, his expression defeated.

"Kendra, she's gone."

"*No*," I growled, gritting my teeth. I tried to shake him off, but he moved his grip to my arm.

"We need to go back. Your father... he needs you."

At the thought of my dad's body lying on the shoreline, I released a heaving breath.

This wasn't happening.

My mother was long dead. My sister and dad were all I'd had, and now, both of them were gone in the same instant. And Melody...

I strained my neck, turning my gaze toward the shoreline, but the beach was empty. My heart skipped a beat—*Melody was gone too*.

"Where's Melody?" I demanded, kicking to stay afloat as rough waves thundered down on us, spraying us with water. Matt turned to follow my gaze. When he realized she was gone, he swore. Clearly, he hadn't intended for her to disappear.

"Come on." He grunted. "The last thing we need is for her to sneak up on us and drag us into one of these ocean currents."

He was right, so we swam back to the beach. As I stumbled onto the warm sand, the cold wind hit me instantly, making me shiver despite the warm day. I slowly walked up to my father's body and collapsed beside it, unable to hide the tremble of my lips as tears filled my eyes.

And then, like a dam that had burst, I was sobbing. I leaned over his body and clung to him, and I tried not to imagine my life without him and Coral. I didn't know how I was going to go on alone. How I was going to clean up the mess Melody had left behind.

Matt waited behind me, giving me space. He didn't speak; maybe it was because he didn't know what to say, or maybe he knew words weren't enough in this moment. But he let me grieve for what seemed like hours until finally, he cleared his throat and said, "I'm going to go and get your car so we can take him back to your house. We can't leave him here."

"What are we going to do with him?" I sniffled, my voice unsteady. Coral had said that everyone was under Melody's spell, so there would be no way to organize a funeral. And we couldn't just bury him without a casket... it didn't feel good enough...

"We'll figure it out once we've moved him. Where do you keep your keys?"

I told him they should be in a small bowl in our house's entryway, and he began to jog back up the beach toward the trail that Melody had chased us down only hours ago.

The sun was still shining down on me, and I could feel the heat burning the back of my neck now. But I didn't care—a numbness had spread through me, making the minutes seem like hours. I was in no rush for Matt to return because I had nowhere to go and nothing worth doing.

"Coral?"

A voice called from behind me, and I turned slowly. A figure had emerged from the waves, wearing a navy-blue uniform that was dripping with water. His hair was wet and

13

slicked back, glowing like a coppery-red beacon in the sunlight. He noticed my face and my layered short hair, and faltered.

"Oh... you must be her sister." He apologized. "I'm sorry... I don't recall your name."

It had been years since anyone had mistaken me for my twin, seeing as everyone on this island knew whom we were. I stared bluntly at the stranger, too caught up in my own feelings to process what was happening. Why did he care whom I was? Why was he searching for Coral?

Lost in my grief, I turned back to my father's body and ignored him. His heavy boots indicated his approach, but he came to stand on the other side of my father's body. There was a moment of pause.

"I'm very sorry for your loss," he said finally, his voice quiet. "Coral was desperate to save you both. She must be devastated."

"Coral's dead," I said quietly, the words floating in the air like a haunting echo as I finally met his gaze. The man paled, eyes widening with shock, but he quickly shook his head.

"That's impossible. The ocean would have responded in turn. She's connected to it now."

I frowned at him, a surge of anger sparking at his nonsense. "What are you talking about?"

He ran a hand through his hair, planting his other hand on his hip as he said, "Well, I felt a bond snap into place between her and King Lysander right after he sent me to check on her. She *must* be alive because that bond hasn't broken yet. The entire Undersea felt it. It's ancient magic that only spreads through the waters when a Reigning Queen steps into power."

14

I buried my head in my hands, trying to make sense of the information. *A Reigning Queen?*

Since I'd woken up, back in my house, I'd only been able to grasp bits and pieces of what was happening. I vaguely understood that Melody had been controlling everyone somehow... that she'd intended to kill our dad. And I'd *seen* Coral do something with the waves, twisting them like a funnel to throw Melody back to shore. And Melody had mentioned Lysander—Coral had been with him while I was asleep—but it still didn't make sense. Why *had* I been asleep for so long?

"Didn't she tell you anything?" The man faltered, gauging my reaction.

"There was no time to explain," I replied, but now my heart was racing again. If there was a possibility that Coral was still alive somehow... I needed to see her. I *needed* my sister.

Before the man could speak again, his gaze landed on something behind me. I turned and spotted Matt skidding down the sandy slope toward us. My car was parked as close as possible, near the palm trees along the road.

He noticed the man and slowed his pace. "Who's this?" he asked, shoulders tensing as he watched him warily.

I looked back at the man, waiting for an explanation.

"I'm Leif," he introduced, with a small smile. "King Lysander's army commander."

The tension left Matt's shoulders, but he shook his head in disbelief.

"Right. You're that Undersea being Coral told me about. She said you'd be nearby if we needed you. Guess she was wrong about that."

15

There was a bitterness to his words, and Matt massaged a gash on his upper arm for emphasis. When I turned back to Leif, he was frowning at both of us.

"My men *were* nearby and ready. Didn't they step in to help?"

I scoffed, earning a quick glance from him, and that was answer enough. Leif's gaze grew more urgent now. He began scanning the beach.

"What happened, precisely? Where did Coral go? And what happened to Melody?"

"If we knew, we wouldn't be sitting around here, would we?" I snapped back, and Leif seemed taken aback.

Matt walked over to stand beside me now, with a resigned expression. His ponytail had come undone in the fight, but now he was tying his locks back again into his usual style. He focused on Leif and said, "We can discuss all of this in a bit. But first, we need to move Mr. Klassan's body. Will you help us?"

Leif was glancing back at the waves now, eyes filled with worry, but he nodded after a moment. Matt lifted my dad's shoulders, Leif took his legs, and together, they heaved him toward the car. It was harder once we reached the slope, and they both grunted from the effort.

I could barely watch as they finally got my dad into the back seat of the car, limp and lifeless. Worse yet, he took up the entire space, so Leif had to sit in the back with Dad's legs over his lap. The car rumbled to life as Matt turned the key, which earned a yelp of surprise from Leif.

Matt drove us back to my house, which seemed too big and empty after everything that had happened. What had once felt like a familiar, safe space felt foreign as we drove through the tropical foliage and pulled up on the gravel right outside the front door. The two men worked to get my dad inside, with me holding the front door open for them, but instead of taking him upstairs, they took him to the sofa in the living room.

I sat on the bottom step of the staircase and waited, nervous energy building up inside of me. I needed to know what was happening. If I waited much longer, I might burst. In the moments that passed, I noticed how the house seemed neglected. Our potted geraniums were wilting in the foyer, and there was a thin layer of dust collecting on surfaces throughout the room.

Finally, Leif and Matt came back to find me, and Leif glanced at the two of us.

"So, tell me what happened." I met Matt's gaze and added, "Start from the *very* beginning. Whatever Coral told you, I want to know as well. I don't have a clue what's going on here."

So, Matt began by telling us how weeks ago, he and Coral went to Maya's grandmother to try to make contact with my mother's ghost; how they'd learned Melody was a siren; how I'd been poisoned by Melody, and my mother's necklace had put me into a deep sleep to protect me.

He explained how Coral had traveled to the Undersea to find answers and had discovered we were both of royal mermaid heritage—which took me a moment to process. He went on to say that King Lysander had needed Coral to break his curse, but he had chosen to let her go. Then Matt had stumbled across her on the beach, and they'd made a plan to break me free and save our dad... but the plan had failed.

17

And then he told Leif what we'd both seen—Coral controlling the waves and disappearing under them forever.

"So, Melody knew you were coming and cornered you both in the kitchen?" Leif pressed finally, turning back to me. I shook my head.

"I don't know—I'd only just woken up. Why wouldn't she have been in the house when we were there?"

"Well, the thing about Melody is that she doesn't just sit around doing nothing," Leif replied darkly. "And if she had the entire island under her control, I doubt she would have been lounging around an empty house waiting for Coral to just show up. No... this had some strategy to it."

I blinked.

"So... what are you saying?" I asked slowly.

"Well, I think Melody might have disarmed my men, for one. They *definitely* would have been at your side the moment Melody engaged in combat against you. I gave them direct orders."

An unsettling feeling came over me.

"So where is Coral now?" Matt asked, folding his arms. Leif pondered for a moment.

"It *sounds* like she unlocked her heart magic to defeat Melody, but that would require a transformation into her mermaid form. And if that's the case, then Coral hasn't come back to land because she *can't*. She's part of the Undersea now and bound to it forever."

I faltered.

"Bound to it?" I whispered. "What do you mean? Am I ever going to see her again?"

Leif bit his lip as he glanced between us.

18

"If you want to see her, I can take you to our kingdom... like we did with her. But I should warn you; it's dangerous down there right now. You're probably safer up here, where Melody can't hurt you anymore."

"Then let's go," Matt said determinedly, unfolding his arms. "I'm not staying here cleaning up after Melody. We need to know how to break her control over the townspeople, and Coral should have a say in what happens to her father too."

"Oh, the townspeople should be fine now," Leif replied. "If Coral truly bound Melody's magic, the spell she had over them would have broken instantly."

I exchanged a glance with Matt. Even if the townspeople had their freedom back, they would be confused. Weeks had passed, and there was no saying whether they had conscious recollection of how they'd spent that time. Someone should stay to let them know what had happened...

And it should be me, because I'm the only Klassan left, I realized. With Coral and my dad gone, the island resort, the residents, and all its duties fell to me. People would be knocking at our door for an explanation, only to find our home abandoned if I didn't stay. And I needed to deal with my dad's body.

That being said... I didn't *want* to. My sister was out there somewhere. She'd spent weeks trying to find a way to rescue us from Melody all by herself. She'd gone to this strange underwater world I'd yet to see for myself, and I'd never felt more disconnected from my twin in my entire life. I hadn't been there for her when she needed me...

But Coral was the one who cared about Dad's legacy the most. She would want me to stay here and take care of the resort, the residents, and make all the necessary arrangements... so I explained all of this to Matt and Leif.

Matt shook his head.

"There's got to be someone higher up that can deal with that. Leave them a letter or something," he insisted. There were definitely resort staff we could promote into management positions... but it didn't seem good enough to just leave a letter and hope someone would find it. Even a phone call wouldn't be enough time to properly explain the situation and make arrangements. And what state would my dad's body be in by the time someone came looking for us?

I was already overwhelmed just thinking about it. And quite honestly, I didn't care enough about Dad's legacy to prioritize cleaning up after Melody either.

One thing was clear though: this would be my one and only opportunity to go with Matt to the Undersea. Leif already seemed restless, shifting from one foot to the other—I doubted he'd make a second trip back for me.

My gaze flicked back and forth from Matt to Leif. In recent years, Coral had spent all her energy living for other people, acting like a martyr for my dad, for me, for Melody. She'd taken the Snack Shack job and never once shared with me what *she* wanted to spend her life doing.

But I wasn't my twin—I lived for *me*.

"We'll only be gone for a few days, won't we?" I asked, glancing toward the living room where my dad's body lay lifeless on the couch. I knew Coral would be pissed, but it would be fine to leave for just a *couple* of days... right? "I can't just leave my dad like that. His body will..."

I couldn't finish the sentence—I nearly gagged just thinking about it.

"You're right." Matt nodded slowly, grimacing. "We need like... a big freezer or something..."

"Or Kendra could just use that necklace around her neck," Leif pointed out, like it was obvious.

I frowned, looking down at the shell necklace that Coral and I had taken turns wearing—the same one that had put me into a sleep to protect me from Melody.

"It crystallized Kendra and kept her in perfect condition. It can do the same for your father until we return," Leif explained.

"But didn't it only work because Coral and I are mermaids?" I asked uncertainly. Leif smiled.

"Yes, but that doesn't mean you can't use it on other people. It contains your mother's heart magic—so *you* can guide the necklace's power and give it purpose."

I hesitated, twisting the shell necklace in my fingers.

"But... how?" I asked, my cheeks heating. I felt foolish asking. Leif waved me over to my father's body, and I followed. He indicated for me to remove the necklace and place it around my father's neck, so I did so as gently as I could.

Then he said, "Touch the necklace with your fingers, and think about what you want it to do. The heart magic that resides within it should follow your command."

I followed his instructions, only half believing this was going to work. As I pressed my fingers to the shell and thought about crystal encasing my dad, I felt stupid. Matt and Leif

21

were both watching in anticipation, and I wished they wouldn't.

But then, crystal burst to life from the necklace, wrapping itself around my dad rapidly, and I leaped back with a cry of shock. The crystal glowed blue and purple as it solidified, and just like that, my dad was in a crystal coffin.

"Well done," Leif commended, and I stared back at him with wide eyes.

"Did I really just do that?" I whispered, staring at my hands. Matt snorted.

"After seeing Coral whip up a tornado of ocean water, I'm surprised you have to ask," he replied, folding his arms. "And speaking of which, we should really get going. We need to find Coral and figure out what happened to Melody."

I nodded in agreement and got to my feet. The three of us headed for the back door so that we could make our way back down to the beach. My heart pounded as we navigated down the same sloping hill that Melody had chased Coral and I down just hours before. So much had changed in such a short amount of time, it felt like years ago already.

Once we reached the beach, I paused for a moment, letting Leif and Matt go on ahead of me as I took it all in.

This is it, I thought, staring at the rolling waves. With my dad dead and my sister trapped in the Undersea, it felt like nothing else mattered anymore. I didn't care about school or the few friends I had there. I didn't care about the stupid island resort or the residents.

I was a mermaid about to set foot in a magical underwater kingdom that, hours ago, I hadn't even known *existed*. I swallowed hard, anticipation building in my stomach, as I tried to imagine it. I didn't know what to expect, but it comforted me somewhat to be with Matt, who seemed a little more clued in on the whole situation. And knowing that I'd find Coral there helped too.

Leif directed us to wade into the waves, the sand and seaweed collecting around my feet as we followed him. When we were waist deep, he turned back to us and pulled two pearl bracelets from his pocket.

"Take these," he told us. "We're going to dive. And when we do, you need to put those on your wrists. You'll probably fall unconscious from the severity of how the enchantment affects your body... but it will keep you alive while we're in Veranis. I'll make sure you both get down there safely."

I hesitated at the thought of falling unconscious in the water. What if I drowned? I knew the whole point was to ensure I *didn't* drown as my body adjusted, but what if something went wrong?

I exchanged a glance with Matt, but he didn't seem fazed by Leif's words. Perhaps he'd already been through enough that he'd expected as much.

Leif nodded, then turned his back to us and made a clean dive under the waves. Inhaling deeply, I attempted to steel my nerves as Matt and I followed suit, and I immediately slipped the bracelet onto my wrist.

A strange sensation spread over my body, like a ripple passing through my body, and then heaviness pulled at my eyelids as my mind drifted away.

CHAPTER TWO

Coral

Pain was everywhere.

My entire body felt as if it were being stabbed by thousands of needles, and my legs felt heavy, like a weight dragging me down, down, *down* into the depths of the ocean. The salty ocean water burned as it shot up my lungs, stung my eyes, and washed over every inch of me. My hair tangled in the currents, blinding me as the water grew darker and darker.

My lungs were screaming. I couldn't breathe, and as much as I tried to fight the current, it kept tugging me under. Black spots formed in my vision, and I knew I was going to drown. There was no way I was getting out of it this time.

Perhaps it was my fate all along, I thought, as pain continued to ripple through every muscle in my body, and my lungs screamed for air. *I should have died that day, in the surfing competition. It was always going to come to this.*

As I continued to sink, it felt like I was drifting in and out of the ebbing darkness. There were moments of overwhelming, flashing pain—everywhere from my toes to my calves to my hips—and then there were moments where I couldn't remember anything, and I relished those moments. When my lungs couldn't take it anymore, I inhaled out of reflex, and water gushed through my lungs, adding to the heaviness.

And then a numbness spread through me, and I finally let go.

The first thing that tugged at my awareness was the sensation of hanging. Slowly, I opened my eyes. To my surprise, it was pleasantly warm, and I was breathing somehow. My sight was blurry at first, and I had to blink a few times to make out the crystal-clear water—which was now far easier to see in despite the darkness.

But when I tried to move, my muscles were stiff with protest. I craned my neck to see that one arm was tangled above me, the other below, in clumps of congested and heavily knotted seaweed. I must have drifted into it, but now I was caught like a spider in a web, hanging miles and miles above seafloor and wedged between two seamounts that made up a valley below.

It seemed that my dislocated shoulder had healed in the time I'd been out. I wasn't sure how, but I could wriggle without sending shooting pain through my body, which was a good sign at least. Yanking my wrists, I tried to get free, but there was too much seaweed holding me in place. I tried to kick my legs, but as my gaze followed the line of seaweed from my wrists and arms, down past my waist, my breath caught in my throat at the sight before me.

I didn't have legs anymore.

Instead, a golden tail was caught in the ribbons of seaweed. I stared at it for a moment, unable to comprehend what I was looking at.

I'd transformed.

25

And I'd lived.

And now I was a mermaid. *Forever.*

I couldn't go back to the surface. I couldn't see Kendra again, or Matt. I couldn't even bury my father—

My throat constricted, and I swallowed hard as all the memories flooded back to me. My dad dying, fighting and binding Melody, giving Lysander my heart...

I blinked hot tears away. I couldn't fall apart here.

Gritting my teeth, I focused on the seaweed again, looking around for a way to free myself. I wasn't close enough to either mountainside of bedrock to rub my wrists against them. As I yanked and tugged, I became more and more certain that I was too tangled to get free on my own. And when I tried to kick my tail, or even just wriggle it, it didn't move at all. It was like my brain had disconnected from any muscles and nerves below my waist.

I had no idea where in the Undersea I'd ended up, nor how anyone would ever find me. But just as I was starting to feel panicked, I heard voices and looked down.

Below me was a patrol of soldiers holding jellyfish lanterns and dressed in navy-blue uniforms. *Just like Leif's uniform.*

"Hey!" I shouted, struggling to get a better look at them, and they swung their lanterns upward to observe the source of the noise. "I'm up here!"

They took a moment to observe me, and then one of them yelled, "We've located the queen!"

They immediately began to scale the seaweed, swimming upward and using each stalk of seaweed like a guide. I breathed a sigh of relief as three of Leif's men finally reached me.

"Are you okay, Your Grace?" one of them asked me, clinging to the clumps of tangled seaweed for support as he kicked to stay afloat in the currents.

Your Grace?

"Why are you calling me that?" I asked, frowning.

The men exchanged glances with each other.

"Because of the new binding," a second replied slowly. "When you defeated Melody. You're the Queen of the Undersea."

I felt the blood drain from my face. *What?*

"I... I don't..." I stammered, as a million questions swarmed through me. What did they mean, *Queen of the Undersea*? The whole Undersea? As in all three kingdoms? Or more, perhaps?

I didn't understand how this had even come to pass—Lysander had never mentioned such a thing. And all I'd done was unlock my heart magic to transform into a mermaid.

That, and give Lysander your heart so he wouldn't be heartless forever, I thought. It had been a heat of the moment decision—I'd had to do it while I was human for it to be effective. After all that had happened between us, I couldn't just leave him with his curse... but I hadn't had time to think of the consequences either. Being trapped down here was just one of them, it seemed. And now, I was a queen?

I couldn't rule. I'd never even so much as managed Dad's resort—I didn't have the experience or knowledge... and these were people's livelihoods at stake. *I couldn't do this!*

"I need to speak to Lysander," I said finally, trying to keep my voice steady but failing. The third solider only nodded, showing no sign of noticing my fear.

"Don't stress, Your Grace, we'll get you down from here. Hold still."

Clinging to a stem of seaweed, he pulled out a dagger and began cutting through the strands binding me. I blinked for a moment, staring at the dagger as a murky detail nagged in the back of my mind, but the solider gave me a reassuring look and hummed softly at me, like he was comforting me. I didn't have time to ponder any of it as the restraints loosened, and I dropped suddenly. But the other two guards were there to catch me, and they guided me back down to the seafloor. My cheeks heated with embarrassment as I clung to them for support, my tail still not responding when I tried to use it.

"Sorry," I blurted finally, stumbling as my tail scraped against the floor. I felt pain singe through the delicate scales, and relief flooded through me. Even if I didn't have a handle on kicking yet, at least I could feel my tail, and the connection was already stirring something in my brain.

"Why don't you ride with me, Your Grace?" the first solider suggested. I nodded, grateful as he climbed atop his seahorse and offered me his sturdy arm. I pulled myself up to sit behind him, the seahorse's skeleton body against the scales on my backside, and the party of men began to make its way along the winding bedrock roads through the dark valley.

I took a moment to get familiar with my new body. When I felt along my neck, I discovered gills—so delicate and concealed that I might have missed them had I not felt the constant ebb and flow of water around that area. And my fingers

28

were slightly webbed now if I looked closely. Even my nails seemed sharper.

"Where are we?" I asked finally, looking around as we rode, and the solider chuckled.

"You're not far from Seer's Peak—you sank a long way from land, actually. It's my fault we didn't reach you in time... I do hope you can forgive me."

Lysander had promised that Leif's men would be nearby if I needed them while facing Melody. But it didn't matter—they were here now, and I told him as much. If I was going to be a queen, I wasn't about to start my rule acting cruel and heartless when someone made a mistake.

We traveled for a little while longer through the valley, and I tried to keep my eyes peeled for familiar sights. But I'd only traveled this particular road once, and it was all too vague. Hours and hours passed, and I tried to recall how close Seer's Peak was to Veranis. Surely, it wouldn't be much farther?

Finally, a familiar sight came into view... but it caused dread to coil in my stomach. My gaze landed on pointy red spires, circling sharks, and towering walls in the distance.

Coronis.

We were going the wrong way.

The solider in front of me must have felt me tense up because he clicked once, and the seahorse began to bob faster—a gallop.

Eyes widening with panic, I glanced around, but the large party of soldiers had closed in around me, blocking any means of escape.

Why were they taking me to Coronis? These were Leif's men... right?

Unless they weren't.

Why hadn't Leif's men come to my aid earlier? How long had it taken for me to transform and sink to the bottom of the sea? How many days had I been missing?

Something wasn't right, and my gut was telling me to get out of there immediately, even if my heart wasn't glowing to indicate danger. Was that only a protective measure that worked in my human form?

I looked up, and resolve settled in my stomach. Concentrating hard, I kicked off the seahorse with all my might. I shot up into the current, soaring through the waters, and glided for a moment. But when I tried to kick my tail again, it was delayed, and I began to sink, losing momentum.

Then an arrow pierced through my tail, sparking a sharp pain, and I cried out. Two more struck, embedding deep, and I was hurdling for the bedrock floor again. I slammed into the hard surface, skinning my arms as I slid, and the heavy sound of footsteps surrounded me. Two soldiers grabbed my now grazed arms, yanking me upright, and clamped a set of iron cuffs on my wrists, forcing my hands behind my back. The cuffs dug tight against my wounds, making me hiss, and the iron rendered my mermaid magic useless—not that I'd learned how to use any of it yet.

I looked up to see the first solider—the one I'd trusted and rode with—approaching me. He was shaking his head and tutting at me.

"Pity. I was hoping you wouldn't figure it out until we got much closer. But it seems our Reigning Queen isn't as familiar with her subjects as she should be," he taunted, flashing his razor-sharp teeth at me.

They were sirens, I realized, and it was like a glamour had been wiped from all of them. They must have used siren song on me, without me realizing. And that's why they had the daggers—a siren's preferred weapon. I glanced down and noticed that their uniforms remained the same. Leif's party must have been attacked, and that's why they hadn't found me sooner.

"Take her to the gates. She'll be dealt with there," the solider said, eyes gleaming as he watched his men drag me toward Coronis. I squirmed, trying to break free of the bonds, trying with all my might to gain control of my tail... but it flapped weakly and helplessly, stinging as the hard ground chafed against it.

Was it true that I was the Undersea queen then, or had they just said that to distract me? And if it was true, had I *really* been captured in my first few hours of stepping into the role? I couldn't help it as shame flooded my cheeks. I already felt like an impostor, unworthy of the title, and this just confirmed it.

We were almost at the gates when a familiar sight greeted my eyes. Melody was standing there, arms folded and waiting, in a regal gown of beige. She had a cold, vengeful look in her eyes, but I noticed her skin had lost its luminous glow, her bouncy hair was duller, and her shapely figure was thinner. When I'd bound her magic, I must have also bound all the aspects of it that enhanced her siren attractiveness.

"So, you've found the little *queen*," she seethed, eyeing me with amusement like the whole concept was a joke. My cheeks turned a deeper shade of red, and my fists trembled from where they were bound as I stared down the female who killed my dad.

The soldiers threw me to the ground before her, scraping my chin. I wriggled, lifting my chin indignantly. The sight of her still made my blood boil, and I remembered my dad's eyes going lifeless as I drove my dagger into his chest. As he fell to the ground, dead.

All because she'd used her siren song on me.

My chest ached remembering it—remembering that *I'd* delivered the killing blow—so I tried to focus on my burning resentment toward this female. After all, none of this would have happened if she hadn't commanded it, if she hadn't weaseled her way into our lives and torn our family apart from the inside out.

"Bring her then," Melody purred, a sadistic smile appearing on her lips. "Our new king wishes to extend his formal congratulations."

CHAPTER THREE

Coral

The soldiers dragged me through the icy streets of Coronis, where sirens watched from the sidelines and jeered. We passed through the market square and continued down a labyrinth of roads that snaked through fancy private estates. I couldn't help feeling like Melody was taking the long route just to drag out my humiliation and put on a show for her kingdom.

I tried to keep my head down, but the onlookers kept calling for my attention, or throwing rocks and litter at me. The harsh ocean currents stalled the momentum and impact a little, but I was covered in bruises before long. My teeth ached from gritting them—I wanted to retaliate, but what good would it do? It was better to put up a strong, unbothered front—at least right now. And especially when I didn't know how to address these people... weren't they technically *my* people? What did it even mean to be the Queen of the Undersea? What responsibilities did that give me? And was there still a need for rulers in other kingdoms?

I assumed yes because clearly, Coronis had a new king I was being dragged to now that Melody was powerless and had lost her title. I didn't know what the hell was going on, why I'd been brought here, or what rights I truly had over the people of Coronis.

33

What I *did* know, however, was that Melody was furious with me. And I had no doubt that if she wasn't bound against doing harm, she would kill me instantly. I sure hoped she didn't find a loophole to my binding while I was under her captivity.

As the moments dragged on, I wished Lysander was here to fill in the gaps, to tell me what to say and how to act. I didn't have any experience ruling, and he'd never said a *single* thing about Undersea queens or what they even did and had jurisdiction over. Any hints at all would have been nice.

Eventually, the streets started to thin, and we reached a set of stairs leading up to the towering castle. Its bloodstone edges were razor sharp, and every roof was adorned with a deadly spire. The entire building was a death trap, and I didn't want to know what it was like on the inside. But that was exactly where we were headed.

Every step knocked my tail so hard that I knew it would be black and bruised by the time we reached the top. Meanwhile, Melody climbed each step gracefully, holding herself poised and perfectly as she led the way. We finally reached the top, and a set of obsidian doors swung open, casting shadows into an already dimly lit foyer. Red crystals grew along the palace walls and roof, lighting our way as I was marched through the cold palace toward a second set of doors. When they opened, they revealed a throne room.

This room was somehow worse—the interior walls made of sharp, jagged onyx, and if I wasn't mistaken, there was dark-red blood coating the tips of the spikes... like prisoners and wrongdoers had been impaled on them many times before. The floor was polished sunstone, and there was a rounded glass ceiling in the roof that revealed the circling sharks and other predators guarding the palace.

As I quickly scanned the room, I noticed guards in every archway, with daggers at their waists. On the wall ahead was a row of severed heads—preserved by some kind of magic and hanging proudly. And lounging on a red coral throne was none other than Eugene Pryor—Melody's brother—whose lips curved upward at the sight of me, to reveal a row of razor-sharp teeth. I noticed the golden crown on his head, and my stomach turned.

So, Eugene was the new king of Coronis? But I didn't think Coronis *had* male rulers...

"The Queen of the Undersea joins us!" Eugene sang joyously, flicking a ring on his finger with his thumb as he studied me. "I've been *most* eager to have your company."

"I don't share the sentiment," I shot back, as the soldiers forced my tail to bend before him. I resisted every inch of the way down, and Eugene smirked as he got to his feet.

"Oh dear, *Your Grace*, don't be so quick to write me off," he chided, taking a few steps toward me. "I sent for you myself, you know. I wanted to extend my congratulations to your bold new title... *and* my thanks."

I held his gaze, trying not to reveal the question in my eyes, but he must have known I was thinking it because he continued with a wave of his hand.

"Thanks to you, I am the new king of Coronis. And there has never been a single king of Coronis in all of existence, so really... you're already making history."

He winked, and my stomach rolled. I wondered if that was why the entire kingdom of Coronis had come to jeer at me as I was dragged through the streets. Lysander had told me that Coronis was a kingdom where females had all the power. So of course, a male king would disrupt the order of things. Were they angry with me for causing this turn of events?

"Seeing as you helped me, I think it's only fair that I help you," Eugene added leisurely, clasping his hands behind his back as if making polite conversation. "So, tell me, Coral... what can I do for you in return?"

I didn't have any intention of making negotiations with Eugene, especially since I was clearly his prisoner and didn't want to give him more leverage. But all the same, a dozen different requests ran through my mind—and I entertained each one mentally. It would be helpful to learn how to use this stupid, useless tail that didn't want to respond to me. It would also be ideal for him to just let me go so I could get back to Lysander, but that seemed unlikely to happen. Still, the thing I desired most came to mind when my gaze fell upon Melody, and I narrowed my eyes.

"My father is dead because of you," I seethed at her. Turning to Eugene, I stated, "You could serve her a death sentence, and that would be a great start."

Nothing would be right until it was done. Nothing would ever come close to justice for what she'd done to our family. All those months of manipulation, all those *years* of biding her time... It wasn't even just my father—my *mother* was dead because of her too! Because she'd *known*, and she'd tried to protect Kendra and I from Melody's cruel hands.

I'd do it myself... but the thought of killing someone, even Melody... I didn't know if I could bring myself to do it again. My soul already felt tarnished after what I'd done to my dad.

"Now, now, Coral, *within reason*," chided Eugene, and I snorted.

"You asked me what I want? *That's* what I want. Are you the kind of king that sticks to your promises, Eugene?"

He scowled, and I sneered back. But I knew he wouldn't kill his own sister—this conversation was going nowhere.

"How about this?" he suggested finally, beginning to circle me as he spoke. "I won't kill you, even though you're a threat to my kingdom and my rule. And while you remain a guest in my palace, you will have the finest quarters to accommodate you. *And*—"

He paused, meeting my gaze as I simmered back at him.

"I will call a temporary truce with Veranis *and* Atlantis, so long as both King Lysander and King Malvin agree to my terms. Which means you don't have to lead an impossible charge against my people to free the mermaids and restore Atlantis to its former glory."

No way. All of that was too good to be true. What did Eugene get out of it? And why did he want to involve Lysander? Why give me *anything* at all when I was already in iron cuffs at his feet?

"If you call a truce with Atlantis, that means you have to free the mermaids immediately," I reminded him, trying to figure out his underlying intentions. I straightened my back, craning my head to watch his movements, and he laughed from behind me as he walked.

"Well, let's not get ahead of ourselves—"

"It's not a truce if you don't," I insisted, and he came fully into view again as he finished his first lap around me.

37

"Well," he huffed, running a lazy hand through his blond hair, "I'm sure we'll work something out once Lysander agrees to my terms."

A feeling of unease developed in my stomach... what if his terms hurt Lysander? Or put him in a position where he had to make an impossible choice?

"What terms?"

He eyed Melody with a smug expression, folding his arms.

"Well, I can't go giving all my secrets away, can I? Didn't you ever learn how to negotiate properly before you decided to go and become Queen of the Undersea?"

"I *didn't* choose to—"

"Hush now," he cut in, and one of the soldiers pressed a firm hand to my shoulders to force me lower to the ground again, in a submissive position. I kept my eyes locked with his, despite the awkward and uncomfortable angle of my neck.

This deal... it meant I'd be kept here, in the Cora Palace, for at *least* a little while. And I still didn't know *why* Eugene wanted me here... unless it was by Melody's request, which would make more sense. But I had to assume that there was something about this arrangement he wasn't telling me... something bad.

However, if I refused, it would be selfish. This was the easiest way to cease war between both kingdoms without any more bloodshed. It would free the mermaids, which is something I already committed myself to doing, and I wasn't about to turn my back on them now. Maybe there was another way to get to these desired outcomes... but we would need a bigger army and more time... and it seemed foolish to send more men to their deaths when Eugene was offering all of this to me on a silver platter.

This deal might not benefit me, but if I was truly Queen of the Undersea, then wasn't it my job to ensure the well-being of *all* its inhabitants? Why put myself through fighting and send more men to their death when this option was available to me? Maybe it wouldn't hurt to accept his terms for now until I figured out another way out of here...

"You would really draw up treaties with both kingdoms and free all the mermaids in return for my compliance?" I asked finally, raising a tentative eyebrow. I had to make sure agreeing to this deal—even if temporarily—was the best course of action for everyone.

Eugene was silent for a moment, then strode forward until he stood a foot away from my craned neck. He knelt down and tilted my chin upward with his slender finger.

"I will draw up the treaties immediately. But I will only free a mermaid for every year that you remain my prisoner."

My stomach dropped—I'd expected *immediate* release of all mermaids. I thought I'd only be in here for a few days. Perhaps a week, if it came to that. But *years*? I'd thought spending my life in the Veranis dungeons was bad. This would be far, *far* worse.

I'd never see Lysander or Leif or anybody I cared about again. And I'd never be able to sleep so long as Melody was under the same roof as me.

"No," I said plainly—I'd rather fight my way out and bring back armies if those were his terms. "Besides, I won't live long enough for you to free all of them." My throat ached as he held my chin up.

"Well then, I guess you'll have to have offspring," he purred, a wicked smile growing across his face, and my stomach rolled with nausea at the thought. He let me go suddenly, and my head snapped back down, relieving the aching pressure.

"I said no," I repeated, my gaze following him, and I tugged on the iron cuffs as panic started to claw through me. "You either release the mermaids immediately, or we have no deal. Without a treaty, Lysander will tear your entire kingdom apart looking for me!"

He smirked.

"The undine king is a fool, but he's not dumb enough to bring his armies to Coronis. Don't you think he, or even his father, would have tried that years ago if they were in any position to do so?"

I faltered and slowly realized he was right. Lysander might be obsessive, but I remembered King Conrad saying as much about their standing with Coronis. Even Leif had been hesitant to challenge Coronis soldiers, knowing Veranis was already outnumbered.

If I didn't take this deal as it stood, I'd have to fight out of here on my own, with an injured, unresponsive tail. And though I was prepared to try... the odds didn't seem to be in my favor. If I took the deal... at least I'd have done *something* for my people—for the mermaids.

Eugene came to stand beside Melody, and I watched as he exchanged low words with her.

"Dear sister, I must commend you for finding her," he said, and I was only just able to overhear them. "You'll make a fine adviser at my side with all your experience and knowledge. There is nobody I would rather employ," he added, and if Melody was pleased by this turn of events, I couldn't tell. Her expression had remained bitter since the moment we'd arrived.

"Then might I propose that we forget this nonsense and dispose of our new queen before she causes any more trouble?" Melody replied stiffly, folding her arms. "She has already bound my magic and sabotaged my chances of becoming a Reigning Queen. That was a plan nearly twenty years in the making!"

Hmm. So Melody *didn't* want me kept here, after all? Which meant this deal *purely* served Eugene somehow...

"I'm afraid not," Eugene replied, his gaze turning back to me, and Melody pursed her lips unhappily. "You see, I have quite a few uses for our little queen yet. You know the power of a mer-heart... and one like *hers* would do us many favors indeed."

Realization slowly washed over me, and a pit of horror formed in my gut. I'd forgotten how valued mer-hearts were among sirens. Of *course* Eugene would be wanting mine. The last time we'd met, he'd intended to deliver my heart as a wedding gift to Melody.

Eugene then snapped his fingers. The soldiers at my side pulled me upward so I was hanging limp once more. I tried once more to kick my tail, but it was useless. I'd never wished more for my legs in my entire life, and I would never see them again.

"Last chance to take the deal, little mermaid," he said with a cruel grin, and my mind raced as I thought it over once

41

more. I was going to be trapped here anyway... the only question was whether any good might come of it for the mermaids.

But if I took the deal... Lysander wouldn't be able to come free me without breaking the treaty. Which meant if I didn't succeed in getting myself out of here... I was going to die here.

"I... agree," I said finally, my voice small as I felt a vow lock into place in the water around me. I couldn't be selfish when taking this deal meant Atlantis would finally be free of war... that my grandfather and all the remaining mermaids could come out of hiding. And each year that I failed to escape would at least mean a mermaid went free. I tried not to resent my choice.

"I knew you'd come around," Eugene purred, his eyes glinting with smugness. "And now that I *truly* have you in my captivity, we can get down to business."

He marched toward a door on the right side of the throne, Melody following and the soldiers dragging me after them. At first, I thought we were heading to a dungeon, but then they steered me through a set of double doors and down a narrow corridor. At the very end was a door leading outside.

"Where are we going?" I demanded, struggling against their sturdy grips as my heart began to race. I imagined all the terrible things they planned to do with me. How was I going to endure years of my life in this palace?

Furthermore, how was I going to get out with so many guards and my useless tail?

We reached the set of glass doors leading out to a balcony, which Eugene threw open vigorously. As he circled the balcony, arms raised proudly, I heard the echoing chorus of *boos* and protests from below. At first, I thought they were for me,

42

and the shame creeped back through me at the thought of being paraded around like this. But as I was made to kneel at the edge of the platform, I realized the attention of the crowd was directed toward Eugene, while the majority of the onlookers ignored me entirely.

Deciding this was an advantage, I studied the balcony—it had no railing, and while it wasn't an ideal drop from here into the claws and teeth of hundreds of sirens, it might be my one chance of escape. If I could escape, it wouldn't matter what vows I'd made to Eugene—I would lead an army into Coronis myself to free the damn mermaids.

But before I could shuffle closer to the edge, the guards around me disconnected my wrists from where they connected behind my back and clamped a set of iron chains to my wrist cuffs instead. Now I was bound to the floor where the chains were firmly embedded—and I knew I wouldn't be able to jump if I wanted to.

Eugene stood behind me, as if presenting a prize to the crowd, but they didn't seem to care. They continued to shout curses at Eugene and scream in protest against their new male ruler.

Unable to help myself, I glanced over my shoulder at Eugene and gave him a pitying look.

"Looks like your subjects don't think much of you," I drawled, raising my eyebrows at him. His eyes gleamed with hunger as he stood closer to me and leaned down to whisper in my ear.

"Oh, they will. When I'm done making an example of you, they won't think twice about bowing down to me." His breath on my ear made me shiver repulsively, and Eugene stepped forward to address the crowd.

"People of Coronis," he began over the noise, which didn't die down as he spoke. "I know you are confused and upset. Your way of life has been threatened. The many rules and ways of being you are accustomed to have been challenged. But let me assure you that the Undersea has *chosen* me to be your ruler. It would not have done so had the choice not been fair and just."

The crowd was beginning to quiet now as he continued his speech. His hand went to his crown, and he removed it, showing it to the people before us.

"In all of existence, there has never been a king of Coronis. And yet, I have been chosen to rule over you by the Undersea itself. I would not be able to wear this crown if it was not the will of its ancient ways." He glanced down at me, that gleam still in his eyes, as he said, "And I will prove it to you."

He slowly walked around my kneeling body until he was directly behind me, and I couldn't see what he was doing. My heart thudded with the anxiety of not knowing, terrified to be presented in front of all these people.

"I have here the Queen of the Undersea," he said softly. "And we all know that when such a rare queen comes about, she makes ruling decisions that impact *all* of our kingdoms. She is the most powerful ruler in existence—a female to be feared."

He chuckled at his own words.

"And yet, I have captured her. I have her in chains before you, and I know for a fact that she does *not* have rule over all of our territories. You see, ours is still the most powerful kingdom of all. Ours is the untouchable kingdom. And while I remain your king, your Reigning Queen cannot use her magic against any of us."

I felt something loom above me, and it vibrated from the proximity. I looked up to see Eugene holding the crown inches from my head.

Something told me I didn't want it to make contact. Not if that powerful vibration was any indicator.

"When a Queen of the Undersea has power over all four territories, she is also the master of all four territories. The kingdom in question bows to her... so long as she can wear its crown. But as you are about to see..."

Eugene placed the heavy crown on my head, and I felt a zap of power.

"She cannot handle the Coronis crown."

A sudden searing pain erupted in my temple and spread like fire over my skull, through my veins, and right down to the tips of my fingers and my tail. It felt like the currents of the ocean had turned on me, flooding through me, suffocating me, and I screamed.

It was like being drowned and buried all at once as currents of ancient magic latched onto me and started ripping me apart. Desperate, I began thrashing against the restraints, trying to reach the crown, but I couldn't. I could hear Eugene's terrible laughter and the crowd cheering vibrantly at the sight of their all-powerful king.

I screamed and screamed as the suffocating pressure built all around me. I toppled forward from exhaustion, the restraints catching me before I could hit the balcony floor, as the crown continued to drain me of all my magic, energy, and willpower. I was panting hard and my skin clammy with sweat by the time Eugene finally lifted the crown, and the unbearable pain finally ceased.

Every muscle in my body ached, and my vision swam. I didn't have the strength to sit up, but I stayed awake, refusing to let the lingering darkness on the edges of my vision whisk me away from this nightmare, even though it was tempting to allow myself to black out. But I would not pass out in front of all these people. They already thought I was weak for not handling the Coronis crown. Gritting my teeth, I held my head as high as I could. But their attitude had completely changed as they cheered on their king.

The king that had conquered me—even though I was supposed to be the most powerful queen. He was wearing the Coronis crown again, and it didn't affect him at all.

The crown of Coronis had not rejected Eugene. So *why* had it rejected me, the queen with ranks above him? Would other crowns reject me too? Was I even the queen they all claimed I was? I wished that I knew more about the role— wished that Lysander had told me *something* before I'd wound up a prisoner in Coronis.

I was still pondering each question as the guards unclasped me from the chains on the balcony and reclasped my hands behind my back. But as I watched the crowd turn their jeers to me, I felt a sudden surge of rage wash through me.

This might be my last chance to escape. I wasn't going to let them march me back inside. Not willingly, anyway. I kicked as hard as I could with my tail in a circular motion, and for once, my tail obeyed. One clean sweep knocked them all out from under their feet. I fell backward but kicked again, more determined this time to stay upright. My tail began to respond, thrashing desperately to get a handle on the currents of the water as I got the hang of staying afloat. It still throbbed from the spearheads wedged into it, but I ignored the pain.

The guards were drawing daggers now, but I let out a cry as I aimed my tail at Eugene's face. My tail collided with it, smacking him with the hardest kick of my life. And it was glorious, watching him recoil backward, blood spurting from his nose.

Except I rebounded off of him, straight into the hands of three ready guards who tackled me to the ground and pulled the tip of my tail back so that it was flush against my backside. I clenched my teeth, heart sinking, as I screamed and thrashed against them, panting furiously. They began to bind my tail with rope as I tried to kick them off. But they had me bound in seconds, and they proceeded to carry me into the palace by my arms, one guard at either side of me.

I turned my head, getting my last look at freedom as I stared longingly at the seamounts in the distance... in the direction of Veranis, where Lysander was undoubtedly waiting for me to return. Where he would soon learn what I'd done and realize he couldn't reach me. Before I knew it, the deafening echo of the palace doors closed behind me, and I was once again a prisoner in the Undersea.

CHAPTER FOUR

Lysander

It had been days since the two bonds had clicked into place—one that gave me my heart and broke my curse, the other that named Coral as the Reigning Queen of the Undersea. And despite all of that... there had been no sign of her or Leif, for that matter. Even Nerissa had been absent—she hadn't been heard from since she went with Leif's men on their scouting mission.

Still, I was doing my best to block out those thoughts, and I returned my attention to a book sprawled on my desk. Notes accompanied it, scattered around and drifting through the water, just within reach. My eyes had been scanning the same line of text over and over for hours, but the words weren't sinking in. I tried to read it again, but I could barely register what I was reading.

The book was from the library—an ancient tome detailing the rules of True Ruler magic. I'd borrowed it out the same day Coral had returned to the surface, determined to find a way to undo my father's binding against me so that I could restore Maya's soul. I'd wanted to surprise Coral by venturing there myself and doing the deed before she returned.

If she returned.

My stomach dropped at the thought. It had been lingering in the back of my mind as a possibility that maybe she'd find a way to stay with her sister and father. That given her new-found power, she wouldn't want me anymore. And as each

48

day passed, the thought ate away at me, smothering my optimism little by little.

It had taken a lot of trust to let her go... and I'd known when I had that she might not return. But I liked to think that we had something *real* forming between us, and if she'd chosen to give me her heart... didn't that mean she felt it too?

My thoughts lingered there for a moment before I snapped out of it. *Focus*, I told myself, shaking my head and returning to the page again. Regardless of whether Coral returned or not, I still had a duty to uphold. I owed it to Maya to help her. I began reading again... but made it halfway down before I found myself zoned out and distracted, and I cursed aloud. Shoving the book away, I rose and stepped back from my desk.

I paced the length of my study and found that I was unable to stop fidgeting. I'd never felt this way before—so restless and stressed, with tension weighing my shoulders and a sick feeling in my gut. The past few days had been a wave of emotions, one after the other, and each one more amplified than the last. It was like my body was no longer my own, my mind no longer a familiar place.

I was going *crazy*.

Finally, I tired of pacing and moved from my study to my attached bedroom, collapsing on the soft bed and placing my head in my hands. My entire *world* had fallen to pieces since she showed up in my life. I couldn't imagine losing her... and yet, I couldn't function without her. I couldn't keep going like this.

There was a knock at the door, and a messenger entered after a moment, stopping briefly to bow.

"Your Grace, the commander has returned. And he has brought humans with him."

I sprang to my feet immediately, frowning. *Humans?* Coral was no longer human, so I couldn't imagine whom else Leif might have brought down here. Unless Coral's family had decided to join her—

My heart lit up with delight. *Of course!* She had returned with her family. They would be *more* than welcome, of course, and we would be married and live happily—

"He's waiting in the throne room for you."

The tumbling thoughts instantly came to a halt, and I shook my head. I was getting ahead of myself. Straightening my jacket, I followed the messenger out of my room, down the staircase, and into the throne room, where Leif stood with his back to me. When I cleared my throat, he turned, and I noticed the heavy bags under his eyes. His hair was more ruffled than usual too.

Defeat settled in my gut when I realized he was alone and clearly troubled.

"Where's Coral?" I asked, scanning the room for her. He grimaced back at me, and my heart continued to sink in a way that was almost unbearable.

"It looks like Eugene Pryor got to her first," he confessed, and my mind went blank. "I found my men on our way back from land... they were dead, and their clothes were gone. I can only guess at what happened next, but..."

He trailed off, but I didn't need him to fill in the blanks. His words already sounded far away, like someone had covered my ears and muffled his voice. A surge of panic and anger flared through me, and Leif tensed at the sight of me. I

50

struggled as my cheeks heated. My hands clenched, and suddenly, I'd pulled my spear from behind my back.

My eyes landed on a pot of seagrass across the room, and with a yell, I threw the spear. It sailed clean through the pot and shattered it before embedding itself into the wall, wobbling there for a moment.

Breathing heavily, I turned back to Leif, who had already moved into a defensive position, one hand raised and the other clutching his own spear. His eyes were wide with horror.

Guilt instantly washed through me, and I staggered back, taking a shuddered breath.

"I—I apologize," I muttered finally, shaking my head. "These new emotions have been... an adjustment."

It was the wrong reaction. Leif's men had died—*our men*. And Nerissa... she'd been with them. Was she dead too? But despite those facts, I couldn't stop imagining what was happening to Coral.

Leif tentatively approached me, sheathing his spear but letting his hand linger on the hilt.

"We will get her back," he promised. "But first, we have to confirm that's what's really happened and figure out where he's keeping her."

I backed right up to the wall near the entry doors and sank down against it, feeling an overwhelming pressure settle around me at the answer I didn't want to hear. I couldn't help the bubbling annoyance that built up inside of me. It was taking all of my restraint not to run out the door, cross the Undersea, and start banging at the gates of Coronis for answers.

I could feel Leif's presence—feel his calming energy. But chaos was swirling inside of me... I couldn't handle his sympathy, couldn't handle how small and pathetic it made me feel.

"The messenger said you brought humans with you?" I pressed finally, desperate to pivot the focus off of me.

"Yes—her sister and her friend are asleep upstairs, recovering from their journey down. I don't think they will be awake for a few hours yet."

My eyes widened with hope, but Leif shook his head.

"They know nothing—trust me, I already asked. They came with me in hopes that we could all find Coral together."

My heart deflated once more, and this time, the disappointment was overwhelming. A surge of anger surfaced, and before I could stop myself, the words were tumbling from my mouth.

"This is the second time your men have failed us," I reminded him, my voice laced with frustration. The first time had been during our journey to Atlantis, costing us our cover while we were passing through enemy territory. "If you can't find better men for these situations, I'll have to find someone who can."

Leif's expression paled again, and he looked like he wanted to protest, but his eyes fell on the crown on my head, and he hesitated. Finally, he responded stiffly.

"I understand your concern, Lysander. We were already short on our best men before your father passed... I'll see to it that new men are trained immediately."

I grunted, and he had the sense to bow and walk away, leaving me to wallow in my own mess of emotions.

As soon as he was gone, I felt immediate regret for my words. Leif's priority had been keeping myself and Coral safe these past few weeks... he hadn't had the time to spend training and overseeing his men. And my father had been using them too, sending them on patrols and scouting while Melody posed a threat.

Letting out a steady breath, I got to my feet once more. I hated this helpless feeling that kept plaguing me, and despite Leif's insistence that Coral's sister knew nothing, I couldn't help thinking about her, asleep upstairs in one of the guest rooms.

I wouldn't disturb her. But even though she didn't know where Coral was... she was the closest thing to Coral I had access to. Perhaps just *talking* to her would ease the ache in my heart, even a little bit.

CHAPTER FIVE

Kendra

Groggily, I came to and blinked a few times to clear my vision.

I was lying on my side, on some kind of soft bed, and the very first thing I saw were towering windows with schools of vibrant rainbow fish swimming by.

Eyes widening, I slowly sat up on the bed and stared at the scene. I could barely recall the events that had led me here. I vaguely remembered following Leif into the ocean, slipping on the pearl bracelet... and now I was here.

It felt like a dream. I looked down at my wrist and saw the pearl bracelet seated perfectly there. *Not a dream then...*

Swinging my legs off the bed, I rose and made my way over to the windows. As I approached, more revealed itself to me. There were sprawling coral gardens in all shades of red and yellow and pink swaying in the current, perfectly paved bedrock paths that formed a courtyard, and braided seaweed that created a waving garden wall. I let out a small laugh of delight, hands pressed against the glass.

It was *beautiful*. Better than anything I'd seen in my textbooks. I was eager to get a closer look at all the fish and the species of plants.

But reality made me turn around and face the room I was standing in. Crystals grew along the ceiling, lighting the space and providing a strange heat that battled away the icy chill of the water. An extravagant bed was centered in the room, the bed frame also made of coral, and a wardrobe stood proudly across the room, along with a comfortable-looking chair and a side table.

I couldn't believe this was real. The *Undersea* was real, and I was standing in it, *breathing* in it...

There was a knock at the door, and a lady entered. She had long black hair and wore a navy gown—the same shade as Leif's uniform.

"Good evening, my lady," she greeted with a small curtsy. "My name is Rue, and I'll be looking after you. Dinner will be served shortly, but first, I must prepare you to dine with the king—he wishes to speak to you and your friend about your sister."

I looked down at my pink gown—the one I'd worn at Melody's dinner party weeks ago. So much had happened that I'd never had a chance to change out of it.

Rue caught my gaze and gestured toward the wardrobe.

"Don't worry—I'll help find something more appropriate for you."

An hour later, Rue had fitted me into a long off-shoulder gown that shimmered between blue and gold hues. Beaded threads trailed from my waist down to my ankles, giving the gown a dazzling effect whenever I spun in it.

I felt like a princess... and that's when I remembered that I *was*. It still hadn't quite sunk in that Coral and I were both royalty... that our mother had been the heir to the Atlantis

55

throne—the mermaid kingdom. But standing here in this dress, it finally *felt* real, and it hit me so suddenly that I nearly had to sit down.

I managed to stay standing as Rue gestured toward the door, and with one final look at myself, I followed her downstairs.

Matt was waiting for us at the foot of the stairs, also dressed in new clothes. He wore a simple white button-up shirt with a beaded blue jacket and matching pants. His eyes seemed to brighten at the sight of me, and I felt the same—it was nice to have a familiar face around, even if I didn't know Matt as well as Coral did.

Following Rue, we pushed through a set of tall doors and into the dining room, where a long table greeted us, piled with strange dishes. I spotted seaweed in fancy arrangements, caviar, raw fish, and even some crab. I knew I wouldn't be touching any of the seafood, but scattered throughout were bowls of red berries that made my mouth water on sight.

Having delivered us successfully to dinner, Rue excused herself, and my gaze trailed her as she left through a side door. That's when I spotted a familiar man standing at the end of the table. He stood tall, with wavy black hair and sea-green eyes which were already locked onto me.

Lysander—the man who came to our house to return Coral's surfboard. My gaze flicked up to his bornite crown, and I remembered that he was a king down here—*the* king we were supposed to be dining with.

Footsteps sounded behind us, and I turned to see Leif approaching. He offered us a kind smile.

"How are you both feeling?" he asked us, as we lingered in the doorway.

"Um... refreshed, I suppose," I said, glancing at Matt. It was still so surreal to be down here, to wrap our heads around it all. I couldn't accurately describe how I was feeling even if I wanted to.

"Good. Let's sit—we need to discuss our next steps," Leif replied, so we moved farther into the room to take our seats. Matt and I sat a few spaces away from Lysander, opting to sit together. Leif circled the table, choosing to sit opposite, and he waved a hand toward us and introduced us to Lysander.

"This is Matt and Kendra."

I turned my gaze back to Lysander, whose lips turned upward as our gazes met again.

"Yes, I've met Kendra," he said, and I nodded in confirmation. He quickly looked away, and I wondered if it was weird seeing someone who looked so much like Coral at his table.

"So, where's Coral?" Matt asked, getting straight to the point as he looked around the room. Leif quietly sank into his chair across from us, and we all looked back to Lysander for answers. His expression was pained now.

"We think Eugene Pryor might have Coral," he admitted finally, in a small voice. I frowned at the familiar name.

"Pryor? You mean like—"

"Melody's brother," Lysander confirmed, and I began to shake my head.

"I didn't know she had a brother," I replied, and it was true. Melody had come into our lives so quickly, we'd never really learned much about her or her family. "And he's a siren too?"

57

"Yes," Lysander said, nodding. "He's already attacked Coral once. He's... rather ruthless."

That made my stomach turn. He'd just *left* my sister in the clutches of a ruthless siren? One *related* to someone as unhinged as Melody?

"Then why are we sitting here?" I exclaimed. "We have to do something—"

"We can't," Leif interrupted, his voice strong, and I turned to him. "Coronis is already a dangerous place to walk into... and right now, it would be impossible to gain entry. We need to know exactly where Coral is being kept before we try to get her back... and we need a plan. A better plan than last time."

"So, what's this plan?" Matt pressed, raising an eyebrow at both of them. They both seemed to hesitate for a moment, and then Leif straightened his back.

"I'll let you know when we have one," he promised with confidence, but Matt pushed on.

"She's in danger *now*. And yet, you don't have a plan?"

"She's a Reigning Queen," Leif reminded us. "She can take care of herself for the time being. Besides... Eugene tends to toy with his victims before he disposes of them. Which means we don't have a lot of time if he plans to kill her... but we do have *some*."

Despite the pained look on his face, he said it so casually, like Coral being tortured wasn't grounds to storm Coronis right this second and get her back. But I decided not to fixate on that fact and instead asked, "What's a Reigning Queen?" I'd heard the term a few times now, with no explanation.

"It's a very rare type of ruler," Leif explained. "They don't come about often. But a Reigning Queen has some kind of

connection to at least three of the four realms—the land, Veranis, Coronis, and Atlantis. It grants them magic power and certain ruling rights over all of the territories—ranking them
higher than anyone else, even Eugene and Lysander. But they
can only make *certain* ruling decisions, and they can't make
decisions that affect other rulers. Whereas a regular king or
queen—a True Ruler—has limited power over a single kingdom, and they must rise to power through the ancient laws tied
to that kingdom," Leif explained.

"So... a True Ruler must be born or marry into royalty?" I
asked, but Leif shook his head.

"Not always," he offered. "In Coronis, they have clans,
and the most powerful clan holds all the power. When a clan
have proven themselves most worthy, they can challenge and
overthrow the ruler at any time. But it's not as easy as it
seems—sirens have done ruthless things to earn their power to
rule. More ruthless than what is common and accepted among
their kind."

Lysander nodded in agreement.

"And that's precisely why it's Melody we should be worried about, not Eugene," he added, as if that helped us feel better. "She may be bound and powerless right now, but she's
worked too hard for too long to come undone this easily. Melody will be up to something... and if she gets her power back,
she won't hesitate to kill Coral."

Just hearing the words made my stomach turn. I opened
my mouth to speak, but Leif cut in again.

"I promise, I'm working on a plan," he said. The doors
opened at that moment with a heavy clink, and a messenger
entered. He looked apologetic for his interruption as he

bowed, but then he hurried to Lysander's side and spoke in a voice so low that I couldn't catch his words. But a moment later, all the color drained from Lysander's face, and he slowly turned to face the messenger.

"What did you just say?" he growled.

The entire room felt as if it had gone very cold and still as we all stared at Lysander. I barely dared to breathe as the messenger cleared his throat and spoke a bit louder.

"*King Eugene*, Your Grace. He's sent word from Coronis. He says Coral has agreed to stay in the Cora Palace indefinitely in return for a truce among the kingdoms... and that a mermaid will be freed from Coronis for every year that she remains there."

What?

I stood abruptly, staring at them both in horror. Lysander was shaking his head like the same thoughts were running through his mind.

"Lysander," Leif warned, and I noticed that Lysander's hands were beginning to shake. The temperature of the water seemed to rise around us. He jumped up just as abruptly as I had and growled.

"We need to get her out. *Now*."

"She's untouchable," Leif reminded him, getting to his feet as well. "We need a *plan*—"

"That was before we learned that Eugene was *king* of Coronis!" he shouted. "Since *when* do they have male rulers? If he's in power, there's nothing he can't do—forget torturing her, we'll *never* get her back!" Lysander was shaking, pacing, and his erratic behavior made me take a step back. I gripped my chair for support, and Matt reached out to grab my arm in a show of comfort. His shoulders were tense, like he was preparing to get us out of there if he had to.

Leif noticed our discomfort, and his expression twisted into one of determination as he took a step toward the king.

"*Calm down,* Lysander!" he demanded finally, and Lysander froze in his tracks, eyes snapping to Leif. "You're scaring our guests."

Lysander stopped pacing, and guilt appeared in his eyes. Leif was shaking his head.

"You need to get ahold of yourself and your emotions. You won't be any help to Coral if you go charging in there recklessly."

Slowly, Lysander nodded and sank back down in his chair. I felt all my muscles go slack with relief. Matt wore an expression of stone—he hadn't let go of my arm yet. Lysander buried his head in his hands for a moment before finally looking directly at Matt and me.

"I apologize for my outburst," he said. "I'm not usually this... *emotional.*"

That earned a snort from Leif.

"That's an understatement," he muttered, and he returned to his seat as well. He began helping himself to the food, albeit warily, and I hesitantly followed suit and grabbed a bowl of berries. Matt didn't touch a thing, choosing to stare down Lysander warily. After a moment, Leif continued talking, and I focused my gaze down at my bowl of berries.

"We can discuss a plan of action after dinner. I'm working on some ideas already... I just need more time. Perhaps you should tell our guests about the kingdom of Veranis while we're eating—"

At the sudden pause, I looked up and followed Leif's line of sight to Lysander's chair. But it was empty—Lysander had slunk away while we were distracted, and Leif sighed with defeat.

"He's embarrassed," he admitted to us, his tone apologetic. "He's been heartless his entire life. I don't think he knows how to handle the weight of what he's feeling. I'll speak to him later about his outbursts, and you have my word; no harm will come to either of you."

My eyes lingered on his chair, and I resonated with what Leif had said about feeling the weight of one's emotions. All the shock and excitement of waking up in the Undersea had given me a temporary reprieve, but since my dad died, I'd felt like my emotions were clawing to burst out of me, and I was struggling to keep it together.

Perhaps it was something the king and I had in common.

CHAPTER SIX

Kendra

After dinner, I was seated at the vanity while Rue undid my hairstyle, trying to process so many thoughts. Moments of silence passed before Rue spoke.

"Is everything alright, my lady?"

I didn't know the answer to that question. The thought of Coral being kept a prisoner was unsettling... even though I knew she was strong. She'd always been the sister I admired and looked up to, even when I didn't admit it. And even with everything that had happened, my father's death still lingered in my mind. I didn't want to leave him for too long... I wanted to give him a proper funeral. And I wanted Coral to be there because she deserved to be.

It wasn't easy to confide all of this to a stranger, someone I'd met mere hours ago... but she was also the only person I had right now. I'd considered going to Matt a couple of times as he was only down the hall... but I didn't want to bring up any old memories of Maya's death by making him relive the death of my father. He'd already done so much to help me... he'd stayed with me, helped me move the body... I couldn't burden him with my thoughts right now.

So, I told Rue about my father's death and how I missed him. She nodded as she listened, running a clam hairbrush through my hair.

"I'm sorry to hear that," she said softly. "It's never easy to lose a loved one. I wish I knew what to say to bring you comfort... but perhaps the king would be better to speak to. He recently lost his father as well."

I tensed at the thought. I hadn't known that. *Another* thing we had in common, perhaps. But to burden the *king* with my troubles? When he was already so troubled? I doubted he'd welcome such a conversation. He'd already run off from dinner after his outburst earlier. I didn't think he could handle any more bad news.

Rue noticed my hesitation and smiled warmly.

"He's quite easy to talk to once you get to know him a little. And I'm sure he wouldn't mind. He's been a bit out of sorts lately, without the queen around, and it might bring him some comfort to have someone who knows the queen to converse with."

I grimaced, but the more I thought about going to sleep without talking to someone, the more I dreaded it. I *needed* to get these feelings out... and I needed to be understood, not sympathized with. It was all good and well for someone to agree with me about my shitty situation, but at the end of the day, they still had a family to go back to.

I didn't. Not anymore.

"Fine... where could I find him?" I asked, a little unsure about this but willing to test the waters. I met Rue's gaze through the mirror, and she beamed.

"He's been in the courtyard since dinner. I can take you there now, if you'd like?"

I shrugged and nodded, rising from my stool. It was a good thing I hadn't changed into any nightwear yet because these gowns seemed to take a painfully long time to change in and out of, despite how pretty they were to wear.

Rue led me back through the hallways and down the staircase, but instead of heading toward the dining room, she led me around the stairs and toward the back of the palace. We finally reached a set of double doors that she pushed open, and the vibrant coral gardens greeted us.

I took a step forward, admiring the beauty of the space, and Rue quietly closed the doors behind me to give us our privacy. I immediately recognized half a dozen species—cup coral, elephant ear, acropora, and fire coral being the closest to me. There were also many species of fish gliding around, too fast for me to get a good look before another would swim past and hide the first school from view.

I spotted Lysander, his back to me, seated under a large stone statue of someone I didn't recognize. Taking a few steps forward, I cleared my throat, and Lysander glanced over his shoulder at me—his mouth pulled in a stiff line and his brows furrowed.

"Uh... hi," I said with uncertainty, already feeling that this was a huge mistake. It took a moment, but finally, Lysander's stiff expression softened.

"Kendra," he greeted, and the way he said my name sent a strange feeling through me. He didn't seem like the same person who had been yelling uncontrollably just a few hours before, and for that, I was grateful. He looked me up and down once before adding, "I'm glad to see Coral was able to rescue you, at the very least."

His tone sounded dejected, and I raised an eyebrow.

"So, you heard about my father's death?"

He nodded and smoothly scooted along the base of the statue to face me head on.

"Leif briefed me before dinner on everything that happened. I'm... quite sorry to hear that Coral wasn't able to save your father."

Leif had said that too, or something like it. Coral must have made her priorities known the entire time she was down here. It seemed like something she would do.

He gestured beside him, silently asking if I wanted to sit, and I accepted the invitation.

"I'm sorry too, about your father," I replied, crossing the space and sitting tentatively beside him. I kept my gaze trained on the bedrock floor as I took a deep breath and added, "Truthfully, I feel awful that Coral was left to try and save both of us alone. I'm glad she had you and Leif, and that you were kind enough to support her."

I finally looked up at him again, and he nodded, listening intently with a gentle expression. Any doubts about me burdening him with my troubles began to fade. "I was under Melody's spell for so long... if only I'd known. I might have been able to help my sister. And I said such horrible things to her while Melody was controlling me..."

Tears had formed in my eyes now, and they blurred my vision as they mixed with the water. I wiped them away, but they didn't stop coming, my bottom lip trembling. I didn't want to cry in front of a stranger... but Lysander was patient and didn't seem alarmed by it.

Oh, hell with it, I thought, and spilled the rest to him.

"Now our dad's dead, and there's nothing either of us can do to bring him back. She took all the burden, right from the very start, trying to protect us from Melody... and I let her down."

I immediately felt better once the words were out, and I was surprised at how easily they had flowed around Lysander. Perhaps it was because I didn't know him well enough to feel judged. He hadn't even said anything about his own father yet, and I suddenly wondered if I was oversharing. He leaned back against the statue and turned his head up toward the swarms of fish passing overhead.

"Yes, she did seem quite burdened," he admitted finally. "But not once did I get the impression that she felt let down by you—she knew you were under a siren spell. Forgive me for saying it, but perhaps you are being too hard on yourself."

I bit my lip to stop myself from crying again as I considered his words.

"However, I understand a little bit about wanting to go back and change the course of things. I didn't have a good relationship with my father, but I still wish things had ended on better terms between us," he confessed quietly, and he tilted his head to the side, and our gazes met. "I realize now that he was only trying to protect me."

"How did he die?" I asked, the curiosity getting the better of me before I could rethink my question, and his eyes grew pained.

"Eugene's men murdered him right after I gave up my heart to save Coral from spending eternity down here." His gaze trailed to the floor. "And now she's stuck here anyway, and I have all these new emotions that I didn't realize would feel so draining to have."

67

I frowned, tilting my head at him. He noticed and continued speaking.

"It's like... I get angry, and it's so overwhelming that I can't control it. Or I get lost in such waves of sadness and grief that I can't seem to find a way out of my negative thoughts. I didn't realize how this was going to feel... and I don't know if I can handle it."

His words resonated so deeply—it was everything I was feeling right now and more. I grimaced and clasped my hands together in my lap to stop myself from reaching out to comfort this stranger I didn't know—a man my sister was *definitely* more involved with. Instead, I offered words of my own.

"I think I understand. I've felt that overpowering sadness since my dad died. It feels like it's never going to go away."

He nodded, meeting my gaze again, and I offered a small smile.

"But maybe we can work on that together while I'm down here?"

He smiled a genuine smile then, and it caught me off guard how handsome he was when he wasn't brooding all over the place. He went on to say, "And how long do you plan to be down here?"

I wasn't sure anymore. At first, it was only meant to be a few days, but I was quickly coming to realize that we might not be able to rescue Coral for some time. And there was no way I could return to the surface until I knew she was safe—townspeople and their questions be damned.

"I don't know," I confessed, and he studied me for a moment.

"Well, I look forward to your company, Kendra," he replied, and I found myself surprised to realize that I was looking forward to his as well.

Lysander offered to walk me back to my quarters so that I didn't get lost, but as we were ascending the stairs in the foyer, Matt appeared at the top. As soon as he saw me, he seemed to sigh in relief and came rushing down the stairs.

"There you are. I've been looking for you everywhere!"

I frowned.

"Why, what happened?"

He shook his head, eyeing Lysander with a grimace and folding his arms.

"Nothing... I just wanted to speak to you about something, but when you weren't in your room, I got worried. And then I couldn't find you anywhere on the upper levels."

"I'm sorry—I didn't mean to worry you. I was just speaking to Lysander," I replied, wondering what he'd been seeking me out so urgently for. After all, we barely knew each other, and if it had anything to do with Coral or the Undersea, then Leif would probably be here too.

Matt's eyes flicked between the two of us, eyeing Lysander with distaste, before finally resting on me.

"Well, it can wait until tomorrow. I can see that you're busy."

"No, it's fine—what is it?" I asked, taking a step up toward him. But just as he opened his mouth to speak again, the front doors rattled open behind us. All three of us whirled around at the disturbance, wondering who might be walking in so late at night.

My eyes widened and my heart dropped into my stomach just as Lysander made a whining noise in the back of his throat. I slowly turned to examine Matt's reaction and was not at all surprised to see that his face had drained of color, and he looked like he might pass out any moment.

Then I slowly glanced back at the figure of my sister's deceased best friend, Maya Rivers, who was standing before us. She wore a strange floaty dress that resembled octopus tentacles. I recognized her arched eyebrows and high cheekbones, but she used to have brown eyes. Now, they had an unusual green shimmer to them as they locked onto Matt—whom I slowly turned back to.

I had no words. But Matt certainly had words as he turned to Lysander and growled.

"What the actual *fuck*?"

CHAPTER SEVEN

Melody

I leaned on the black obsidian railing overlooking the courtroom, tapping my long, slender fingernails on the smooth stone. Below, my brother lounged on his newfound throne, listening attentively as a long line of people waited to speak with him. Guards stood posted by the walls around the room, ready to strike if anyone tried anything.

It used to be me on that throne. And now, I was *nobody.* The king's adviser was just a glorified title so that Eugene could bounce his ideas off of me, but I knew he was smart enough to make his own decisions. And he no doubt had plans of his own that had been in the making since the day we struck our deal, which I'd foolishly believed would never come to pass.

I'd been *so sure* I would succeed. Twenty years on the throne, and I never thought that Lorraine's two meddling daughters could wreak such havoc on my plans. Or that the Veranis prince—now *king*—would prove to be such a problem, with all the stories I'd heard of his aloof approach to his royal duties.

As I stood there, watching the day's court duties unfold below me, I noticed that there were very few females in the crowd—a significant number of sirens were still unhappy with the gendered change in rulership and refused to meet with the king. But the males had embraced it, flocking to Eugene with requests and praise. They hadn't stopped coming since Eugene

71

had put on his display of power with Coral. My blood simmered at the memory of her writhing on the balcony for all to see, and I sneered at how easily she'd been captured.

How had I come undone by such a weak human being just days prior to her capture? Especially now that she was locked up in our prisoner's suite when she supposedly had all the power of the Undersea at her fingertips? I nearly laughed at the thought... two iron cuffs, and she'd been rendered helpless.

The line moved as a male siren bowed to Eugene before striding away, and a couple took his place. But in the shadows near the back entry door, I noticed a figure in a deep-crimson dress, her dark-brown hair slicked back, and her hair adorned with glittering rubies.

Sloane Drakos.

She was a member of one of the top five siren clans in our kingdom. My mother had tried to pair Eugene up with Sloane the same way she'd tried to marry me off to Nikolai Galanis. But that was twenty years ago—and Sloane had shown no interest in Eugene back then. Why was she here now, lurking in the shadows instead of waiting in line?

As if sensing my stare, she looked up calmly and met my gaze. Her amber eyes glittered, and I deepened my frown. Her lips curled up, and she turned and disappeared into the shadows.

Where was she going?

I turned and set off at a brisk pace down the corridor. I sensed trouble, and I needed to stamp it out quietly. My brother continued to hear out his people, completely oblivious to Sloane's mysterious lurking, and I didn't want to alert the guards and cause a panic just yet. Eugene might have been sitting on the throne, but as far as I was concerned, this was still *my* palace.

I took a back route and marched down the spiral onyx stairs, which led to the court room. Sticking to the shadows, I tracked to Sloane's last-seen location. She was gone, but she couldn't have gone far—after all, the palace was not free for outsiders to roam. If she didn't take the back exit into the courtyard, she'd have left through the front doors, so I weaved through the crowd to check that route first.

I'd barely stepped through the front doors when a small laugh sounded from behind me, and I whisked around.

"I didn't expect you to fall for such an easy trick. You make luring you out so easy."

She stood in the doorway, leaning casually against the obsidian frame. I straightened my stance and folded my arms, pointedly showing off my freshly manicured claws.

"Why are you here?" I asked coolly. She raised an eyebrow at me, a smirk tugging at her lips.

"You and I are going for a drink," she said in a matter-of-fact tone, pushing off the doorframe and striding toward me.

"And why would I abandon my court duties?" I drawled slowly.

She stood close enough to touch, a mischievous look in her eyes now.

"Because I have a proposal that I believe you'll be *very* interested in."

Sloane Drakos took me to a downtown bar that was classy by siren standards, though I much preferred the elegance of a restaurant or café. Seagrass and kelp decorated the ceiling, and golden glow crystals backlit the bar where they were serving cheap alcohol and wine sourced from the human lands. It was far from the upscale dining I was used to, with glittering chandeliers and lush white tablecloths, where waiters would bring Christopher and I the finest aged wines, and I'd indulge in seven courses of gourmet meals...

I shook the thoughts away. The memory of Christopher was like a dull ache now. Nothing but a lost victory I'd come too close to claiming.

Sloane strode through the space like she owned it, pulling up a stool at a private table in the corner. She waved over the waiter and ordered a boozy cocktail, then looked to me and raised an eyebrow.

"I'll just have wine," I told the waiter briskly, and he hurried off to make our drinks. Sloane leaned forward in her seat, clasping her hands together under her chin and studying me with an amused expression.

"So, tell me," she mused finally. "How did the most feared and powerful siren in all of Coronis come undone *so easily* by a little mermaid?"

I glared daggers at her.

"Careful," I warned her, my tone dark. "Just because I'm no longer the queen, doesn't mean I won't gut you if you piss me off."

She hummed at me like she didn't quite believe it.

"Maybe I want you angry," she said finally, a hint of delight in her voice. "Maybe our plan depends on it."

"What plan?" I snapped, becoming increasingly more frustrated. I shouldn't have followed her all the way out here if she was going to be vague and useless. Why didn't I just throw her in a cell and torture the information out of her?

"*Patience.* First, I need to make sure I can trust you," she said lightly as our drinks arrived.

Fully irritated by Sloane's confident teasing, I'd never been so thankful to see alcohol in my life. I took the glass of red wine that was meant for me, removed the weighted stopper that kept the liquid concealed, and downed half the drink in one hit.

Sloane watched with a fascinated expression. She merely sipped her own drink daintily before replacing her stopper and said, "Now, I know you didn't go to the trouble of exiling the Atlantis princess, overthrowing Queen Chora, and taking your war to the human lands *just* to settle as your brother's adviser while he rules all of Coronis. You want your brother off the throne, don't you?"

Her words stirred something in me, and it took everything I had to keep my expression blank. She was right—it should have been *me* on that throne. As much as I loved my brother, this was the one thing I desired more than anything, and it pained me to see him rule the kingdom I'd worked so hard to claim, to *build.*

Not to mention I would have been Queen of the Undersea by now; the Reigning Queen of three territories, tearing Veranis to the ground, building a new kingdom better than any-

75

thing that had come before us... I would have been all-powerful, untouchable. *Nobody* would ever be able to control me again. Control *us*...

It wasn't just for my benefit. It was for Eugene's too. But he had other plans... *different* plans. He didn't see things the way I did.

I conveyed none of this to Sloane though.

"Such an accusation could land you in a cell," I warned.

"And yet, you don't deny it," she replied, grinning as she leaned back with amusement. If she wasn't wearing a dress fit for court, I imagined she'd be leaning back in her chair with her feet up on the table—she had that kind of demeanor about her.

"I also know that you and your brother had a deal, which is how he became king. What intrigues me is why someone as relentless and powerful as you could have any reason to strike a deal so damaging to your years of hard work. Unless you were trying to protect a bigger secret?"

Something twisted in my gut as I remembered my secret meetings with Lorraine—and momentarily, a vision of her with the past sea witch that I didn't recall with great clarity—but it blurred and faded as a sudden bolt of panic made my hands go clammy.

"That's none of your business," I snarled, surprised at my tone as I rode the strange emotion. It was gone as soon as it had come, and I realized I hadn't felt that kind of fear in so long, I'd almost forgotten what it was like. Now, it was lost in the abyss once more. *Pointless and forgotten.*

Sloane leaned forward, her voice a husky whisper. "You want to know what I think?"

I barely dared to move, to breathe, as I caught a whiff of her perfume—ocean blossoms and coconut and a hint of *spice*.

"I think you were in *love* with the Atlantis princess. That Eugene caught you, and you swore him to secrecy with a deal you couldn't refuse, lest your mother find out. I do remember how vicious she used to be."

I slowly leaned back, sizing Sloane up. Perhaps I could rip out her vocal cords so she might never repeat these words to anybody ever again.

"Whether you're right or not, it changes nothing," I told Sloane carefully. "Eugene now sits on the throne, and I'm bound to do no harm. I cannot change things."

Though I'd certainly been trying. Bindings were particularly difficult things to break—they could only be undone by the caster, unless there was a rare artifact involved in the spell, which there hadn't been. The only way I'd get my powers back was by asking Coral to undo them, and that thought was laughable. *Me?* Grovel at the feet of Lorraine's treacherous daughter to beg for my power back? Knowing full well my request would fall on deaf ears? I would *never*.

But perhaps after rotting in a cell for ten years and being subject to Eugene's daily torture, she might be open to discussing the subject. Or perhaps if I found a way to capture her precious little undine king, she might cooperate. I savored the ideas—they were the only things keeping me sane right now.

"And that brings me to my proposal," Sloane mused, tapping her claws on the table. "We share a common goal, Melody. Myself and... a select few other sirens are unhappy with the change in leadership. We want to put you back on the throne, and we're prepared to help you get your power back to do it."

I pursed my lips, considering her words.

"Well, as delightful as that sentiment is, I think you'll find it exceptionally hard to overthrow Eugene, along with the palace guards, while the ocean backs his rule. We would need a *massive* show of power and strength to flip the scales again—last time, I had to exile the heir of another kingdom."

"So, we go higher," Sloane suggested, waving her hand casually. "You have the *Undersea queen* in your grasp now. All you need to do is dethrone her, and we'll have our calling card."

"Easier said than done when I can't *harm* anybody with these bindings in place," I shot back bitterly. I couldn't do anything that would lead to damaging a living being's well-being—dethroning included.

"Then we'll just have to earn our new Undersea queen's trust, won't we?" Sloane insisted, her eyes darkening with mischief. "After all, you are quite the skilled manipulator these days."

The more I thought about it, the more plausible it seemed. It would be difficult, yes... but if I could get Coral to trust me, then I might be able to trick her into breaking my bindings. And then I could dispose of her and go up against my brother with the ocean backing my challenge.

Sloane picked up her drink and began sipping it again, before adding, "So, what do you say?"

If I did nothing, then I would be back where I started—a puppet to those who sought to use me. This time, it would be my brother controlling me, using me as his adviser. The thought made visions of my mother swim through my head... of her controlling, manipulative ways. I thought of Nikolai Galanis, whose head hung in the throne room of the Cora Palace. Who had nearly trapped me in a miserable eternity...

I couldn't go back there again. I had to break these bindings, and I had to get the throne back. And then I would *never* let anybody take away my power ever again. Even if it meant befriending the Undersea queen and gaining her trust... I would do whatever it took.

CHAPTER EIGHT

Coral

I stared up at the glittering black spikes that covered the ceiling of my cage. Every limb in my body felt like it had been sapped of energy and repeatedly hit with a sledgehammer for good measure. I could barely keep my eyes open, and it was taking all of my focus to flex my tail.

Over and over.

Despite the iron cuffs pinning me to the bed and the one around my tail fin, I'd been stretching my tail muscles nonstop since they'd left me in here, trying to become familiar with my new body. And while I couldn't move it much under the restraints, I felt like I had a better understanding now.

My tail kicked in a back-and-forth motion, it appeared. And the faster I kicked, the more momentum I'd build. Plus, my tail fin had all sorts of muscles and nerves for balance, which I'd have to utilize and test out once I got free again.

They hadn't treated my wounds, and every movement was agony. But with clenched teeth, I kept going, refusing to yield just because there was an arrow tip still wedged into the tender flesh, and refusing to acknowledge how it was starting to swell and turn a nasty shade of brown.

The doors to the prisoner suites opened somewhere up the hallway, and dread coiled in my gut immediately. Had a whole day passed already? I didn't have a good sense of time down here. They weren't bringing me regular meals, and I kept drifting in and out of consciousness. But it seemed like once a day,

Eugene had been coming down here to drain my power for himself with his terrible crown. And now he was back... what was it, a third time?

So I've only been down here for three days, I thought wearily, as the footsteps grew closer and closer. Three days of this miserable eternity. I strained to look over my bound body at the golden bars surrounding my small space of imprisonment. At least the room was somewhat tasteful—unlike the mossy Veranis dungeons where barnacles had threatened to cut me the entire time.

As I listened to the footsteps, I tried to steady my breathing, to prepare myself for the immense pain that was about to wreak through my body again. But then I realized the footsteps sounded different. It was more of a *click* than a *thud*.

Suddenly, Melody strode into view on the other side of the bars, wearing another one of her signature cream dresses and studying me with folded arms. My head slapped back against the bed, and I found myself wishing Eugene was here after all. I would have taken the crown any day over having to face the female who forced me to murder my own father.

"Darling Daughter," Melody said coldly, and I didn't bother correcting her this time. I knew she was doing it just to spite me. "We need to talk."

I didn't respond—I didn't have *anything* to say to her, and I wouldn't give her anything ever again. Not my time, not my energy, and certainly not a conversation. But she continued on as I focused my gaze up at the ceiling and tried to drown out her words.

"It appears that you and I share a common desire. We would both like to see my brother dethroned... and thanks to you, that is not something I can take care of alone."

Good, I thought bitterly. For once, Melody wouldn't get everything she ever wanted. That thought alone made my suffering more worthwhile—Eugene could take all the power he desired if it would keep him on the throne and spite Melody more.

"Tell me, Coral... do you really think that having Eugene on the throne is for the best? You're Reigning Queen now. You have a responsibility to provide well-being in all four territories, and you'd let Eugene wreak havoc while you play prisoner down here?"

"Well, he's already created a truce with two kingdoms thanks to my negotiations, which is better than anything you ever did," I shot back finally. "Maybe I *want* Eugene on the Coronis throne. Maybe this is all part of my bigger plan."

Melody laughed—a sound that had once been musical, but now echoed like untuned piano strings that filled the hollows of my ears and made my insides twist.

"Oh, don't be *foolish.* Eugene has plans of his own—this will end in tragedy for everyone; you just wait and see."

"Well, if only I wasn't chained up down here, maybe I could do something about it," I drawled, wriggling my cuffed hands for emphasis and glaring at her.

"And that is precisely why I am here," Melody mused softly, curling her clawed fingers around a bar of the golden cage. "What if I could help you escape? And in exchange, you'd do something for me?"

82

"Forget it," I snarled, breaking eye contact with her and returning my gaze to the ceiling. Melody made a sound in the back of her throat like she was losing patience.

"I heard you seek to restore the sea witch's soul—that you plan to venture to the Sea of Souls to do so," Melody said finally, all softness devoid from her voice now.

Ah yes, another thing on my to-do list once I got out of here. I'd nearly forgotten with everything else I'd been dealing with—the grief, the mermaids, the *torture*...

"Rarely does anybody return from that place alive. In fact, the only two people who were last known to return from there were your mother and myself."

I looked up now, meeting her gaze, and she raised her eyebrows knowingly at me.

"The *only* reason we returned from that place is because the sea witch herself—the last one, that is—allowed us to do so. Otherwise, we would have been swallowed by the currents, lost forever until we perished. Do you *really* think that the ancient magic tied to that place will allow you to just swim in, take a soul of your choosing, and leave so freely?"

"I'm the Reigning Queen..." I trailed off, but Melody shook her head and laughed again.

"That means *nothing*. It is still forbidden. The dead are meant to stay dead. You don't get to meddle with such things just because you hold the most power—at the end of the day, the ocean is still the *most* powerful entity of all, and it always will be."

"So, what are you suggesting?" I asked hollowly, and Melody's eyes glittered like she'd been waiting for this question.

83

"If you are going to go venture there, you need someone familiar with the waters. Someone the ocean already recognizes to be ruthless and powerful. I will take you there myself, in return for one thing."

I already knew what she was after. It was a trap—it *had* to be. She would never waste her time helping me. And besides...

"Do you really think I would go anywhere with you after what you did?" I asked icily, narrowing my gaze at her. She returned the expression, straightening her stance.

"Trust me, Coral, I do not desire to help you in the slightest after you meddled with my plans. But it is clear to me that we need each other. That if we are to *both* get what we want... we need work together."

"I'll never help you," I seethed, and I pointedly returned my gaze to the ceiling. This conversation was over—she could go rot in a hole.

Melody sighed from the other side of the cage.

"Fine," she said, and I heard something clatter to the ground. Unable to help myself, I strained my neck and saw a glint of silver, which she kicked with her heel. It skimmed across the polished floor until it was hidden deep under my bed.

A dagger.

I glanced up at Melody, who simply said, "Think it over won't you, darling Daughter?"

And then she strode off back down the corridor. I was left staring up at the ceiling, my mind racing at the thought of the deadly weapon beneath me that was *just* out of reach, just waiting to be used so that I could escape.

If only I could figure out a way to get to it.

CHAPTER NINE

Lysander

Leif came to personally escort me to breakfast that morning, followed by half a dozen more guards. He was wearing his usual navy uniform and shaking his head at me the moment I stepped out of my room.

"Lysander, your colossal fuckups never cease to amaze me," he chastised, placing a hand on his spear hilt for good measure as he turned, and we marched through the corridors together. I'd been awake all night thinking about it—another problem to add to my avalanche of worries right now.

"I was waiting for the right time to reunite them," I replied carefully through gritted teeth. I hadn't slept well—tossing and turning as nightmares of being murdered in my sleep jolted me again and again. "And besides, I thought Coral would have told him what had happened."

Evidently, that had not been the case. Because after Matt's outburst, he'd proceeded to demand answers, spent a good while trying to talk to his lifeless dead girlfriend, and when Maya said nothing, he stormed upstairs and didn't emerge from his room again for the rest of the evening. The hairs stood up on the back of my neck at the memory of his face—the anger that had blazed in his eyes—and I glanced subtly over my shoulders for any sign of him as we walked.

"He already doesn't trust you, and now you'll be lucky to make it through each night alive. Speaking of which, I've stationed more guards outside your room this morning—I have a feeling you're going to need them," Leif said, lowering his voice as we passed through the guest suites corridor and turned onto the staircase. "I have to say, serving your father was never this stressful, Lysander. I'm thinking I should request a pay raise."

"Don't push it," I warned, but I caught the hint of a smile on his lips and appreciated him trying to lighten the mood.

Leif placed a hand on the dining room doors to push them open, but then he paused and turned to me, blocking my entry.

"Also, maybe don't mention that you're the reason she drowned, or he might *seriously* try to plunge a knife into your throat."

And with that, he pushed the doors open, and we stepped into the dining room. Kendra was already seated at the table, helping herself to the same berries that Coral liked so much. She seemed a little on edge, and when I spotted Maya at the end of the table, I realized why. Maya was her usual, lifeless self, but it was unsettling all the same. Thankfully, there was no sign of Matt, but to my surprise, a familiar face was seated opposite Kendra.

"Nerissa!" Leif cried, clearly shocked to see her as well. She smiled mischievously at us and swam over the dining table to greet us. Kendra watched with wide eyes, particularly drawn to Nerissa's shimmering green-and-blue tail.

"So, you're alive then," I said, eyeing a nasty bruise above her right eyebrow and a gash on her upper left arm as she came to settle in front of us.

"As if Eugene's men could take me down so easily," she scoffed, rolling her eyes. "They originally captured me—they were going to take my heart. But I managed to escape right before we reached Coronis." She turned her gaze to Leif and added, "I went back for your men... but by the time I arrived, it was too late. I'm sorry."

Leif shook his head. "It's not your fault. I'm glad you survived."

"Well, so am I," Nerissa replied, her upper lip curving. "I believe we merpeople still have an agreement to uphold with your kind. I'm supposed to teach Coral how to use her magic... and I can only imagine how much she's struggling without any training."

She glanced over at Kendra and added, "I was just filling in our *other* Atlantis princess about her magical capabilities, seeing as they both have heart magic. She seems eager to access the magic and rescue her sister—oh, and she told me Coral's been captured," she said, looking back at me and raising an eyebrow. "I'm surprised you're not halfway to Coronis by now, Your Grace."

Kendra's eyes were shining with determination as Nerissa recounted their conversation, but Leif faltered, exchanging a knowing look with me. I knew what he was trying to convey.

I took a step toward Kendra and cleared my throat, summoning her gaze to mine.

"You know that the only way to unlock your heart magic is to become a mermaid, right?" I asked quietly. "And that's precisely why Coral's trapped here now?"

Kendra's excitement faded, and she nodded solemnly.

"Yes... Nerissa explained it to me. I just... I don't think I'd mind the trade-off."

I frowned at her, tilting my head. Coral had been so against staying down here. She'd fought for her freedom, wanting nothing more than to return to land. But Kendra seemed to like it down here, and I couldn't fathom why. Weren't they supposed to be twins?

More so in looks than personality, I found myself thinking. But I was drawn out of my thoughts by a hollow laugh from the doorway, and we all spun and noticed Matt standing there, listening to our conversation.

"And why in the *hell* would you want to stay down here, Kendra?" he drawled, glaring daggers at me. "When these people are so quick to trap and drown their guests?"

"Matt—" I began, but he took a step toward me. Leif was back at my side in an instant.

"That's what you did to Coral, didn't you?" he accused, raising an eyebrow and continuing his determined approach. My guards had spears pointed at him now, and Leif casually angled himself in front of me, hand on the hilt of his own spear. Matt sneered at the guards.

"Wait," I said, more firmly, directing the order to everybody. "You're not understanding the whole situation. My father had a lot to do with her imprisonment, but I let her go."

"He's right," Nerissa added, and the sound of a chair scraping on the floor indicated that she'd pulled up a seat. "Didn't you give up your heart or something to free her?"

I nodded but kept my eyes trained on Matt.

"Before you and Kendra arrived here, I was working on a way to restore Maya's soul. I'm doing *everything* I can to make it right."

"Then why has it already been a whole year?" Matt drawled, gesturing to where Maya was sitting, and I caught the pain in his eyes. "I thought she was *dead!* I'd finally come to accept it... but she's been down here the entire time?"

I gestured for my guards to lower their weapons, which they did reluctantly, and took a careful step toward Matt. He tensed, but I didn't back down.

"There is a way to restore her soul if we can reach the Sea of Souls. The only trouble is my own father bound me from going there before he died, so if I try to set foot there, I'll turn to sea-foam."

"How convenient," he snarled, eyes blazing. "Send someone else then."

"Only a Reigning Queen can save me," Maya said, her haunting, eerie voice filling the room. Matt faltered as she stood and drifted over to us, eyes still blank but looking more alert than usual. After all of his attempts to get a word out of her last night, he seemed shocked to have heard her speak.

Leif cleared his throat to defuse the tension. "Yes, apparently that's a critical element of this operation. And given our current circumstances, we've had to put it on hold while we get Coral back because, as you can see, *Coral* is the one who needs to do it."

Matt finally shook his head and stumbled into a nearby chair. The guards finally stepped away, giving us our space, and Kendra scooted her chair around next to Matt's side and placed her hand on his comfortingly. Nerissa frowned at the two of them, then flicked her tail as she averted her gaze.

"And there's no other way?" Matt asked quietly. I nodded, my expression apologetic.

"I swear it. If there was any other way, I can assure you I would have already done it."

Matt watched Maya for a moment, looking close to his breaking point at the sight of her.

"Is she always like this?" he asked, his voice cracked, and we nodded. Maya drifted around the room like she was seeing things that only she could see, whispering to herself as she went. Matt shook his head and added, "Does Coral know about this? About... what happened to her?"

Matt's anger seemed to be gone, so I pulled up a chair next to Kendra, adding to the disarray of the dining room.

"Yes. She... didn't take it too well when she first found out. But thankfully, she forgave me."

Matt's eyes immediately flashed with anger, and Leif quickly stepped in.

"What our king means," he said, giving me a warning look, "is that Coral realized it wasn't Lysander's *direct* fault because of his unusual curse."

Matt continued shooting daggers at me with his eyes, and I swallowed hard.

"The point is, Maya can return to her old life and her old self if we can bring back her soul. She will still be the sea witch and still maintain her powers and duties... but this is a curse we can break if you'll give us a chance to do it."

Matt turned to face Kendra and asked, "And you're okay with this?"

Kendra's eyes widened with surprise, and she held up her hands in protest.

"I'm staying out of this. I don't know *any* of you here well enough to—"

Matt leaped to his feet, and the guards drew their weapons again.

"That's bullshit!" he growled at her, and Kendra flinched. "Maya is Coral's best friend, and you're Coral's *twin!* You're either with me on this, or you're as spineless as *this* guy!"

He jabbed his thumb at me, and I frowned at the weird gesture. Leif and Nerissa were silent, watching the exchange unfold.

"Matt... that's not fair," Kendra stammered, eyes darting between each of us. "Listen to what they're saying. They're working on a solution—"

"I'm done listening," Matt snapped, shoving his chair aside and storming out of the room. Maya watched with a glazed expression, but she didn't go after him. Kendra let out a shaky breath, and after a moment, she turned her chair back toward the food. She didn't return to eating immediately, but as we began to gather around the table to dine properly, she slowly began popping berries into her mouth again.

I took a seat on her left and watched her for a moment, entranced somehow. She'd defended me... but why?

She finally noticed me staring and raised an eyebrow at me.

"What is it?" she asked, and I noticed her tense tone. I quickly looked away and shook my head.

"Nothing. I just... thank you for what you said."

91

After a moment, I snuck a glance back at her, and she was still watching me with an expression I couldn't decipher. But finally, she shrugged.

"Like I said—I'm not taking sides. I just... I felt like he wasn't acknowledging the fact that you've been trying to help her."

"Well, maybe he doesn't have to," I admitted, helping myself to some salmon. "He has a right to be angry."

Kendra hesitated for a moment, and then she said, "I'm surprised Coral forgave you. I think about what Melody did to our dad... and I could *never* forgive her. Maya and Coral were best friends—the inseparable kind. They took the same classes, had the same hobbies, and I'm pretty sure they would have applied to the same colleges if they'd gone. She was a mess when Maya died... I can only imagine how she handled it when she found out Maya was down here."

Not well, I thought, as I chewed the salmon. And something told me that Matt wouldn't be as quick to forgive me... if he ever did.

But then Kendra surprised me by saying, "If she forgave you, then she must see something *really* decent in you. So... I'm choosing to see the good in you too."

She met my gaze, her upper lip curving into a soft smile that did something to my heart.

"Even if your emotional outbursts scare the *shit* out of me," she added, though her tone was playful, and I thought of how ridiculous my outbursts truly were. We both broke into a chuckle, and all lingering tension was gone by the time we finished eating.

Leif and Nerissa went to the strategy room after breakfast to work on the rescue operation, so I decided to head to the library and see if I could find any more books on True Ruler magic. Matt's anger had renewed my determination to find a loophole and restore Maya's soul sooner, if a way could be found.

Upon hearing that we had a library, Kendra insisted on joining me.

"You like to read?" I asked, as we climbed the raw alexandrite staircase together, and she nodded enthusiastically.

"I'm probably the *least* adventurous person in our family," Kendra admitted, with a guilty smile. "Coral loves surfing, my dad loved sailing, and *heck*—my mother left behind a whole kingdom to come to land. I've always been content to curl up with a book and read about such things."

"Well, you're welcome to as many books in the library as you desire," I told her earnestly, unable to help the smile that tugged at the corners of my mouth. "They don't get nearly as much use as they should."

I strode a few paces ahead to hold the library doors open for her, and she gave me a shy smile in thanks.

It was that moment that the likeness between Coral and Kendra split in two, that my mind was able to separate their identical features and see past the exterior to the two very different souls within. Where in Coral, strength and stubbornness dominated. I saw more overarching gentleness and curiosity in Kendra. And now their features were embedded in my mind to resemble as much—the same face, but Coral's cheekbones and eyes were sharp, where Kendra's were softer.

93

This was further solidified watching Kendra step into the library. The moment she entered, her eyes widened, and her jaw dropped—her entire being captivated by the endless shelves of books, the towering windows showcasing the passing schools of fish, and the plush kelp-stitched armchairs that promised hours of comfortable reading. She noticed me watching and turned a shade of red, recovering quickly.

"So, what are we looking for, exactly?" she asked, shifting to plant her hands on her hips.

I was more than content to indulge her attempt to play it cool and casually gestured to the far left, where most of the magical tomes were stored, and replied, "Anything to do with True Ruler magic. I'm looking for a loophole to my father's binding."

Kendra raised an eyebrow at me as I ran my hand along a bookshelf.

"We're not going to wait until we rescue Coral to restore Maya's soul?"

I paused and debated airing my true thoughts. After a moment, I glanced toward her.

"Truthfully, what happened to Maya is my fault. I want to fix it before Coral gets back so that she can just... not have to deal with any more burdens I've created for her. But on top of that... the Sea of Souls is a dangerous place. I don't want her to venture there alone if I can help it."

Kendra slowly nodded. "I see." The weight of my words hung in the air, and she took a moment to think, then asked, "Remind me again why we don't just barge into Coronis and take Coral back?"

I shook my head, humbled by how naive she was.

"Passing through Coronis is one thing. Trying to gain access to the Cora Palace undetected is a whole other thing. If the guards don't catch us first, Eugene or Melody are sure to spot us, and we'd be done for. That's without factoring in that my presence at the Cora Palace could be considered an act of war, given Eugene's treaty and the fact that Coral solidified it by agreeing to it. She's not just Reigning Queen but bound to become the future queen of Veranis, so all decisions she makes impact our kingdom. And so far... Veranis has avoided conflicts of war with Coronis. We're not in a position to defend ourselves against them."

"But it's only a matter of time until they attack, I take it?" Kendra pressed, her gaze fixated on mine. I nodded, grimacing.

"Eugene's truce is only temporary—that much I can say for certain. He would never let the other kingdoms live in peace while he holds so much power. But because Coronis has technically made peace with us, the consequences of *us* retaliating now would be far worse than under normal circumstances."

I stepped back to a nearby armchair and collapsed, already feeling the weight of the choices I had to consider. This is *exactly* why I hadn't desired to be king.

"What if we were to rescue Coral under the guise of delivering a peace treaty delegation?" Kendra suggested, surprising me. Perhaps she wasn't as naive as I first thought. "We could use the delegation to honor the treaty, but it would really be a distraction while someone else sneaks in and grabs Coral. After all... Eugene plans to break this truce eventually. It would be better to ensure any collateral damage—*a.k.a. Coral*—is safely removed from his palace before he tries to use it against us in a direct act of war."

I considered the idea.

"How would we get away undetected?" I asked finally, not wanting to dismiss her ideas—to snuff out the light of hope in her eyes. But if this plan was to lead to a dead end, she'd soon talk her way into it anyway. "Our chances of not being detected are slim, so perhaps a better question is how we might get away *quickly* without bringing a whole army down on our kingdom's doorstep."

Seahorses wouldn't be fast enough. We needed something bigger—like a manta ray. But the manta rays were exclusive to Coronis territory, and we'd owe the sea witch another favor if we called one to our command to balance the ancient laws of the Undersea.

"Well... I think Nerissa said something about the Alta Palace being protected by crystal? Maybe we could do something similar here..."

I shook my head. *Kendra* might be strong enough for such a stunt, but she was in her human form, her heart magic safely locked away.

"Nerissa isn't strong enough to crystallize our kingdom's entry points and defend it alone," I told Kendra gently. "The Atlantis royals were able to pull off such a stunt because royal heart magic is more powerful than regular heart magic."

"Which is why you're going to help me transform into a mermaid," Kendra said finally, eyes full of determination, and I nearly fell out of my chair in shock. Nerissa had mentioned her interest... but I wasn't expecting her to just drop the command on me so suddenly. The world had suddenly gone very hollow and quiet with her words.

I slowly leaned forward in the armchair, knees weak at the idea.

"I'm pretty sure Coral would *kill* me if I did that."

"Coral doesn't get to dictate my life decisions."

"I understand, but she also went through a lot to save your life... to ensure you had a *future*. If I let you—or even *assist* you—in throwing that all away just to help rescue her from the Cora Palace—"

"Do you have a better plan?" Kendra pressed, folding her arms, and for the first time since her arrival, I saw a glimpse of her sister in her, beyond their identical appearance. Strangely enough... I didn't welcome the reminder, didn't cherish their similarities at all. I hadn't expected to like Kendra being her own individual person so much.

Desperate to wave away such thoughts, I gestured wildly to the door.

"Leif is working on a plan right now," I insisted, but she shook her head. A hint of a desperate plea strained in her voice.

"It's already been *days*. I can't lose my sister on top of my father. And if I have to stay down here as a result of my actions, then so be it."

She didn't know what she was saying. I rose from the armchair, running a hand through my hair as I ran her request through my mind over and over. Coral aside... it was too soon to let her make a decision like this. I'd nearly made that mistake with Coral, and I was glad in hindsight that she had initially refused to transform so quickly.

"You've only been down here for a single day. You know nothing of life outside this palace."

"I've seen enough," she said softly. "I've seen the fish... the coral... I've seen *you*. It's enough for me."

She met my gaze again, and there was something in it I couldn't quite place. Something anchoring her to this place. But I couldn't let her do this. Couldn't give her what she wanted. Again, I couldn't bring myself to tell her no directly, to shut down that hope, so I walked past her and avoided meeting her eyes, trying to buy myself time.

She sensed my hesitation anyway.

"Fine. Then I'll ask Nerissa to help me," she called after me, and I paused, letting out an exasperated breath.

Turning back to face her, I summoned as much order to my voice as I could and said, "I'm the king, and I won't allow it."

It pained me to order her around this way.

"You're not *our* king," Kendra reminded me, and I recoiled—the rejection was as good as a slap in the face. "Nerissa and I are mermaids—we answer to the Atlantis royals, not you. So if I want Nerissa to help me transform, then that's what's going to happen."

Damn Nerissa for educating her about the mermaid kingdom before she even knew what she was getting into! I could tell Kendra was dead serious and wasn't going to be swayed otherwise. I wished she would at least give it a week—I could have taken her out on the seahorses and shown her what life down here was really like first.

I caved, letting my "king act" crumble.

"Please... there has to be another way," I begged finally, but Kendra's lips were a thin line, and she refused to budge. I could already feel the wrath Coral would bring down on me if I let this happen. And I didn't want to resort to throwing Kendra in the dungeon just to keep her put.

"Tell me something, Lysander," Kendra said finally, closing the distance between us. Her proximity did things to my heart, to my *body*, that I didn't quite understand. "If we took Coral out of this discussion, then would you still be opposed to this?"

I swallowed hard, trying not to fixate on how sweaty my hands were, how alluring the slender arch of her neck was, how much I liked gazing at her in general.

"I would let you make your own decision—but I would also encourage you to go out and actually *see* what you'd be getting involved in first. Life above land is very different to life down here."

"Let me do this," Kendra insisted, her delicate hands taking mine. My heart leaped in protest, like the act alone might reveal all the thoughts in my mind. "Coral tried to protect me. Now it's my turn to protect her. And by doing this, we don't have to wait any longer—we can save Coral *now* without putting Veranis at risk of attack. Don't you want to get her back?"

Coral...

Guilt plunged through me. For just a moment, all thought of her existence had escaped me. I found myself hastily nodding. *Yes*, of course I wanted Coral back as soon as possible. Or at least, that was what I ought to want.

"Then let me handle my sister," Kendra said, an edge of order to her tone that I found unreasonably attractive, "and help me save her."

CHAPTER TEN

Kendra

The coming days were filled with preparations. Lysander filled Leif in on the plan we had come up with together, and along with Nerissa, we'd spent hours in the strategy room working out the specifics.

"There were siren guard uniforms discarded near the site where our men were slaughtered," Nerissa said, as we gathered around a table centered in the strategy room. Sprawled from one end to the other was a map of the three kingdoms. All of Leif's markers were clustered around Coronis, trying to decide on the best pathway in, but until now, he hadn't been able to find a strategy that wouldn't require hundreds of men and brute force. "We could stop by the site on the way to Coronis and salvage whatever uniforms are left—if a current hasn't swept them away by now."

"Good idea," Leif agreed, studying the map. "We can disguise ourselves using the uniforms to sneak in and grab Coral. But we need to decide who's doing what first."

So far, we'd narrowed the operation down into three groups. The delegation would be sent directly into the palace as a distraction. Whoever delivered it would need to be able to defend themselves and get away fast, possibly without additional help if things went south fast. So Leif was considering pairing Nerissa and I together for that task because mermaids could manipulate the ocean currents to swim almost three times as fast as any other being in the Undersea.

Though I had to admit, the idea of venturing directly into the Cora Palace scared me. I knew we'd be entering the belly of the beast, and there would be sirens *everywhere*. But I was determined to help Coral, and if this was the best way to do it... I was willing to do my part.

Next, we had the rescue team, and Leif wanted to pair himself with Matt for that task. Lysander couldn't enter the Cora Palace without directly risking an act of war, and with Eugene's men, they'd both agreed he'd be lucky to get anywhere near it. But Matt and Leif could sneak around if they got their hands on those uniforms Nerissa mentioned.

"The only problem is if we run into trouble, Matt is a liability," Leif grimaced, folding his arms as he debated his options. "He doesn't have years of training to defend himself, and I don't have enough time to train him."

Matt had been avoiding us—taking meals in his room—so thankfully, he wasn't here to be offended by Leif's blunt statement. But I cleared my throat.

"Matt fought off three siren guards on the beach—he saved my life," I said in defense.

"It's not that he can't hold his own in a fight," Leif replied firmly. "But we're talking *hundreds* of guards this time. It'll be risky to involve him... However, we're short on men as it is, and everyone else is accounted for and required to defend the people of Veranis if we bring Eugene's men back to our doorstep."

I frowned. I understood where he was coming from, but if it was risky to involve Matt, then it would be risky to involve *me* as well. Just because my mermaid transformation would give me access to my heart magic didn't mean I'd be any good at using it if we were surrounded by hundreds of siren guards. If they were going to trust me, they should trust Matt too.

"I agree," Lysander cut in, surprising me. "I'd rather Leif carry Matt's weight in the mission than us be one man short on our borders. Because if Eugene's men discover a weak spot in our defenses, they'll be able to sneak through and use their siren song to turn our kingdom on each other. We'll be destroyed from the inside if that happens."

Leif nodded like that had been his thought process too, and I grimaced. But I believed in Matt—he'd show them both what he was really capable of if it came down to it.

"Okay, the getaway team..." Leif huffed, bringing us to the final leg of our plan. This was where the manta rays came into play.

"I don't like this because borrowing a manta ray means owing another favor to the sea witch to balance out the magic," Lysander informed us, leaning his palms on the table. He'd discarded his formal court-appropriate jacket over the back of a nearby chair, and I couldn't help noticing how his shoulder muscles flexed under his white button-down shirt.

"I don't think we have another choice," Leif replied, his expression firm. "Like last time—nothing else can get us in and out of the city fast enough, and anything smaller can be shot down quickly. At least a manta ray can withstand a few arrows."

The current plan was for Lysander and Maya to wait outside Coronis until Leif sounded the conch shell. It was the only undetectable signal that would travel from within the Cora Palace to the outskirts of Coronis. Once the signal was

103

made, Lysander and Maya would ride a manta ray into Coronis so that we could escape. But we would only get one shot at this—especially with the predators that circled and guarded the Cora Palace. We couldn't afford to miss our window, or we'd be trapped inside at the mercy of the guards' siren songs.

The entire plan had risks—there was so much that could go wrong. But it was the best plan we had unless we were to spend weeks, or even months, waiting for a better opportunity to come by. The thought of leaving Coral in that place any longer... it made my insides twist with dread.

Two days before we were set to head out, Leif insisted that everyone be present during dinner so that we could discuss final preparations. Matt wasn't happy to be summoned, and Leif made sure he was seated at the opposite end of the dining table, away from Lysander, who sat at the head of the table. I took the seat beside Lysander.

"If Kendra is going to be in her mermaid form, she needs to transform tonight," Nerissa said from midway down the table, helping herself to a plate of mussels. "It'll take her some time to adjust, to learn how to swim again, and then I'll need to train her in the basics of magic."

A thrill went through me at the suggestion. *Finally*. Since getting Lysander on board, I'd been eager to go through with the transformation, but he'd convinced me to wait these past few days until we had a solidified plan.

Leif, who was nodding in agreement, turned to Matt.

"Likewise—we should do some training of our own," he suggested. "I'll find you a sword from our barracks. Providing you don't use it to stab Lysander, that is."

Matt's eyes glowered back at him.

"I make no promises," he replied witheringly. "But until we rescue Coral... I'll try to refrain from murdering your king."

I glanced at Lysander, who shifted uncomfortably beside me, and I resisted the urge to reassure him that Matt wasn't being serious. But around us, the guards' hands had gone to their spears, refusing to ignore the threat. Leif held up a hand to stop them from moving any closer.

"He's joking," he assured them, though he looked strained in his efforts to defuse the tension. He turned back to Nerissa. "Okay, we'll go ahead with Kendra's transformation. What do you need for tonight?"

"Well," Nerissa huffed, drumming her fingers on the table. "I'm not sure what to expect—it's not like us merpeople go trading our tail for legs every day, and vice versa. And none of us were present to witness Coral's transformation... so this could go smoothly, or it might not. Either way, I think we'll need somewhere with lots of space. Maybe some pain relief too, if you have anything on hand."

"You can have the ballroom," Lysander told her. "It's huge—there's lots of space to practice swimming if you need it. And I can have a bed sent down there too. We might have some herbs, and I could have a tonic made for the pain..."

I felt the blood drain from my face as they casually discussed the agony that might arise from having my freaking *legs* fused into a tail. I suddenly found that I couldn't eat another sea berry from my plate, feeling sick to my stomach at the thought.

Lysander glanced back at me, and guilt immediately crossed his face as he noticed my expression. He cleared his throat and stood.

"Make the arrangements you need to make," he ordered suddenly, and offered me his arm. "I will escort Kendra to her quarters so she can rest until it is time."

Relieved, I reached for his arm and let him guide me out of the dining room. It wasn't until we were up the stairs and well away from the others before I dropped my hand from his arm, and he turned to me.

"I'm sorry—that was very careless of me," he said, sincere guilt shining in his eyes. "I didn't scare you, did I?"

"If it was a tactic to get me to change my mind, it wasn't good enough," I reassured him. "But I appreciate you escorting me out like that."

He reached for my hand, then stopped himself, realizing what he was doing. Clearing his throat again, he clasped his hands behind his back formally and asked, "Will you be okay? If you want, I can be there with you when it happens."

The sentiment was kind, but... I'd noticed the strange connection Lysander and I had developed. It had only been a few days, and he was the easiest person down here to talk to. And I noticed the way he looked at me from time to time—nobody had ever looked at me that way, made me *feel* the things he did.

But Coral had given up her *heart* for this male, and she was my sister.

"I need to clarify something," I said finally, and he bristled like he'd been waiting for this, dread flickering across his expression for just a moment. "You and my sister... what exactly is the nature of your relationship?"

He hesitated, looking strained.

"It's not really been defined," he replied carefully, running a hand through his hair. "We left things on good terms... *promising* terms, the last I saw her. And I care about your sister, I *truly* do. But since the bond snapped in place between us... since she gave me her heart... my emotions have been difficult to read."

I raised an eyebrow at him. He had to give me more than that, and he grimaced at the look on my face.

"What I know for certain is that we are corulers, bound by her breaking my curse. I'm not sure what it would mean for her title if we were to dishonor that—I'm her tie to Veranis, and the only thing giving her reign over three territories right now. But our relationship never really progressed anywhere solid, what with my cursed nature and the whole Maya thing..."

"But do you want to be with her?" I asked, and he hesitated.

"I *care* about your sister," he repeated slowly, like he wasn't entirely sure. "For the first time in my life, I have a moral compass and an obligation to do the right thing by her. The way we left things... I think I owe it to both of us to see where it leads."

"I see," I said, and disappointment settled in my stomach.

"And this coruler thing is bound by the ocean—I don't want to mess with that while she's in Eugene's clutches. It could be the only thing keeping her alive right now, giving her power as Reigning Queen."

"Understood," I replied tautly, not wanting to hear any more. It was like I'd thought, and that was fine. I wasn't about to mess with my sister's happiness. I was here to rescue her, and then I'd get out of this palace, make a new life for myself as a mermaid—

Lysander caught my arm before I could turn away, and our gazes caught. For a moment, neither of us could stop staring at one another.

"I say all of that, and I mean it, *but*..." he breathed, and I could have sworn I saw fear in his eyes. Like this was the most vulnerable he'd ever been with anyone. "Ever since *you* got here, I've felt more confused than ever. And at first, I thought it was just that you're twins and that I miss Coral... but I'm starting to think it's more than that."

My heart skipped a beat, and somehow, the hope that flittered to life inside of me felt worse than the disappointment in my gut a moment ago.

"Well, if there's any reason *not* to act on this, other than maintaining our morals, it's the fact that doing so could jeopardize Coral's safety," I replied quietly. "So perhaps it's best if we limit our time together, and we just focus on getting Coral back in one piece."

Lysander faltered, letting go of my arm, but nodded.

"Yes, I agree," he said, but I saw the disappointment in his eyes. I wonder if he saw the same in mine. I took a step back from him, turning toward the stairs again.

"Don't bother walking me to my room. I'm ready for Nerissa to begin now," I told him, before looking away and descending back down. Trading my legs for a tail might be painful, but I doubted it would be any more painful than what I was already feeling in my heart.

CHAPTER ELEVEN

Coral

I'd lost track of time again, unable to tell if hours or days had passed since Melody's visit. My stomach gnawed painfully, but everything else felt hazy and numb, including the stabbing pain that had been erupting from my tail nonstop these past few days.

I'd thought long and hard about how I was going to reach the dagger under my bed, and I came to the conclusion that I'd have to get out of these iron bonds first. Even if I swiped a key or a weapon, my hands were positioned too awkwardly to free myself. And I couldn't see them freeing me of the cuffs unless I urgently needed to be whisked out of here.

One thing was for certain though: Eugene needed me alive—if only to steal my power with his crown—and I was willing to bet that he'd do anything to stop me from dying down here. If my tail became too infected, it would threaten my well-being, and with the wound already festering, all I needed to do was *appear* more ill than I truly was.

For the past few days, I'd wriggled my tail fin until it was pressed against the iron, and I pressed with all of my might, irritating the already infected wound. Agonizing pain had shot through my tail, making me grit my teeth, but I'd continued to wedge the arrow tip deeper for hours and hours, day after day, until I couldn't take the pain anymore. A mix of fresh and stale metallic blood now floated freely within the cage, adding to the haze that indicated my vision was fading, along with my strength.

My thoughts were still clear, but the pain in my tail was almost unbearable, and I felt noticeably sluggish. I was beginning to think I'd made a grave mistake. Had I dug myself an early grave trying to push myself to the edge of death? Perhaps I'd been bleeding for too long, and my body lacked the substance to fight my way out of here.

My head lulled to the side of the bed, trying to ignore the pain in my tail as I waited. I realized I'd dozed off because I didn't hear footsteps approaching, and suddenly, a key was rattling in the lock of my cage. I felt more than one presence fill the room, but I didn't open my eyes, my heart hammering in my chest. This was it—if I could merely *appear* more ill than I was, I might just be able to get out of here.

Two fingers pressed against my throat, and I fought back the urge to shift away, letting my body stay limp.

"She's dying," one of them said, and I heard something clink against the floor. "You—send for a healer."

There was a pause, and I focused on keeping my breathing steady and shallow. One of the sirens slapped me all of a sudden, and my head jolted sideways, but I bit my cheek to avoid crying out in pain. It took all my focus to keep myself limp and lifeless.

"I don't think a healer will arrive in time—not with the right supplies. We should deliver her ourselves."

"We've been ordered not to move the Undersea queen for any reason."

Another pause, but I felt a strange tension in the air.

111

"Then perhaps you can be the one to tell the king that his source of magic perished overnight because of *your* poor judgment."

Another pause, and then a grunt.

"Fine. But be quick—I don't want to be caught and punished for doing this."

Finally, I thought, as hands appeared on my wrists and tail. In moments, they had me unhooked from the cuffs, and I continued to stay limp as they attempted to heave me off the bed. But my heart was pounding, adrenaline coursing through me, a surge of energy building for just the right moment. I waited until my tail hit the ice-cold floor, and then my eyes sprung open.

I kicked upward, so hard my tail wound throbbed with hot white pain, and smacked the first siren in the nose. He went flying backward, letting me go, and I sank below the frame of the bed.

Head turning, I spied the dagger and swiped it. Just as the second siren came at me, weapon drawn, I swung my arm around and swiped the siren's heels. He let out a yell and collapsed, his tendons ruptured and his ability to stand impacted. The two sirens collided with each other in the chaos, and I brought the dagger upward. In a clean sweep, I'd stabbed the first siren in the stomach, blood flowing fast and free into the water. Gritting my teeth as all my muscles protested, I drove the second blow into the other siren's gut and kicked both of them down with my tail. Their eyes rolled into the back of their head as they hit the floor, out cold.

I drifted back to the floor, and I lay there for a moment, watching the blood collect in the water above me, and panted hard. I didn't think the sirens would die, but their injuries would definitely need treatment. I needed to get out of here before someone discovered us—or worse, the sirens came to.

Wincing, I sat upward and waved the blood out of my face, then studied my bloodied mess of a tail. There was puss and blackened bruising all over the scales, and it was still bleeding. Grimacing, I reached for the first siren and tore half of his undershirt off using the dagger, tying a temporary bandage around my tail fin. It hurt like hell as I pulled the fabric tight, but I pushed on and bit my bottom lip to stop from crying out and attracting attention. I didn't have time to waste.

Using the bed for support, I pulled myself upright—dagger clutched in my right hand—and gave my tail a few kicks for momentum. Every single movement sent pain through my lower body, but I gritted my teeth and pushed forward to the open cage door. Using my tail was like having a severely injured leg *without* having the other leg to lean on for relief. Plus, the sensation of my tail working at half capacity was similar to having a limp, and I could tell my movements were sluggish and delayed as a result. It was agony and torture all at once.

Once I was out in the hallway, I broke into a swim, pushing as hard and fast as I could down the hallway. My T-shirt was soaked in blood and grime—it was obvious I was a prisoner, and I'd be caught instantly if I wasn't careful. By the time I reached the end of the hallway, I felt clammy and shaky all over. I hadn't realized how weak I was until now. I had to pause for a moment, leaning against the door, and I used that moment to press my ear to it to listen for signs of life on the other side. Then, I carefully opened it and peered out.

113

The hallway stretched on endlessly, and I could go either way with no real assurance that I'd be heading toward an exit. I knew I couldn't go out the front entrance—there would be too many guards. I'd have to find a more discreet way out, and then I could worry about getting through the city. I already dreaded the thought of having to swim that far on my own.

I staggered a few paces out into the hallway, then turned left and found I didn't have the energy left for strong, broad strokes anymore. I was down to a weakened doggy paddle as I sluggishly pushed past a few rooms and finally spotted a staircase leading down.

But there were guards positioned below, and I heard voices from somewhere farther down the hall. Swearing under my breath, I drifted sideways into an alcove and sank down to the floor, hoping I was concealed enough not to be noticed. My vision was swimming, and I tried shaking my head to clear it. *How long had it been since I'd eaten, again?*

Then I noticed the trail of blood that had been leaking from my tail into the water, and my blood turned to ice. *I'd led a trail directly to my hiding spot.*

The voices were growing closer now, and I squeezed my eyes shut. I was going to have to fight again, and I didn't know if I could do it a second time.

The voices stopped, and footsteps paused. They were right around the corner—no doubt that they'd seen the trail of blood and were moments from discovering me. My breathing turned erratic as a tall siren came into view, slowly glancing toward me. When he spotted me, his eyes glinted, and a smile curved on his lips.

"Trying to escape, were we?" he chastised, eyeing my wounded tail. He glanced over his shoulder at his companion who was still out of view, and ordered, "Send word that the Undersea queen is out of her cage, and fortify the palace."

I inhaled deeply, knowing this was it. I'd be back in my cage in a matter of minutes, and I doubted I'd get another opportunity to escape.

"Of course," a light, calm voice replied, and the second figure walked behind the first as if walking past him.

He turned, and a dagger swiftly appeared in his hand, slicing clean through the siren's chest. The siren barely had time to gasp before he sank to the ground, and standing there was Leif—dressed in a red siren guard uniform.

Everything slowed for a moment as I tried to process it. As my heart pounded, relief sagged through me. His eyes hardened at the sight of me curled into the crevice, at my wounded tail, and he snarled.

"*Fuck*. What did they do to you?"

He immediately kneeled to offer me his steady hand. I couldn't stop staring, my eyes wide with shock. "It's okay, I've got you," he breathed, more quietly this time, as he glanced over his shoulder before turning back to examine me from head to toe. "Can you get up?"

Slowly, I swallowed hard and nodded, not trusting myself to speak. His eyes shone with relief, copper-red hair swaying in the gentle drifting water.

"Good. Matt will be here any second, and then we're going to get you out of here."

"H-h-how are you here?" I stammered, as I finally realized I wouldn't be going back into the cage. *I was getting out of here.*

He motioned with his extended hand, which I took, and he pulled me upright. I had to lean on him for support, but he didn't protest once. His body was warm and comforting next to the cage I'd been in these past few days.

"Long story. I'll explain on the way back," he promised, and we navigated out into the hallway again. That's when I spotted Matt sprinting toward us, and the shameful part is that he was *still* twice as fast in his human form as I was with my injured tail. He was also dressed in a red guard uniform.

"Eugene and Melody are too busy taunting Kendra and Nerissa—but neither have made a move to harm them yet," he breathed, coming to a stop before us. My heart rate spiked, and a hand clamped over my mouth.

"They have *Kendra?*" My shout was muffled thanks to Leif's well-timed reaction. He must have known I would panic.

"It's part of the plan—don't worry," he reassured me, his voice low next to my ear. *Don't worry?* Was he *insane?* I opened my mouth to protest again, but Leif handed me over to Matt.

"Lean on him for a second—I've got to signal to Lysander and Maya," he told me, and Matt wrapped an arm around me for support. I'd never been so relieved to see the people I care about, but at any moment, we could be caught, and then we'd all be screwed. Leif pulled a familiar-looking conch shell out from his trouser pocket and blew into it once. Like last time, I didn't hear anything, but I could sense a shift in the water around me.

"We've got less than a minute to prepare," Leif said, and motioned for us to move. The three of us navigated closer to the stairs, toward a black railing. When I looked down, I saw the Cora Palace throne room, where Eugene was seated and sneering at Kendra and Nerissa, Melody standing behind him. I nearly gasped aloud at the sight of Kendra—at her *lilac mermaid tail*—but Leif anticipated my reaction and clamped his hand over my mouth a second time.

I struggled against him in outrage as he took the moment to observe my wounded tail again, then glanced up toward the glass dome overhead—and that's when I saw a large shadow pass overhead, drowning the throne room in darkness.

"I was hoping your tail would be in better condition for this, but I guess we'll have to improvise," he muttered.

"Now or never, Leif," Matt whispered quickly, peering over the railing stealthily and noting how the guards' gazes had drifted upward toward the shadowy disturbance. When I glanced back at Leif, he had unsheathed his dagger a second time. With a single throw, it sailed through the water, long and hard, and pierced the glass dome. It shattered, and screams erupted from the throne room below as thousands of tiny shards rained down. Even I threw my hands up as the currents turned wild and scattered the glass our way.

"That's our cue!" Nerissa sang from below, her voice filled with mischief. I peered back over the railing, and before I knew what was happening, she and Kendra had begun swimming in circles around the throne room, zigzagging around guards and beckoning with their hands. I watched as they use

117

their magic to tug at the currents of the water, and in moments, a whirlpool had come to life. It reminded me of the whirlpools Kendra and I used to make in my father's outdoor spa as kids, but this one was far more powerful. It swept up every siren except Eugene and Melody, who were safe in the center of the room.

"Time to go!" Leif shouted over the chaos, racing over to a polished redwood side table, which had six cupboard doors attached. I didn't have time to ask what he was doing. Eugene looked up and spotted us, and his growl erupted through the entire throne room, deafening over the raging water.

"*Stop them!*" he screamed, and I heard footsteps echoing up the nearby staircases leading to the second floor.

"How are we getting up there?" Matt demanded, panic shining in his eyes now as Leif began yanking and cutting through three of the six doors with his dagger. "I thought Coral was going to swim us up."

"New plan," Leif said quickly, ripping the last door free and racing back to our sides. He thrust a door into each of our hands. "We're going to ride Nerissa and Kendra's current up to the top."

I went pale.

"You want me to paddleboard," I said in realization, staring at the narrow door in my hands. It reminded me of the swim boards Kendra and I had learned to swim on as kids—barely large enough to support my whole weight. "This is essentially surfing. And I haven't surfed since Maya died... I don't know if I can do this—"

"If you want to get out of here alive, you don't have a choice," Leif replied briskly. "Now show me how it's done, and do it fast."

I swore, this time not bothering to keep it under my breath. But as I looked up at the ceiling, resolve settled in me. Leif and Matt had given me a newfound strength. We *just* needed to make it to the top of the dome.

I could do this.

I shifted my weight off of Matt and clambered onto the obsidian railing, shaking with nerves and feeling woozy from my weak limbs. One jump, and we'd be in the current, using the cupboard doors to guide and navigate our way through it.

Heaving a deep breath, I kicked as hard as I could with my tail and was instantly swept up. It took all of my strength to stay balanced, to keep the board positioned under my chest. Shouts were all around us now, and arrows were starting to pierce the current as Leif and Matt jumped in behind me, following my lead. It was a tangle of bubbles and foam and fins.

"Take us up!" Leif shouted to Nerissa and Kendra as they whizzed past. They were a blur of lilac and green and blue, and they spiraled up to the top of the dome to wait for us. I looked up and locked my gaze onto the open dome above as the current lifted us higher—but it lifted the sirens caught up in it higher too. They lashed out at us as we rode around and around, and I had to swerve with the cupboard to dodge their deadly claws. Jumbled echoes of siren song floated in and out of my ears, indistinguishable under the roar of the current, but strong enough to knock my balance once or twice. My grasp nearly slipped from the cupboard, and splinters dug into my fingers from how tightly I held on.

119

We pushed through shards of glass, dodged arrow after arrow, and before long, my arms and cheeks were covered in tiny nicks and cuts. Not to mention my tail was screaming in protest from swerving and balancing, the pain growing unbearable, but we were so close now—*so close...*

"Don't let them escape!" Eugene roared from below, his voice echoing above all. "Shoot the queen down! She's already injured!"

The open dome loomed, and my hand reached for the broken ring, ready to haul myself up to freedom—

Something shot clean through my upper tail, and I let out a cry, my grasp slipping from the board as pain rippled through me. The board fell away as I tumbled past Leif and Matt, who both strained to reach me but weren't fast enough.

I tried to fight the current, but I couldn't move my tail—something had pieced a critical nerve, and it wouldn't respond. I was caught in a tangle, an endless roll, I couldn't separate down from up—

"Coral!" Leif bellowed, tugging my awareness upward. I caught a glimpse of him reaching for me as he and Matt clung to the dome rim. I struggled against the current, but it was too strong. I was going to be thrown back out, down onto the second level of the palace.

That's when I realized a group of sirens were waiting to catch me and subdue me. And Eugene stood with them, watching with a greedy, satisfied gleam in his eye. It stirred something deep inside of me, and I snarled, pushing my hands out in front of me.

I won't be a prisoner again, I thought, and pushed hard against the currents.

120

They obeyed.

With the iron cuffs gone, the water responded to me, swirling up around my arms like jets gaining a grip. And then there was a massive surge, and I flew back up toward the dome, riding the currents.

Leif and Matt were caught up in my current too, and we all tumbled upward, rushing through the open dome space until we were floating in the calmer chilled water above the Cora Palace. My head was spinning. Nerissa and Kendra were nowhere to be seen, but Leif reached for me with his hand, and I grabbed hold. I reached for Matt with my other hand so that we wouldn't be separated.

As we twirled, I heard snarling, and it was only then that I realized we were surrounded by the predators that guarded the Cora Palace—each one more deadly than the last, with razor-sharp jaws and beady eyes.

"Brace yourself!" someone screamed from behind us, but before we even had time to look, something swept under us like a flying carpet and then pushed upward, trapping us against a large flat expanse of flesh as it sailed away from the palace. My tail throbbed from impact.

Hands held me steady as I took a moment to process where I was. A manta ray had scooped us up and was now zigzagging through a swarm of vicious sharks. They snapped at us, eyes dark at the sight of all the blood trailing from my tail. Nerissa and Leif were on both sides of me, and to my surprise, Maya was in front of us as if leading the manta ray.

"Lysander, do something!" Nerissa snapped, ducking as a shark lunged at her. She drew an arrow and shot it between the eyes to deter it, and it faltered.

I looked over my shoulder, and my heart swelled when I realized it was Lysander holding me steady. Kendra was sitting to his left, pale as a ghost as she fought to hold on, and Matt was on his other side. I didn't have time to ask about Kendra's tail because the manta ray took a sudden dive to avoid a shark, and we all screamed. My stomach dropped like I was riding a roller coaster as we glided over the city of Coronis and headed toward a valley of seamounts in the distance.

Lysander looked around at the sharks that were still chasing us and said, "Leave us!" The sharks didn't stop, snarling at him in response, and Lysander's cheeks turned red. "They're loyal to Eugene—they won't listen to me," he admitted finally, earning an eye roll from Nerissa. And at that moment, another shark lunged at us. Lysander covered my head and pushed us flat against the manta ray to avoid it. My nose stung from being shoved down, and when I twisted around, I saw Leif bury his dagger into the shark's side, which caused it to slow and sink.

"We're not going to lose them with that wound in Coral's tail." Leif panted, crouching next to me again. "They'll track the blood all the way back to Veranis. We need to shake them somehow."

"What was that thing she did before?" Nerissa demanded, keeping her eyes trained on another approaching shark.

"I-I don't know," I stammered, staring down at my hands. "I just... was determined not be caught, so I made a pushing motion, and the current took us up—"

The manta ray took another sweeping dive and curved as we sailed around a seamount. Instinctively, I shifted my weight for balance with the others—but Matt dove to clutch the manta ray's right fin, grunting as he was nearly thrown off. Lysander reached back to grab his wrist as we turned upright again, and Matt glared at him like he'd been assaulted. Frowning, I recalled the trouble I'd had with my balance the last time I rode a manta ray, and I remembered Lysander saying he understood the currents so well he could predict them. That's when I realized that perhaps I had similar instincts now that I was transformed—and it was why Matt was struggling in human form.

"Whatever it was, just do it again!" Nerissa yelled, shooting another two arrows at the sharks snapping at our heels. I realized she meant me, and I tried making a movement with my hands.

Come on, I thought, trying to remember how I'd taken control of the water around me. Lysander was watching me anxiously, one hand gripping Matt—who wore a bitter expression—and the other placed gently on my back to support me.

Nerissa was almost out of arrows now, and Leif's dagger was long gone with the shark he'd killed.

I let out a cry as a surge of power washed through me from head to tail, and the water around us rippled out from my hands, expanding as far as the eye could see. The sharks tumbled away in the powerful current, smacking into nearby seamounts, which then proceeded to rumble dangerously around us.

Kendra let out a gasp as rocks began to tremble and shift, rolling down the mounts.

"Go up! *Up, up, now!*" she bellowed, pointing desperately above us. Lysander let out a low whistling sound, and the manta ray cut upward just as the mounts began to give way around us. Bedrock crumbled, and sand shifted into haze beneath us as we glided out of the wreckage. Leif peered over the edge of the manta ray, at the well-worn paths that had now become buried, and swore.

I took a moment to recover my breath, then remembered everything—Kendra's tail, Matt and Maya's presence, and I rounded on Lysander with wide eyes.

"Are you *crazy?*" I demanded shrilly, and he recoiled from my outburst. "Why did you endanger my friends? And my *sister?*"

I peered around at Kendra, who was still pale in the face and clutching onto Lysander for support. Lysander frowned at me.

"The plan only *worked* because of them," he insisted, sounding offended. "If there had been another way, then I would have done it."

"Then you should have left me there!" I hissed back. "Why risk all of their lives for just me? I was *fine*—Eugene wasn't going to kill me!"

Annoyance flared in his eyes, and he opened his mouth to argue back, but sudden white-hot pain erupted through my tail fin, knocking my balance. I tumbled backward, my vision splitting. Lysander let out a yelp that sounded very far away, and I felt his arms around me just as the world faded to black.

CHAPTER TWELVE

Coral

I awoke with a start in an unfamiliar bed in the Vera Palace. Before I could so much as sit upright, there was movement beside me, and Lysander's face came into view, eyebrows creased with worry.

"You're awake," he stated, reaching for my hand with his. "How are you feeling?"

I winced as many aches and pains returned to my body all at once. I was clearly still suffering from some overexertion. But my tail wasn't throbbing anymore, and I flexed the muscles in my tail fin as a test. When there was no pain, I pulled the blankets up to examine it and noticed that all arrows had been removed. My tail had been bandaged properly with kelp, cleaned thoroughly, and the swelling had gone down.

I rested my head back against the pillows, letting the blankets drift down again, and turned toward Lysander.

"A lot better," I told him finally, and he smiled warmly, his sea-green eyes sparkling with relief. He sat gently beside me on the bed, running his other hand through my hair softly, like he still couldn't quite believe I was here. His hand in my hair felt nice... but something felt off. I'd spent *days* imagining this very moment—being reunited with him. I thought I would gravitate toward him, unable to keep my hands off of him. But I was quite content to stay where I was.

Why wasn't I overcome with happiness? All I felt toward him was annoyance for the fact that he'd endangered the people I cared about.

"You scared me," he whispered finally. "At first, I didn't think you were coming back. And then when I heard you'd been captured... I realized I was foolish to think such a thing. I wasn't there to protect you when you needed me most... and I'm so, so sorry."

It was nice to hear his words—to hear that he *cared*—and I realized I'd become familiar with his nonemotional self. It was unusual to see him this way, to hear him speak from his heart.

My heart, I realized. The heart we now shared that gave him the capacity to feel things.

I slowly pushed upright in the bed, noticing the protest in his eyes but ignoring it. So much had happened... and I recounted the last moments before I'd blacked out. I remembered the manta ray, Kendra, and Matt—and *Maya*.

Crap!

Guilt flooded through me. *Matt knew about Maya.* I'd meant to tell him. I just... I wanted to wait until I'd restored her soul, rather than put him through more pain.

He must be so angry with me...

Pushing the thought aside, I mentally played out the rest of the rescue operation. I realized I might have overreacted in the heat of our narrow escape. All that sat before me was a gentle, sincere being who had clearly been worried out of his mind about me. And he'd come for me, even though it put his kingdom in danger, and it went against the treaty. So, though the annoyance still lingered, I reigned it in.

"I'm sorry I yelled at you before," I said, meaning it, and reached to slip my hand into his. His fingers tightened around mine, firm and steady. "But you need to tell me—why are Kendra and Matt down here? What happened while I was gone?"

Lysander shook his head at me.

"There's no need to worry about all of that right now. Just focus on resting up—"

"I'm fine, Lysander," I insisted. "Tell me why they're here. Did *you* bring them here?"

Hurt flashed through Lysander's eyes, and I grimaced.

"I would never do that," he replied thinly. "It was *Leif* who brought them here—at their request, I might add. I may have been desperate to find you, but I would never endanger your loved ones."

I bit back a retort because *clearly*, he had been willing to bring them on the rescue mission. But I was trying to be reasonable, to see it from his point of view.

"Alright, fine. Well, I have some questions about being the Undersea queen... and I want to talk about some of the things that happened with Eugene," I said, my thought namely going to the crown and why it had rejected me. There were so many things I wish he'd thought to mention before—had he *known* I would become the Undersea queen? "But *first*, I want to know why my sister has a tail."

Lysander winced.

"Perhaps we could circle back to Eugene first?"

"*No.*"

He let out a breath.

127

"It was her decision... and I tried to talk her out of it, but she was determined. We couldn't risk rescuing you sooner without a way to defend Veranis, and her magic combined with Nerissa's..."

He trailed off, but I understood enough. *That* was why he'd risked his kingdom's safety—because Kendra was his fail-safe. I couldn't believe he'd let her talk him into it... but I also knew it was typical of my sister.

My blood boiled, seething anger building toward *both* of them.

"Send her in."

Lysander flinched at my tone and nodded, getting to his feet. He seemed almost relieved to have an excuse to leave, given my impending wrath.

"Just call for me if you need me," he said hesitantly, and promptly left.

I lay there for some time, mulling over everything else that had happened. There was a plate of food on the bedside table, but I couldn't bring myself to eat despite the gnawing in my stomach.

Lysander and I were supposed to be king and queen... *equals*. But we'd talked all of two minutes, and it had ended with me sending him out, fueled by anger. How were we supposed to make decisions together when we couldn't even *talk* to each other?

Not to mention, he seemed like a completely different person with his newfound emotional depth, and I couldn't grasp the connection we'd once had anymore. Surely, this was supposed to be a happy time, being back in each other's arms, talking about our plans for the future together... but all we'd done is argue. Was this what Eugene had wanted?

As I lay there, staring across the room at his dozens of bookcases, I realized I was relieved to be alone again. I'd spent all that time as Eugene's prisoner wondering if I'd ever see Lysander again, yearning for the aloof male I'd once fallen for... but *that* Lysander was gone. In his place was a new Lysander, and it wasn't the same...

Could this really work? I felt like I was having to get to know a whole new person, and it was like a final boulder falling into place as I realized just how much I'd lost over the past week. My father, Lysander, my mortal body... Tears formed in my eyes. For the first time, I felt safe to grieve, in a quiet place where I wouldn't be judged, where I didn't have to stay strong. And so, I let the tears flow, sobbing into the sheets and wiping my nose. It felt good to let it all out.

After a few minutes, there was a knock at the door, and I hurriedly wiped my eyes as best I could before plastering a half smile on my face.

"Come in," I called, trying to hide the waver in my voice. The door opened, and Kendra peered around tentatively. But she noticed my smile, and her eyes lit up at the sight of me.

"Coral!" she cried, zooming into the room with a laugh. Despite my initial anger, I broke into a genuine smile at the sight of her, and she collided with me, wrapping her arms around me tightly. I squeezed her, so relieved to have her with me. "I thought I'd never see you again!"

"Me too," I admitted, and Kendra scooted into bed with me, pushing me aside to make space. When I transformed, I thought that was it—my old life was gone, and my sister and Matt would be left wondering about me forever.

"We thought you had drowned until Leif showed up," Kendra replied earnestly, laying on her side to face me. "Like seriously, don't ever do that again! And Leif explained a lot of stuff to us... but not everything. Like why did you come down here for help against Melody? How did you even *know* to come down here?"

I stared at my precious sister, whom I'd fought so hard to protect, and held back a small laugh at her many questions.

"I didn't mean to end up down here," I admitted finally. "I jumped off the balcony into the ocean, trying to get away from Melody at her dinner party, but a current pulled me under. Lysander's men saved me and brought me down here..."

I paused, thinking about how to explain the rest.

"He didn't let me leave immediately, but he never hurt me. The longer I was here, the more I came to understand his curse, and we grew closer."

Kendra rolled her eyes.

"So, *you* ran off to have a fairytale romance while I was stuck sleeping in a crystal coffin," she scoffed, and I swatted her on the arm.

"You *know* that's not true—every moment I was down here, I was looking for a way to stop Melody. I knew it wouldn't be enough to just show up as I was... and I was right. That's why we lost Dad."

The words hit hard, and a heaviness settled between us. Kendra's eyes grew solemn.

"About that... I may have crystallized him and left him in our house," she said quietly. "I couldn't just bury him. Not if

130

we could throw a proper funeral. And I didn't want to say goodbye without you."

She sat up, tucking her tail under her bottom, looking very delicate all of a sudden.

"We should probably go back in the next days or so and do something about it."

"We *can't* go back," I reminded her firmly, nudging her tail with an accusing look as anger surfaced again. "Also, what the hell is this? Didn't anyone tell you that if we set foot on land after our transformation, we'll turn to sea-foam? Tell me, Kendra, what are we supposed to do about Dad now?"

"Maybe... Matt or Lysander could help us bring the funeral down here..."

It didn't look like we had any other choice, and I sighed. Our mother had once saved our father from drowning, and he was going to end up at the bottom of the ocean anyway. What a cruel twist of fate.

"So, why did you do it?" I asked finally, and she frowned. "And don't give me that bullshit excuse that Lysander gave me—you wouldn't have traded your *entire life* above on the off chance that Eugene's army might follow us back to Vera-nis."

"Well, they still could!" Kendra protested, and she poked me for emphasis as she added, "Besides, *you're* not in any condition to fight right now."

"Give me a day and I'll be perfectly capable," I scoffed back, folding my arms.

There was a moment of pause and then, "Truthfully? I wanted to stay here with you."

She avoided my gaze, and I tried to reel in my frustration.

131

"Kendra, are you kidding me right now? After *everything* I've done, just so that you could have a chance at a real future?" Kendra pursed her lips at me, and I shook my head, letting out a single hollow laugh. "You do realize that we're *stuck* down here for the rest of our lives, right?" I added, gesturing to the room. "I'm stuck with this tail, stuck with the likes of Eugene and Melody, and I'm never going to be able to set foot on land again. I didn't *want* that for you! I can never drink smoothies or go surfing or do *anything* I actually like doing. And yet, you decided to throw away your chance to go to university and become a marine biologist to stay stuck down here with me?"

Her eyes blazed now.

"Why can't you just be happy that I sacrificed so much so you wouldn't be alone!" she bellowed, gesturing around wildly.

"Is it *really* a sacrifice for you?" I pressed, my blood thrumming.

"You know what? *No*, it isn't! Did you ever consider that maybe I don't *want* to be a marine biologist anymore? That maybe I changed my mind *long* before you dropped out of school to protect my precious future from Melody?" she yelled, using air quotes with the word *future*.

"Kendra, you *love* studying the ocean!"

"Exactly!" she shot back, jumping up now and drifting in the water above the bed as her arms extended wildly. "This is *so* much better than anything I could do on land, Coral! Being down here, living *among* the marine life and the organisms... I want to stay here! And I want to know what it was like for our mother to live down here as a mermaid."

I narrowed my gaze, heart thudding in my chest. She glared back with determination.

"Anyway, I don't know why we're fighting about this when it's already done," she snapped coldly, folding her arms. "It's my life, Coral. Stop trying to control it! You're only in this mess because you keep trying to protect me. Maybe, for once in your life, you should put yourself first and let me make my own decisions!"

With a hard kick of her tail, she stormed off out of the room. I watched with a heavy heart as the door slowly closed after her and finally clicked shut.

CHAPTER THIRTEEN

Coral

The next morning, Nerissa helped me dress in a golden bralette that was embedded with dozens of blue crystals. Beaded threads hung down over my stomach, adding to the extravagance of the outfit, and a glittering deep-blue silk wrap was tied around my waist as well.

Then she braided a crown around my head, letting the rest of my blonde waves float loosely down my back. By the time she was finished, I looked like a sparkly jewel, and Nerissa seemed satisfied.

"When you're ready to join the others, they'll be waiting for you down in the strategy room," she told me, before curtsying and exiting the room.

I flicked my tail, which had almost completely healed overnight. A mix of carefully crafted ointments, along with me being a mermaid, had accelerated the healing process immensely. It also explained why my dislocated shoulder had healed so quickly during my transformation—after all, it had only needed to click back into place.

My fight yesterday with Kendra had sobered me. Perhaps she was right—perhaps I *was* too controlling, and maybe I *did* act like a bit of a martyr when it came to those I cared about. I'd tried to figure out why and realized it was because I was *so* afraid of losing people the way we'd lost our mother.

Even when I'd resisted Lysander's initial request to give him my heart and stay down here with him... it had been because I cared more about saving my family from Melody. But in the heat of the moment, I *still* hadn't been able to let Lysander live with his curse... and I'd trapped myself down here as a result of my actions.

I didn't even owe him anything! We weren't together. We weren't married. And yet... I'd given up everything for him.

It had to stop. From this day forward, I was ready to consider what living for *me* might look like. What would I do if I put nobody but myself first?

Turning to the door, I took a deep breath. I was ready to face everyone, and I hoped today would go much smoother. *No more drama*, I thought, then swam over to the door and pushed it open.

A figure was standing there, his back to me, but he turned at the sound of the door opening. Leif's gaze met mine, and he offered me a soft smile that made my heart flutter. All my thoughts went out of my brain.

"Your Grace," he said, bowing once, then offering me his arm. "I've been instructed to escort you to the throne room. Just an... added safety measure," he explained.

I raised an eyebrow.

"Well, I assume that's code for *Lysander's paranoid that I'll be kidnapped again in his absence*," I replied, and he smirked at me.

"Something like that," he agreed, and the way his eyes sparkled with amusement sent a thrill through me. I still hadn't forgotten the way he'd saved me from the Cora Palace—the

135

way he'd looked me up and down for signs of injury when he'd found me scared and alone. The words he'd said.

I placed my hand on his arm, and it wasn't until we were heading down the corridor that it occurred to me that we didn't necessarily need to be touching at all to make it down to the strategy room. But for some reason, I didn't let go of his arm, and he didn't pull away either.

"I don't think I ever got a chance to thank you," I said finally, my voice low. "If you hadn't shown up when you did, I'd definitely be back in a cage right now. Or dead, even."

Leif glanced at me, and there was something about the way he was looking at me—*again* with the looks—that made my heart skip a beat.

"I can assure you, Your Grace, that I wouldn't have walked out of that palace without you," he replied softly, his eyes flickering with a sort of possessiveness. My stomach flipped, and I held his gaze for a moment, studying him.

"Because Lysander ordered it, right?" I replied, and he was silent for a moment as we turned onto the staircase.

"Of course," he said finally, looking away. "Lysander was eager to free you. It was my job to ensure your safe return."

Well... that was that then.

We reached the bottom of the stairs, and in the same instant that Leif stepped away from me, the doors to the dining room swung open on the left, and Nerissa swam out. She waved at us casually as we made our way around the staircase in silence, and the physical space between Leif and I felt tense. Too open... too empty.

I shook my head. What was I even *doing?* I needed to pull myself together.

136

When we reached the strategy room, Lysander was moving markers around on a huge map sprawled across a stone table. Kendra and Matt were there too, but only Matt offered me a stiff nod. Beside him, Kendra refused to look at me, her arms folded tensely. I guessed she was still angry with me, and I made a mental note to deal with that later.

"Our men are in position," Leif informed Lysander, shutting the door behind us as he came to stand at Lysander's side. I took a seat in a nearby chair as they studied the map and shuffled the markers. "If any of Eugene's men pass Seer's Peak, they'll send scouts back ahead of time to inform us. I have men on standby, should we need to rally our defenses."

"Good." Lysander nodded, looking relieved as he glanced over at me. "I have no doubts he'll try and counter attack... I want to be prepared."

He offered me a reassuring smile, but my gaze was drawn to his bornite crown shimmering on his head. Suddenly, I was back in that room with Eugene's crown on my head, and I shifted uncomfortably in my seat, avoiding his gaze.

I still had so many questions about what it meant to be the Undersea queen... but a part of me wanted to bury the responsibility and avoid it.

"Coral?" Lysander asked, and I looked up to see that everyone was staring at me now. I raised an eyebrow at them, feigning nonchalance.

"What?" I asked, but my tone was too sharp.

"I asked if you were okay," he said, making his way around the table toward me. "You don't have to be here if you're still not fully recovered—"

137

"I'm fine," I insisted, rising from my chair and swimming over to the table, unable to meet his gaze. "I'm the queen—I should be here to know what's going on."

"About that..." Lysander trailed off from beside me, and I turned my head sharply to look at him. "You *are* the Undersea queen... but you're not officially queen of Veranis yet. Under law, we still require that a formal coronation take place before we can grant you proper ruling permissions."

My stomach dropped at his words.

"I don't understand," I said, shaking my head. "What's the difference between the two?"

"Well, True Rulers like myself take care of day-to-day operations within kingdoms," Lysander explained. "While Reigning Queens oversee the growth and prosperity of all the Undersea as a whole. Reigning Queens are *physically* and *magically* stronger than True Rulers—but they don't have permissions to dictate how True Rulers govern their own territories."

Right. So when I was Eugene's prisoner, I wouldn't have been able to order him to let me go... but if I'd gotten my iron cuffs off sooner and unbound my magic, I might have been able to physically overthrow him. That would have been helpful to know sooner...

"All that being said, your magic can serve to assist the lands, the people, and in some cases, you can work with the sea witch to change or create new bindings."

My eyes widened, and I swam a foot closer to him.

"Wait... does that mean I could restore Maya's soul *without* going to the Sea of Souls?" I whispered, my heart skipping a beat, but Lysander's expression fell.

"Oh... no. Because your duties as Reigning Queen require you to oversee the well-being of the Undersea as a whole, any bindings you create using Reigning Queen magic must serve the *entire* Undersea, not just a single individual, including yourself. As such, opportunities to create bindings are rare, but they do present themselves from time to time," he told me, looking apologetic. My heart sank, but it made sense.

"However, True Ruler magic works a little bit differently," he countered, his tone lighter now as he exchanged a glance with Leif across the table. "As queen of Veranis, you can bind anyone who threatens the well-being of the kingdom—like my father did when he bound me from venturing to the Sea of Souls."

Right. King Conrad bound Lysander to ensure Veranis would have a king.

"But I still wouldn't be able to shift Maya's binding—I still need to physically venture to the Sea of Souls to find Maya's soul," I said, and after a moment's pause, Lysander nodded.

"Yes," he said quietly, and his hand came to rest on the strategy table. His expression looked strained as he added, "But we have plenty of time for that. We should do the coronation ceremony *first,* to restore your credibility and enforce your title. And besides, you shouldn't leave the kingdom without me so soon after escaping Eugene's clutches."

I must have still looked confused because Leif added, "News has spread through the Undersea of how Eugene captured you. This would be a chance to show your citizens that you are not so easily defeated. It... would defeat the purpose if you were captured again so quickly."

My heart sank. Neither of them believed that I could take care of myself. And why should they? I *had* been captured easily. And I probably never would have gotten out of the Cora Palace alive without everyone's help. Again, I thought of Eugene's crown. How easily I'd been stripped of my power and strength day after day. I wasn't ready to rule a kingdom, let alone the entire *Undersea*.

But it still hurt to know that they didn't trust me—that they felt burdened by me and felt the need to cage me here in the kingdom for my own protection. I couldn't meet either of their gazes, staring down at the stone strategy table with a hard expression.

"And really, the ceremony is quite short," Lysander added lightly, misreading my mood. "There's a ball afterward, which is much more exciting!"

"Coral's not much of a dancer," Kendra pointed out coldly. It was the first words she'd spoken the entire time.

"I don't think this is a good idea," I said finally, lurching away from the strategy table and swimming across the room toward a row of bookcases. I was aware that I was letting my fear get the better of me, but they already thought the worst of me... so why hide it?

Lysander tried to track my movements, but I spun and raised my hands to give him pause. "You don't understand what happened back there... I already failed at being Reigning Queen, and I don't even understand how I came to *be* Reigning Queen!"

Leif took a step toward me.

"Well, that's easily explained—you became Reigning Queen because you hold rights in three out of four kingdoms."

I stared at him blankly, so he continued.

"You're the heir to Atlantis *and* the land, and your relationship with Lysander grants you power over Veranis too. So, your ties to each territory give you a personal connection to each kingdom and their people. That's why Reigning Queens are so rare—very few people are able to secure rights in three territories, let alone all four. Most try it through seizing kingdoms by force because they don't have the patience or the means to develop family ties to each kingdom."

"So, if anybody is fit to rule the Undersea, it's someone who is personally connected to all the kingdoms," Lysander finished. "Especially given the fact that you *inherited* the title, rather than taking it by force."

"But... Coronis *rejected* me!" I blurted out, tears brimming in my eyes, and they both faltered, looking alarmed by the outburst. "I don't know how to rule a kingdom, let alone the entire Undersea... and I wasn't strong enough for the Coronis crown. Eugene..." I swallowed hard, trying to get the words out despite the haunting memory. "He put me on display in front of all his people and forced his crown onto me. It was like... like it was trying to rip me apart from the inside. Split my magic and soul and humanity all at once and strip me bare. The crown drained me of my power, my magic... and he did that every single day. He was using me as his own personal power source because he *knew* the crown would never accept me—that his *people* would never accept me. So how am I supposed to rule over the entire Undersea when there's a whole kingdom out there that *hates* me?"

141

The temperatures of the water dropped, an icy chill settled over my skin, and everyone glanced at Lysander. His eyes had darkened.

"Lysander?" I whispered.

The water turned stormy around us as he growled.

"*I'll kill him*."

"Here we go again," Matt muttered under his breath with raised eyebrows.

Leif sighed in agreement, before adding, "Lysander, will you *calm yourself*?" Something told me this wasn't the first time Lysander had snapped, from Leif's exasperated expression. "We will find a way to dethrone Eugene Pryor, and he will be dealt with accordingly then."

I wrapped my arms around my torso, wanting nothing more than to sink into the floor and disappear. Leif turned back to me as I said, "What if the other crowns reject me too? What if they *know* I'm not good enough to do this?"

He crossed the room in two strides and looked me firmly in the eyes. "The Coronis crown only rejected you because you don't have a solid tie to Coronis. It doesn't mean you can't do this."

There was something about the way he held his stance, the way he gently held me by the shoulders and looked at me with such conveyance... like he wanted me to really *hear* him and understand him.

"Coral, listen to me," he said firmly. "If you want to keep your title as Reigning Queen, you have to fulfill queenly duties. If you lose your status... we can't restore Maya's soul. This coronation is a queenly duty—it will solidify the fragile connection between you and Lysander that is barely keeping your title in place. I know this is a lot... but don't get hung up on ruling the entire Undersea yet. Just focus on Maya and the steps you can take to keep your title until we can devise a plan to visit the Sea of Souls."

He was right. Only a Reigning Queen could restore Maya's soul... and I owed it to her to do just that. I was heir to Atlantis and the land by birthright, but *not* to Veranis... so I'd have to work to maintain that connection.

I took a few breaths to steady myself, then glanced at Lysander again. He'd finally calmed down too—ducking his head like he was embarrassed for his outburst. Kendra was watching him with a strange expression I couldn't quite place. When she realized we'd stopped discussing ruler responsibilities, she cleared her throat and turned to me.

"There's another matter we need to deal with before any of that—laying our dad to rest."

Lysander's shoulder's sagged at the reminder.

"You're right," he said, nodding. "Why don't you tell your sister the idea we came up with."

I raised an eyebrow at them both, and Kendra finally looked me in the eye. She spoke thinly.

"We came up with the idea to send a boat out to sea with Dad laid inside of it. We'll guide it far enough out for a private funeral and burn it."

My heart warmed at the idea. I liked it—and it meant both Kendra and I could be there, in the water. I think Dad would have liked it too, with his love of sailing. Much more preferable than bringing him down here for a burial.

"Okay," I agreed with a nod. "When will we do it?"

Leif shifted forward in his seat.

"I will go back to land and prepare the body."

That was smart. Matt could have gone, but we'd lose more days waiting for his body to adjust to land again. Leif looked me in the eyes and added, "I could use your help guiding the boat out—with your magic, I mean."

"Sure," I replied quietly, though I glanced at Lysander, wondering if he would let me leave the kingdom without him. He didn't protest though, nodding with approval, so I guessed he trusted Leif enough to think that I wouldn't be kidnapped again in his presence.

I hadn't been able to save my father, so I could at least help give him a proper funeral by guiding the boat. And it meant I didn't have to talk to Kendra again anytime soon.

"Lysander will escort Kendra and Matt to the funeral location while we fetch the body. If we work quickly, we should be able to lay your father to rest by sundown."

My throat was closing up now. It was beginning to feel too real.

"Okay. Let's get going then," I said, unable to stay still any longer. I hadn't realized how much I'd needed the closure until now, and I'd buried the thoughts of my father's death into the back of my mind while I was Eugene's prisoner. After all, I hadn't even expected that I'd be able to say goodbye to him after I'd transformed, so it had been easier to just avoid thinking about it at all.

But *I'd* been the one who stabbed him. Even if Melody influenced me to do it, it had been my actions that ended his life. I didn't know how I was going to live with myself knowing it was partially my fault. I didn't deserve the opportunity to

144

apologize and say my final goodbyes... but I was thankful all the same.

Leif and I used an air bubble to travel to the surface quickly, but he popped it right before we reached land. Now that I was a mermaid, I was able to stay awake for the entire trip as the fast-changing pressures of the ocean washed passed us, which was nice, for a change.

Promising to be back, Leif waded to the shoreline while I stayed in the shallows near the fringing outcrops I'd first met Lysander on. I didn't expect Leif to be back anytime soon—he first had to source a boat from the marina, then smuggle my dad's body out of our house. And I couldn't see much from the water, but when I peered my head out, the beach was fairly busy, which meant the islanders were returning to normal life again.

While I waited, I noticed that the surf was excellent today too, and my heart panged as I watched people out on their surfboards. I couldn't believe I'd never get to ride the surf ever again. Having a tail just wasn't the same thing, and my ability to predict the currents took all the fun out of riding the waves. I missed the thrill of finding that perfect balance. I missed the spray of the ocean gently caressing my face. I missed the way the waves would form a tunnel, making me feel as if I'd been transported to a brand-new world. It was all ruined for me now after everything I'd seen and done in the Undersea.

I'd spent so much time refusing to surf, feeling guilty over Maya. Now I realized that it was precious time wasted. She'd tried to save me so that I might live doing what I love, and now that opportunity was gone.

I couldn't make the same mistake with my dad, who was gone for *real* this time. He'd died to protect Kendra—to protect me from the guilt of killing her. So I owed it to him to do something with my life this time... perhaps I'd put everything I had into ruling Veranis.

Then I thought of spending a lifetime ruling alongside Lysander and cringed. Was that what I *really* wanted?

An hour later, I sensed something approaching on the current, and that's when I spotted the underbelly of a sailing skiff approaching. It was an older model to what they made nowadays, made of both wood and aluminum. Perhaps it had been easier to steal due to its outdated value. Leif was perched up front, using an oar to steer it, but once he reached me, he discarded the oar and slipped into the green-blue water beside me.

I swam up to the boat and peered inside. There, my dad lay peacefully, still crystallized but decorated in sand dollars, clams, shells, and vibrant seagrass. My eyes stung, and before I realized what was happening, tears were running down my cheeks and sobs were wreaking through me. Leif's hand slipped into mine comfortingly and gave it a squeeze.

"You did all of this?" I sniveled, and he nodded.

"I wanted it to be nice," he said gently, shifting a little closer to me in the water. "I know how much he meant to you."

His presence was strangely welcomed, and I leaned into him for support as I continued to cry. He smelled like seaweed and citrus.

"It's my fault he's dead," I whispered between sobs. He shook his head and wrapped his arms around me, holding me tight.

"This is *not* your fault," he murmured, and I clung to his shoulders. "You did everything you could to try and save him. He wouldn't blame you for this."

"I don't know how I'm going to forgive myself," I breathed, finally wiping the tears from my eyes. His expression was pained as he watched me.

"I know it's hard... but blaming yourself won't bring him back," he replied softly. "Today is about celebrating the amazing life your father lived and all of his accomplishments. He wouldn't want you to be grieving."

I nodded, realizing he was right. He waited patiently while I pulled myself together. My throat still felt tight as we submerged under the water, but I felt much better having let it all out. I was grateful Leif was with me during all of this.

Once we were a few paces ahead of the boat, I felt into the currents with my magic. They swirled around my fingertips, then my wrists and arms, and before long, I was guiding the boat along behind us, parting the waves to make a path as we swam farther out to sea.

We traveled for another hour before we reached the location Leif and Lysander had picked. It was out in the middle of the reef, the fringing coral forming a circle around the boat as it floated into place.

I swam back up to the boat, leaned in, and melted Kendra's crystal with the touch of my hand before plunging down into the ocean to unite with the others. Kendra and Matt were sitting on nearby bedrock on the edge of the reef, and I swam over to greet them.

After we were seated, Lysander and Leif approached the boat and worked together, hoisting themselves steadily up into it. Leif must have brought a lighter with him—perhaps Kendra told him where to find one—because after a moment, a flame flickered to life, and the two men splashed back down into the water. By the time they joined us on the reef, the boat was fully aflame and smoking. Lysander took up residence on my left side, with Kendra on my right, and Leif swimming down to sit beside Matt. I didn't expect the distance between Leif and I to bother me so much.

"Would you like to say a few words?" Lysander asked Kendra and I, wrapping an arm around me for support. He seemed strangely stiff—maybe funerals made him uncomfortable. Did he even get a chance to throw a funeral for his own father?

Kendra went first. She spoke about some of her favorite childhood memories with our dad—trips out to the reef on his boat, eating gelato down on the boardwalk, and Dad reading us bedtime stories as kids.

"Thanks for saving me, Dad," Kendra whispered, her eyes shining with tears that she had to keep wiping away to stop her vision blurring. "You were the best."

I nodded in agreement, finding it hard to speak. He'd raised us almost entirely on his own, worked relentlessly to provide for us, and he'd always tried to be there for us, even when we missed our mother and wished she was there to help us sometimes. I'd known he wanted to resume traveling one day... but now he'd never get to set sail and explore more of the world like he'd wanted to.

I didn't know what happened after death. Even though my mother's ghost had been appearing to me every now and again, I didn't fully understand why. Was it because she was a mermaid? Because she had magic? Either way, I didn't expect to see Dad's ghost appearing to us anytime soon, and I had a feeling that wherever he was now, he was gone for good.

The boat was beginning to fall apart, with bits of wood drifting down into the depths of the ocean. But past that, there was a beautiful sunset—with hues of red, orange, and pink rippling on the ocean's surface.

I swallowed hard to clear my tight throat and finally spoke.

"Goodbye, Dad... I hope wherever you are now, you find your next adventure."

PART TWO

CHAPTER FOURTEEN

Melody

"Do you want to explain how the Undersea queen was able to disarm *two* of our most highly trained siren guards and escape?"

"*Not particularly.*"

Eugene stood in the doorway of my room as I sat at my vanity, filing my claws with a ruby-encrusted dagger. I'd expected my brother to be furious, expected him to come to me for answers, but he couldn't trace anything back to me. The dagger I'd slid to Coral was from the guards' personal weapons rack—any of them could have dropped it, or she could have swiped it.

I flashed him a sweet smile and added, "Don't worry, dearest Brother—she can't threaten your throne anytime soon. You made sure of that when you put her on display and demonstrated your own power. Our kingdom would be foolish to rally behind some feeble little mermaid princess who fell into her title on dumb luck."

Just saying the words aloud reminded me of how severely I'd failed in my plans to claim the land territory as my own, and I hid a sour frown by returning to my filing.

"Well clearly, she's not as feeble as we thought her to be," Eugene scowled, and I glanced up at my mirror to see him striding across the room and perching on the end of my sandstone bed. My entire bedroom was done in tones of cream—the creamy drapes in the windows, the brown kelp-woven rug

151

and sheets—which matched nicely with the obsidian walls and floors. "She bound *your* magic, and she managed to escape over twenty guards and our most vicious predators."

"She had help," I mused simply, placing the dagger down on the vanity and turning to face him once more. "The Veranis king, with his entourage. She wouldn't have made it had they not timed the rescue perfectly."

"So how *did* they time it perfectly?" Eugene snarled, and I let out a withering sigh. I didn't know, but I also didn't particularly care. All that mattered was that she'd gotten out alive.

"Over the years, I've learned not to dwell on my failures," I told him, rising from my stool and crossing the room to pat him on the back. He tensed at my touch. "You should take it in stride, Brother—a bit of wisdom from your former ruler."

He narrowed his gaze at me, but I feigned a yawn.

"Now if you please—I need my beauty sleep."

He rose from the bed, giving me a once over.

"Yes. I suppose you do," he drawled finally, and my blood simmered. I restrained myself from looking back in the mirror until he'd shut the door behind him, but then my gaze locked onto my sullen features—the gaunt cheekbones, the pale skin, the stick-thin figure that had lost its curvy appeal. All my enhanced beauty had faded with my bound magic, and it was a different kind of daily torture.

Soon, I thought, flexing my claws. The first leg of the plan was done—Coral had escaped with her precious king in tow. And over time, I would gain her trust... gain back my magic, and then my kingdom.

"Well, I bet he's fun at parties," came a low voice from the window, and I whirled around, claws sharp and ready. Sloane

152

was perched on the sill—the window ajar as she'd let herself in.

"How did you get inside?" I demanded, holding my attack stance, and she smirked.

"I picked the lock?" she offered, waving a lockpick at me. "You should invest in something more heavyweight if you want to keep beings out."

I'd thought the predatory sharks would be enough to deter beings from breaking in, but apparently not. She hopped down from the sill, landing with perfect grace, and crossed the room. Within moments, she had draped herself over my bed leisurely, and I bit back another sigh—I'd been *serious* about wanting to sleep.

"So, what's next?" she asked, tracing circles on my sheets as she looked up at me through long lashes.

"I assume you're referring to the plan," I replied stiffly, crossing to the wardrobe to fetch a simple silk nightgown and draping it over my forearm. "I don't see why we couldn't discuss this during the day."

"Because if we're seen together too often, word is bound to make its way back to the king," Sloane replied simply. "Therefore, a little stealth is required. But don't worry—I'm happy to do all the legwork."

She winked at me, and I sneered back.

"Well, make it quick. I'm turning out the lights in thirty minutes."

"Ooh, saucy." She grinned, stretching out on the bed for emphasis. I did my best to ignore how nice her figure was and folded my arms.

153

"I need to gain the Undersea queen's trust somehow. Helping to free her wouldn't have been enough, and I know she won't associate with me unless she has good reason to."

"So we make her an offer she can't refuse," Sloane suggested, lying on her stomach and clasping her hands together so that her cherry-red gauzy dress showed off the valley of her breasts. My eyes lingered momentarily before I dragged my gaze away, inhaling a steady breath. I needed to get this female out of my bedroom.

"Well, you seem invested, so what do you suggest?" I asked stonily, pretending to pick at minuscule dirt on my nightgown.

"You don't know what her deepest desire is?"

I let out a low laugh.

"Oh, there are many things she wants—her dead parents back, for one. And me dead, for another. Neither of which are things I can do for her."

"There *has* to be something else," Sloane insisted. "Perhaps we could kidnap someone important to her?"

"That would just cause more mistrust," I countered, crossing the room and perching on my vanity stool again. "No, this has to be something pure. Something she *really* wants and would do anything for. I'd send a spy out to collect info... but getting into Veranis is bound to be difficult right now. And such a thing wouldn't go unnoticed by my brother."

"Well, when you figure out what she wants, I know how you can gain her trust," Sloane said finally, shifting into a seated position. "Have you ever heard of the First Sea Witch?"

I shook my head, curious now.

154

"She was the *original* sea witch, from thousands and thousands of centuries ago. Her soul still lives on inside the Sea of Souls, and she is said to be able to grant *one* binding to anyone who can find her—any binding you desire. But the chances of finding her among the other souls is... rare."

A chill went down my spine. Even *I* wouldn't set foot that deep in the Sea of Souls—I had no desire to walk among my dead enemies, among their vengeful, lingering souls, even for the *slim* chance of getting my power back.

But this was perfect. Coral already planned to venture to the Sea of Souls for her best friend. If we could trick her somehow, and I could just direct her deep enough into the sea... well, she would never return. Her body would be devoured and left to rot, and not even her precious king would be able to find her and bring back the corpse without turning to sea-foam himself.

"As irritating as you are, you're a genius sometimes," I told her as I crossed to the window, and she gave me a mocking bow.

"I try."

I opened the window and jabbed a finger through it. "Now get out. I want to go to bed."

"So *bossy*." She pouted and began crawling off the bed at a sensually slow pace that made me forget how to breathe momentarily. I averted my gaze, waiting for her to hurry up and leave. She finally reached the edge of the bed, slipped her feet to the floor, and plodded across the room to the window. But she paused at my side, and I inhaled her sweet coconut-and-ocean-blossom scent.

"We make a good team, Melody," she purred. "Perhaps next time, you'll offer a girl a drink when she scales the side of a palace to see you."

I scowled at her as she effortlessly swung herself out the window, hanging off the ledge, and began to climb back down the spikes of the Cora Palace exterior. I couldn't look away, fascinated that she did it with such confidence and precision. It would have been so easy for her to slip and impale herself. But she made it all the way to the bottom, and only then did she look up to find that I was still watching her.

She grinned at me, and heat flushed at my cheeks. I lifted my gaze haughtily and didn't spare her another moment of attention as I slammed my window shut.

CHAPTER FIFTEEN

Coral

The first few days after the funeral were difficult and had brought up all kinds of feelings that I'd buried while I was Eugene's prisoner, making it hard to function. I spent many days alone, curled up in bed in one of the guest rooms of the Vera Palace. Lysander had offered for me to stay in his room with him, but I'd wanted to be on my own.

I'd never felt grief like this before. Not even when I'd thought Maya was dead, and I'd blamed myself for her trying to save me. But people had constantly told me it wasn't my fault, that she had chosen to go after me. This time, it was different because I could still feel that knife plunging into my dad's chest. I *knew* I was the reason he was dead, even if it had been Melody's command that drove me to it. I couldn't stop replaying it in my head... the scene haunting me every waking moment of the day.

Rue brought me food every day, and Kendra and Matt checked on me a couple of times. But other than that, I slept and cried and stayed hidden under the blankets, keeping the lights dimmed. I knew I needed to get up eventually, and Leif's words about fulfilling my queenly duties kept echoing in my head... but right now, I couldn't find the will to do anything.

It wasn't until the third day that Lysander finally knocked on my door. My heart didn't exactly leap at the sight of him—which I chalked up to wanting to be alone—but I wasn't upset either. He let himself in and slowly crossed the room to perch on the end of my bed.

"Coral, let's go for a seahorse ride," he prompted gently, placing a hand on my lower tail. His dark hair drifted in the current, swirling like shadow in the dim lights. "It will do you some good to clear your head."

I shook my head at him.

"Not yet," I mumbled, turning away from him and facing the other side of the room. I knew I couldn't stay here forever... but I needed more time.

He hesitated, then crawled farther up the bed to my side, lay down, and wrapped his arms around me from behind. My heart rate increased as his hands locked around my waist, and his body pressed close to me, emitting warmth. I was surprised at how nice it felt to have someone hugging me like this.

"I miss you," he murmured into my ear, sending goosebumps down my arms. "I want to be here for you. Won't you come sleep in my room at night, at the very least?"

I grimaced thinking about it. Something still felt disconnected between us, and I wasn't sure if I was ready to dig into fixing it, wasn't sure if I even had the capacity to while I was feeling so much grief in my heart. But at the same time, I knew avoiding him wasn't going to fix it. And he'd been so patient already, giving me the space I needed. I felt guilty for shutting him out.

"We don't need to... *do* anything," he added carefully, like it had been an afterthought. "I just feel better when you're close to me. Maybe it will help you sleep as well."

Admittedly, just having his arms around me was helping a great deal. I thought about what it would be like to sleep like

158

this every night. Would I still wake up in tears, shaken by nightmares of how I'd killed my own father?

Slowly, I turned to face him, and his dazzling green eyes softened. He reached up to cup my cheek, and I closed my eyes, leaning into the touch.

He pressed a light, soft kiss to my lips—just once, before pulling away—and brushed his thumb down my jaw before letting me go again. My eyes blinked open to see him getting to his feet.

"If you change your mind about your sleeping arrangements, my door is always open to you," he told me, before crossing the room and leaving me in peace again. Suddenly, I felt very alone, the space too big and quiet to bear, and I found myself pulling the blankets over me to rekindle a sense of comfort again.

A week later, I finally emerged from my room and headed downstairs for breakfast in the early hours of the morning. I wasn't expecting anybody to be awake at this time, which is why I'd picked it—I still wasn't ready to face everyone—but I found Matt down there, helping himself to a plate of prawns.

"You're still here?" I asked, lingering in the doorway. Matt glanced up at me, then raised an eyebrow.

"Should I not be?" he replied slowly, and I realized how my comment had sounded. I blushed and shook my head, swimming over to take a seat across from him.

"No... never mind. I didn't mean it like that."

159

It had already been a week since the funeral... since they'd rescued me from the Cora Palace. And so far, no signs of a retaliation from Eugene or his men. So I guess I was just surprised that Matt hadn't returned to the surface yet while it was safe to do so. All was well here... or at least as well as it could have been.

Matt studied me for a moment, then passed me a bowl of sea berries and said, "It's good to see you, Coral."

I smiled at his gesture—he knew me too well. Taking the bowl, I popped a handful into my mouth and let the juicy taste consume my tongue.

"So how come you're up so early when everyone else is still asleep?" I asked, looking around the empty dining room. Matt leaned back in his chair and folded his arms.

"Actually, Lysander and Kendra are out on a seahorse ride," he told me in a matter-of-fact tone. I stared at him for a moment, the words not quite registering.

"What do you mean?" I asked finally, shaking my head.

"Yeah—for the past couple of days, they've been doing it every morning. Or so I hear," he told me, taking a slow bite of a prawn. "You didn't know?"

My heart sank with a strange sort of disappointment. Lysander had come to my room just *days* ago, offering to take me on a seahorse ride, and I'd refused him. Why did I think the offer had been reserved for me alone?

A strange, smug look in Matt's eyes told me he'd been waiting to drop this information on me. I sat back in my chair and frowned at him. I didn't know why it hurt so much... it's not like Lysander had been ignoring me. I'd been the one avoiding him. But regardless, he was out on leisurely rides with my sister while I'd been curled up in bed mourning... and it didn't feel right.

Still, I tried to see it from a positive angle.

"Okay, so they're bonding then," I said simply, waving my hand like it was nothing, and Matt's expression fell. "That's a good thing—the guy I'm bound to rule with *should* have a good relationship with my sister."

He scoffed and dropped the prawn onto his plate.

"Seriously? I don't trust him, and you shouldn't either—*especially* not with your sister."

I rolled my eyes at him.

"Come on, Matt, he wouldn't hurt me. If the past few weeks have taught me anything, it's that Lysander is head over heels obsessed with me—that whole stunt he pulled to get me out of the Cora Palace proves it. He knows doing anything with Kendra would be crossing a line."

Matt narrowed his gaze at me.

"It didn't stop him from drowning Maya. *Your best friend.*"

Guilt plunged through me as soon as he brought it up. I still hadn't had a chance to apologize or explain myself. I leaned forward in my chair.

"Matt... I'm *so* sorry that I didn't tell you. I didn't want to cause you unnecessary pain. And I thought I'd be able to re-store her soul before you found out."

"I know, Coral," he replied bitterly, folding his arms. "I was able to figure that much out on my own."

I winced at his reaction, but I didn't get to say anything else because Matt continued.

161

"I say this as your friend, but... you're not *really* in love with Lysander, are you?"

I hesitated, words catching in my throat when I tried to speak. I avoided his gaze after a moment and thought about it.

"I don't know," I admitted finally, my voice tiny and fragile. I wrapped my hands around my chest. "I *thought* I was... but maybe I just need more time..."

Everything had been so... *rushed* before my father's death. Sure, I *liked* Lysander. I'd gotten to know a part of him that had been hidden beneath his curse—a kind, doting, generous being who had good intentions, even if he hadn't known how to communicate those intentions in the best way. I'd felt attracted to him... I'd let him woo me...

And then I'd found out about Maya, and things had changed.

I could see that he was trying to make things right. He sacrificed the one thing that meant anything to him—his heart—so that I could return to the surface and rescue my family. He could have easily kept me in Veranis, but he didn't. So maybe I'd felt a sense of obligation toward him when I finally gave him my heart. Maybe I felt like I *owed* it to him to see where this relationship would go. We both cared enough to make sacrifices for each other... but did we *really* care about each other? Or did we just care about doing what we thought was *right* for each other?

I didn't know anymore. But what I *did* know is that I wasn't yearning for his company each night. And his presence was always a fleeting comfort—a friendly face and a warm hug at best. It faded so quickly whenever he left.

Matt leaned forward in his seat, placing his arms flat on the table for balance.

"I think you should leave. I don't like that he kept you here against your will."

I shook my head at him.

"It wasn't like that—"

"Open your eyes, Coral!" Matt insisted. "I'm not going to let you lie to yourself. That guy isn't good for you, and I'm worried about what will happen if you stay here with him."

I let out a shaky breath.

"Well, too bad I don't have a choice anymore," I replied quietly, and my tail twitched as if confirming it. There was a moment of pause between us, and then Matt sighed and got to his feet.

"There has to be a way to change your fate. But you've got to be willing to look for it," he told me firmly, before walking away. I heard the dining room doors open and close behind him.

Change it? No, that was just wishful thinking. There was no way to change this. I was fully transformed... I'd made my choice. My mother had done the same, and she'd suffered the same fate.

At the thought of my mother, I wondered if she had ever missed having a tail. I still wasn't completely sold on mine. I felt like I'd lost a major part of myself when I'd traded away my legs... and I couldn't surf with a tail. It was the one thing I'd really loved to do.

Half an hour later, Lysander and Kendra finally returned from their ride, and I was still mulling over Matt's words, having barely eaten. The sound of their laughter echoed through the palace before the doors even opened, startling me, and I swiped a handful of berries to try and look as if I hadn't been spacing out.

"You're finally up!" Kendra cried as soon as she saw me, and I plastered a smile on my face as she came over to wrap her arms around me. She was wearing a deep-blue riding jacket under a white shirt. I offered her some berries, which she took without question, before shifting my gaze to Lysander.

"So, you two have been out seahorse riding?"

Lysander beamed at me.

"I wanted to show her the sea turtles near Veranis," he explained, and Kendra giggled.

"Oh Coral—there's just *so much* marine life here!" she gushed, collapsing into the seat beside me. "It's *amazing*! I can't believe some of the things Lysander has shown me."

I nodded, my gaze flicking between the two of them as a scowl appeared on my face. Lysander quickly realized my irritation because he cleared his throat hastily and crossed to the other side of the dining table.

"Shall we eat together?" he suggested, taking a seat across from me. He seemed very flustered all of a sudden, avoiding my gaze as he reached for a plate of shellfish. "We, uh, were actually discussing some of the land affairs we still need to take care of while out on our ride."

I raised an eyebrow at him.

"Like what?" I pressed.

"Well," Kendra began carefully, "Matt wants to return to the surface once Maya's soul has been restored, so he's not going anywhere anytime soon. And you and I are staying here.

So we need to figure out what we're going to tell people back on land, and what we'll do with the house, the resort... all of it."

Lysander eyed me with shining eyes, like he was proud to be so on top of things. I fought the urge to grind my teeth.

"You both discussed this without me?"

"Well, *you* were cooped up in your room for a week and refused to come out, so I thought I'd take care of it," she shot back, a hint of annoyance in her tone. "I've already decided on what we could tell people and what we could do with the house."

I let out a dry laugh.

"Oh, do tell!" I drawled, and she straightened her stance defensively.

"Melody's already gone, and the only person from land who knows that Dad is dead is Matt. But Melody already announced at the dinner party that Dad would be retiring, right? So, we can just say they decided to elope last minute and took off sailing together. We promote one of Dad's staff members into a management position, sell the house—"

"Hold on—slow down!" I interrupted, my mind racing a million miles a minute now. "We can't sell the house!"

"Why not?" Kendra challenged. "We can't go back to land anyway. We don't need it anymore. In fact, we don't need the family fortune or any of it! We might as well give it all away."

"Kendra, that was Dad's legacy!" I exclaimed, my heart racing now. "You can't just give it all away! It's not right!"

"Well, what do *you* want to do with it?" she asked finally, sighing with exasperation. I shook my head, at a loss for words. I hadn't yet adjusted to the idea of Kendra staying

165

down here, and a small part of me wanted to hold on to the house in hopes that one day, I might find a way to send her back. But her gaze was determined and set, and I knew she wasn't going anywhere. I needed to propose a better reason than keeping it for her.

"Look, it's an asset," I sighed finally. "It's not smart to just sell everything. We should at least keep the house... maybe we could rent it out to someone."

"We don't need the money," she reminded me. "It's no good to us down here."

"But we *do* need to pay the resort staff's wages," I pushed back. "The resort makes enough, but we also need money for maintenance and whatever else the resort might need. Maybe Matt can help us employ someone to oversee all of that."

"Okay," she agreed. "But you're happy with the cover story for Melody and Dad?"

I nodded slowly. It would work, and it would be far easier than explaining what actually happened. Melody had done us a favor when she announced the retirement at the dinner party... and the story wasn't coming out of left field, so it should be believable too.

"So... all resolved then?" Lysander asked carefully. I shot him a glare, and he shrank back in his chair.

"I'll speak with you later about this," I told him firmly, before grabbing another handful of berries and shoving them into my mouth. I hadn't planned on being downstairs for very long or speaking to anybody... but this whole conversation had been a wake-up call for me. I couldn't afford to mope around any longer. I had a kingdom to run, decisions to make... and a best friend's soul to restore. It was time to get my butt back into action.

"Has Nerissa started training you yet?" I asked Kendra, and she nodded. "Good—then I want in too."

CHAPTER SIXTEEN

Coral

I followed Kendra out into the courtyard and down a nar-row set of bedrock stairs that curved farther into the enormous cave side. As we descended, tails swishing in wake, I spotted three large training rings separated by blooming coral gardens, and a small, narrow building similar in build to the Vera Pal-ace. It didn't take me long to realize it was for the palace guards when I saw the uniformed soldiers coming and going.

Two of the training rings were in use by soldiers, but Ne-rissa was waiting for us in the third one. There was a weapons rack off to the side, but it went untouched.

"Finally," Nerissa beamed, flashing her unusually sharp teeth when she saw me. "I was wondering when the queen might finally join us."

"Are we going to have to go over the basics again?" Ken-dra asked, swishing her tail in annoyance as she observed me. Nerissa waved us closer.

"Yes, but it never hurts to go over basics," she replied, and turned to me. "Coral, what do you already know about mer-magic?"

I only knew what I'd read about in the library many weeks ago and what I'd learned through trial and error. So, not much.

"The core of a mermaid's power comes from the heart," I said, and Nerissa nodded. "Which is why mermaids are hunted. Our hearts alone can be used in spells and potions, and we can draw from our hearts to manipulate the ocean."

"Correct." She smiled. "When we create crystal as a protection mechanism, even that is manipulation of the ocean—water turning to ice and magically transforming to crystal."

She swam a lap around us—fast as lightning, and said, "We can manipulate ocean currents to swim faster than any Undersea being—but it *will* give you a terrible stitch if you overexert yourself, and you won't be able to swim that fast again for at least a day, which is why we don't do it often."

I nodded. I knew a lot of this, or I'd at least *guessed* as much, but it was starting to make sense now.

"So, what kind of things can I do with the ocean?" I asked. The water tornado I'd summoned to throw Melody to shore had been created on a desperate whim, and I'd seen Nerissa and Kendra create a whirlpool... but there *had* to be more I could do."

"We'll get there," Nerissa promised, a sparkle in her eye. "But first, you need basic training—so we're going to start with breath work to get in tune with your heart so you can access your magic quickly and swiftly on command."

So, we spent the morning practicing breathing exercises. Deep breaths, short breaths, inhaling and feeling into our magic, exhaling and bringing it to the surface of our fingertips. It took two hours before I was summoning and ceasing magic on command—before I could feel it thrumming beneath my fingers, like pins and needles, waiting to be unleashed.

"Good," Nerissa said, observing both of us. Kendra looked bored—she'd already covered this last week, and apparently, she was miles ahead of me with what she could do. I felt bad bringing her back to basics.

"Why don't you and Kendra demonstrate some real magic for me?" I asked finally, needing a break anyway. "So I know what I have to look forward to."

Kendra's eyes lit up, and Nerissa agreed, so I swam over to sit on the narrow steps that led down from the Vera Palace and watched. Nerissa led her through a series of actions and movements—like a dance routine. First, Kendra manipulated the currents around us to change directions on command, to slow down and speed up as water rippled past. Then, she brought a ball of swirling white water to her fingertips and released wave after wave, blasting each one across the training ring. Finally, she raised her hands above her, and I noticed how the tips of her fingers turned blue. The water stilled above us, the temperatures growing colder and colder as bubbles rose from the bedrock ground around her. Each bubble solidified into a jagged piece of ice, and she brought them hurtling down around her until they shattered on impact.

By the time she turned back, she was beaming, but I couldn't bring myself to smile back. I didn't understand what was wrong with me... I should have been happy for my sister. *Glad* that she could protect herself without me. But all I could think about was how naturally she'd been able to adapt to being a mermaid, how easily she was getting along with Lysander, how much better she'd been at staying on top of our urgent, pressing affairs like our father's funeral and the cover story for his disappearance.

And for the first time in my life, I felt a like a dagger was twisting in my heart, and I couldn't shake the deep desire to upstage my sister in everything she was doing and being.

"What do you think?" Kendra prompted, and I plastered a smile on my face.

"You were great," I said quickly, kicking up from the stairs. "But I'm exhausted, so I think I'm done for today— let's continue tomorrow."

Before they could protest, I turned my back on them both. At the end of two hours, all I had were *breathing exercises* to show for my efforts. Well, Kendra might have the upper hand in magic, but I was going to get the upper hand in something else.

I rapped on Leif's study door repeatedly until he opened it, looking me up and down, and I planted my hands on my hips.

"I need your help," I insisted, and his brow furrowed.

"What is it?" he asked, scanning our surroundings like he was anticipating a threat.

"I need you to teach me sword fighting," I ordered, and he stared back blankly for a moment. "I only survived as a human by dumb luck with my dagger—if it comes down to it, I need to know how to disarm my enemies and deflect various weapons."

Leif finally let out a breath.

"Look, I'm happy to teach you... but it took me *months* to learn the basics of sword fighting. *Years* to master it. When

Eugene finally attacks, you'll be better off using your mer-magic—it'll come more naturally and be twice as powerful."

I gritted my teeth and threw my hands in the air.

"Well, then I'm *screwed* because all I know how to do is breathe my way into summoning magic," I replied, rolling my eyes. He studied me, then stepped aside as if to let me into his office. I obliged, swimming a few paces inside. It felt different than the strategy room—more cozy, less cluttered—and the distinct scent of citrus and seaweed clung to the water.

"Well, that sounds pretty promising to me. After all, sum-moning your magic is the first step to using it," he replied, with a quirked eyebrow. "Why don't you tell me what this is *really* about?"

Guilt plunged through me at the thought of admitting how I truly felt about my sister... and it was only then that I real-ized how hasty I'd been to run straight to Leif for sword-fighting lessons to upstage her.

What the hell was *wrong* with me? I was a *terrible* sister.

I shook my head, plastering a smile on my face, and let out a short laugh.

"You know what? You're right," I said quickly, meeting his gaze. "I'm being silly, acting prematurely... I *should* stick to learning magic right now. I'm sorry I bothered you," I re-plied, and swam past him again as I exited the office. He made a noise like he wanted to protest, but I felt into my heart, willed the ocean around me to do my bidding, and in a blink of an eye, I'd already reached the top of the palace stairs and was gone.

More days passed. More breathing exercises, more basics of magic, more pathetic attempts at waves next to Kendra's strong and forceful ones. More watching Kendra and Lysander return from their morning seahorse rides, laughing and joking. More joining Lysander at court, picking coronation decor, and learning about my queenly duties. More awkward dinners by Lysander's side where he tried to pay me compliments and told me I was *doing so well.*

As the days dragged on, that jealous feeling clawing through me became harder and harder to stifle. I felt like I was in a dream—like none of it was real. Like I was standing outside, watching everything through a window. Because everyone around me seemed fine—they smiled, they laughed, they talked and joked. Even Matt, who distanced himself from Lysander as much as possible, was joining us for meals and conversing with Leif. There was a veil between us, and I could see through it, but I couldn't pass it, couldn't reach any of them. No matter how hard I tried to show up, fit in, and join their conversations... I couldn't seem to find my way back to them. It was as if a hollow shell had taken my place and was going through the motions with them.

When I watched Lysander at court, taking note of how he listened to his subjects and made decisions, I tried to envision myself ruling beside him. But every time I did, my heart began racing, and I had the overwhelming urge to start swimming. To swim as fast and far as I could and never stop.

But I'd chosen this. I had to stay now. I had to become queen of Veranis and sit on that throne beside him and oversee his people with him. It was my fate, and I couldn't escape it.

"Which ones shall we display, Your Grace?" a servant asked, as she walked me through the displays of vibrant, colorful seaflowers and seagrass. A whole week had passed, and the coronation was just days away. Lysander had wanted me to have final say on all the arrangements.

"I like the green ones," I said, pointing to the plain seagrass. I honestly didn't care that much—I would happily let them do whatever they felt would look best. Watching the ballroom be transformed before my eyes—with ornate displays and statues and tables for catering—made my chest constrict and my throat close up. I tried to stay calm, but I felt like I couldn't breathe.

It was starting to feel too real, and once I was queen of Veranis? It *would* be.

I still couldn't believe that, weeks ago, I'd been human. My father had been alive. The most exciting part of my day was getting to eat the leftover sorbet after my shift at Snack Shack. I'd never *asked* for any of this to happen... and I missed my old life. I missed life on land, the sun on my skin, the waves I used to surf...

Now, I was going to be chained to a throne for all eternity... stuck by Lysander's side forever. Eating nothing but *sea berries* for the rest of my life! I didn't know if I could do it... but I also knew I didn't have a choice.

When I'd decided to live for myself... this wasn't what I'd had in mind. Did my wants and needs even matter to Lysander? Did he *care* if I spent the rest of my life feeling trapped in his kingdom?

Dread clawed its way up my throat as we moved on to a table full of catering samples. It was all seafood, and I wrinkled my nose as I stared.

"What would you like to serve, Your Grace?" the servant asked, turning to me. "You're welcome to try anything here."

I stared dully at the food, nausea building in my stomach.

"Just serve anything," I said, turning away from it. It wasn't like there was an abundance of options, and I'd only be able to eat berries and seaweed anyway. I swam a few paces into the center of the room, my stomach churning, my heart racing. It felt like my chest had entirely closed itself off... like I couldn't get any air.

"Your Grace?"

The voices sounded muffled, and I tried to inhale. I couldn't get any air down. My heart was pounding now, and panic seized me.

Without warning, I bolted from the room, ignoring the cries of protest around me. I made it up two flights of stairs using my heart magic before I paused and managed to rasp down a breath. My hand clutched the railing as I gasped, the breaths coming back slowly, each one a slow, painful knife to my chest as my lungs greedily soaked up the oxygen. My vision was spotty around the edges, but the blackness was fading now.

175

I couldn't go back to that room. I *couldn't*. If I did, reality would set in again, and I couldn't bear the thought of being trapped down here for eternity. Even though I *knew* there was no other way... my fate was sealed. But despite that, I couldn't help it as I dragged myself away to the one place I didn't think I'd ever venture into again—the palace library.

My gaze landed on the sprawling shelves of books, and as I swam past them, I tried to recall the volume I'd picked up weeks ago that detailed about the sea witch. Curses and bindings could be broken... maybe there had been a way to break my mother's binding that she never knew of. Maybe I could find it and get my legs back. I'd give almost *anything* to walk on land again.

It took some time, but I eventually located the book, recognizing the faded, worn cover. When I flicked it open, the same illustration of the ethereal sea witch stared back at me. The text was still in an unfamiliar language, making it impossible to read. But I had an idea.

"Deandra?" I called, swimming around the library in search for her. I eventually spotted the palace librarian behind a desk—her spectacles sliding down her nose as she sat hunched over a stack of books, taking notes from them, and her graying brown hair done up in her usual crown of braids. I called out again as I approached, and she looked up.

"Your Grace," she greeted, inclining her head at me. "What brings you back to the library?"

I placed the book down in front of her, and I knew she recognized it from last time from the way she stared at me.

"I know you weren't permitted to tell me anything about the sea witch before, but things are different now, right?"

She lifted her gaze to meet mine and nodded.

"Well," I huffed, planting my hands on my hips. "Could you transcribe it for me? I want to know if there's a way to reverse my binding."

Deandra paused.

"The king has already tasked me with researching ways to undo *his* binding," she advised carefully. "While I'm happy to assist, I'm afraid I won't have as much time to dedicate to your request."

I wanted to insist—I *needed* answers before the coronation. But that was mere days away, and I didn't expect her to be able to transcribe the entire book before then.

"Then forget transcribing the book—just, please, if you could read it and take note of anything that might help me..." I trailed off finally, and her gaze softened. After a moment, she reached out and dragged the book across the table toward her.

"I will see what I can do," she told me, and I let out a breath. Tension lifted from my shoulders, and I immediately felt better. Even if nothing came from this, I'd at least have done *something* to try and get myself out of this mess.

I left her to her work, swimming back to the library doors, and headed downstairs to the training rings for my daily training session with Nerissa.

CHAPTER SEVENTEEN

Coral

Nerissa took us through a quick warm-up before we dove into the magic training for the day. We'd finally moved on from currents and waves and were learning how to heat and cool the water. This was how Kendra had created the ice shower—and it's as far as she'd gotten with her own training before we'd gone back to basics.

This time, Lysander came to watch us on the sidelines, eyes filled with pride and admiration as he watched us. But I couldn't tell whom his gaze was directed at.

The first hour went poorly because I was so distracted by Lysander's presence, and I couldn't shake the thought of how close Kendra and Lysander were becoming. Where were they going on their morning seahorse rides anyway? Would they let me join them if I asked?

Did I even want to join them?

Bitterness surged through me, and out of nowhere, I sent a particularly rough wave hurtling toward Nerissa. She deflected it using her own magic and frowned at me.

"Coral! You're meant to be freezing the water," she scolded, and I muttered an apology. She shook her head at me and added, "If Loverboy here is too distracting for you, I'm going to have to ask him to leave."

I grimaced, not wanting to respond to that. The truth was that I *wished* he would leave, but I knew saying as much

178

would hurt his feelings—or worse, bring up a discussion around why. And that would make things so much worse.

I spared a glance at Kendra, who was oblivious to my simmering. I knew the feelings were childish—there was nothing to be jealous about. But I couldn't help the way my gut twisted when I thought of them together, laughing together and conversing with ease.

Meanwhile... I'd been struggling to reach for what we had before. I'd debated going to his room so many times, but it felt awkward, like I wasn't welcome there. The intimate moments we'd shared at the Alta Palace felt like a faraway dream now.

Not to mention that before, I'd been in a totally different headspace. I'd been desperate to lose myself in a feeling, trying to escape from my reality. I thought maybe I could let Lysander in, and I thought that perhaps I *had*... so why did it feel so different now?

I thought of Deandra transcribing the sea witch book in the library. Of me running away from this place. Of me abandoning Lysander and my promise to rule alongside him. Guilt clawed its way through me like an angry, vicious monster, tangling with the jealousy and resentment until—

"Coral!" came Nerissa's urgent warning, and I snapped out of my thoughts. It was only then that I realized the water had turned so chillingly cold that my skin was turning blue, and a flurry of ice shards was circling overhead. My eyes widened with shock.

"*Very* carefully, dissolve it," Nerissa guided, her expression strained as she watched the deadly spikes overhead. "Focus on warming the water."

The ocean had turned as cold as my bruised heart. I didn't know if I had a lick of warmth left inside of me after these past few weeks. I didn't know how to find that person I'd once been again. But when I looked at Nerissa and Kendra—at Lysander—and I thought of my ice hurting them...

The shards shattered overhead, causing Nerissa to yelp and throw her hands up. But the ice sprinkled down on us like glitter, except cold to the touch. Kendra breathed a sigh of relief, and Lysander came rushing over to us.

"What happened?" he demanded, looking to me for an explanation. I shook my head, my hands trembling from what I'd nearly done. I was a danger to the people around me. Something was *wrong* with me—deep in my heart.

Jealousy and grief were pulling me deeper into a hole that I couldn't seem to escape from. I wasn't turning *heartless*, was I? Had I received Lysander's old curse?

No... impossible, I realized. If that were the case, I wouldn't feel anything at all, and I'd been on a roller coaster of grief and anger since my father had died. This was something else... something darker than a curse.

"I'm sorry," I blurted finally, before leveraging the currents to flee. In less than a minute, I was back in my room, my back pressed to the door, and I sank down to the floor and wrapped my arms around my tail.

If I was going to hurt the people I loved, then I wouldn't leave this room again. I would stay in here... and make my ruling decisions from here if I had to.

Time passed, but then a sudden knock at the door jolted me out of my skin, and I breathed a steadying breath.

"Coral?" Lysander demanded. "Let me in."

"I want to be alone!" I called back, trying to keep my voice steady, but the ocean currents seemed to rumble in response to that.

"I'm ordering you, as the king, to open this door," he commanded, and his tone had some kind of influence to it that rippled through the ocean itself. *Damn it*, I realized, as I unwillingly got up from the floor. He was using his True Ruler magic on me.

Well, two can play that game, I decided, and opened the door to let him in. Lysander stormed into the room, bringing a current of frustration with him. He spun to face me and glared at me.

"What the *hell* is going on with you?" he demanded finally, clenching his fists. "You nearly killed your sister back there!"

I kicked the door shut with my tail and folded my arms.

"What's going on with *me*? What the hell is going on with *you two*?" I shot back, unable to hide my true feelings anymore. "I feel like a stranger in your home, Lysander—like I'm some third wheel you don't want around anymore!"

His expression turned exasperated. "What gave you that impression?"

"Oh, just the daily seahorse rides you've been doing together, to *who knows where*, doing *who knows what*. The awful dinners where I feel like some broken toy you've been trying to put back together with *careful,* gentle words of appreciation."

His clenched hands loosened.

"I invited you to come seahorse riding with me," he reminded me quietly.

"*Once!*" I snapped, tears brimming in my eyes now. "When I was still mourning my father! But I guess you couldn't be patient enough to wait for me, huh? So my sister was available, and you decided to take her instead?"

Lysander tensed, taking a step forward.

"Your sister asked me to show her the kingdom and surroundings. She likes studying the plants and marine life... it took her mind off of her own grief. You're not the only one still mourning him, Coral."

I swallowed hard, trying not to fall apart in front of him. It was like everything had been building up to this moment.

"It's inappropriate," I said finally, and I felt stupid even saying it aloud. I wasn't the jealous type—I never *had* been—and had always thought it stupid when girls at school felt the need to snoop through their boyfriends' phones instead of working on trust and communication within the relationship. But I couldn't help feeling this way. "I feel like I've been alone in this whole thing, Lysander. Trying to work through my grief and forget the torture Eugene put me through. But you haven't been here for me. Why am I coming second to my sister when, weeks ago, I was the center of your entire world?"

I knew it was the curse that had caused that obsession, and it hadn't been healthy... but it felt like we'd gone from one extreme to the other. I didn't want to be the only person Lysander cared about... but I *did* want to come first, especially when I was dealing with difficult things and needed emotional support.

My bottom lip began to tremble, and all the defensiveness in Lysander melted away. In two quick strides, he had me in his arms, his hand stroking my hair.

182

"I'm sorry... I didn't consider it that way," he admitted softly. I slowly wrapped my arms around his torso, but it felt foreign. Like I didn't know this person anymore.

Something was *definitely* wrong with me. Why couldn't I accept that Lysander had changed? Why couldn't we just build on what had been there before? Why was it so hard for me to open up to this new version of him that actually had the capacity to understand me, to *feel* things with me?

It wasn't that we didn't have a connection. But it wasn't the same as it had once been, and it *definitely* wasn't the same kind of connection I saw between Kendra and Lysander. Something told me that it hadn't just been the marine life and me that had influenced Kendra's decision to transform and stay down here.

After a long moment in his arms, I looked up and met his gaze.

"You and my sister..." I trailed off finally, and Lysander immediately shook his head.

"We're *just* friends," he insisted, a determined look in his eyes. I raised my eyebrow at him.

"You clearly get along."

"But so do you and I," he insisted, his voice weaker now. "Or at least... we *did*." I looked away, and he sighed. "Coral, I like your sister, but I've spent weeks worrying over *you*. I fought for you, defied my father for you—hell, my men have *died* trying to protect you!"

"I don't think it's enough," I whispered, and I'd never felt more selfish in my life. "Lysander... I never wanted this. I *thought* I could love you... that I could compromise and give

183

up everything for you... but I feel like I'm losing myself down here. I don't *want* to be queen of Veranis."

His gaze hardened.

"You think *I* wanted any of this?" he growled, and I recoiled. He stepped away, gesturing around the room. "You think *you're* the only one who feels trapped? I never wanted to rule either, Coral, but I'm the sole heir to Veranis! If it wasn't for Maya, you could run off anytime you wanted. But me? I'm *truly* stuck in this, so don't talk to me about choice and compromise! I am doing *everything* I can think of to make this easier for you, and you keep shutting me out! I thought this was something we could navigate and endure together, but you *refuse* to be part of it!"

I stared at him, mouth gaping, too stunned to speak. But then words came flooding out.

"You've been raised to fit the role!" I retorted, my voice shaky now as I tried to defend my point. "I feel like I'm swimming around in the dark in comparison. I don't know the *first thing* about ruling a kingdom!"

"Then let me help you!" he insisted, his voice exasperated as he ran a hand through his hair and took a step forward again, but I buried my head in my hands. The truth teetered on my lips, and I couldn't stop myself as I spoke quietly.

"I just... I don't know how to do this when I don't want to be here. I don't want to be with *you*."

The words echoed around the room hauntingly, and he was silent. Slowly, I managed to meet his gaze again, and devastation had filled his eyes. I felt sick to my stomach. I hadn't meant it to come out quite like that, and I desperately wanted to backtrack. But how did I explain that the person I'd been

184

falling for was his cursed self? That it wasn't *him* I didn't want to be with, but this new version of him that felt foreign and unfamiliar?

How did you tell someone you preferred the worst part of themselves?

"Ah," he said finally, his voice hard and gravelly. He averted his gaze for a moment, swallowing hard as he composed his next words. "Well, in order to maintain your title as Reigning Queen—"

"I know, I know, I have to fulfill queenly duties," I replied stiffly, folding my arms, but he shook his head.

"It's not just that. You gave me your heart, which is what ties you to me. To *Veranis*," he emphasized, referring to the personal connections that maintained my status. "So, in order to maintain that connection... I have to stay loyal to you. Or else I'll turn heartless again."

My blood ran cold, and I saw fear flash in his eyes at the thought of reverting back to his old, cursed self.

Oh *God*... this was such a *mess*...

It was all my fault. I shouldn't have broken his curse in the first place. And now that he knew what it was like to be uncursed, it would be so much worse to go back. To lose that part of himself he'd uncovered. He'd already made such progress mastering his emotions over the past few weeks. I couldn't take that from him for my own selfish gain!

And yet... I didn't want Lysander's loyalty. Or his love. Or *anything*. I just wanted to be free. But I *needed* to restore Maya's soul first... and there was no way Lysander would let me go anytime soon, with Eugene's men out on the prowl. I

185

felt more trapped than ever before, and I suddenly I couldn't stand to be near him any longer.

"I think you should go," I whispered, tears filling my eyes as I stepped back from him. "I'm so sorry, Lysander..."

He looked like he might protest—like he was determined to stay and resolve this, right here and now. I wondered if he feared he would revert to his cursed self if we didn't make amends. But after a moment, he turned and refused to meet my gaze. Without another word, he left me alone in silence, and I realized that the isolation I'd felt before was *nothing* compared to what I was feeling now.

Not long after Lysander had gone, I'd thrown on the first nightgown I'd found in my wardrobe, not caring that it was one of the more skimpier ones Nerissa had stocked for me, and slumped straight into bed. I'd skipped dinner and break-fast, and now I was ignoring the gnawing in my stomach as I lay there, feeling like an absolute monster.

I didn't deserve food, and I was never leaving this room again. Not if it meant risking running into Lysander—whom I wasn't ready to face and could probably *never* face again. Just the thought of bumping into him made me feel sick. I'd broken his heart... and we somehow still had a kingdom to run together and a coronation to endure by the end of this week.

I couldn't fathom it. Couldn't even entertain the idea right now. A part of me wanted to run away from it all, but that would entail leaving my room.

A quiet knock pulled me from my thoughts, and I shot upward, my heart hammering as dread filled my gut. He wasn't *back*, was he?

Before I had time to question whom it was, Leif let himself in. He was carrying a wooden sword and wearing his armor.

"Hey, I thought I'd come see what was taking you so lo—"

He paused midsentence, his jaw dropping at the sight of my bold red nightgown. It was sheer lace with gold seaflowers stitched into it, and it left very little to the imagination.

He immediately turned a shade darker than his hair and turned around, covering his eyes as he stammered.

"I—I apologize—I thought you'd be up by now—"

I mentally cursed Nerissa—she'd probably stocked the stupid nightgown thinking I'd wear it for Lysander. Blushing furiously, I pulled my blankets up to cover myself and snapped, "What do you want?"

"I, uh... Nerissa said I was training you today," he managed, his throat hoarse as he continued to avert his gaze. "She said there was an incident yesterday and that you guys were taking a break from magic practice, so I was to step in and teach you sword fighting instead. Kendra's already waiting at the training ring."

"I'm not going," I told him bluntly, curling back into the pillows. "Kendra can have a solo session."

He risked another look, and his shoulders relaxed when he noticed I'd pulled the blankets over myself. His boots thudded on the flecked stone-and-bedrock floors as he came to stand next to me.

"Coral," he said, his voice gentle. "What happened?"

187

"I don't want to talk about it," I muttered, pressing my face farther into the pillow so I didn't have to look at him. Even though I always enjoyed looking at him *immensely*.

I heard a sigh and then the clink of his armor as he shifted his stance.

"Come on, you were doing so well. I'm not going to let you fall back into this routine of hiding in your room."

"Too late," I mumbled bitterly.

"I'm training you," he said assertively. "So get up, or I'm going to drag you out of bed—sheer nightgown and all."

"You can't do that, I'm your queen—"

"You're not queen of Veranis yet, you haven't been coronated," he reminded me. "And the coronation is only days away. You need to be ready for an attack."

I rolled over so I could look at him again. He was staring down at me with determined eyes.

"You'd really rip these sheets off of me and risk seeing me practically naked again?" I challenged. His eyes darkened slightly in response.

"If I must," he replied, and something about his tone sent a shiver down my spine. "Though I'd suggest finding something more appropriate to train in. Your sister might not appreciate the view as much as I would."

My throat went dry. Was he *allowed* to say things like that? I imagined how Lysander would react, and pain stabbed through my heart once more. It sobered me up quickly, and I waved him away.

"Give me five minutes, and I'll meet you outside," I relented, clutching the sheets to my chest as I sat up again. He told me he'd be waiting before leaving me in privacy to change.

Thankfully, we didn't run into Lysander on our way down to the training ring, though I couldn't shake the thought of him curled up in his room the way I had been, riddled with misery.

Kendra was doing tail stretches when we arrived, and the sight of her made something twist in my stomach. Leif crossed to the weapons rack and threw Kendra a wooden practice sword similar to the one he'd brought to my room.

"No warm-up exercises?" I asked him, thinking of how Nerissa always made us start with our breathing routine.

"I think we're past the basics," he replied, grabbing a practice sword of his own and striding back over. "Though, another day, I want to take you through some defensive techniques. But today, I just want to get a sense for how well you can each hold your own in a proper fight."

He gestured for us to face each other, and we did. Kendra had her gaze trained on me, and I remembered how I'd nearly killed her yesterday. A part of me hesitated, lowering the sword.

But then she spoke, and my stomach dropped.

"What did you say to Lysander yesterday? He wouldn't talk to me about it this morning on our ride."

After everything he'd said about caring about me, about needing to stay loyal to me, about wanting to resolve matters with me... *he'd still gone seahorse riding with her?*

189

Unbridled rage coursed through me. I snapped, letting out a low growl, and hurled myself at her. She dodged at the last moment, eyes wide with surprise. Her sword flung up to meet mine as I brought it down, aiming for her head.

I screamed in her face, letting every ounce of frustration out as I attempted to jab at her.

She was the reason Lysander had grown distant from me—my relationship was *ruined* because of her! Because she'd just *had* to stay down here, to get in the middle of it all, to make my life even *more* complicated—

"Coral!" Leif cried, trying to intervene, but we were too fast as our swords clashed back and forth, echoing through the training ring with vicious ferocity.

"What the hell is wrong with you?" Kendra snapped, panting hard as she deflected me. I smacked her in the upper arm, and she cried out—then discarded the sword and brought up a wave of water to shield herself.

Oh, so she wanted to fight *dirty*?

I summoned a ball of water and hurled it at the shield, using the force to repeatedly break down the shield.

"You're the *worst*, you know that?" I screamed at her, finally breaking through her defenses and blasting her across the training ring with a wave. Leif swore and waved over a handful of guards. I was preparing to hammer Kendra with another wave when two arms grabbed me, pulling me back from her. Two more guards stepped in to disarm Kendra.

I thrashed, still yelling—but the pain was turning to grief in my heart, and tears began flowing, blurring the water around me. I fell limp in the guards' arms, and they let me crumple on the ground as I curled into myself and sobbed.

190

It wasn't Kendra's fault. It was *mine*. I shouldn't have pushed him away. I should have tried harder to connect with his new self. *I'd* been the one to let jealousy eat away at me.

I had nobody to blame but myself.

Kendra was breathing heavily, staring down at me like she didn't know me. Leif crouched by my side, eyes filled with genuine concern that made me resent myself even more.

"Come on," he prompted, offering me his hand. "We're getting out of here."

CHAPTER EIGHTEEN

Leif

I hadn't been home in weeks.

Before Coral had arrived, I would usually try to visit home once a week, even though I hadn't lived there in years. But with everything that had been happening, there hadn't been a spare moment for it.

Needing to get Coral away from Kendra, and out of the palace entirely, had given me the perfect excuse to return. So, I fetched her a cloak and led her out of the front doors of the palace, down the sloping path surrounded by coral gardens, and through the palace gates.

The kingdom awaited below—thousands of homes dotting the sloping canyon that filled the massive cavern Veranis had been built inside. We navigated down a path that led to the back roads, as it was the fastest way to my family's home. Tendrils of blonde hair drifted out from beneath the hood of her cloak. Underneath, she wore a plated blue corset over a button-up shirt. I thought back to what she'd been wearing this morning and swallowed hard—I *really* shouldn't think about that right now when I was blocks away from my own mother.

We navigated around the back roads, down slate staircases that had been built into the slope, past minuscule stacked homes sprawling with algae tresses. It was less busy in this part of the kingdom, but there were still plenty of people, so I stuck close to Coral for good measure. Finally, we reached a small two-story abode. The front door seemed more weathered than I remembered it, tucked under a curved stone arch. Potted anubias flowers were placed on either side, under two wide windows. I smiled knowingly at the decorative touch.

"Where are we?" Coral asked, lifting her hood to get a better look at the building. Before I could answer, there were heavy, thudding footsteps from inside, and the front door burst open.

"Leif!" came a shrill cry, and I was tackled three steps back by strong arms around my waist. "Where have you *been*?"

I looked down to see my youngest sister, Storm, hugging me tightly. I ruffled her choppy short hair in response. She was wearing dark leather pants and a vest over a green shirt, which enhanced her coppery-red hair.

"I missed you too!" I replied, grinning, and she beamed up at me before glancing over her shoulder.

"Mother! Leif's home!"

"Well *that* much was obvious from the racket you just caused," a different voice called back from somewhere inside. I gestured for Coral to follow as I shuffled through the door, Storm still attached to my waist with her vice-like grip. There was movement from the staircase on my right as we entered the foyer, and a third voice chided.

"You'll have to let him go eventually, Storm."

Leaning against the railing was my second-youngest sister, Juniper. She was wearing a dark-turquoise shift dress with lace on the cuffs and hem, and her hair was pulled into a messy bun.

"Storm! Come help me in the kitchen!" the second voice added, and my mother peered around a doorway a little farther up the hallway. "Leif, dear—welcome home!"

My mother's gaze landed on Coral, and she went still.

"Oh—I didn't realize you had a girl with you," she breathed, and I smiled, gesturing to Coral.

"This is Queen Coral," I introduced, and Coral seemed to cringe at the title. My mother let out a squawk, blushing furiously, and instantly sank into a curtsy. Even Juniper blushed, bowing her head respectfully. But Storm just stared up at Coral with wide eyes.

"Whoa! Are you a royal? Where's your crown?" she asked, and my mother's eyes nearly bulged out of her head at her boldness. Coral let out a laugh, looking relieved by Storm's presence.

"I am a royal, but I haven't been coronated yet," she replied gently, and bent down so that she was eye level with Storm. The movement caused her cloak to shift and reveal her mermaid tail. Storm's eyes grew wide like saucers, and her jaw dropped at the sight.

"You're a *mermaid*!" she gasped. "I've never seen one of you before!"

My mother glared at Storm from the doorway and cleared her throat, pointing at her feet to order Storm away from us. But Storm proceeded to swing on my arm repeatedly, completely oblivious to the situation.

"Can... can I get you anything, Your Grace?" my mother sighed finally. Coral opened her mouth to protest, but I stepped forward.

"Have you been baking lately, Mother?" I asked. "I think Coral would love to try one of your cakes."

Her eyes lit up, and she clasped her hands together with delight.

"Why *yes*! Come on through—I have just the thing," she said, waving us through. Storm ran on ahead, giggling with delight, and Juniper followed calmly after us. There was a small rustic table squished in the corner of the kitchen. I remembered eating at this table when I was growing up, and my sisters loved it when Mother baked for us. I wasn't as fond of the sweets.

We all took a seat around the table, and my mother placed a large layered cake onto the table. It was white and lime green and specked with colorful blobs throughout. Coral seemed hesitant at first, but I nodded my head toward it as my mother cut her a slice.

"Trust me. Just try it," I said, and I watched as she tentatively scooped it up with her fork and studied it. Finally, she took a bite, and the moment it touched her tongue, her eyes widened with delight.

"What *is* this?" she asked, and I laughed, my heart warming.

"It's layered coconut and a special type of seaweed that you'd probably only find this deep in the ocean, mixed with those dried fruits you like," I explained. "Sweet, isn't it?"

"Why don't you guys serve this up in the palace?" she asked, devouring it hungrily. My mother beamed at the reaction and offered her another slice before taking a seat across the table.

"It's difficult to source those dried fruits," my mother replied. "Especially nowadays, with all the changes in leadership and added security in Coronis. But Leif is so good at bringing them back when he travels for work."

"Did you stab any bad guys lately?" Storm asked me, and Juniper scowled at her.

"Storm, he doesn't just go around stabbing people. He protects the royals, who barely ever leave Veranis anyway," she replied sternly. My mother shifted in her chair at the mention of the royals.

"I heard about that attack a couple of weeks ago, when the late king was killed," she said. "So, you're serving Lysander as king now? Is that why you haven't had time to come visit us?"

Coral was halfway through her second cake slice, but I noticed her shift uncomfortably as soon as his name came up. *Interesting.*

I cleared my throat.

"That's correct," I answered curtly, and my mother shook her head.

"I think you should ask for a raise."

I grinned at her. "That's what I said."

She waved her fork at me. "Well, did you get one?"

I shook my head at her, still smiling. "Maybe one day I'll convince him."

We talked a little more, and I steered the conversation in a different direction for Coral's sake. Clearly, something had happened between them.

"Tell me more about what's been happening here. Where's Daphne?"

I'd been listening for sounds of a third person in the house since we got here, but it didn't seem like she was around.

"She's out with her boyfriend," Juniper sniggered, and my heart leaped into my throat.

"Daphne has a boyfriend?" I exclaimed, thinking of my sweet, innocent sister and feeling very protective all of a sudden. "Who is it?"

"It's Atlas—that guy that kept bringing her the seaflowers each morning."

I groaned. Not *him*. He was so confident and outgoing that it made me suspicious of him—most males were too shy to approach the likes of Daphne. By undine standards, Daphne had the looks of a goddess.

"Is Leif *your* boyfriend?" Storm asked Coral pointedly, and my mother choked on her slice of cake as Coral went red.

"Storm!" she hissed. "That's *extremely* disrespectful. You can't ask a queen questions like that!"

"And besides, she's obviously courting King Lysander," Juniper added, rolling her eyes at Storm.

I felt my throat tighten, but Juniper didn't pick up on how Coral's shoulder's tensed as she tried to educate our little sister. "I heard there was a coronation of sorts taking place in a few days. Are we attending that, Mother?"

"Well, I don't see why not," my mother replied, placing her fork down. "You girls love a good ball—we can rent out those nice dresses from the shop in the square."

"What if the sirens attack again?" Storm asked, and I shook my head at her.

"I'll be there to protect you," I promised. "That's my job, remember?"

"I thought your job was protecting the royals," she frowned, and Juniper sighed in defeat.

"If there's ever an attack, my sisters would always come first," I explained, reaching across the table to poke her playfully in the ribs, and she laughed with delight.

Coral was watching us with a soft smile on her face, and my heart fluttered. I swallowed, pushing the feelings down. *I can't let myself go there...*

My mother and sisters continued discussing the ball, so I got to my feet and said, "I'm going to show Coral the rest of the house. Thank you for the cake."

"Oh, are you sure you've had enough?" my mother responded, and Coral nodded.

"It's the best thing I've had down here. *Truly*," she told her, and my mother blushed with pride. I held out my arm to guide Coral out of the room, though I didn't touch her. We headed back toward the staircase, and I pointed upward.

"Let's go the roof," I said, allowing her to go first. She raised an eyebrow at me.

"The roof?" she repeated, and I nodded.

"It's quiet up there. And Storm hasn't figured out how to climb the trellis yet."

Coral's eyes lit up with understanding, and I directed her upstairs, down the hall, and into Daphne's bedroom so that we could slip out the window and up the trellis.

There was a portrait of all my sisters hanging in Daphne's room over a vase of seaflowers. Daphne was the tallest, with lovely red hair that cascaded down her shoulders and pearls in her hair. Juniper's hair was tied back in a neater bun this time, but she still had a rough look to her. And Storm stood in front

198

of them both, the shortest, with her choppy hair, her full cheeks, and her radiant smile. Coral paused for a moment to observe it before we finally reached the window.

The trellis was a little slippery with the algae, but we managed, and soon, we were nestled together on the rooftop, overlooking Veranis and the thousands of fish gliding overhead. It was a comfortable silence, and Coral didn't speak for a while. I think she was grateful for the privacy and the peace and quiet.

"Your sisters are lovely," she said after a while, finally meeting my eyes. I chuckled.

"Daphne and Juniper are fine. Storm is a *menace* most of the time."

"I think I like her best." Coral grinned. "She adds a bit of spice."

"Spice, huh?" I cocked my head at her, not sure what she was referring to, and she laughed. My heart warmed at the sight of her. I liked seeing her like this... she hadn't looked this happy in a long time.

There was another pause, and then I finally willed the courage to ask.

"It's none of my business, so you don't have to tell me... but... may I ask what happened?"

She fixed her gaze ahead for a moment, bringing her tail up to her chest and hugging it.

"We had a big fight," she said finally. "I think... it might be over between us."

I blinked at her, too stunned to respond. She lifted her finger and traced swirls of water through the rippling currents with her magic.

199

"But ever since I got back, I've felt like something was different between us. Like... whatever connection was there before is gone. And I'm not sure why."

I was pretty sure I knew why. Lysander and Kendra hadn't exactly been subtle, even if they were blatantly denying their attraction to each other out loud. But that being said... there *had* been a connection between Lysander and Coral before, however small. Sure, things had been rocky between them... but to think it was over already...

He'd given up his claim on Coral's heart for her freedom. And then she'd given up her heart and her freedom for him. How did those kinds of feelings disappear in the space of a few *weeks*? Lysander was more than my employer and my king... he was my friend. And despite my own feelings, which I'd been pushing down for weeks now, I felt like I owed it to him to try and fix this.

"If I may... you've only known him a couple of weeks," I pointed out. "It's normal for these things to take time. Especially with someone like him."

She finally met my gaze.

"What do you mean?" she asked, unclasping her hands and leaning back on her two palms.

"Well, his curse meant your relationship was unusual from the very start. I don't blame you for having doubts and feeling confused."

She grimaced and straightened her posture.

"So what? You think I'm just *confused*? That I should go back to him?"

Absolutely not.

I shook the thought from my mind, from my lips, and said, "Perhaps you could give him another chance. There has to be *something* there for the two of you to give up all that you had for each other."

Her gaze fell, and I couldn't help feeling I'd said the wrong thing. A part of me wanted to backtrack, to tell her how I really felt... but deep down, her reaction sparked hope in me. Because if she *truly* felt this way... if she really didn't want to go back... then maybe I had a chance after all.

You can't, my mind reminded me. The moment I acted on my feelings, I'd lose everything I'd worked for. I'd lose my best friend. I wasn't about to throw it all away because I'd developed a small crush.

"What if it was just the curse influencing the both of us?" she asked finally. "I feel like everything we did for each other was out of moral obligation... because it was *right*, not necessarily because it was what either of us wanted. Maybe he was only attracted to me because I could restore his heart. What if I was attracted to him for the same reason? What if there were no real feelings involved from the very start?"

I didn't have an answer for her because I couldn't let myself give in to this kernel of hope she'd created. She returned to watching the fish swimming by, but I couldn't take my eyes off of her. I longed to reach for her hand, to tell her everything would be okay.

Finally, she glanced at me again and asked, "Do you think your mother would let me take her cake back to the palace?"

A smile cracked across my face as I thought of how my mother would react to this request. "I'm sure she'd love nothing more."

201

CHAPTER NINETEEN

Coral

I rapped at Kendra's bedroom door, and she scowled the moment she opened it and saw me waiting there.

"Wait!" I insisted, as she went to slam the door in my face, and I caught the door before it closed. "I came to apologize."

"Apology not accepted," Kendra shot back, but I barged my way into her room. With a sigh, she swam back to her bed and sank down on it, refusing to meet my gaze.

"Look... I'll admit, I got jealous," I said, swimming slowly over to her. "And Lysander and I had a fight, and I took it out on you. That was wrong of me—I shouldn't have let a boy come between us. We're better than that."

"You're damn right we are!" she snapped back. "I can't believe you *did* that to me! You could have seriously hurt me!"

"I know," I said. She was right—and I had to take full responsibility for it. "I want to make a vow with you. An official, legally binding one as future queen of Veranis, that we will not harm each other anymore. *Ever*."

The words rippled through the air with magical promise. I didn't think I'd be able to create bindings until I was coronated... but it looked like the ocean was willing to work with me.

"So, you're still going to rule alongside Lysander?" Kendra asked, raising an eyebrow. "Even now that you guys are..." she didn't finish the sentence, like she didn't know how to.

I shrugged hesitantly and came to sit beside her.

"I guess I am. I'm still Queen of the Undersea, so I'm still bound to Lysander through my heart binding that broke his curse. I can't just run away from my royal duties."

And I couldn't jeopardize my status as Reigning Queen. I owed it to Maya to restore her soul. Talking with Leif had helped clear my head and woken me up to how I'd been acting lately. I'd been drowning in my resentment for my current situation, but I only had myself to blame for it. And I'd been entertaining stupid fantasies thinking somehow, I could escape it... but that was never going to happen.

This was my life now, and my time being selfish and lost in my own grief was done. I needed to figure out how to move on with my life and find happiness down here in Veranis. If Kendra could do it, surely, I could too.

"Well, that's going to be awkward as hell," Kendra breathed, and I couldn't agree with her more. I still wasn't ready to face Lysander, but Leif had convinced me to come back to the palace and to keep coming to training until the day of coronation.

I'll handle Lysander—keep him distracted and out of your way, he'd promised me, and that had eased my nerves a little. *Except for tomorrow morning, of course—you'll have to see him at the coronation rehearsal. But you don't have to talk to him.*

It wasn't a permanent solution... we would have to talk to each other eventually. But it would get us through the next few days—and hopefully, the entire two-hour rehearsal where I would be memorizing lines and learning a dance for the ball afterward. I cringed at the thought of having to *dance.*

203

"I'm sorry if I... caused a rift between you two," Kendra said finally, and she kept her gaze on the floor. I slipped my hand into hers.

"No—I overreacted," I said firmly, drawing her attention. "It would have been fine if Lysander and I weren't having problems to begin with. I *wanted* to be happy that you were bonding. Why wouldn't I want my sister to get along with my... romantic partner?" I said the last part with uncertainty. I wasn't really sure *what* to call him or how to define our relationship at all. "I projected my own insecurities onto you, and that was wrong of me."

Kendra didn't look convinced—and I could have sworn there was guilt in her eyes.

"If we're being honest with each other?" she began finally, "I... think I have feelings for Lysander."

It should have shocked me, but it didn't.

"And does Lysander have feelings for you?" I asked quietly. A part of me didn't want to know the answer. But we were past pretending, past avoiding this strange turn of events.

"I think he does, but he won't admit it because of you," she replied earnestly, and guilt shone in her eyes. "I told him we shouldn't be around each other... but after Dad's funeral, you weren't there. And he was so kind, so easy to talk to..."

I thought I'd be angry, but it had actually helped to know that Lysander had been holding out because of me. He'd been trying to fight his newfound emotions and feelings to do the right thing by me—even if it was only to maintain his un-cursed self—and it was touching. I mean, weeks ago, he didn't even fully grasp what morals were. This was real progress.

"Thank you for being honest with me," I said, squeezing her hand. "I meant what I said—I don't want us to fight anymore. I... might need some time to process this, but I'm not angry that you feel the way you do."

Her eyes glimmered with relief.

"Really?" she breathed, and I reached over to hug her. She squeezed me back, and I realized I'd missed this warmth, this feeling of not being so alone in the world.

"Dad wouldn't want us to fight either," I said firmly, leaning back from the hug.

Kendra let out a laugh and added, "Dad would have grounded us for six months for letting a man come between us—and then banned us from dating at all."

I laughed with her, knowing she was right. I didn't even want to think about how Melody would have reveled in such drama, seizing her opportunity to step in as the "stepmother" and punish us.

"I'm going to go change out of these clothes," I told her—I was still wearing the plated corset and top that I'd fought Kendra in, and sweat from our fight still lingered. Relieved that I'd been able to mend things with my sister, I exited her room and swam down to my quarters.

As I swam, I thought about the hours I'd spent with Leif earlier. It had been surprisingly easy to talk with him about Lysander... though Leif had always been easy to talk to. He'd been there for me since I first came here, and he'd always been thoughtful toward me. I appreciated that he'd taken me to his family home, even if it had just been as a distraction and to get me out of the palace for a while. I liked his family as much as I liked him...

I slowed in my tracks as the thought hit me. What *did* I feel for Leif? Because lately, I'd noticed more and more how handsome he was, and every time I saw him, it made my stomach flutter and my heart race. But with all the turmoil with Lysander, I hadn't had much time to consider the way he made me feel until now.

When I entered my quarters, I was so preoccupied in my thoughts and finding a fresh bralette to change clothes that I didn't spot the sealed scroll on my bed until afterward. Frowning, I swam over to it and found no hints of whom the scroll was from. Curiosity got the better of me as I opened the scroll and read what was scribbled there in familiar swirly handwriting.

Dearest Coral,

A little fish told me you've been having trouble adjusting to your new life as a mermaid. Boy problems, rulership doubts, and a deep craving for the sun and surf you used to love so much.

I'm willing to give you something that will restore your old life and eliminate all of these problems in return for something of equal value of course. Come meet me and my associate at Seer's Peak this evening. We'll wait until midnight for you—and we expect you to come alone.

Kisses,

Melody.

PS: Eugene is desperate to get you back into his captivity. He's planning to torture your fellow kin as punishment for your escape. If you're having second thoughts about meeting me, well, I might have a solution for this too. Show up if you want to know more.

I read the letter again, then reread it a third time.

Sinking onto the bed, I considered her words. It could be a trap, a lie... but I knew she wanted her power back. I was the only person who could undo that binding for her.

I couldn't get her words about the mermaids out of my brain. Guilt plunged through me all over again—I'd failed them. In fact, I'd completely forgotten about them in my selfish grief these past few weeks. And according to Eugene's story, I'd *vowed* to stay his prisoner to free them. I wondered what they thought of me now that I'd escaped and abandoned them to a monster's fate.

Then there was Melody's vague promise about restoring my old life. Was there *really* a way to go back to land? To get my *legs* back? I hadn't heard back from Deandra yet... If there was a way, was it worth waiting for her to finish reading the sea witch book and tell me her findings? Or maybe she wouldn't find anything, and I'd lose my one and only opportunity to discover the method from Melody.

I didn't want to get my hopes up... my mother had warned me this was a permanent transformation. She'd given up her entire *life* below to go to land, and she'd paid the price in the end. I'd only asked Deandra to transcribe the book out of sheer desperation, but deep down, I'd never expected anything to come of it.

But what if my mother had been wrong? What if my inkling to dig deeper had been *right*? I could free myself from this situation... I could escape my fate ruling Veranis forever with Lysander. I didn't have to act on it immediately... I just had to know *how* it was possible.

I debated back and forth about going, and I couldn't help wondering how far Melody was willing to go to get what she wanted. If I didn't show up tonight, would she start threatening the people I loved? Maybe it was worth going just to appease her, even if I didn't accept her proposal.

Thoughts swirled through my head. I would have to make a choice soon if I was going to make the journey by midnight. But again... what if it was a trap?

Then it's a risk you'll have to take, I thought finally, rising from the bed. If not for me, then for the mermaids—I at *least* owed it to them to find out if Melody had a real solution to that problem. After all, I'd stood up to King Malvin because he'd been too content and cowardly to save his own people. I wasn't about to follow in his footsteps by abandoning the mermaids when I'd promised to free them one way or another. So, I quickly found a traveling cloak to throw over my bralette, tied a silk wrap around my tail, and slipped out of my room.

I was halfway down the stairs when a voice cleared from behind me. Spinning around, I saw Matt standing there, leaning on the railing.

"Running away?" he mused, and I grimaced.

"Just going for a seahorse ride," I lied, and I hated that I had to lie to him. It was already going to be challenging enough to sneak past the guards without tipping off Lysander.

Matt descended a few more steps.

"Great. I'll join you."

I paled. Melody had warned me to come alone—I couldn't show up with Matt at my side.

"Uh, actually... I kind of wanted to go alone..."

He threw me a knowing look.

"You're running away," he confirmed, folding his arms. "Either that, or you're doing something you shouldn't be." I let out a sigh as he finally reached the same step I was on, and he continued, "Come on, haven't I always been your partner in crime?"

I rolled my eyes at him.

"This is different. It's too dangerous," I replied, thinking of the last time we faced off against Melody and he'd nearly been killed.

"Good. I was getting bored sitting around here," he replied firmly, and strode down the rest of the steps. "Lead the way, *Your Grace*." He gestured sweepingly to the foyer door, a hint of mocking in his tone, and it was in that moment that I knew I was stuck with him. But it did occur to me that I was more likely to be allowed outside the kingdom with an escort, so maybe having Matt at my side *would* be helpful.

With a relenting sigh, I beckoned him to follow me, and I hoped Melody would be merciful.

We snuck past the guard towers, mounted two seahorses, and rode to Seer's Peak. By the time we arrived, it was close to midnight. I'd never been to the top of the overlook and was thankful we had the seahorses to carry us up the winding path. Rough currents ripped at my hair the entire way to the top.

We dismounted our seahorses and left them tethered to a rock nearby, next to two other seahorses that I assumed belonged to Melody and her associate. But there was no sign of either of them as we navigated to the edge of the seamount, where the most breathtaking view awaited.

I saw the glittering lights of Veranis in the far distance and thought of how angry everyone at the Vera Palace would be if they knew we'd snuck out to meet with Melody. Shifting uncomfortably, I continued gazing to the left, where rocky, mountainous valleys loomed in shadow and deadly creatures swished in and out of the darkness, barely visible from here.

And directly ahead? The Sea of Souls—a swirling mass of wispy white streaks that clouded the territory from view. Just looking at it sent a shiver up my spine.

"So, you came," a voice drawled from behind us, and Matt and I whirled around to face Melody—dressed in crème traveling pants with a white fitted jacket. She was accompanied by a slender female whom I didn't recognize, whose dark-brown hair was somehow slick and perfect next to my unruly blonde waves that had been battered by the currents. The female wore a crimson-red riding jacket and black leather pants with laced up boots.

Melody paused, planting a hand on her hip as her eyes flicked to Matt, and scowled. "I see you still struggle to follow directions, dear Daughter."

I glared back at her.

"We're expected back at dawn for a coronation rehearsal—so don't try anything funny, or you'll have Veranis guards tracking you all the way back to Coronis."

"A scary threat from a meddling princess," the female said to Melody, her lips curving into a smile.

But Melody patted her shoulder lightly and taunted, "Now, now, Sloane—Coral here is a *queen* now, which means we must obey her every command."

I huffed, not wanting to spend a moment longer in Melody's wretched company than I had to. So, I pivoted to my questions.

"How did you get your letter to my room undetected?"

Sloane raised an eyebrow at me like I was stupid.

"Um, I handed it to the messenger?" she replied dully. "Do your staff not do their jobs in your kingdom?"

"She probably used siren spell on him," Matt muttered to me under his breath, and I nodded in agreement.

"Okay, next question—"

"Aw, how cute. I didn't know she was old enough to play twenty questions." Sloane sniggered to Melody, who smirked back, and my blood thrummed.

"We can leave if you're so bothered by our company," I snapped, taking a step toward the seahorses. Melody sighed.

"Oh, don't be so dramatic, darling Daughter—"

"*Don't call me that—*"

Melody tutted. "Clearly, you're a very busy queen. Shall we get down to business then, so you can return to screwing your little undine king? Or do you both *make love* now that he has his emotions to guide him?"

Heat flushed through my cheeks as I tensed, and Matt put a hand on my shoulder to steady me.

"She's just trying to rile you up," he growled, throwing Melody a glare. Then he stepped forward and spoke up. "You said you had a plan to free the mermaids? What can you tell us?"

She strode slowly across the space of the lookout like she enjoyed harboring the information. Finally, she met my gaze again.

"It's simple—I'll free them once I claim back my kingdom. My *Queendom*. In return for you breaking these damned bindings that limit my power."

I let out a hollow laugh. *She* was going to free them? I should have known better than to come here.

"Why the hell would you do that?" I drawled, folding my arms, and she shrugged.

"Well, Veranis and Atlantis are allies now, thanks to your sweet little ceremony with King Lysander a few weeks ago. And you've already defeated me once when I was so close to getting everything I wanted."

She paused, looking pained to say the next words.

"I lost it all because I was too ambitious. Now, I know better. All I want is my kingdom back—*without* the threat of losing it again to you or Atlantis. I'll free the mermaids to secure our peace between kingdoms."

I frowned at her, looking for any hint that she might be lying. But she kept her face neutral, her stance poised.

I would be *stupid* to give her back her powers. *Utterly stupid.* But the offer was promising...

"You also mentioned that you had a way to restore my old life," I prompted, wanting to hear the rest. "Why offer that when this deal seems as good as any?"

"Because I know you're not dumb enough to give me back my powers while *you* hold the power to storm and seize Coronis on your own," Melody replied pointedly. "Sure, it would take some planning, and you might lose a lot of men, but you could do it. For you to *really* consider my offer... I must give you something you can't refuse. And I'm willing to do just that."

Sloane stepped forward and added, "Of course, the alternative is that you let Eugene skin the mermaids alive like he's already started doing—as punishment for your selfish escape." She grinned savagely, and another chill went down my spine. "I wonder how many he would get through before you pulled together a plan to take on Coronis? Our way would be much faster, much *easier*."

I grimaced, realizing she was right. And yet, I couldn't risk giving Melody back her powers without something more solid, more worthwhile in exchange.

"Tell me how you'd restore my old life," I pressed, and Melody's eyes gleamed.

"Deep in the heart of the Sea of Souls, you will find the First Sea Witch," she explained, making her way back toward Sloane. "She is difficult to find... but *should* you find her, she will grant you any binding you desire. And I just happen to know where she is."

My eyes widened. Yes, that could work... but if it was true, then how come Melody hadn't sought out the witch's soul on her own to get her power back? Why did she need me?

As if reading my thoughts, Melody added, "When I say she is difficult to find... even I have struggled to find her. But I know of her location within the sea, and I'm willing to take

213

you that far—in exchange for my powers back, of course. And once that is done, I shall leave you to find our current sea witch's soul and make your deal with the First Sea Witch. You won't have to worry about me ever again."

I was tempted. *Extremely* tempted. I wanted my legs back more than anything, wanted to escape Veranis and walk on land again. I *needed* to feel the sunshine in my hair, to feel the spray of the surf on my skin as I rode a wave... I felt like I would slowly wither away down here otherwise.

I didn't know how I'd navigate Lysander's heartless curse, but right now, I didn't care. I could only focus on one problem at a time, and this was the opportunity being presented to me. If I didn't take this... I'd have no one to blame but myself for the life I ended up trapped in.

Live for yourself, Coral.

The words echoed through my mind—a reminder.

"Coral, I don't like this," Matt muttered under his breath to me. "It sounds too good to be true."

He was right. I shouldn't say yes. I shouldn't be fooled by Melody, the cunning, manipulative female who had forced me to kill my own father, who had destroyed my family, who had led me to transform and sacrifice my entire life on land...

That thought snapped in me.

"I'll do it," I said finally, and a ripple in the current locked my vow in place. Matt let out a groan of protest as Melody's lips curled into a smile, and Sloane's eyes glimmered with excitement.

"So glad you've come to see reason, my dear daughter," Melody purred, and turned toward the seahorses. "Well then— we've no time to waste."

I faltered.

"Wait... we're doing this *now*?" I protested, and she looked over her shoulder at me.

"Oh yes—this is a one-time deal. We either go now, or we don't go at all."

I sucked in a breath. The rehearsal... I wasn't going to make it back in time. And before long, Lysander and Leif would realize we were missing. I was going to be in *so* much trouble afterward.

But... I couldn't let this opportunity slip through my fingers. And it meant I didn't have to wait any longer to restore Maya's soul. Maybe I could avoid the coronation altogether!

So, I gestured for Matt to follow, and we mounted our seahorses and set off back down the seamount—on a direct path to the Sea of Souls.

CHAPTER TWENTY

Lysander

I felt sluggish as I pulled on a peacock-green button-down shirt and pants, and I was nursing a terrible pounding headache. The past few days had been... draining.

Between the twisting in my stomach and the hollow aching in my heart, I couldn't tell if I was angry at Coral, devastated that she'd rejected me... or guilty over the fact that I was secretly relieved. It felt like a massive jumble in my brain that I was eager to numb, and I'd ordered my staff to bring me two bottles of hard liquor to get through the night.

No wonder humans drink so much, I thought. It had helped... if only temporarily.

The only reason I was bothering to get up was because of the stupid coronation rehearsal I'd agreed to. I should have postponed the entire event... but I couldn't. The entire kingdom was already planning to be there, and they were counting on Coral and me to display our power and strength, to ease the whispers of war that were spreading like weeds throughout our people.

I dragged myself downstairs and made my way to the ballroom where servants continued to haul statues, ocean blossoms, woven kelp streamers, and crystal lights inside to decorate for the grand event. Leif and Kendra were already awake and waiting near the ballroom entrance, eyes trained on the decor, but there was no sign of Coral or Matt.

I didn't even have the strength to chuckle as a passing servant shoved a crystal statue of Coral and me into Leif's empty arms, eliciting a look of shock from him as she told him to hold it before rushing over to help with the streamers. I came to stand next to him as he stared down at the statue with distaste, not sure what to make of it. In the statue, we looked happily in love, caught up mid-dance.

Leif glanced at me as I said, "They've overslept."

This earned a raised eyebrow from him. I bit back a sigh. I was tiring of this routine with Coral—the constant hiding and her avoidance of duties. But I didn't want to be the one to say anything while she was still grieving and recovering. But she acted like she was the only one—like her own *sister* hadn't lost her father too. And yet, *Kendra* had managed to show up on time, so why couldn't Coral?

"Actually, neither of them is in their room," Leif countered back quietly, shifting the weight of the statue from one arm to the other. "I already checked—I was going to escort Coral myself to ensure she arrived on time. But I found out that two seahorses are missing. They must have gone on an early morning ride, and they're running late in their return."

I grimaced. Well, that was only slightly better. Though it was strange that the guards hadn't mentioned anything.

"We'll have to start without them," I announced finally, turning to face them both. "I have a fitting this afternoon and some other duties to attend to, so I can't delay the rehearsal. Whatever training Coral misses, she'll just have to figure out for herself on the day."

It was harsh, but I was past caring. Past making excuses for the mermaid who had thoroughly rejected me, *all* of me, who hadn't even been willing to *try* and see the real me. She'd shut me out and then she'd blamed me, and every time I thought about it, my heart felt heavier and heavier.

I hadn't been good enough for her after all.

Storming across the ballroom toward the dais, I approached the officiant, who was supposed to be practicing lines with Coral, to dismiss him. But before I'd made it halfway, a swarm of glimmering neon dwarf fish—seven of them, to be exact—spiraled into my path, frenzied and sending whispers along the ocean currents to my ears.

I froze, my blood running cold as their words met my ears, and my heart began to race.

Instant guilt flooded through me; here I'd been simmering and cursing Coral for her absence without considering that *maybe* there was another explanation for it.

I turned back to Leif, who noticed my abrupt movements and glanced at me. He saw the panic on my face and began heading for me, statue still in tow.

"Coral and Matt aren't out on a seahorse ride," I informed him, my hands clammy, and his expression went slack. Kendra, overhearing, swam a few paces forward.

"What do you mean?" she demanded. "Where are they?"

I listened to the fish darting around my head, to their whispers of how an associate of Melody's tortured their kin with siren song for personal intel about Coral before they lured her out last night. About how she and Matt had met with Melody, and where they'd ventured off to together. I was the only one who could understand the fish, but Kendra's face grew slack, which I only half registered, as pure fear coursed through me.

I wanted to slump to the ground—I couldn't help her. I was *angry* with her, but not angry enough to leave her in the clutches of the monster who had destroyed her family. And her sister... Her face was white and full of apprehension. She would be devastated to lose her, and the very thought made my heart ache with a new kind of sorrow.

But my father's binding... it would turn me to sea-foam. And then I'd be forever useless.

"Lysander," Leif pressed, a sense of urgency to his tone as his gaze flickered from the fish to me. "*Where is she?*"

I heaved a shaky breath.

"Melody has her—and they're venturing to the Sea of Souls."

Pure, undiluted fear flickered across Leif's face. Then he dropped the crystal statue, which shattered all over the polished stone floor, and ran.

PART THREE

CHAPTER TWENTY-ONE

Leif

My mind was whirling as I urged my seahorse to ride faster, faster, *faster*—across desolate bedrock plains, rocky seamounts, and rolling hills of Neptune grass.

She was with Melody—or at least, that's what the dwarf fish had said. But I'd been with her only hours before she'd snuck out. *How* had this happened? What could have possibly swayed her to leave without saying something to one of us? Why had she taken Matt with her?

I didn't trust Melody. Not within an inch of my life, not after everything the Pryor clan had done to the Undersea. I *had* to reach her before anything happened. If I didn't...

My heart was pounding. I couldn't think about that. Every moment that passed was a moment wasted, and I pushed on, colors blurring around me as I rode.

The seahorse began wheezing when we reached the last leg before the Sea of Souls—but it was well timed, as I couldn't take the seahorse any farther. Even as we approached the swirling sea of mist, a chill skittered up my arms, and the seahorse slowed and bucked in protest.

Gritting my teeth, I hastily dismounted and ran the rest of the way on foot, water swirling past me. The moment I reached the mist, the temperature plummeted, but I pushed through. The mist was so thick, I could barely see a foot in front of me as I ventured deeper and deeper into the frigid opalescent water. And with each passing minute, the water

221

turned from white to a sickly moss green—murky and forbidding.

She could have gone in so many directions... how was I ever going to find her? Desperation clawed at my throat as I searched for clues, but the bedrock floor left no tracks, and it was too thick to see anything anyway.

I kept running, knowing I couldn't afford to stay still. The water grew deeper, darker, thicker... and a strange stiffness began to cling at my armor and skin, swirling around me with such staleness that it felt suffocating.

"Is it just me, or does it feel like the water has stopped moving?" A faint, faraway voice drifted, and I froze. Listening intently, I heard a low chuckle.

"They have, dear Daughter," another voice echoed—louder, like the female was calling out. "Because we've almost reached the heart now—the place where souls of the sea go to rest. Where there is no life, only death, and time stands still to let them pass through the veil."

It's them, I realized, and I raced toward the sound. I couldn't tell how close or how far they were in the mist—was the ocean carrying the sound to me intentionally, or were they mere feet away? Either way, I didn't dare call out, as much as I wanted to. I didn't want to alert Melody and prompt her to act prematurely—not when I didn't have my eyes on Coral. I needed to know that she was safe first, and I had the element of surprise on my side.

As I raced deeper and deeper through the water, the chill on my arms became even more prominent. I shuddered, feeling a strange tug in my gut—like it was pleading for me to turn around. To get far, far away from this place.

But I pushed on.

Up ahead, the mist was clearing, revealing a stretch of bedrock surrounded by a thick rounded wall of stagnant seawater. And cutting through the ground was a gaping chasm—the edges glowing luminescent like the cavernous sky of Veranis.

I spotted them and halted in the misty shadows before the clearing. Melody and another female were paused at the edges, peering down the chasm. Coral was a few paces down with Matt, and she spared the chasm a quick glance. Matt's eyes were trained on the two sirens, and the unknown female grinned fiendishly at him while Melody held her chin high.

"So, my dear daughter, I have brought you as far as I am willing. *As promised*."

Coral frowned at Melody, then looked back down into the chasm.

"Are you saying that what I'm looking for is down there?"

Melody nodded, a slow smile creeping onto her pink lips. *What was she looking for?*

"*All* that you wish to seek, you will find on the other side of that veil. But I must warn you... no one makes it back from that chasm alive—hence the stories about the Sea of Souls. There are horrors down there worse than anything you've experienced up here."

I couldn't let Coral go any farther. I began to scan my surroundings, looking for a way to take Melody and the other siren out without alerting them.

"Now, I believe we had a deal," Melody continued pointedly, staring Coral down with fierce, determined eyes. Coral hesitated, looking pained, and dread filled my core as I watched. It was like she was being forced by an invisible

223

hand—like *ancient magic*—as she grudgingly waved her fingers through the water slowly. Silvery-blue tendrils of current curled up her forearm before sweeping into the current and flowing over to Melody. The tendrils of water encased her body from head to toe and rippled over her.

Horror slammed into me as I watched Melody's binding come undone—her hair began to take on a glossy shine, her gaunt cheeks appeared more contoured, and her skin developed an alluring golden glow. Very slowly and quietly, I drew my spear. I was going to have to sneak around and take her out.

Melody flaunted her arms and legs for a moment, admiring herself with gleaming eyes, then threw Coral a savage smile that made me halt in my tracks.

"At last," she breathed, a gentle lull of song to her voice again. "I've been waiting for this moment."

Before I could even blink, the other siren had lunged across the clearing for Matt, a flash of silver in her hand. Matt barely had time to dodge, and a dagger sank into his thigh. He cried out, attempting to shove the siren off of him.

I ran straight for them without thinking.

"*No!*" Coral screamed and went to swim for Matt, but the gentle hum of a song stopped her in her tracks. The sound washed over me, enticing me for a split second, but I resisted—it wasn't meant for me.

But Melody, with a cruel smile on her face, was holding Coral to the spot with her siren song while she thrashed and cried out. Matt, clutching his leg as blood seeped around them, was staggering away from the other siren, who grinned maliciously.

224

I let out a cry as I brought my spear down into Melody's shoulder, and her siren song turned shrill and off-key as the blade sank into her skin. More blood joined the water as she stumbled, hissing, and swiped at me with razor-sharp claws.

Coral was already moving to defend Matt, who'd finally drawn his sword. Melody's eyes blazed as she looked over me.

"The king couldn't come himself, so he sends his commander?" She purred at me, rolling her shoulder like she was merely working a kink out of it and not nursing a bloody wound. I held my spear steady in my hands as she prowled toward me.

I heard the clash of swords and the whoosh of water as Coral and the other siren began to fight. We all needed to get out of here, *fast*, or this was going to end in a bloodbath.

"You have your power back," I reminded her calmly, matching her every step as we began to circle. "Now leave before I drive my spear through your heart."

"I'd like to see you try," she snarled, and lunged for me again. She was fast, but years of training kicked in, and I side stepped, bringing my spear around hard. Out of nowhere, she'd drawn a dagger, and despite its short length, the weapons clashed and held. Baring her perfect teeth, she pushed back with all her might, and I gritted my teeth as I deflected her.

There was a scream from behind me, and a blast of current washed past. My mind urged me to turn, to see what was happening with Coral, but the moment I turned my head would be the moment Melody landed her killing blow. I heard cries from behind me, a grunt of pain from Matt, a shriek of terror...

225

"Uh-oh," Melody mused with a smirk, as her gaze flicked back and forth between what was happening behind me. I lunged, our weapons dancing, and shifted my gaze for a moment.

The other siren had backed Coral and Matt up against the edge of the chasm, and Matt was still injured. Her eyes glimmered as she spoke.

"Jump."

Matt staggered, caught in the spell, then turned and—

"*No!*" Coral shrieked, diving to grab his arm. But she missed, and Matt gracefully tumbled over the edge.

My mind was racing as I locked my gaze back on Melody, our weapons meeting again. But Coral's anguished scream hit my ears, and a surge of adrenaline hit me. Grabbing Melody's upper arm, I knocked the blade from her hand and twisted until she was forced to kneel. I brought my knee up, slamming it into her chin, and she crumbled to the ground—even if only for just a moment—letting out a low groan.

Then I sprinted over to Coral, who had landed in a heap at the edge of the chasm. I was surprised she hadn't dove down after Matt—but then I realized she wasn't moving, even with the other siren inches away. I heard a low hum and realized she *couldn't.*

"What a pity," the siren taunted as she approached. "The souls of the Undersea will be quick to devour your friend— that is, if the sharks don't sniff out his bleeding leg first."

Coral growled in response. "*Let me go!*"

As I gained on the edge, I saw a thin veil of silver light stretching from one side of the chasm to the other. But the siren suddenly held up a hand in my direction, and my legs snapped frozen—the sudden movement causing me to drop my spear, which skidded a few paces away. Her gaze slowly drifted to me.

"Your prey is getting away, Melody," she sang out, without taking her gaze off of me, and I heard a grunt from behind me. *Crap.*

I couldn't move. Couldn't see Melody. My heart pounded harder than ever as the siren's lips curved upward. Coral's frantic panting echoed throughout the clearing. I let out a strangled noise, trying to shift a muscle, lift a finger, *anything.*

Melody's low, musical chuckle sounded from behind me, and I felt sick to my stomach.

"I'm bored of him. And stop toying with my poor daughter, Sloane," she purred, walking past me like I wasn't even there. She came to stand between me and Coral, who was still trapped on the edge of the chasm. "If she wants to join her friend and be devoured, then let her. But before that, I really should mention a small detail."

She paused to admire her clawed nails like she had all the time in the world. Coral was practically sobbing—how far down the chasm was Matt now? Was he dead?

"The veil only allows *living* beings to pass through. If you die on the other side... well, you're trapped there forever," Melody mused slowly, meeting Coral's gaze. "So when you bring a soul back from the other side, I *do* hope you won't have to choose between precious Matt or Maya."

A cruel smile appeared on her lips, and I could *feel* Coral's rage and desperation radiating off of her. My own blood was thrumming with hatred for Melody, for the way they were taunting Coral in this very moment, for what they'd done to Matt.

Dismissively, she motioned to Sloane, who waved her hand. Coral slouched forward, but I was still stuck. I couldn't so much as yell out in protest as she kicked her tail and swiftly dove into the chasm.

Damn it!

Now they were both down there—beyond the realm of the living—where vicious souls devoured the living. My eyes flicked to Melody, who gave me a withering look.

"Now, what to do with this one?" she mused, striding over to me. The wound on her shoulder was slick with blood, and she had a nasty bruise on her lower jaw from my knee. But otherwise, she looked radiant again—*powerful.*

Sloane lurked behind, noticing Melody's wounds and frowning.

"We should return," she prompted, and my ears felt hollow with the sudden absence of her humming. My muscles unlocked, and I realized I could move again. "This one tracked the mermaid all the way out here—let him track her until he meets his own demise down there."

Melody didn't look convinced, but then Sloane slung an arm around Melody's shoulder and purred into her ear.

"Now that you've got your power back, we've got a kingdom to overthrow."

Melody's eyes lit up at the suggestion, and I didn't bother to hide my frown. Were they talking about Veranis? Or Coronis? Either way, I needed to stop them—but I also needed to go after Coral and Matt.

I still didn't have my spear, and if I went for it, Melody would react before I could wield it and attack. I needed something faster, something more effective...

"Why bring Coral all the way out here?" I asked, trying to deter them as they turned to leave. Melody planted a hand on her hip as she observed me.

"Because there's no better place to dispose of a body," she replied slowly. "Like I said, only the living can return from the other side, and Coral can't bring back a soul without making an equal trade. We *both* know she's not selfish enough to trade Matt's life for Maya's."

I felt sick hearing the words, and Melody grinned at me.

"So yes, Coral may be a Reigning Queen... but there's *no way* she'll survive down in that chasm."

She meant for Coral to sacrifice herself.

My hands clenched, and I snarled back, "Neither will you."

Before she could blink, I hurled forward, slammed into her, wrapped my arms around her waist—and took her over the edge of the chasm with me.

CHAPTER TWENTY-TWO

Coral

I remembered falling like a strong current was sucking me down, down, *down* into endless depths of darkness. The moment I'd passed through the veil separating life from death inside the chasm, every inch of my skin had been drowned in a deep cold so numbing, I could no longer feel my hands, my tail fin, or anything.

I hadn't seen Matt. Hadn't seen the bottom. And then I'd blacked out, and I'd dreamed of my mother again.

It had been a long time since she'd appeared to me, and this time, she was more transparent than ever. Her long brown hair was faded, her triangular face and dimples barely visible. She stood in front of four crowns, each one sitting on a stone pillar surrounded by near darkness. And she said, "*Meet me here.*"

But before I could say more, she faded entirely, and I was left staring at the four crowns. They were familiar—one resembled Lysander's crown, made of bornite. The gold one was the Coronis crown. The copper one reminded me of what my grandfather, King Malvin, had worn. But the silver one was new. I stared at them, trying to figure it out, until—

"*Coral!*"

Someone was shaking me awake, giving life to my senses again. I barely registered the hands on my shoulders as my body was so numb from the cold. But the shaking motion had stirred me, and my eyes fluttered open. It was too dark, too blurry...

"Wake up, Coral!" the familiar voice begged. I tried to move, and a sharp pain in my shoulder bit through the numbing cold. I winced, hissing as I pushed up from the floor, and registered two hands cradling my face. Gentle, calloused hands that handled me with such delicacy that my heart fluttered. I could have sworn whoever it was let out a quiet, relieved huff.

My surroundings were starting to take shape, though blanketed by murky darkness. It was strange not being able to see because since transforming into a mermaid, my vision had greatly improved to cater to the depths of the ocean. But as I waited for my eyes to adjust, I was able to make out cavernous walls around us, a bedrock floor so cold it stung my hands, and kneeling before me was Leif. I realized it was his hands caressing my cheeks, but he swiftly moved them to steady me by the arms as I tried to get up.

"Careful—I think your shoulder is injured," he told me, and on cue, a sharp stab of pain rippled through me again from that spot. I slouched forward, leaning into him for support, but he held me without protest. I must have landed poorly on a rock or something.

"Where's Matt?" I ground out, barely able to speak through the pain. "His leg... it was bleeding..."

"He's over here," Leif said, keeping me in his grasp as we navigated a few paces over. I spotted Matt's body on the floor and let out a choked gasp. The only thing that stopped me from collapsing at his side was my shoulder.

231

"I already bandaged his leg with some of his pants fabric," he told me reassuringly. "But he could use some proper healing. I think... *you* might be able to do that."

He was right. I'd never done it before, never even researched any spells around it... but I *knew* mer-hearts had healing properties. It had to work. I couldn't let Matt die down here.

Leif eased me down beside Matt, and I gritted my teeth against the pain in my shoulder. Matt was unconscious. I didn't know how much blood he'd lost, and as far as I could tell, his skin was ice cold like the rest of us down here, which told me nothing about his actual condition.

I did my best to find his bandaged wound in the dark. Eventually, my hands grazed something sticky—barely distinguishable with how numb my fingers were—and when I brought my fingers to my nose, I inhaled a metallic scent.

"Hold on Matt," I begged, and began to channel and focus my magic on the wound. I felt my fingertips warm as golden light began to spread across his leg where the wound was thick with blood loss. I put everything I had into it—my entire heart, my soul, every ounce of my being.

Heal him, I begged silently, hoping my body would understand what I wanted my magic to do.

"Not to add pressure to an already tense situation," Leif added after a moment, glancing over his shoulder, "but you might want to hurry. Melody's down here too, and she could wake at any moment."

My heart leaped into my throat, and I spared a quick look over my shoulder, but it was too dark to see anything else.

232

"How long have we all been down here?" I asked finally, focusing my gaze back on Matt. "How did *you* get down here?"

"I'm not sure how long it's been—I woke only minutes ago—and the last thing I remember is following you," he said, and I met his gaze. He quickly looked away, like he was embarrassed or something.

"And Melody followed too?" I asked, raising an eyebrow at him. He raised a hand to the back of his neck, looking sheepish.

"Well, uh, she was talking about overthrowing a kingdom. I didn't think it best to let her go, so... I brought her down here with me."

Well, that was just *great*. On top of being unable to see a damn thing, my murderous almost stepmother was down here too—and something told me she'd get a kick out of hunting us in the dark.

"Come on, Matt," I breathed, my magic still spilling over him, but I didn't notice any changes.

"Why did you agree to come out here with Melody?" Leif asked finally, his voice more tense this time. I let out a breath. For some reason, it felt stupid to admit out loud. *Selfish.*

"She promised me something," I replied quietly, unable to meet his gaze. How could I tell him that I'd been so willing to leave him? To abandon the *entire* Undersea, and all my duties, to get my life back on land? All because I preferred having legs and missed the sunshine.

I was no better than my mother in that regard. No wonder people had been so angry when she fled to land and never came back. I didn't think I'd have to face Leif while making the decision... or face the aftermath of my actions.

233

"And you *believed* her?"

"She also promised to free the mermaids—her plan was more effective than anything we could have done. I only met with her because of that. What she promised me *after* that was... well, it was what sealed the deal."

"Well, it must have been a pretty good promise for you to abandon all reason and allow yourself to be lured into her *obvious* trap like this," he ground out. "She had *no* intention of letting you live, Coral! So, who's to say she'd even stick to this *mysterious* promise she offered?"

"It was sealed by ancient magic," I said finally, turning to him. "So she *has* to let the mermaids go, at the very least—I already upheld my end of the deal by undoing her binding."

Leif's expression softened a little.

"Well, at least this wasn't all for nothing then," he huffed finally, and slumped down onto a nearby rock. "Anyway, I overheard you both talking earlier—there's something down here that you want. What is it?"

"Maya's soul is down here," I replied quickly, avoiding any mention of the First Sea Witch. "I was going to restore it anyway... but I wanted to go after it alone. It's too dangerous for you and Matt to stay down here with me. Once I heal him, you should both go back together."

"Don't be stupid," Leif growled. "There's no way I'm leaving you down here alone. And *especially* not with the likes of Melody. And Coral, there's something you should know—"

"Stop it!" I snapped, making him falter, and my blood thrummed in my veins. I let out a shaky breath. I couldn't stand the thought of him trying to protect me... and the fact that he'd *chased* me out here was embarrassing enough. "I know what you think about me, okay? You and Lysander *both* think I can't take care of myself—you won't even let me outside the kingdom on my own! Well, you don't have to worry about me anymore. I'm going to do better from now on. I've trained, and I can handle my stepmother," I assured him, my expression firm. He made a noise like he wanted to say more, but then Matt finally stirred and groaned. I gasped, my heart racing.

"Matt?" I cried, and he jolted upright, wincing. His hand flew to his leg, clutching it, and I let out a shaky, relieved laugh. "You're okay!" I flung my arms around him, close to tears and shaking, and felt the arm that wasn't nursing his leg wrap around me in response. It had *worked*.

He took a moment to recover and get his bearings, before asking, "We're still going after Maya's soul, right?"

I offered him my hand, helping him to his feet. "Yeah, but... it's so dark down here," I replied, straining to make anything out in the darkness. "I don't know how we're going to find it."

Leif rose from the rock, a murky blur in the darkness that made Matt leap aside.

"Who's there?" Matt demanded, reaching frantically for his sword. But he found himself patting an empty hilt—the sword had been left above. In fact, none of us had our weapons thanks to Melody and Sloane's siren spells.

"Don't worry, it's just Leif." I shushed Matt, glancing over my shoulder again. "But we should go—I'm the only one down here with magic, and neither of you is armed against Melody."

235

"*Melody's* here too?" Matt groaned, and I exchanged a grimace with him that he probably couldn't see. "Coral, I am so damn tired of fighting your evil siren stepmother!"

"That makes three of us," Leif grumbled. "Let's go this way."

Blindly, we followed his blurry figure in the darkness. As we walked, I reached up and used my healing magic to ease the pain in my shoulder, wincing from the difficult angle. But once the pain faded, I kept my hands outstretched, worried we'd run into something—even though Leif would be the first to hit anything anyway.

I didn't have a clue where we were going or what we might find... but we couldn't turn back now. Maya's soul was down here, and we *had* to find it. That, as well as the First Sea Witch.

"How big do you think this place is?" Matt asked after a while, and I shook my head as we walked.

"Maybe it's endless," I replied. Eternal, like the souls that resided here. Maybe we would be wandering forever trying to find what we were looking for. I had *no* idea how we were going to find a way out of here in the darkness—even if we did mark our tracks somehow.

Leif led us around a bend—warning us to put our hands against the rocky walls of the chasm so we could navigate— and we began down a spiraling slope, coming out at the edge of a cliff where, *finally*, there was light ahead.

Except it wasn't light. I gasped, and Matt's eyes went wide beside me.

There was an endless ocean ahead, filled with wispy glowing orbs that were flying in every direction. Each one flickered in a different luminescent color—red and green and orange and yellow...

"Are those the souls?" I whispered, coming to stand beside Leif, and he nodded grimly.

"There's got to be thousands of them," he replied in a low voice, watching the masses spiraling through the space. "*Hundreds* of thousands. We're never going to find Maya by just observing them."

There was just blackness below and blackness above. If I kicked off the cliff, I would have to swim through the souls to find Maya—checking each one individually. Leif and Matt wouldn't be able to follow with the current so strong.

Leif was looking at me like he could read my mind. Immediately, his hand gripped my wrist, stopping me.

"Don't," he insisted, his voice low and pleading. "We'll find another way."

"What if there isn't another way?" I asked, meeting his gaze. There was a pained look in his eyes as he observed me. Before I could ask what was wrong, a soul glided past leisurely, glowing light blue. Leif reached up to grasp it, but his hand went straight through it as if it were smoke. A low, musical chuckle sounded from behind us, and the three of us spun around.

Melody was leaning against the chasm wall, arms folded as she watched us.

"Poor Coral," she purred. "Coming all this way for a soul you'll *never* be able to find."

Leif and Matt were tense beside me, but I stepped forward.

"So, help me find it, and we can all get out of here," I suggested. "Unless you want to stay trapped down here forever?"

"Oh, don't worry about that. Sloane will find a way to get me out," Melody said lightly, examining her clawed hand. "You three, on the other hand..."

I swallowed hard. Lysander couldn't set foot in the Sea of Souls without turning to sea-foam. And Kendra... I prayed Lysander would never let her come after us. It was *far* too dangerous.

"Why can't I grasp the soul?" Leif asked, and Melody raised an eyebrow at him.

"I already told you," she mused, and I looked between Leif and Melody with a frown. She tutted and shook her head, stepping forward as she spoke. "For one, you're not a Reigning Queen," she said pointedly at Leif, before glancing at me with distaste. "And *even* a Reigning Queen has to offer a sacrifice to grasp a soul. Meaning that you'll never be able to take Maya's soul out of here without trading something valuable in return—such as a *life*."

Horror washed through me, and she smirked in cruel satisfaction. I hadn't realized... if we wanted to take a soul out of here, then someone else would need to stay behind. *A life for a life.*

I glanced to Leif and Matt, and I knew I would *never* subject them to that kind of fate.

But Melody... *she* had killed my father. *She* was the reason I'd grown up motherless. She was the root of *all* my pain and suffering. She could stay behind, and in that moment, I was sure that I wouldn't feel a shred of remorse.

I slowly glanced back at her, and she narrowed her gaze. Clearly, she hadn't planned to be down here with us, so in a way, Leif had given us a way out of this. But could I really do that to Melody? I may hate her... but I didn't know if I could have any more bloodshed on my conscience.

Melody smiled with amusement, like she knew the exact moral argument going through my mind. She *knew* I couldn't leave her behind—that I couldn't bring myself to murder her with my own two hands. Hopelessness flickered through me as I considered the only other option.

Me.

It was like everything kept leading back to this. It seemed fair that I would stay behind—that's how it should have been from the very start. Maya *never* should have drowned that day... and it had already been more than a year that she'd been trapped down here as the sea witch.

It should have been me. So, if I had to take her place to restore her soul, then so be it.

Another soul whizzed past—this one red. It ebbed with a sort of urgency as it flittered around our heads. I stared at it for a moment, wondering what it could mean, and my gaze fell back to Melody.

She had gone white as a sheet as she stared at it, and I frowned.

The soul floated closer, like it was *urging* me to grab it. But it didn't *feel* like it was Maya's soul. I tried to think of something I could give up to grab the soul in front of me.

"Coral?" Leif asked tentatively, staring at the soul. Melody took a step back from us.

That was *fear* on her face. Pure, undiluted terror. What in the *world* scared Melody so bad that she was on the verge of running from us?

Curious, I reached up and locked my fingers around the soul. It materialized in the same moment that I felt five years of my life flow through my fingers, traded away forever. The soul glowed red—so angry and pulsing and burning so hot that I couldn't keep my hold on it. With a cry, I threw it down to the ground, and it exploded in a mass of red shadow and smoke.

Melody was flat against the chasm wall, her lips pulled thin, her claws at the ready as a male with slicked back blond hair rose from the smoke and stepped forward. His cheekbones were skeleton like—gaunt and narrow—and his eyes glowered as he stared down Melody.

I *knew* him from somewhere. I'd seen his face, but I couldn't place where...

He strode toward Melody like he was a hunter, and she was his prey.

Melody took off running the way we'd come like a spooked mouse. But the male chuckled in a different kind of song. His voice was low and velvety and instantly alluring as it washed over us. Melody froze in her tracks and turned to face him, eyes wide with terror.

"I've been waiting for this moment for a very long time," he sang at her, sensual and dark. And *that's* when it finally clicked; on the wall in the Cora Palace throne room, there had been a row of heads. And one of them had been *this* male.

"Nikolai," Melody whispered, her voice filled with dread.

Leif's hand circled around my elbow, tugging quietly. He pointed to a slope behind us, silently urging us to go while they were distracted. I looked back at Melody, at her pleading eyes, and thought of all the things she'd done to my family. I thought I heard a faint screaming in my head—like someone was begging me to save her.

But if I left her here... I could get Maya's soul out. We could *all* get out. And technically, the bloodshed wasn't on my hands this time. Melody *deserved* this fate after everything she'd done. All I needed to do was turn around...

The male looked back at me once, like he knew—like he was fulfilling my wish. His ice-blue eyes were deadly cold, filled with malicious promise.

Go, he seemed to say.

And so, we did.

CHAPTER TWENTY-THREE

Lysander

The events of the day did not pass quickly nor productively.

With Coral, Matt, and Leif all gone, our rehearsal lasted all of thirty minutes before I dismissed everyone and stormed upstairs for my fitting. It was too hard to concentrate, not knowing what was happening, and I loathed how powerless I felt.

The fitting took two hours, where my servants fussed over my lapelled jacket and fitted pants, working expertly with their hands to avoid pricking me with the pins and needles. I'd settled on a dull tone that struck between blue and purple for the fine clothes, believing they would complement Coral's golden tail nicely. But the more I stared in the mirror, looking at myself, I couldn't help realizing how much nicer it would look with lilac... with *Kendra's* tail.

My gaze drifted across the room, to the decanter of liquor on my nightstand, and I yearned to dismiss everyone and drown out my thoughts. But we'd had enough interruptions, and it was critical that this coronation take place.

Finally, the servants finished, and I changed back into what I'd been wearing before. When I was done, I forced myself to walk away from the liquor, opting to head downstairs and eat something instead. But I only made it a third of the way down before I paused and found myself sitting on the steps, head in my hands. I let out a breath, feeling the stress in my shoulders, the constant nagging worry in my gut, and I hated it. *All* of it. Things had been so much simpler when I was a cursed prince. Now, I was a tormented king.

"Your Grace?" a voice sounded from the top of the steps, and I looked up to find Rue peering down at me with a furrowed brow. "Are you well?"

"I'm fine," I said quickly, getting to my feet. "Just... a little drained."

"Perhaps some time outside will help clear your head?" she suggested, coming to stand next to me. "I can bring you something to eat as well."

I was at a loss for what to do, so I agreed—if only to ease her worrying and escape the rest of the palace staff. She rushed off to prepare the food, and I stalked through the palace toward the courtyard, expecting it to be empty. But when I pushed the doors open, I spotted Kendra at the far end, surrounded in coral gardens and fish.

My heart softened at the sight of her, and instinctively, I headed for her. As I got closer, I heard talking, and I frowned. *Whom was she speaking to?* My eyes scanned the space for another being, but there was nobody but her... and the *fish*.

I cocked my head curiously, coming to a pause near the statue of my great-great-great-grandfather. She was nodding at the fish, and her eyes gleamed as she spoke in soft tones to them. They flittered around her, full of energy and delight in her presence. How unusual...

Only undine royals could speak to fish, so she *must* have just been speaking to them for her own amusement and not because she could understand them. But as I watched them, listening to the whispers of the fish and her responses, my breathing slowed.

243

"Sun coral?" she breathed to a blue dwarf fish, gently tracing the protruding tip of a staghorn coral. "In the tunnels?"

Yes, the fish whispered. *Atlantis had many beauties before its destruction.*

"I would have loved to see it," she murmured, her eyes dulling, and the fish seemed to drift closer in comfort. I shook my head, closing the rest of the distance.

"You can *hear* them?" I asked, mind reeling, and her gaze whipped to meet mine.

"Lysander!" she exclaimed, straightening up to face me. "Of course I can hear them... I thought that was normal!"

I stared at the seven dwarf fish as they rode the currents over to greet me. *Our King*, they trilled, sending a shiver down my spine. I was beyond confused... I'd *never* heard of this happening before. This was an exclusive ability reserved for our kind, and as far as I could tell, not even *Coral* had absorbed it when she bonded with me.

"They've been telling me about Atlantis... saying they traveled from there," Kendra added casually, like this was no big deal. She held out a hand, and the fish spiraled up her arm, grazing her soft skin and eliciting a giggle from her. The sound tugged at something inside of me.

"They seem fond of you," I noted, watching the fish as their chittering whispers echoed on the currents. This was some kind of trick—a *torment*. Another way that Kendra was everything Coral was not. The fact that we shared an *ability*...

It was like she was meant for me. Glaringly, obviously... and I couldn't have her. Not without causing more damage, creating more conflict between her sister and me. And especially not before we restored Maya's soul.

244

Kendra tilted her head as she watched me.

"Any news about the others?" she asked quietly, and I shook my head. With a grimace, she took my hand in hers. A show of comfort, nothing more, but...

Her gaze met mine again, and I wanted to kiss her. I *hated* myself for it, and at the same time, I wanted to throw caution to the wind and do it anyway.

"Are we going to cancel the coronation?" she asked me, and I shook my head.

"It can't be canceled," I replied grimly, and the weight of rulership clung to me like an anchor. "If we cancel it... our people will know something is wrong. We need them strong, not divided and feeding off of the rumors that have already begun to spread. They need to be able to believe in their queen... and *me*, for that matter. They know Eugene is threatening war, that he could be on our doorstep any day. This coronation... it's more than a ceremony. It's a show of strength and hope."

"But what if Coral doesn't make it back in time?" Kendra asked. The thought had crossed my mind more than once over the past few hours. And an idea had been in the back of my mind, but I didn't know how Kendra would react. In front of me now, she waited—eyes firm and demanding a response—and I knew I couldn't keep it from her much longer anyway.

"Well... you're both twins," I began, gesturing to her. "So I thought that perhaps you could *pose* as her. Just for the sake of the event, not because you'd be taking her place or anything like that. We could do a proper initiation ceremony when she gets back, behind closed doors."

Her eyes widened, and she drifted backward a fraction.

"Me?" she whispered. "Pretend to be my sister? In front of all those people?"

I nodded, and I wanted to tell her she didn't have to, that she had a choice... but we *didn't* have another choice.

"I'm sorry... I know it's unfair on you—"

"No, it's okay. I'll do it," she agreed, and I was taken aback. She tucked her hair behind her ear as she added, "It's to keep the kingdom united, right? I'm sure Coral would do the same... she would want this."

A slow smile grew on my lips.

"Well, that's settled then," I said, and then a thought occurred to me. "Speaking of which... you'll need to learn the dance Coral was supposed to learn today. For the ball afterward."

Her eyes softened, looking up at me through long lashes, and she offered me her other hand.

"Why don't you teach me then?" she suggested. "Here and now?"

I glanced around the courtyard. It was spacious enough and private—nobody except me tended to come out here. And apparently Kendra now, when she was talking to fish behind my back. I wondered what other secret talents she might be hiding from me.

"A little difficult to learn without music... but I'm sure we'll manage," I agreed, taking her hand and guiding her back into the courtyard. We had to adapt the dance to accommodate for Coral's tail, but I was pretty familiar with the core steps. I positioned her left hand onto my shoulder and kept her right hand in mine, bending our elbows upward.

"Follow my lead," I told her, and she kept her gaze locked on mine as I stepped back slowly. She kicked her tail ever so slightly, drifting with me. Above us, fish swam in swarms, rippling rainbows above our heads.

I found that I couldn't look away from her as I took her through the series of steps, moving slowly so she could memorize them. But from the way she was looking at me, I wasn't sure she was paying much attention to the steps. She was close enough to radiate body heat, and her intoxicatingly sweet scent wrapped around me—guava and honeysuckle. I yearned to lean in and press my lips against her to see if she tasted as sweet as she smelled.

"Are you paying attention?" I asked, my voice surprisingly low and husky.

"Hmm... To one thing, yes," she replied, her lips curving, and I knew it wasn't the dance steps from the way she spoke. We did a full lap of the courtyard, and I guided her through a spin. She turned just a little too fast, coming back to me hard and fast and crashing into my chest. I caught her, and she let out a breathless gasp. I wondered if she could feel how my heart pounded.

Her hands snaked up my torso, against the fabric of my shirt, and her lips hovered dangerously close to mine. I almost leaned in—*almost*—but...

I let her go, stepping away, and disappointment flashed in her eyes. My chest crumpled, but I heaved a breath. "I—I can't," I said finally, straining to hold her gaze. I could at least look her in the eye and tell her why. "Coral..."

"What about Coral?" she huffed, and I sensed the rejection in her voice. "I spoke to Coral—she knows how I feel. How we *both* feel. Why are you still holding back?"

"Because of the binding," I said, and fear rose in my chest. "Because... I'm afraid that if I break it, I'll turn heartless again. And the being I was before was not a decent one, Kendra... He would not treat you the way you deserve to be treated."

Her shoulders sagged.

"My sister gave her heart to break your curse." She remembered, as understanding washed over her finally. "So you're afraid to reject it. To let it go..."

I nodded and was surprised at how much better I felt admitting the words. It felt even better to be heard by Kendra and validated.

She drifted closer again, reaching for my hand. I didn't stop her as her fingers entwined with mine.

"What if I could love you heartless?" she whispered, and I pulled my hand away, shaking my head.

"*No.* Kendra, you didn't know me before. I killed Maya without a second thought... I was possessive and obsessive. I *hunted* your sister's heart to break my curse for my own selfish gain. I won't subject you to that."

"So, you're going to decide for me? Like Coral is always trying to do?" she stated, her tone turning sour. My own gaze hardened.

"I'm doing this to protect you—because I *know* I'll hurt you."

"Well, congratulations," she seethed back, flicking her tail angrily. "You've hurt me anyway." Without another word, she swam across the courtyard and disappeared inside, and I crossed a few steps to sit at the fountain statue.

This was for the best. Coral hadn't accepted me once I changed. If I changed back... I *knew* Kendra would reject me too. It was better to keep her at a distance, where she wouldn't be hurt. Because heartless or not, hurting people was the only thing I seemed to be good at doing.

The doors opened again, and I swallowed hard. I didn't think I had the emotional energy for another argument or the strength to continue resisting Kendra if she continued pushing for me. But to my relief, it was Nerissa who swam into view— with urgency in her eyes.

My gut turned over, and I stood as she spoke.

"We have a problem. Our scouts just reported that Eugene's army is marching on Veranis. We've only got a day— maybe two—to prepare for the attack."

CHAPTER TWENTY-FOUR

Coral

We'd stopped to rest against the wall of the chasm, after running for what seemed like hours but could only have been minutes.

My head was pressed against the wall as I stared up at the circling souls, miles and miles away.

We'd *left* Melody back there. And for some reason, despite everything she'd done, I felt like a monster for it.

"She's going to die," I said finally, my voice hoarse with regret. "That male—*Nikolai*—he'll kill her."

"Good riddance!" Matt exclaimed, pushing off the wall and nursing his stiff leg. My healing had stopped the bleeding and eased the pain, but it was a shoddy first attempt at healing magic, and clearly, he was still sore. "Let's just find Maya's soul and get the hell out of here!"

Leif was sitting on my other side, but he didn't meet my gaze.

"We had no choice, Coral," he said quietly. "It was you or her. And I know you were considering the alternative... I wasn't about to let you do that."

There was a lump in my throat and a deep pit of regret in my stomach. I couldn't do this. I couldn't keep going knowing that male would do more than give her a swift death. His eyes had promised torture.

"Nobody deserves to die that way," I protested, pushing off the ground, but Leif grabbed my arm.

"If you go back there, you'll just end up dead too," he insisted. "Maya needs *you*. You're the only one who can grab souls down here. And if you go back and save Melody, there'll be nothing to bargain with when we find Maya's soul."

He was right, of course. I knew I wouldn't be able to sit around any longer, so I gestured for Leif to get up.

"Fine. Let's continue on then," I huffed finally, and forced myself to keep swimming away from Melody and Nikolai and all the horrors that were undoubtedly happening in that moment.

We continued down the slope for some time before reaching a fork in the path. One sloped down, and the other continued on straight into a cave. For a moment, we just stared at the paths until Matt gestured to the one that sloped down and said, "I'll go this way, and you two go that way."

I shook my head. "No way—we're *not* splitting up!"

But Matt's stance was firm. "We need to find Maya's soul fast. The only other person who knows her as well as you do is me. It doesn't make sense to send Leif on his own because he won't *sense* her the way we will."

I wanted to argue, but Leif stepped in.

"He's right," he said, and ran a hand through his hair. "If we split up, we can search this place faster. Let's agree to meet back here in ten minutes."

I didn't like it, but with a sigh, I relented. Matt headed off down the slope, and Leif and I continued ahead through the frigid water. I hadn't been able to stop shivering for some time now. That split second of holding Nikolai's soul had reminded

251

me what it felt like to feel heat, and I would do *anything* for a shred of warmth again.

We reached the mouth of the cave, and Leif spoke.

"If I had a jacket, I'd offer it to you."

I glanced at him—at his armor—and grimaced.

"Thanks, but I wouldn't take it—you'd need it as much as I do," I replied, noticing the subtle tremble in his own hands. This place wasn't meant for people like us. I wondered how long we'd survive down here before we froze to death.

"Don't worry about me," he replied gently. "I've braved icy temperatures before. But you're from a land of sunshine and warmth. Are you sure you're okay?"

I stopped a few paces into the cave and held his stare for a moment. He always noticed these things about me.

"I'm okay," I promised slowly, frowning as I considered his concern. "Leif... why did you come after me?"

He hesitated, averting his gaze.

"Because Lysander couldn't," he replied finally, and I shook my head.

"He could have sent anyone. Why *you*?"

He finally met my gaze and took a step closer to me. My heartbeat sped up. I remembered the way he'd held my face before... the delicacy in his touch.

"Because I wanted to make sure Melody didn't harm you," he said finally, his voice low, his gaze possessive, and my skin flushed—warmth seeping through the mind-numbing cold. I could barely breathe from the proximity as I inhaled his citrus and seaweed scent. I'd thought about it once or twice—what his lips might feel like on mine—but...

"I see," I said finally, thinking about Lysander, about the words left unsaid with him, about our duties as corulers of Veranis. I didn't need any more complications when it was already the biggest hot mess. And besides, if I found the First Sea Witch down here... I would choose to go back to land. I would leave everything and everyone behind without question.

I just wasn't made to be trapped down here. If I stayed, my soul would slowly wither and die.

If Leif knew how I was feeling, he didn't mention it and didn't try to stop me as I swam ahead into the cave.

It didn't take long for us to stumble upon a mirror embedded into the rocky wall of the cave. The border was made of an intricate golden carving, broken away in some places from years of age. My familiar blonde locks and brown eyes greeted me as I stared into it, and Leif came up behind me, his coppery-red hair flowing gently in the current.

"What is this?" I asked, approaching it slowly. Why would a mirror be down here? Had somebody once lived in this cave?

As I got closer, the mirror shimmered, and I froze in my tracks. A voice echoed in my mind suddenly.

"I am a looking glass. What do you seek to find?"

I stumbled backward, and Leif reached out to steady me.

"What is it?" he asked urgently, and I blinked at the mirror.

"You can show me anything?" I asked, earning a frown from Leif, but the mirror shimmered again, as if in confirmation.

I stepped forward once more.

"Show me where to find Maya's soul."

253

The mirror changed, showing us a vision of a soul drifting among the others—in a vibrant shade of emerald green. It glowed brighter than the others, and I *knew* just by looking at it: it was Maya, without question. I could swim to her, grab her...

But in the background, I saw the cliffside. I saw Nikolai and Melody at each other's throats, claws swiping. And my stomach dropped.

Melody was covered in blood and limping. Nikolai stalked her, like a predator, as she continued to dodge. She seemed winded, like she couldn't hold out much longer.

Once again, that guilt slammed into me full force. She was still alive... there was still a chance to save her...

I whirled around, fully intending to race back to Melody, but then I noticed what had been behind us, against the far wall, this entire time.

The crowns.

The ones from my dream, when my mother had told me to meet her here.

They glimmered with promise, and I stared at them in confusion. What were they *doing* here? What were they for?

"You came," a voice echoed, startling both Leif and me out of our skin, and we whirled around once more to see my mother standing behind us.

She was as real as I'd ever seen her. Clearly still a spirit, with her translucent skin, but for once, she wasn't at a distance or appearing to me in a dream. She was *here*, mere feet from me, close enough that I could reach out and touch her—

"Coral," she breathed, tears shining in her eyes, and I burst into tears of my own as I raced forward. I couldn't feel her when I wrapped my arms around her, but I knew she was hugging me regardless.

My mother pulled back and held me by the shoulders, her expression firm.

"Listen to me very carefully," she said. "You don't have much time, but you *must* go back and save Melody from Nikolai."

"*Hell* no!" Leif stated from behind me, but I was relieved to hear the words from my own mother.

"You can *all* get out of here alive—including Maya—but first, you must break a curse, and to do so, Melody must live."

"What curse?" I asked, frowning as my mother's expression turned grim.

"My curse," she whispered, tears flowing down her cheeks now. "The one I caused. It's the reason Melody is heartless—she wasn't always like that. And it's why all Undersea beings except merpeople aren't capable of true, unconditional love and kindness. It's all my fault."

"What are you talking about?" I shook my head as I stepped back, and my mother wrapped her arms around her torso, letting out a heaving breath.

"Melody and I weren't just friends," she said finally, and she couldn't meet my gaze. "I had feelings for her... and I think she had them for me too. But she was under pressure from her mother to marry Nikolai Galanis so that their clan could increase their power and status. We never... we didn't admit how we felt about each other, and in the end, it was too late."

I blinked stupidly at her. This couldn't be true... what about my dad? Had she ever really loved him?

255

My mother's eyes widened at the look on my face.

"Coral, I really did love your father," she insisted. "But it was *after* everything that happened with Melody. I went to land because Melody threatened him, and what started out as concern for him blossomed into love. But Melody was my first love... and your first love is different than all the rest."

I was reeling.

My mother *loved* Melody.

The same female who tormented our family, tried to marry my father, and *killed* him.

"Please, Coral, you have to understand," my mother pleaded, her eyes full of sorrow. "It's the *curse*. Melody had a heart once! She tried to stop me from going to land, and the last sea witch cursed her for it, turning her heart to stone. *Her heart is literally stone*, and until you break that curse, she will remain bitter and cruel. She's capable of remorse, of love... if you give her a chance to show you."

"I don't understand what you're asking me to do," I said hollowly, taking another step back. My mother's eyes were full of pain.

"There is another way for you to make a large sacrifice and restore Maya's soul *without* trading a life—you can give up your title of Reigning Queen."

My heart skipped a beat. I'd never considered that to be an option.

"But it will only work if you master all four crowns," she added, and my gut plummeted. I glanced at the Coronis crown, and the memory of the soul-sucking pain washed over me. *No... I couldn't do that...*

"How is she supposed to master the Coronis crown without a tie to Coronis?" Leif asked, stepping forward.

"Isn't it obvious?" my mother asked, her voice filled with sadness. "You need Melody—you need her to accept you as her daughter *for real*, and vice versa."

I let out a laugh—I'd never heard such a stupid, *ridiculous* statement in my entire life.

"You want *Melody* to essentially adopt me as her step-daughter?" I shot back. "After *everything* she's done? You think I could just forgive her that easily?"

"I'm not making excuses for what she's done," my mother said firmly. "But it was not all *her*—the curse has influenced her choices. If you break the curse... everything will be different. And you can solidify that final bond that will give you the power to get out of here safely—*all of you*."

I shook my head, refusing to meet her gaze.

"I *can't*," I said, a dry laugh building in my throat. This was *nuts*. Melody was the reason my father was dead. There was *no way* I could accept her into my life...

"You found a way to forgive Lysander for what he did to Maya," my mother insisted desperately. I looked back at her, and she was growing more transparent with each passing minute.

"Yeah, because he was *heartless*, and his father influenced him not to tell me the truth—"

"How is this any different?" she asked pointedly. "Melody is heartless too."

I hesitated, blinking back tears that threatened to spill. This was too much...

"Coral... please..." my mother whispered, as she began to fade. "This is our last conversation we'll have—I'm using the last of my heart magic to ask this of you. After this... I'll *truly* be nothing but sea-foam."

My lips trembled, and I shook my head in protest. This wasn't *fair*. My mother was using her last moments with me to plead for Melody's life. I would never see her again...

"I *beg* you—save Melody. Save *yourself*. Do it for me... because I can't save either one of you."

Her last words echoed around the cave as she faded, and sea-foam bubbled in place of where she'd been, drifting calmly away. A sob heaved in my throat, and then Leif's arms were around me again as I stumbled backward.

Melody was fighting for her life *right this second*. And if we didn't go, she wouldn't make it. It had been my mother's final wish for me to save her. To give her that second chance. To break her curse—and with it, break the curse affecting *everyone* in the Undersea.

But I still felt so *angry* toward Melody. I didn't know how I was going to do this.

"So, I will admit... this is not my favorite plan," Leif said finally. "But if you're going to go back for Melody... I'll help you. There's not much time left to decide though."

I pushed up off the ground, wiping the tears from my eyes and inhaling deeply to steady myself.

I could do it for my mother. *Not* for Melody... but for whomever my mother had known before the curse. For the female my mother had fallen in love with. I knew enough about that sort of thing from my relationship with Lysander, which now lay in ruins.

I managed to turn and face Leif.

"Help me grab the crowns," I said finally. "We have a curse to break."

CHAPTER TWENTY-FIVE

Melody

"Get up," Nikolai growled over his endless siren song, and I trembled as I tried to push myself up off the ground. My body ached and throbbed in protest, there was a deep gash in my arm screaming with pain, and a near-fatal slice up my left side that made it difficult to breathe.

I'd made it to my knees when Nikolai's fist collided with my face again, and I tumbled backward.

It was over.

I'd known from the moment I saw him I wasn't leaving here alive. The wretched mermaid and her entourage had abandoned me and left me to face the wrath of the siren who once threatened to make my life miserable. He'd never gotten the chance, but he was making up for it now. I flinched as another blow came down on my face, and pain shuddered through me.

My mother wanted me to marry this male. To submit to him. All so that she could bask in the power and glory of our clan's status. And I'd been dumb enough to think that I could be rid of him forever.

"My death was sheer luck on your part," Nikolai hissed, squatting down to meet my blurred, bloody gaze. He was right—it had been his own foolish fault that he'd summoned sea snakes and been bitten. I'd merely taken the credit for his death by not intervening. "You think you're more powerful than me? You only know how to manipulate a situation, not do the dirty work required to win. You're *weak*, Melody."

"*Hey!*"

A thunderous voice echoed across the cliffside, drawing Nikolai's gaze away.

"Get the *fuck* away from her."

My body protested as I strained my neck to see a familiar pair of heavy boots striding toward us. I caught a glimpse of the long brown hair before my vision split in two, my body begging to give out. *No more*, it whispered, defeat settling in my stomach.

Nikolai sneered at the newcomer.

"Well, well," he mused. "Don't you look so much like Lorraine? I guess Melody still has a type."

"And I guess you're still a piece of shit," Sloane growled, angling a dagger toward Nikolai.

"Don't," I croaked at Sloane. She shouldn't be here. Why would she waste her energy trying to save me? Nikolai was going to make chum of us both.

Nikolai's lip curled as he considered us both, then he said to me, "Oh, I'm going to enjoy making you suffer as you watch her die."

My heart beat frantically, and I dug my nails against the bedrock, trying to muster the strength to stand. Nikolai lunged at Sloane, who dodged and nicked his shoulder with her blade. But he was fast... and his siren song was dizzying. It was already preventing me from singing back at him or summoning any ocean predators for help. Like a persistent lull in my ears, it was driving me to the brink of insanity.

"Nikolai!" I rasped, but neither of them could hear me. Or they were choosing to ignore me. I knew I shouldn't beg—it only revealed my weaknesses—but I was powerless to do anything else. At this point, I just wanted Sloane to live, even if I perished down here.

Nikolai's foot collided with Sloane's chest and sent her hurling to the edge of the cliffside, her dagger skidding across the ground. As she scrambled to her feet, Nikolai casually picked up the dagger. She lunged, but he knocked her back and grabbed her by the throat, lifting her into the air. She gasped for breath, kicking helplessly as Nikolai angled the dagger against her chest—where her heart would be.

Something cracked in my own heart. A sliver of pain emerged—screaming and pleading for this not to happen.

Out of nowhere, someone came hurtling through the mass of souls drifting out in the ocean and knocked Sloane and Nikolai back from the edge of the cliffside. A tumble of gold scales and golden hair rolled aside, and then Coral was there. My eyes widened with shock as she snatched up Sloane's dagger and threw it hard over the edge of the cliff.

Nikolai snarled as he leaped to his feet, glaring at Coral. A sudden hand appeared on my shoulder, and I jolted, but when I looked up it was her entourage—the commander and her human friend—both trying to help me to my feet. I wanted to snap at them, to tell them I didn't need their help... but I didn't have the strength to shake them off.

"I'm reversing the trade," Coral said to Nikolai. "Give me my years back and return to the other souls."

Nikolai sneered.

"It doesn't work like that," he sang slowly, circling the little mermaid. "You traded those years away—and now, I get to have my revenge. So why don't you get what you came here for and leave us?"

"Oh, we did," Coral grinned, and that's when I noticed Matt was holding a clamshell that had a faint green glow to it. *There was a soul inside—Maya's soul.* So, they'd found it after all.

"Well, run along home then," he insisted. "Before I decide to play rough with you and your friends too."

"Not until you leave Melody *alone*," Coral ordered, and she straightened her stance. "I am your *Reigning Queen* and I order it."

"And I am already *dead*," Nikolai growled. "So I don't answer to you."

He grabbed Coral and threw her aside, which caused Leif to tense beside me. But before he could turn away, she reached out and grabbed Nikolai's ankle.

"I didn't want to do this, but..." she grunted, and Nikolai began to glow red. His eyes widened with surprise as the red spread into her fingertips, and Nikolai turned smokey.

"*No!*" he screamed, his eyes flying to me. To the unfinished job. But it was too late—he returned to smoke and shadow and was reduced to nothing more than an angry, pulsing orb that could no longer touch any of us. Wincing, Coral pushed upward and kicked her tail to swim over to us.

"What did you do?" Leif asked her, and she grimaced.

"Traded another five years to reverse my actions," she replied, looking less than thrilled about it. "So, I guess I'll just

263

miss out on ten years of being an epic grandmother to my grandkids."

Assuming nothing killed her sooner, that is.

"Why did you do that?" Sloane asked, limping across the cliffside to join us. I was curious too, and *conflicted*. She'd left me here to die—I'd *seen* her hesitate and make that choice—but then she'd come back to save me. *Why*?

Coral's eyes flickered to me, and they were cold.

"Because I know the truth," she said finally. "I know what you did to try and stop my mother from going to land. What you... felt for her."

Anger bubbled inside of me.

"I felt *nothing* for your mother!" I snarled, and again, that strange tangle of fear and dread emerged from the abyss. Except this time, it was stronger—fighting to escape the crack in my stone heart. The memories I'd fought so hard to bury resurfaced, and I blinked back tears. It had all been a lie. An *illusion*. She wouldn't have left me if she'd felt the same. I'd been a *fool* to go after her that day.

It was the truth... wasn't it?

Coral offered me her hand, and I frowned at it.

"Let me heal you," she said, and I recoiled back into Leif and Matt's steady hands.

"I don't need your help," I hissed, but my wounds screamed in protest. And I was in no position to fight back, to run. Even Sloane gave me a pointed look that made my stomach turn over—I must have been in bad shape for even *her* to insist that I accept Coral's help.

With a sigh, I reached out and gripped Coral's hand. Almost instantly, I felt the healing magic flow through her fingers, warming my aching, numb muscles as it traveled through me.

Slowly, it worked to heal my wounds, ease the pain, and I felt it reach every inch of my body before it turned inward.

And then it touched my heart, and something snapped—a binding of some kind that I hadn't even known was there. I frowned, clutching at my chest as I felt every inch of my heart crack open, until—

A swirl of color and memory rose up, blinding my vision. Emotions burst and bloomed, and a flurry of grief and fear tumbled through me as it all came back. A current rippled out from my heart, racing to caress every inch of water in the Undersea and strip the curse from every being residing in it.

It was a lie, I realized, recalling everything that had happened.

I'd gone after Lorraine that day... but I'd been moments too late. I tried to stop her from drinking the tonic that would trade her tail for legs, and the sea witch had unleashed her wrath on me. I didn't remember anything after that except waking up in a shadow of darkness and despair, convinced that Lorraine had *never* loved me. That she had betrayed me and left me for that wretched human.

My heart had been struck with a curse, turned to stone... I hadn't been able to feel love. To feel *remorse*. I'd been blinded by hatred and anger all these years. Unable to see the truth.

I'd ruined so much... *taken* so much for Lorraine...

I was lost in the feeling, heaving heavy breaths, and I didn't realize tears were streaming down my cheeks until gentle hands touched them, wiping them away. It was only then that I realized everyone was gone... and Lorraine stood in front of me, entirely ethereal.

She was barely visible, like a fleck of a memory on the current. But she wrapped her arms around me and buried her face in my hair as she whispered, "I loved you, Melody. And a part of me never stopped loving you."

I cracked, and I couldn't stop the flow of tears.

"I'm so sorry." I sobbed into her shoulder, though she was barely there to grasp. "For everything... I never wanted to hurt you—"

"I know," she said gently, and leaned back to trace my cheek with her hand. "And now you can make it up to me by taking care of my girls."

I swallowed hard. I'd hardly earned the right—I was the reason they'd lost their parents. How would they *ever* allow me to take care of them?

"Tell me you'll take care of them," Lorraine insisted faintly—desperately—and I knew I had mere moments left with her. I nodded, too caught up in the moment to overthink it.

"I will. I promise," I replied, my voice a whisper on the current. Relief crossed her face, and then she was gone—and Coral was back again, in her place. She seemed uncertain and closed off as she watched me, like she was expecting me to lash out at her.

The full weight of what I'd done sank in. No apology would ever come close to erasing the harm I'd caused. I didn't even know where to begin mending things with her.

"How do you feel?" she asked finally, and I took a moment to fully feel into it.

"Like myself again," I replied, my voice small and unrecognizable, and Coral nodded.

"Then perhaps we could agree to start over—and you could show me who you really are," she said, relaxing her shoulders. "Though it's going to take some time... and I don't make any promises... I'm prepared to give you this second chance."

I understood everything her words conveyed.

She didn't offer me so much as a smile as she swam past me, and that's when I spotted four crowns waiting on the ground behind us. They must have been dumped in the conflict.

"What are you doing *now*?" Sloane asked, looking stressed from the recent events. Coral picked up the first two crowns and pressed them together so that they glowed and merged. She did that with all four crowns until she held a single crown in her hands, made up of bornite and gold and silver and copper.

I noticed how her hands trembled, and I remembered what Eugene had put her through. It dawned on me what her *true* intent had been in reversing my curse.

She hadn't done it for me.

I expected to feel angrier... but Lorraine's words echoed in my head.

Take care of my girls.

It wasn't going to be easy or happen overnight... but this was the first step. So I got to my feet and approached Coral, who stared down at the crown in terror.

"I don't have the words to make this right," I admitted, offering her my hand. "But from this moment forward... I vow to do *everything* in my power to make it up to you and your sister. If we can both agree to work together on behalf of your mother... perhaps we can make this work."

She swallowed hard, then reached out and took my hand. The crown glimmered with promise as she lifted it to her head, and she flinched the moment it touched her, as if expecting a bout of pain to strike her.

But instead, the crown glowed, and her eyes widened.

"It's working," she breathed, examining her hands as magic coursed through her, dancing on her fingertips. She looked to Matt and Leif, who both beamed at her, then to me. Her words echoed with power as she spoke.

"*I hereby give up my title as Reigning Queen to grant us all passage out of here.*"

The binding rippled through the Undersea, felt by *all* beings as the rare queen that had risen was stripped of power. The magic coursing through her faded until she was nothing more than a regular mermaid with regular abilities again, and the crown on her head disintegrated into glittering dust.

"So, we can get out of here now?" Matt asked, and Coral nodded, a resolve settling in her eyes.

"*You* four can get out of here. There's something else I need to do first."

Ah. She was still going to go after the First Sea Witch then.

268

"What do you mean?" Matt asked, stepping toward her. "We're not leaving you down here alone."

But Coral shook her head.

"You need to get Maya's soul out of here safely," Coral advised, nodding to the glowing clam he cradled in his hands. "Go and get her from Veranis and take her to land so that you can restore her soul without risk of her drowning when she wakes up."

Understanding passed through Matt's eyes.

"You're going to meet us there, aren't you?" he said, which made Leif frown in confusion, and Coral nodded.

"I'm going after the First Sea Witch... and I'll meet you on land when I'm done," she confirmed. Now Leif was wide eyed, shaking his head in confusion.

"I don't understand—" he cut in, but Coral threw him a firm look.

"Go with Matt," she ordered. There was something unsaid in her eyes... something filled with sadness.

"Daughter... are you sure about this?" I asked softly, and Coral cringed at the name I'd used to tease her for so many months. I found myself instantly regretting my words, but Coral offered me a grimace.

"I didn't come all this way for me to give up now," she replied, and despite her cringing, her tone had no hint of malice to it. "Go and free the mermaids like you said you would. We can talk again when you've upheld that end of our bargain."

I nodded in agreement, and slowly, we turned away from her. She watched us as Sloane led us back toward the pitch-black chasm path, away from the light of the swirling souls.

Matt cracked open the clam hosting Maya's soul just a fraction to light our path as we hurried along, and shadows snaked in on us as we rounded the chasm bend. I looked back once and saw Coral heading back down the slope, deeper into the Sea of Souls.

"How are we going to get out of here?" I asked Sloane, thinking of the massive chasm we have to swim back up and how difficult it would be without a mermaid to combat the current, but she grinned at me.

"There's a staircase leading down into the chasm—just below the veil."

"There was a *staircase*?" Matt cried. "And you made me jump?"

"Well, you weren't supposed to live!" she snapped back, and the two began bickering, Matt eyeing the both of us warily the entire time we walked. I kept my gaze ahead, and after a while, realized that Leif had been strangely silent. I glanced in his direction and paused.

He was gone—and I could only assume he'd gone back for Coral.

CHAPTER TWENTY-SIX

Leif

I found Coral back in the cave, consulting the magic mirror for the location of the First Sea Witch. When the mirror ceased flickering and returned to its reflective state, she saw me behind her and let out a short squeal and whirling around.

"You scared the *crap* out of me!" she scolded, her hand flying to her chest as she recovered. "What are you doing here? I told you to go back."

"Why didn't you tell me that you're trying to go back to land?" I threw back, simmering. I was still trying to wrap my head around it. Sure, she and Lysander were having issues right now, and maybe she hadn't *chosen* her fate in ruling Veranis... but giving up *everything* to go back to land?

What about Lysander's heartless curse?

Would I even see her again?

Her expression fell, and she wrapped her arms around her torso.

"I'm sorry," she replied, her gaze falling to the floor. "I just... Melody said there was a way—if I can find the First Sea Witch. That she can grant me a single binding and restore my old life."

"So, you're not happy down here?" I asked, my voice like gravel. Her eyes met mine, wild and pleading.

"It's not that! But I never *wanted* to be trapped down here—why do you think I trekked across the Undersea searching for another way?"

She slumped against the wall of the cave, looking defeated.

"I *hate* having a tail—it's so foreign and unfamiliar. I *hate* feeling scales when I expect to feel skin. I miss my old life on land—the food, the smoothies, the surfing, the *sunshine*. And it was only when it was all taken away from me that I realized how much I took for granted above."

I looked away and grimaced.

"I see."

I'd been a fool to come after her. Such a damn *fool* chasing after this mermaid when she intended to leave the entire time. I should have known she wouldn't be dumb enough to come out here with Melody unless there was deeper reason to. And clearly, she could look after herself.

"What is it?"

I shook my head, turning away from her. "It's nothing."

Fine then. Let her seek out this First Sea Witch. Soon, she'd have everything she wanted—her best friend back, her life on land. I would return to Lysander and we'd both lick our wounds of rejection over her.

"Leif!"

She grabbed my wrist and tugged, and I restrained myself from looking back at her. Because I knew if I did, my heart might break into a million pieces, and I didn't think I could bear it.

"Leif, please look at me."

I closed my eyes, swallowing once. I willed myself the strength and slowly turned around. One look, and I didn't know how I'd ever look away again. How I'd ever let her go. *Damn it*, when had I started feeling so deeply for her? How had I become so consumed and enthralled by her?

She squeezed my hand, eyes blazing determinedly.

"Just because I don't want to be tethered to the Undersea doesn't mean I don't want *you*."

I slackened, the words hitting hard as the confession floated between us.

"You want me?" I repeated, the words barely manageable as my throat constricted. I had to stay strong to resist this stubborn, *devastatingly* beautiful mermaid. Because it would never work. *It would never work...*

She closed her eyes like she was fighting back tears.

"I couldn't tell you because I knew I'd be leaving you," she breathed finally, meeting my gaze again. "And I didn't know if I would ever see you again. I couldn't ask you to come with me... but I'm just not prepared to let this opportunity go."

My heart softened, walls crumbling, and I yearned to wrap my arms around her. I wanted to kiss her, *touch* her... but we couldn't start something we already knew was never going to happen.

"I understand," I said, my voice rough as I swallowed the lump in my throat. "You're right—I'm still Lysander's commander. I'm not prepared to give up everything I've worked for... as much as I want you too."

She nodded, biting her lip to keep her composure as tears threatened to spill, and something in my heart cracked at the sight of it. Of *her*, so vulnerable, and all because of me.

Because she wanted me.

Like some cruel twist of fate, I'd gotten my wish as fast as I'd lost it.

"I should get going," she said, ducking her head as she went to swim past me. To leave me, *forever*. And I wanted to let her go... I wanted to...

But I couldn't.

I grabbed her arm and pulled her toward me. My lips crashed against hers and a noise escaped her throat before she responded in kind. I clung to her, pulling her as close as physically possible, my fingers snaking into her hair, deepening the kiss. Her hands circled my neck, her tail fin grazing my ankle, and I scooped her up into my arms, breaking the kiss and pressing my forehead against hers. She nuzzled against me, like she'd been craving the proximity, fingers grazing the sensitive nape of my neck as she gazed into my eyes. All the words that threatened to spill teetered on my lips: *Don't go. Don't leave me...*

But I wouldn't do that to her. I would let her go because I was not Lysander. I wouldn't keep her tethered to the Undersea against her wishes for even a single second if she desired otherwise. Even if it meant Lysander might turn heartless again.

Carefully, I put her back down, her tail flicking to regain balance as it touched the ground. She was blushing furiously, a touch breathless as she regarded me. But that sorrow remained in her eyes.

"I'm coming with you," I blurted without thinking, and her eyes widened with surprise. "To the First Sea Witch," I added quickly, before things got misconstrued. "I'll... I'll be with you until the very last moment."

She bit her bottom lip again and nodded once in agreement. Together, we navigated out of the cave with her leading the way.

We went deeper into the Sea of Souls than ever before, reaching the bottom of the slope and venturing out in the darkness. The vibrant rainbow souls were drifting so far above our heads now that they were near specks. As we walked, the memory of kissing Coral still danced on my lips, threatening to distract me the entire time. But as much as I wanted to savor the moment... I also wanted to be present in these last moments I had with her.

Finally, Coral stopped before a boulder—rugged and mossy—and it didn't stand out compared to the other boulders around it. But Coral tapped on it three times, and it grumbled, sliding aside to reveal a glowing white orb hiding in a hole beneath the boulder.

"*So, you found me,*" a dull voice echoed. This soul wasn't like the rest, and it materialized on its own. A transparent curvy female stood before us, with curling hair that seemed to float all around her. "Kudos to you, *Coral the Cursebreaker*."

Coral took a polite step back to give her some space.

"I've come with a request," she began, and the female inclined her head.

"I am well aware of your request," she replied, her voice echoing through the endless space around us. "You wish to walk on land again. But I must ask if you are sure... as I wonder if your priorities are in order."

Coral frowned. "What do you mean?"

The female chuckled.

"You have not thought this through very well, have you?" she droned. "How do you hope to get back to the surface once you have traded your tail for legs? Without a pearl bracelet to keep you alive?"

Coral paled, and I patted my pockets for a spare, but I had none on me. The female gave us a small smile.

"I do not believe you are ready to make your request. Come back when you've thought it over," she purred, and she began to dematerialize. But Coral stepped forward and grabbed the soul through the middle with her hand, keeping her essence solid.

"Hold on," she pressed. "Is there another way? A way I might bypass needing a bracelet?" I tried not to take offense to Coral's eagerness to get this over with and abandon me *right* after we had just kissed—after all, if we had to come back all this way through the Sea of Souls, it would be equally frustrating.

The female paused, studying Coral as she narrowed her gaze.

"Well, it's all a matter of perspective," she hinted finally. "I can grant other requests, you know. And you are quite the unique individual, my dear—with the soul of a human and the heart of a mermaid, all in the same body. It does make one wonder what else you could add or take... or perhaps *change*."

Coral's gaze flicked to me, frowning as she considered the First Sea Witch's words. She stared at me for a moment, her gaze flicking up and down my body before widening like she'd realized something.

"Leif, why is it that sirens and undines can cross between the land and sea, but not mermaids?" she asked. I shrugged—I'd never really considered it.

"Our bodies, I guess," I replied slowly. "It's a lot harder for a mermaid to venture on land without legs."

Her eyes shone with excitement, and my heartbeat slowed as I watched her.

"Heart of a mermaid... soul of a human... *body of an un-dine*," she breathed, and looked back at the First Sea Witch. "I don't want to trade my tail for human legs—I want to trade it for the body of an undine!"

I held my breath as hope skittered through my body. *Why hadn't we thought of this before?* Why did we just *assume* that the way Lorraine Quarte went to land was the only way to do so? If this worked... and without trade-offs... Coral would be able to cross between sea and land at will! Because her body would be adapted for *both*.

"Will this keep me from turning to sea-foam?" Coral pressed, and the First Sea Witch smirked at her.

"It will keep you from turning to sea-foam *and* drowning down here without a pearl bracelet. But I must warn you—the transformation is immediate. Once started, I cannot stop it. And it will be painful enough that you black out for some time, I imagine."

Coral's eyes remained determined, unwavering. I couldn't believe we'd found this loophole... It changed *everything*.

"There is one more thing I'd like to bestow upon you before you go," The First Sea Witch said, reaching to the

277

ground. She waved her hand over the plain stones beneath our feet, and two of them glimmered opalescent as if enchanted. She indicated toward them, and Coral bent to collect them.

"I have decided to be generous and grant you *two* bindings," she said, and Coral faltered as she straightened up.

"Why?" Coral asked, a hint of wariness to her voice.

"Well, my dear... you are the first Cursebreaker to come along in quite some time," she replied. "And you have done us a service by breaking two long-lasting curses already. So as a token of my gratitude, I will grant you an extra binding of your choosing."

Coral raised an eyebrow at me.

"Um, thank you... but I don't even know what I'd use it for," she replied, staring down at the stones she'd plucked from the ground.

"You will know," the First Sea Witch promised vaguely, sending a chill down my spine. "And when you are ready, all you need to do is hold the stone in your hand and speak your request out loud. But use it wisely, my dear... I see dangers in your future."

A troubled look crossed Coral's face, and she turned to me.

"Can you hold onto it for now?" she requested, handing me one of the stones. "I don't have any pockets, so..."

I took the stone and stored it safely in my own pants pocket. It felt smooth to the touch in my hands. Coral clutched the other stone in her palm, turning back to the First Sea Witch.

"Now, my dear... are you ready?" she asked, and Coral nodded.

"*I wish to trade my tail for the body of an undine,*" she spoke, the words resounding around us and tangling with the First Sea Witch's lingering echo. She immediately tumbled forward as her tail began to twitch. I lunged and caught her, and pain flickered across her face as her tail began to rip in two.

"I've got you," I promised. She gritted her teeth against the pain, clutching my arms so tightly, it pierced the numbing cold I'd grown so accustomed to down here. I knelt, cradling her in my lap and stroking her hair gently, trying to ease her discomfort. A scream tore up her throat, but I continued to hold her, whispering that it would be okay, telling her to let go, and pressing a kiss against her forehead. Her eyes glazed over from the pain, fluttering closed as she slumped in my arms. I waited for her tail to cease shedding, blood and scales drifting off into the currents, as her legs melded into shape once more.

I only let her go for a moment to unbuckle my armor and sheath and to strip off my shirt. It was barely big enough to cover her backside, but it was better than nothing. Then I clasped the armor back into place, carefully positioned my arm under her tender knees to lift her into my arms, and walked her out of the Sea of Souls.

CHAPTER TWENTY-SEVEN

Lysander

I sat in my study, a glass of liquor in my hand, staring blankly down at the reports my men had handed me. The hour was late, but I couldn't sleep—not while knowing that Eugene's army was marching on us this very moment. That they would be here in a matter of hours.

So much for the coronation.

I didn't know what to expect from a full out attack. I'd grown up studying about how to handle such matters, but my mind had been elsewhere in those days. Now, I wished I'd paid more attention to my tutors. My men were ready, fortifying the kingdom, and the people had been warned to prepare, but it wasn't enough.

I slipped the stopper off my drink and took a swig. A knock sounded, causing me to place the glass down without replacing the stopper, and the liquor drifted, mingling with ocean water. I glanced toward the door as Rue entered.

"Your Grace," she spoke, with a quick curtsy. "Matt has returned."

I stood abruptly.

"*Just* Matt?" I asked, and she nodded in confirmation. Running a hand through my already-unruly hair, I let out a breath and waved for her to lead the way. I followed her downstairs and into the foyer, where people were rushing in and out, making preparations for the battle. Matt had his eyes trained on the men, lips pulled in a thin line. When he spotted me walking toward him, his eyes seemed to harden even more.

"Matt," I greeted politely, coming to a pause in front of him. "It's good to see you."

He raised an eyebrow at me.

"Wish I could say the same," he drawled, folding his arms, and I fought the urge to scowl back.

"So, where are the others? What happened?" I prompted, and Matt shrugged.

"Melody went back to Coronis. Coral and Leif are still in the Sea of Souls."

I raised an eyebrow.

"Why are they still there?" I pressed, glancing up and down for signs of clues, injury... *anything* to point to why he'd returned alone.

Matt's lips curved into a smug smile, like he enjoyed seeing me so distressed.

"Coral's not coming back, Lysander," he spoke slowly, his tone laced with satisfaction. "She's trading her tail for legs as we speak."

I felt like ice water had washed over me. *What?*

"What do you mean?" I growled, trying to keep my anger in check. Matt was smirking now, shaking his head.

"It means she's *done* with you. With this entire place. *We all are.*"

He pulled out a clam from his pants pocket and held it up—it had a faint green glow emanating from inside. My eyes grew wide.

"I'm taking Maya, and we're getting the *fuck* out of here. So good luck to you, Lysander, with whatever mess you've gotten yourself into now," he grated, nodding to the rushing men around us and turning for the doors.

"Wait!" I demanded sharply, my heart racing with panic. Shit... *Shit...* we needed Maya! The *only* thing that had stopped Eugene and his men last time had been Maya. She couldn't leave now when we were on the verge of an all-out *attack*!

"No," Matt spat back, turning but holding the clam out of reach. "You don't get to keep prisoners anymore. We're leaving."

"Matt, please," I begged, following him out the front door and down the steps. "Eugene's men are coming... they'll destroy everything without Maya's help defending the front lines!"

Matt snorted as he walked. "Good. It's what you deserve."

His words struck hard, and I stopped in my tracks, watching him march toward the gates. I could have stopped him... could have called guards on him... but I couldn't bring myself to do it. The old Lysander would have done it... the desperate, obsessive male I'd been once. But I didn't have a shred of desire to be him again.

I watched him go, and I knew that without Maya, we were royally fucked.

Hanging my head, I muttered a string of curses under my breath and turned toward the front doors.

"He's wrong, you know," a voice said, and I looked up. Kendra was on the steps—apparently unable to sleep either—and watched me with a severe gaze. "Your kingdom doesn't deserve to suffer because of whom you were before. It's not who you are now."

"Kendra, please don't," I replied warily, marching up the front steps past her. The stress, the tension... it was all coming to a head. I felt like I might break at any moment. She reached for my hand as I passed but I shook her off.

"Why don't you believe in yourself?" she demanded, following me through the doors and across the foyer. "I can see it. *Coral* saw it in you. The only person who thinks you're truly heartless and undeserving is *you*, Lysander!"

I whirled on her, blood thrumming.

"Coral thought I was a monster!" I snapped at her, and she flinched. She'd hated me so much that she was running away, trading her tails for legs to do as much. "She *hated* me for what I did to Maya. She only agreed to stay down here with me because she was trying to protect *you*!"

"You're wrong," she said simply, recovering from the shock. "Matt is only saying those things about you because you hurt his girlfriend. It doesn't mean they're true—people can *change*, Lysander."

I shook my head at her. I couldn't do this. Not right now...

"I need you to go," I told her, and confusion flashed in her eyes. I pointed to the front doors. "Take a seahorse. Get far, far away from here. Without Maya... I don't think we're going to..."

I couldn't finish the sentence. *We were going to die.*

"I'm *not* leaving you, Lysander," she ground back, moving closer. "I'm with you until the end." I took a step forward so that our noses were almost touching.

"I'll make you go," I whispered in her face, and her eyes blazed back.

"No, you won't. You're not that kind of being anymore."

283

Her breath was warm as her gaze flicked between my lips and my eyes. Her words were a challenge as much as they were a gentle reminder. My heart ached with longing and torturous restraint—she was close enough that I could kiss her. But I wouldn't do it. She *couldn't* stay here, in imminent danger.

Suddenly, the earth trembled, and a loud bang erupted from down below, in the kingdom. Eyes wide, we raced back out the front doors and down the steps to the gates, peering down on Veranis to see rubble surrounding the houses near the kingdom entrance.

They were here, I realized, and men began shouting and sprinting all around us. I grabbed Kendra by the shoulders.

"Go!" I insisted, before joining my men and sprinting down the hill to the source of damage. The cavernous walls surrounding the kingdom would keep it sheltered at every other side for now, but once the sirens got through the entrance...

A chill went down my spine.

"Lysander!" Someone cried from in front of me, and Nerissa was at my side in moments, having used her magic to zigzag through the crowd. "They're in—they glamoured themselves as scouts and took out one of our watchtowers."

"Get as many undines into the palace as you can, and fortify it," I ordered, and she nodded. In moments, she was gone again, and I drew my spear as we approached a gruesome battle.

I reached the mountainside of stacked houses, skidding down the slope with our army, navigating twists and turns in the narrow pathways. There was little space to fight, and soon, we ran into sirens who were ripping and shredding flesh with their claws, metal clashing as spears and daggers collided. Song rippled through the air—a scattered tune of melodies that made my ears ring and my head throb. I gritted my teeth, pushing through the skull-splitting pain as I drove a spear into the first siren I saw.

I worked my way through the crowd, stabbing and fighting. My clothes were quick to splatter with blood and mud, tears ripping through the fabric. I hadn't had time to put on armor, but I had to get to the front line and help.

The temperature around us seemed to plummet as my men and I continued to push back against Eugene's army. I didn't think anything of it until a voice shouted.

"Get down!"

One of my men collided with me, dragging me to the ground and covering me as a sudden series of cries and echoes sounded. I looked up after a moment to see a shower of deadly ice shards had taken out dozens of sirens around us. Looking over my shoulder, I spotted Kendra a few paces back, channeling her magic with outstretched hands.

I wanted to protest. To scream at her. But I recognized the defiance in her eyes—the same defiance I'd seen in Coral. I knew she wouldn't run, wouldn't save herself.

I'm with you until the end, she'd said, and she met my gaze for only a moment. The sentiment echoed there, and I gave a relenting nod.

Together, we worked on and on through the kingdom. Kendra made quick work of clearing our path any way she could—with currents and blasts and strategic showers of icicles. Our men and I took care of the stragglers, driving our weapons through them over and over as each one fell to the ground.

We were nearly there when a siren came out of nowhere and tackled me. Grunting, I writhed, trying to push him off. His dagger came down on my left side, and I felt a stab of pain as I rolled. I brought my elbow up into his nose and drove my spear through his chest, staggering to my feet.

"Are you okay, Your Grace?" one of my men asked, coming over. My side throbbed, but I nodded, fixing my jacket stiffly. My legs ached from the running, the fighting, and the last few paces felt like an eternity. But then, we were at the entrance, near the stables and watchtowers, which had been blasted to rubble by giant boulders in catapults. There were dead bodies everywhere, and my stomach twisted at the thought of how many were innocent undines that I'd failed to protect.

Being tackled to the ground had knocked me more than I initially realized. My side was aching... *throbbing*... and I instinctively pressed a hand to clutch my ribs. Breathing felt difficult, and I pressed a little tighter. But more shouts sounded in the distance, and I knew time was short. My gaze was drawn to the giant mouth of the cavern sheltering Veranis.

I turned to Kendra.

"Can you use your crystal to seal the entrance?" I asked her. If we could stop sirens from getting through, we could clear out the kingdom and move the defenses up to the palace where, hopefully, most of the undines would be rounded up by Nerissa.

"I'll try," Kendra promised, and I forced a smile at her. The pain in my side was getting worse.

"When you're done, head back to the palace—Nerissa is sending everyone there. She'll need your help."

"What about you?" Kendra asked, her voice light and innocent, and I fought to hide the strain, the way my hands were growing clammy.

"I'm going to check for stragglers," I told her with a firm look, and her eyes flickered with relief as she nodded again.

"Okay. I'll see you back at the palace," she promised, and swam off toward the cave entrance. Once she was gone, I let out a heaving breath and brought my hand away from my side. My palm was covered in watery red blood, and I looked down to see the tip of a dagger embedded in my side. I'd thought it had just been a cut, but perhaps that had been the adrenaline numbing the pain...

Immediately, my hand returned to the wound, and I staggered. Drawing all of my strength, I threw my shoulders back and managed to walk a straight line past my men, who were too occupied preparing to fight again anyway. I didn't want to alert Kendra. Didn't want her to come back for me when the kingdom needed her magic more.

Once I slipped past a building, I let my shoulders sag, stumbling between a silvery stone cottage and a rocky slope. I collapsed in the shadows behind the building, grunting as pain ricocheted through my side. I was panting hard now, sweat beading on my forehead.

"Well, well..." A chuckle sounded, and I tensed. Someone had followed me.

Turning my head, I saw Eugene striding toward me with an expression of amusement.

287

"The undine king... *hiding* from battle," he taunted, and I gritted my teeth. I didn't have the strength to get up again. "That looks particularly nasty," Eugene added, examining my bloody wound mockingly.

"What do you want?" I ground out, wincing from movement, and he squatted so he was eye level with me.

"Why, I'm here for Coral, of course," he purred. "Tell me, where are you hiding her?"

I wouldn't say anything. If he didn't know where she was, then she would be safer. He observed my silence and straightened again.

"Well, then. Perhaps I'll go ask her sister. I'm sure she'll tell me everything if I give her enough... *incentive*," he said slowly, and a low snarl escaped me. I tried to stand, but my legs gave out instantly. Eugene chuckled and reached toward me, plucking my crown off of my head and slipping it into a satchel. Shallow breaths escaped me now as my strength ebbed away.

"I'll take this too. I doubt you'll be needing it much longer," he added, with a twisted smile. Feeling woozy, my head fell back against the building as he walked away.

He was heading for Kendra. I had to... *I had to...*

I couldn't move.

Reluctantly, I told myself I would take just a moment to recover, then try again. *Just a minute... and I would get up again...*

But a minute passed. And then another minute. And then another... and I still didn't get up.

CHAPTER TWENTY-EIGHT

Kendra

The sirens kept coming, but I swam to one edge of the cave mouth and focused my magic. I felt it building under the surface of my fingertips as I focused, swirling to life like the currents of the water around me. I'd never attempted anything like this other than crystallizing my dad's body using my mother's necklace. But that had been different. It had been *her* magic, not mine.

The water at my fingertips began to solidify in clusters of milky-white crystal. Then jagged clusters of light pink appeared and then pale blue and then purple. They grew all over the edge of the cave and began to expand out.

But not fast enough.

The sirens were storming through the cave mouth now, and our army did its best to push back to stop them. But before long, we were swarmed, and I had to pause to defend myself with an outward blast of water. I gritted my teeth, kicking with my tail as I fought them off. I needed to seal the cave mouth so they wouldn't just keep coming, but I couldn't turn my back without getting stabbed.

Then all of a sudden, a colossal wave of water washed past us with such intensity, I could feel it tugging against my skin as it passed. It left all undines untouched but swept the sirens back into the walls of nearby houses, stunning them. I looked up to see Nerissa circling above us, hands outstretched to attack again. She looked to me.

289

"Do it now!" she yelled, and I nodded. Nerissa focused on keeping the sirens away from me as I returned my attention back to the cave mouth. It was slow work—the crystal was impenetrable, but it took so much of my energy to create. I'd not even covered a third of the cave mouth before I was panting, sweating, giving it everything I had.

Sirens tried to tackle the crystal but failed to break it as it continued to spread.

"Keep going!" Nerissa urged from above, and I willed my magic to work faster. A surge of power burst through my fingers, but the staggering effect of exhaustion took a toll. I stumbled back, glimpsing the cave mouth. It was halfway sealed.

"Look out!"

I whirled as something slammed into my gut and threw me back against the cavernous wall. I gasped as the air left my lungs, and I slumped. Looking up, I saw a familiar mop of blond hair as he threw me a lazy grin.

"*Kendra*. Just whom I've been looking for," Eugene purred, tilting his head at me as he started toward me.

I scrambled up, preparing to blast him back.

"Oh no," he sang, and my arms and tail felt sluggish all of a sudden. "You're not going to hurt me. You're going to tell me where your sweet sister is."

"Go to hell!" I growled back, and his eyes turned cold.

"Pity," he muttered, and lunged with a clawed hand. Nerissa hurled into him from the side, tackling him to the bedrock floor. The spell broke, and I immediately rushed to help pin him.

"Seal the cave!" Nerissa protested, as she grappled with Eugene. "I've got this!"

But I swam close and kicked him hard in the ribs with my tail fin. He let out a cry, and I seethed at him.

"That's for my sister," I growled. "Too bad she's not here to do it herself."

His eyes were full of anger and confusion, and only then did I consider Eugene's words. It suddenly dawned on me that he hadn't known Coral was with Melody. *His own adviser.*

I floated inches above him, thrusting my tail as I spoke, "Melody has Coral, you absolute *dimwit*. But I'm guessing you didn't order that, so I wonder if you can really trust your own adviser."

His eyes darkened, and I smirked at him. *Any* mistrust I could create between him and his sister, I would gladly do because I loathed both of them.

"The cave, Kendra!" Nerissa shouted, and with a kick of my tail, I glided back over to the cave mouth to channel the rest of my magic. Anger had renewed my resolve.

I was so focused on the task that I barely noticed the ongoing struggle behind me until a sudden cry of pain pulled me from my work again. I spared a quick glance toward Nerissa. She pulled a bloody dagger from her upper tail as Eugene bolted for the cave mouth. Gritting my teeth, I tried to speed up the process, tried to seal him in.

You're not getting away, I thought. My head whipped back and forth as I watched him push through the crowd. Sweat began to bead on my forehead. The crystal spread and spread, closer and closer. I was going to make it!

Eugene was mere inches from the cave mouth when he let out a low hum. His song made everyone in his vicinity pause. Throwing me a savage glare, he slipped past the jagged crystal

291

just as it spread over the final lip, sealing shut. I cursed and threw my hands down. A moment later, I whirled to face Nerissa, expecting her to need help—but she was already healing herself, the dagger lying discarded on the ground.

"Never mind," she grunted, noting my fury. "You've blocked off access to the rest of Eugene's army, and that's a win. We'll get Eugene another time."

"It won't be a win if we don't clear out these remaining sirens," I replied. The crowd was still thick with the ones who had snuck through—now trapped and more desperate than ever to stand victorious, lest they be slaughtered or taken prisoner.

"Then let's see that it's done," Nerissa said, rising from the ground, and together, we swam to join the Veranis army who was still clashing weapons and echoing battle cries.

We continued fighting for what felt like hours. But eventually, we managed to take down the last of the sirens, and our army cheered victoriously. Nerissa slumped against a stone fence, breathing hard. Her face was weary with exhaustion, and I joined her.

"We should go back to the palace," I said, looking around. I hadn't seen Lysander for some time, and he did say he'd meet us back there. Perhaps he was tending to his people.

Nerissa nodded in agreement, and we began the trek back up the slopes of Veranis to the palace.

When we reached the palace, it was alive with chatter. People had been crammed into every single inch of space available—crowding the foyer, the ballroom, the dining room, the staircase, and all the upper levels. A couple of guards were positioned in alcoves or patrolling, checking on beings, but most of the palace staff had been left to tend to everyone. I wormed my way through the crowd, scanning for any sign of Lysander, but it was near impossible to spot him in this thick crowd.

"Where's Leif?" a voice echoed from behind me. "He said he'd be here to protect us!"

I glanced over my shoulder and spotted a family near the door—a mother with three red-haired girls. The shortest of the three was peering around the crowd with a frown, and the eldest crouched down. She was stunning, with luscious waves and thick eyelashes.

"We have to assume he's out fighting with everyone else," she replied. "But I'm sure he's fine—he always is."

The youngest hugged her sister, clinging tightly, and they huddled into a group hug.

Pulling my gaze away, I made my way over to one of the nearby guards.

"Have you seen the king?" I asked him, and he shook his head. I grimaced and kept going, asking every servant and guard I came across. It was after the seventh "no" that I began to grow concerned that not a *single* one had seen him. Surely, someone had?

My gaze drifted back to the foyer doors. I could go upstairs, spend the next hour checking all the rooms... or I could go back out into the streets and look. Something instinctive tugged in my gut, urging me toward the door, and without second thought, I pushed back through the crowd toward it.

Fresh, spacious water hit me as soon as I made it through the crowd, and I swam back down the front steps into the coral gardens. The gates leading down into Veranis had been left open, and beings were still making their way back and forth. I swam past them, my mind a flurry of thought and panic.

Where is he? I thought, staring down at the huge kingdom. *How will I ever find him?*

Something nuzzled at my ear, making me jolt, and a fish came into my field of vision. Then two more, and in moments, seven familiar dwarf fish were circling me, trilling urgently.

Come quick, they urged, and I nodded for them to lead the way. I used my magic to pull the currents around me, and we sped through the winding streets and down the slopes, past hundreds of bodies and dozens of injured beings. My eyes trailed over the death and destruction before me, and I began to fear the worst.

We finally came to a stop outside an empty house, and the fish flittered around the side gate. I pushed it open, swimming around the wall of the house, and found him slumped there.

Unmoving and lifeless.

"Lysander!" I cried, dropping next to him and grabbing him by the shoulders. Blood drifted in the water around us, clumping from a wound in his side. His hand lay beside it on the ground, palm still watery with settled blood, and he was cold to the touch. "No... *no*..."

Hot tears filled my eyes, and I clung to him. He wasn't moving. Was barely breathing. I shook him, but he didn't respond. My hand went to his cheek as I sobbed.

When had this happened? How long had he been here? If only I'd known, I could have healed him...

I touched his wound carefully. I tried to heal him, but even as the wound closed, he didn't wake. Didn't move. His skin remained like ice. I began screaming for help, not knowing if anyone would hear. But I screamed anyway and clutched his lifeless body and shook as sobs wreaked through me.

I was too late.

Voices sounded. Footsteps thudded. More and more, and then we were found. Beings gathered—his men, mostly. But I continued screaming, sobbing, wouldn't let them near him. He hadn't been with the other bodies—this was no accident. He'd hidden himself here, away from his people where they might save him.

Because of me, I realized. Because he knew I'd come for him if I'd known. That I wouldn't have sealed the cave mouth. He'd sacrificed himself to save everyone else.

I gently brushed his wavy dark hair from his eyes. Those mesmerizing sea-green eyes. I wished I could see them one last time—sparkling and full of light. My throat tightened in response.

"I love you," I half whispered, half sobbed, pressing my forehead against his. "I would have loved you no matter what."

Then I leaned in and gently brushed my lips against his. Just once.

Lysander's fingers twitched against my tail, and my eyes snapped open.

The color had returned to his cheeks, warmth seeping through him, and he let out a rasping breath as he opened his eyes, saw me, and stared.

"Lysander?" I whispered. I didn't dare breathe, unable to believe this was real.

Slowly, he lifted a hand to cup my face, his thumb brushing the corner of my mouth.

"Kendra," he breathed, and I began to shake. He was *alive*!

Something between a relieved laugh and a sob escaped me. I leaned in and kissed him again, and this time, his lips were warm and responsive. One hand pressed against my back, the other cupping the nape of my neck as he pulled me close to him and deepened the kiss. When we broke away, tears welled again, but this time, from joy.

"How is this possible?" I breathed, and his gaze softened as he traced gentle circles on my back.

"I believe it's called true love's kiss," he replied, quirking his lips as he gazed at me with appreciation. "Love is the most powerful magic of all—and I think your love for me mixed with your mer-magic effectively healed me from the brink of death."

Slowly, a smile spread over my lips, and this time, it was him who leaned forward to kiss me. His lips were slow and gentle against mine.

"For the record, I love you too," he breathed finally, and the confession washed through me like a tidal wave. I'd been waiting so long, *wanting* for so long.

There was an entire palace of people waiting for him and an audience watching us. But they slowly began to disband as we stayed there, wrapped in each other's embrace, for a good, long while.

CHAPTER TWENTY-NINE

Coral

The gentle sound of waves stirred me awake.

Slowly, I blinked my eyes open, but instead of dark water, I was greeted by blinding blue skies and sunlight. I held my breath for a moment, barely daring to believe that this was real.

Then I looked down at my tail—and found legs instead. Furthermore, an arm was hooked under them, and that's when I realized I was being carried.

"You're finally awake," Leif said, peering down at me with his honey-brown eyes. His hair was dripping wet, like we'd stepped out of the ocean not too long ago, and the sun warmed his armor—which, pressed against me, took the chill out of my bones.

"I have legs again," I breathed, wriggling my toes. A laugh of delight escaped my lips, and Leif smiled at my reaction. "Put me down—I want to feel my feet!"

He paused, letting me slip from his arms as my toes touched the sand. The first step sent pins and needles through my foot, and I hissed, but after a few steps, it eased off.

I twirled around and let out a laugh.

"I can't believe it!" I cried, and Leif was smiling with adoration at my sheer joy. With another laugh, I ran toward the ocean waves to test that it had truly, *truly* worked. Dipping a toe into the ocean, I felt nothing. No devastating pull of fate that might turn me to sea-foam, not a single hint of my tail threatening to return.

"I'm me again!" I whispered, feeling it finally sink in, and turned to face Leif. He was right behind me, having followed me, and he gripped my wrist and pulled me flush against him.

Cupping my cheeks in both hands, he kissed me—slow and intentional, like he'd been waiting for this moment and wanted to take his time. I moaned against his lips—I was the happiest I'd ever been in my entire life, and this was the damn cherry on top.

My mind went blank as he placed his hands on my waist and backed me up across the beach, pushing me against the rough trunk of a palm tree. My hands slid up the polished copper plates of his armor, and I let out a frustrated sound when I couldn't find a way to access his shoulders and chest. There was too much metal, not enough of *him*—

In a swift movement, he reached up to unclasp the armor on his torso and legs, and it fell to the ground. Kicking it aside with his foot, he pressed his body against mine and kissed me again. This time, my hands ran across his muscles, his warm skin, and his beating heart against my chest, and my mind went haywire.

His hands trailed down my waist, slowly and tantalizing, like he was memorizing every touch, and my cheeks heated as I remembered I was wearing nothing below my waist, where the hem of his oversized shirt barely covered me. Despite the ache building between my legs, I tensed, remembering how I'd rushed things with Lysander, how I'd let my emotions drive me, and how quickly things had fallen apart in a matter

299

of weeks. Leif noticed my reaction and immediately let go, instead reaching for one of my hands. He kissed my knuckles, then said, "Relax—I'm in no rush."

Relief crashed through me. I was still reeling from the kiss—unlike any of the kisses with Lysander, it left me feeling sort of tingly all over. And as I looked up at Leif, I felt my body completely relax. I knew he meant his words—he had never said or done anything to deceive me.

I reached up and gently kissed him once more, cupping the nape of his neck, and he deepened the kiss like he couldn't help himself.

"*Ahem*."

I broke the kiss and glanced over Leif's shoulder. Matt and Maya were standing at the shoreline, dripping from head to toe like they'd just arrived. Maya still had that wistful, absent look in her eyes, but Matt seemed uncomfortable.

I stepped away from Leif, blush heating my face, and stammered, "Oh! You made it! I, uh, I guess we should go somewhere where Maya would be more comfortable..."

Matt eyed the two of us like he was thinking *anywhere* would be more comfortable than here on this beach right now.

"Your house is closest," Matt replied. "She'll know where she is, so let's head there."

I nodded, and the four of us began trekking along the beach, around the bend toward the road. As Leif and I trailed behind Matt and Maya, I couldn't help smiling as he shifted closer and brushed his fingers against mine.

An hour later, we were gathered in my living room, which felt stuffy from the lack of breeze and use. Matt coaxed Maya onto the plush white sofa, while I cracked the balcony doors open. The pink bougainvillea flowers that usually grew along the balcony railing were limp and dying, as were most of our other potted plants in the foyer. It made my throat close up, remembering the once-happy life we'd lived here. Now, nobody remained to bring life to the house.

Still, I was thankful we hadn't gotten around to renting the house out yet, or else we would have had to find somewhere else private.

I turned around and found Matt waiting for me in the center of the room, holding the clam that contained Maya's soul. It continued to glow faintly, emitting a green light. I crossed the room to join him—we'd agreed to do this together.

"She deserves to have people she knows and trusts with her when she comes to," Matt had said on our walk up to the house, and I'd fully agreed. I didn't know what was going to happen, how she would react, how much she'd remember. What if her last memories were her death? What if she didn't recall anything about being a sea witch? I couldn't imagine the pain we'd have to hold her through, but I was determined to be there for her regardless.

Maya waited on the sofa, still ethereal and blank faced, as Matt and I both put our hands on the clam and held it inches away from her. Together, we pulled back the head, and emerald-green light poured into the room. The soul flew out and immediately enveloped Maya—like she'd been a magnet drawing the soul in. Slowly, the green light spread over every inch of her before sinking through her black skin. A glossy glow appeared as her skin began to materialize before our eyes. Her eyes closed, and the first hint of emotion appeared as her brows furrowed.

"Maya?" Matt whispered, watching intently. After a moment, the glow faded, and her eyes snapped open.

She stared at the both of us, and I held my breath as I waited. Then her gaze drifted to Matt, and she burst into tears. In a matter of moments, we were all crying. Maya leaped up from the couch and wrapped her arms around Matt, who buried his face into her hair and spun her around. Tears streamed down my face as I watched them, and I felt nothing but joy and relief in my heart.

Then Maya looked at me—and it was her. My best friend. The person I'd grown up surfing with, laughing with, sharing *everything* with.

"You *lived*," she breathed, and I shook my head as she enveloped me in a gentle hug. Something cracked in my heart as I clung to her, and she trembled with tears of her own.

"Don't say that," I said, my throat thick from crying. "You *died* because of me—why did you try to save me in that current?"

She pulled back and looked at me firmly.

"Because I *love* you, Coral," she stated. "Because you're my best friend, and I would do anything for you. Just like I know you'd do anything for me."

I simply didn't have the words. All I could do was hug her and sob. Matt wrapped his arms around both of us, and we sank to the floor in a messy group hug.

After all this time, things had been made right—and we were reunited again.

CHAPTER THIRTY

Coral

The sun was setting as the three of us walked along the boardwalk, eating ice cream.

Leif had stayed behind at the house to give us our privacy. Maya had wanted to eat anything other than fish after spending over a year in the Undersea, and Matt and I had eagerly agreed. We'd all changed into dry clothes before setting off. Maya was now wearing one of Kendra's white sundresses, and Matt had found a fresh shirt in my dad's closet, though it was a little large on him. I'd found a flowy periwinkle-blue play-suit to wear, and I was relieved to have something other than a bralette and silk wrap on my body.

The warm summer air on my skin felt better than ever before, and I didn't even mind the humidity. After spending weeks down in the Undersea in endless cold and wet, it was a refreshing change. Fireflies danced by as our footsteps creaked on the wood beneath our feet, and the waves crashed in the distance like a summer song.

We both had a lot of questions for Maya, but I hadn't wanted to bring up any trauma or push her too soon. She'd seemed very open to sharing though.

"So, do you remember anything about being the sea witch?" I asked carefully.

"Oh, bits and pieces," she replied, before biting into her boysenberry scoop. "It was all very vague—half the time, I

303

wasn't even conscious. The strongest memories are ones where you and Matt were around—probably because the part of me who remembered my old life recognized you."

"And... are you *still* the sea witch?" Matt asked.

"I am," she confirmed with a nod. "I can still create bindings and curses... and I know there are things I can and cannot do... but now I have full control over my actions."

"Will you have to return to the Undersea?" I asked, raising an eyebrow as I licked my watermelon sorbet scoop.

"Every now and again," she said, with an absent wave of her hand. "But I believe I could mostly return to living here on land if I wanted to."

"And... *do* you want to?" Matt asked, raising an eyebrow. "Because for reference, I am *not* a fan of being underwater for weeks on end."

We all laughed, and Maya gazed at Matt with an adoring expression.

"Don't worry—I plan on sticking around," she told him, before slowing in her tracks. "But... we might need to come up with a story. My parents are going to *freak* when they see me, and I can't avoid them forever."

Nor would she want to, I imagined. We all paused, pressing our backs against the boardwalk railing to let other people pass us.

"Is it plausible that you got washed up and stranded on a nearby island?" Matt suggested. "Maybe we can say that you survived on coconuts and fish for a year until a passing boat rescued you."

Maya snorted.

"Yeah, except they're never going to believe that I was smart enough to make my own water filtration system. We all know I dropped out of science as soon as I could."

"Maybe there was a stream?" I suggested. "We have streams here."

We pondered it for a moment.

"Well, unless we want to make up some crap about you being kidnapped by pirates..." Matt trailed off, and she began to cackle with laughter.

"Or tell them the *truth*, which they'll never believe," I added, with a smirk. The thought of telling them the truth was *truly* ridiculous.

The laughter died down, and Maya grew very quiet all of a sudden, wrapping her arms around her torso like she was trying to make herself smaller.

"I'm scared to approach them," she admitted finally. "I can only imagine how much pain they went through over the past year. I know they'll be happy to see me, but... there will be so many questions and so many emotions to navigate."

I completely understood—I'd felt that way about telling Matt too. I wrapped my arm around her, and Matt slipped his hand into hers.

"We can come with you," he offered. "Say that we found you, or that you found us first."

But my gut turned over at the thought, and I shook my head.

"I'm sorry... I *can't* go with you," I said, and Maya frowned at me. "Your parents... after you died, they blamed me. And rightfully so. But they won't speak to me or acknowledge me anymore. They were *so angry* when I showed up at your funeral... they wanted me to leave."

Her eyes flashed with hurt.

"That's not fair," she muttered. "I *chose* to save you, Coral. It was my choice, and I don't regret it."

"I don't think they see it that way," I replied quietly. "And can you really blame them?"

She pushed off the boardwalk railing, discarding her ice-cream cone in a nearby bin.

"They'll come around," she promised. "Especially if we feed them a different story."

She set off down the boardwalk again, and Matt and I jogged to catch up with her.

We pivoted the conversation away from her parents as Matt and Maya began talking about resuming their life on land. I didn't mention that I was one-third undine now—and that I could return to the Undersea and planned to. Especially when Maya brought up surfing, and the three of us agreed to surf together regularly again.

It wasn't until an hour later, when the sky had turned black and the lights from every boardwalk restaurant glittered around us, that Maya finally faced us and said, "Okay... I think I'm ready to go see my parents now."

She looked to Matt, and he nodded, taking her hand in his.

"We'll go together," he promised, and she leaned her head on his shoulder.

"Good luck," I said, waving as they began to head toward the main street.

I stood there, considering whether to head back to the house, to where Leif was waiting. But I couldn't help thinking that he'd shown me so much of his world... and he knew hardly anything about mine. There were so many things I wanted to share with him—I wanted him to know me, *all* of me.

Before I'd left, I'd taught Leif how to use the housephone in case of an emergency. But as I dialed my house number on my cell and listened for the ring, I wondered how he'd react.

A moment later, the receiver picked up, and he spoke.

"Coral?"

His voice was tentative, uncertain, and I nearly snickered at the thought of him handling the phone with such uncertainty.

"Hey," I said softly, relishing the sound of his voice on the other end.

"What's wrong?" he prompted with urgency, and I remembered I told him I'd call in an emergency. Guilt plunged through me.

"Oh, no, nothing... I just..." I trailed off, looking to the shops dotting the boardwalk. "Do you want to have dinner with me?"

There was a pause.

"What did you have in mind?" he asked finally, his voice lower, and I smiled.

"Come meet me at the boardwalk, and I'll show you."

CHAPTER THIRTY-ONE

Leif

Coral had offered her dad's closet to me before she left, so I changed into a fresh shirt and pants. Our clothes in the Undersea were made differently to avoid weighing us down in the water, but these clothes were lighter—with strange, airy fabric. I felt near naked wearing them, and I couldn't stop thinking about kissing Coral earlier while she wore nothing but a borrowed shirt.

I took one look at myself in the mirror of her dad's closet and mentally scolded myself. *Don't think like that right now*, I decided. We'd already agreed not to go any further, and I wasn't going to break her trust or push her into anything.

I had a vague idea of the boardwalk location from my various visits to the island, and I followed her instructions—heading down the slope behind her house and across the beach. It was easy from there because the boardwalk was lit up like a beacon.

She was waiting near Snack Shack, sitting on the edge of the boardwalk with her bare feet in the sand. There was a contented look on her face as she wriggled her toes, feeling the sand sift over her skin. She looked so beautiful—her playsuit brought out her eyes, which sparkled when she looked up and spotted me.

"You found it," she beamed, jumping to her feet and slipping her sandals on. "Come on—I have a place in mind, and I'm curious to see your reaction."

Intrigued, I followed her down the boardwalk. My gaze was drawn to all the little golden lights hanging on strings overhead and threaded through the lush cypress trees that swayed in the breeze. The chatter from the taverns and restaurants we passed seemed quieter than I was used to—probably because noise traveled differently in the Undersea.

Coral led me into a posh-looking restaurant with palm trees framing the entryway. A server dressed in a black apron greeted us and showed us to a small table in the corner. My knees brushed against a white tablecloth as I took a seat across from Coral, and my gaze landed on a lit candle in the center of the table. Soft music played from somewhere inside, and everyone spoke in much softer tones around us.

"My family loves—well, *loved* Italian food," she told me, reaching for a glossy menu and handing me one. "So I thought you might like to try it."

I raised an eyebrow at her and glanced down at the menu. My eyes scanned the appetizers, and I frowned at all the unfamiliar names—*garlic bread, bruschetta, garden salad...* Why would anyone want to eat a garden? I thought of the coral gardens back home and wrinkled my nose.

Coral was grinning as she watched my expressions, and my heart warmed at the sight.

"I'm going to order the bruschetta and a Margherita pizza—you can have some of mine," she told me, after we'd spent a few minutes looking. Noticing my undecided expression, she leaned over the table to tap my menu, and I caught a whiff of fragrant lily and grapefruit.

"I think you'd like this—it has seafood in it."

I glanced down to the name of her suggestion. *Marinara risotto*.

"Okay, I trust you," I said, placing my menu down on top of hers as she told the waiter our order and asked for drinks. Her hand lingered near the menus, and I couldn't help myself as I reached forward to entwine our hands. She glanced at me, and a small smile appeared.

Once the waiter left, we were alone, and I wanted to make the most of it. But there were things on my mind that lingered. I would have to return to the Undersea soon... and I didn't know if she would join me. I didn't know how *any* of this was going to work—with her and Lysander's coruling duties and my duties as a commander. Would she even bother coruling Veranis now that Maya had her soul back? I wondered if Lysander would see this as a massive betrayal once he learned about Coral and me and that she could return to land. I'd been hesitant to even *kiss* Coral in fear of losing everything I'd worked so hard to achieve.

A part of me didn't want to have this conversation. I wanted to pretend like it didn't matter—like we were the only two people in the world. But I couldn't bring myself to spend such precious moments with her if they would end in heartbreak for both of us.

"We need to talk about Lysander," I said, and Coral's expression faltered. But then she nodded and drew her hand from mine.

"I know," she agreed, placing her hands in her lap. "I've been thinking about it. About... what I'm going to do now that I'm not Reigning Queen anymore, and I have my legs back. I suppose I don't need to become queen of Veranis anymore either... but I would feel bad if Lysander went heartless again. Is there a way to break the binding between us without restoring his curse?"

If there was, it could change a lot of things—and it would make matters less complicated on both sides. But...

"If we found a way to do that... you wouldn't be queen of anything anymore," I reminder her, and she nodded.

"And maybe that's for the best."

Did that mean she would stay by my side in Veranis? We could build a different kind of life together... I wondered for a moment how it might look.

"So how would we do it?" I asked, and she paused to think, drumming her fingernails on the table. I wanted her to be free of Lysander as much as she wanted to be... not only because she craved freedom so badly, but because I wanted her to be *mine*. I hadn't dared say the words aloud, knowing how obsessive Lysander had acted around her... but while that binding existed between them, a part of her would always be tethered to him, and I hated the thought.

"Well, I was considering using the stone that the First Sea Witch gifted me... but she said to use it wisely. Is this really the best thing to use it on?"

I'd completely forgotten about the stone in the turn of events—it was still in my pants pocket back at the house.

"Well, what else would we use it for?" I asked, and she shrugged.

311

"I'm really not sure yet. But I don't have magic anymore, and I'm not Reigning Queen, so I'm limited in my capabilities... unless I go through with becoming queen of Veranis and find a loophole somehow. Or, I suppose could ask Maya for help... but I want to give her some time with her family first. I'm not in a rush to drag her back down to the Undersea."

And I wasn't in a rush to return without Coral.

"I guess I just need to know something before this goes any further," I said finally, and met her gaze. "Do you... want to be with me?"

Do you want to be mine? I thought a moment later, the words dancing on the tip of my tongue, but I held them back. Surprise flickered in her eyes, and I leaned forward to place my hand over hers again. "I know that's... bold, and it's sudden. But I don't want to start something and then have to live my life without you. If you want a life here on land... I understand, and I don't want to take that away from you. But my life is below... and I've built a career as a commander. I've worked too hard to give it all up."

Her gaze softened, and she scooted her chair around so it was closer to mine, ignoring the way people near us stared. She took both my hands in hers.

"Yes, I want to be with you," she replied, and my shoulders sagged in relief. "And I don't want to be apart from my sister, who is bound to spend the rest of her life in the Undersea. We still have so much work to do freeing the mermaids and rebuilding Atlantis. I think... we could have it both ways. That I could return to the surface a few times a month, perhaps, and spend the rest of my time below, in Veranis, with you. And it would be different because I'm now free to go be-tween both realms." She paused, gauging my reaction, before adding, "What do you think?"

In answer, I leaned forward, caressed her cheek, and kissed her softly. She leaned into the kiss, her hand snaking up my arm to keep me there, and I was breathless by the time she pulled away.

There was movement beside us, and we jolted, realizing the waiter had returned with our drinks. Blushing furiously, Coral shifted her chair a few inches back to where it was and took the drinks, thanking him quickly and handing one to me. The waiter promised to be back with our food, and I watched as Coral busied herself sipping her drink, sneaking a quick glance my way.

I couldn't help smirking at how flustered she'd become. It made my thoughts drift to all the other things I could do to her... all the other ways she might react for me, and I had to force myself to stop imagining such things.

"Do you, uh... like the drink?" she asked finally, gesturing to the pink concoction she'd handed me. Ice swirled in the tall glass, and I poked a thin tube sticking out from it curiously. "It's soda, cranberry, and lime," she clarified, amusement crossing her face at my uncertain gaze. I discarded the tube thing and took a sip, and I let out a noise of surprise.

"It's good!" I exclaimed, savoring the taste. It was fizzy and tangy and... *delicious*. I didn't like fruit very much, but to be fair, I'd only tried the dried variety in my life. She beamed at me as I took another sip, and in that moment, our meals arrived. It smelled as good as it looked, and I was glad to see that among the strange, stringy yellow clumps in my bowl there were clams and shrimps and other familiar foods.

We ate and we talked and she offered me a slice of her pizza, which I enjoyed. The risotto was especially good, and I cleaned the entire bowl. After we ate, she ordered something called tiramisu, which I took a bite of but didn't enjoy as much. I watched her devour it with hungry eyes and made a mental note about the tiramisu. Perhaps my mother could experiment with her baking...

After dinner, Coral suggested going for a walk, so we left the restaurant and headed back out onto the boardwalk. She slipped her hand into mine as we walked back toward the slope leading up to her house. It was getting late—the stars twinkled in the sky above us, and I imagined she must be tired after the draining events of the past couple of days.

But she paused at the end of the boardwalk and pulled me close by the neck of my shirt, kissing me deeply. My hands circled her, holding her close, and I savored the feel of her lips on mine. She met my gaze as we stood under a cloudless sky, basking in the light of the moon.

"Thank you," she said suddenly, and I frowned at her.

"What for?" I inquired, tilting my head as she stared at me.

"For everything you've ever done for me," she said. "You always looked out for me... always thought of me... you've been there from the moment I met you."

I thought back to the moment I'd first seen her in Lysander's throne room, with no idea how much I'd come to like her, how much I'd admire her strength and resolve. I wondered how different things might have been if I hadn't spent the first few weeks trying to help Lysander woo her heart.

"I rushed things with Lysander," she admitted finally, looking away sheepishly. "So, it's not that I don't want things to go further... but whenever I rush things, they seem to fall apart. And I don't want this to fall apart."

My gaze softened, and I held her close as she buried her head against my chest. Perhaps it should have frustrated me, but I appreciated her honest communication... and I knew she was serious about me if she wanted to go slow. It was as if she had no goal to rush toward, but rather, wanted to savor every moment we had together... and I liked that thought.

"We have all the time in the world," I promised her, kissing the top of her head. "Take as long as you need."

CHAPTER THIRTY-TWO

Eugene

I rode through the gates of Coronis—my kingdom—but I sensed an immediate shift in the water. Frowning, I scanned the city streets as my seahorse bobbed through the townspeople, each of them averting their gazes. And I noticed less mermaids—usually they were slaving in the streets.

I knew it had taken some time for people to adjust to having a male ruler... but over the past few weeks, beings had become more and more adjusted to it. Now, however... it was like they were afraid of me.

It didn't make sense—sirens were ruthless. We weren't afraid of anything, lest not a king who rode into war on an opposing kingdom. And *certainly* not one who had lost, though I was sure word of that couldn't have reached this far yet. The reminder of our failed siege—the sirens we'd lost in battle—stung like a slap to the face.

But at least I have the Veranis crown, I thought, hand slipping to my satchel to check its weight. Regardless of whether the king had lived or perished, I'd bested him in my attack—just as we'd bested King Malvin years and years ago. His crown was stored safely in the Cora Palace, while the king himself cowered in his crystal palace. *Pathetic*.

I arrived at the steps of the palace and climbed the length of them, striding through the foyer with my head held high. I wouldn't show an ounce of defeat on my face. But my mood soured when I reached the throne room and found my sister lounging on my throne.

My eyes narrowed at her. What was she doing on my throne?

"Feeling nostalgic, Sister?" I inquired cautiously as I approached. She wore a bold golden gown with long sheer sleeves dotted with tiny ruby gemstones. Her clawed nails curled along the armrests of the throne. My gaze swept the entire throne room, wondering why my guards had allowed her to sit there...

Slowly, my eyes widened. The court room wasn't filled with guards—it was filled with female sirens from the highest clans. I looked back at Melody, whose lips curved into a smile.

"Welcome back, Brother," she purred. "Were your efforts against Veranis victorious?"

I came to a stop, noticing the glow in her cheeks, her lyrical voice, and realization washed over me. I resisted the urge to snarl at her, taking a more diplomatic approach.

"You've broken your binding..." I said slowly, running my eyes over her. I didn't think it was possible—that she could get her power back and the throne with it. Not when she needed Coral Klassan to break her binding, and I was so *certain* that wretched mermaid would never do it.

But her sister had spoken of Melody and Coral being together somewhere. I didn't know where—or what—Melody had been up to behind my back, but if I knew my sister, and she had her power back, then I could only assume one thing:

Coral must be dead.

317

Melody leaned forward—slowly, leisurely—and crossed one leg over the other.

"Quite amateur of you to take most of our army and leave your kingdom near deserted of guards. Taking back my throne was hardly a challenge," she replied, examining her nails casually. "You forget that I sat on this throne for twenty years before you took over. Did you *really* think I wouldn't know my own palace's weaknesses? That I couldn't lead a siege?"

"Well, unfortunately for you, you need the ocean's favor to take back your *crown*," I reminded her, temper rising now. "So, I am *still* your king, and I must ask you to vacate *my* throne."

She didn't move, but a golden crown appeared on her head. Shock rippled through me, and my eyes widened.

"How did you—?"

"It's a long story, Brother, and I'm tired from my journey," she pouted, rising from the chair. I took a step forward, and the low hum of siren song echoed from the court, freezing me in place.

"Tell me!" I growled, trying to fight the siren spell.

Had dethroning a Reigning Queen tipped the scales in her favor somehow? I *needed* to know what had happened in my absence.

"I said I'm *tired*," she drawled back, her voice stormy and gaze dark.

"*How did you come unbound*?" I demanded, eyes blazing at her. A weary look crossed her face, and she sighed.

"Dear Brother, if you *must* know, it turns out that love is the most powerful magic of all," she replied carefully. "More powerful than any siren song, as you and I are well aware.

318

And as it happens, my love for Lorraine and my willingness to put her wishes before my own was favored as a strength by the ocean. So I won its favor, and taking back the throne was child's play after that."

I was scrambling to understand. *Lorraine*? But the Atlantis princess was long dead. Where had Melody been to create this turn of events?

"I don't understand... did you kill Coral Klassan or not?" I pressed, digging for information. I wasn't about to let this go—I'd worked too hard, waited *too* long to let my sister take back her throne. And she'd spent the past twenty years of rulership chasing a revenge fantasy. I had far bigger, far *better* plans for our kingdom... for the entire Undersea.

"No," she said softly. "I have decided to let her live."

I wanted to start laughing. This was *stupidity*! My sister had finally lost all of her good sense.

"And I suppose that's why all the mermaids are missing too, is it?" I ground, noting the empty hallways and surroundings. We were now a kingdom with a court of female sirens instead of guards, with *no* servants to fulfill our labor, and if Atlantis went on to rebuild...

The thought of the chaos that would ensue made my stomach turn. She'd gone from one extreme to the other. All because of some *stupid* mermaid she'd loved twenty years ago.

I thought I'd been helping her when I told her to go after Lorraine. When she finally stood up to our mother and rid herself of Nikolai Galanis. I was *proud* to see her transform into a strong, powerful siren who took charge of her own life, that day she came from the Sea of Souls, like she'd become a totally new person—*renewed and relentless.*

319

But I realized now, I'd planted toxic seeds in her mind. And over the years, they'd festered like a poison. She was *obsessed* with Lorraine, and it was going to destroy our kingdom.

"You mustn't be upset, Eugene," she said, treading down the steps to place a hand on my shoulder. "It's all just experience, and unfortunately, I have plenty in ruling, whereas you have very little. But worry not—I will still need a strong army commander, and I have recommended you highly."

I simmered at her as she strutted off across the throne room toward the stairs, her court following her. My precious sister... whom I loved dearly but couldn't help resenting at the same time. I had only ever wanted the best for her... and she didn't yet realize that *me* being in power was best for everybody. But landing the title of king the first time had been difficult enough—*years* in the making—with the way Coronis hierarchy was structured. It was going to take something bigger to overthrow my sister this time... something that outranked *even* her.

Something that would make me *so* powerful, not even her siren song could stop me.

I thought of the Veranis crown in my satchel and the Atlantis crown stored in the chambers below the palace. I thought of Melody's original plan to rule the Undersea through brute force... and an idea came together in my mind.

CHAPTER THIRTY-THREE

Lysander

The cleanup took days and days. I found myself working morning to night—rising early to assist men in clearing debris, bodies, and rubble, then stumbling into bed late at night with whatever food I'd first spotted in the dining hall and scoffed down. I knew Kendra was busy too—she and Nerissa spent their days in the infirmary, healing the wounded.

Without Leif, I was sought on to consult on strategy and advise on fortification tactics in case of a second attack. We couldn't afford such a thing while we were still in recovery. Kendra still hadn't melted the crystal keeping Veranis contained, and we had *some* farmland within its walls... but not enough to sustain the kingdom for long. Sooner or later, we would have to expose ourselves again and open up for trade.

By the third day, I had a moment of pause as I returned to the palace for lunch. Rue had come looking for me and insisted that I have a proper meal before heading back out. So I found myself picking at a plate of shellfish in the dining hall, my thoughts drifting to Leif.

He still wasn't back, and I could only assume he was with Coral, back on land. I didn't know whether to expect his return or not. I knew not to expect Coral's.

Not that it matters anymore, I thought. Technically, we still had a kingdom to run... but I seemed to be doing fine on my own. And Kendra had been a wonderful help, even though we'd barely spoken two words since the day she'd healed me.

We'd simply been too busy and far too exhausted at the end of each day.

It didn't stop me yearning to kiss her. I hadn't been able to get her out of my mind, and I was starting to feel like I was going crazy. A *different* kind of crazy to when I'd been with Coral.

I finished eating, and no sooner than I had left the dining hall, a messenger found me.

"Your Grace, a message for you from Coronis," he said, offering me a scroll, and my gut rolled. *So soon?*

"What does Eugene want now?" I muttered, taking the scroll from him and uncurling it.

"Actually, it's from Queen Melody, Your Grace," he corrected, and I paused. *Indeed?*

I glanced down at the letter and read the writing there. The messenger waited as I read the page, and my jaw slackened.

He noticed my reaction, hesitated, but then asked, "If I may, Your Grace... what does it say?"

"Melody has freed the mermaids," I said, as my eyes scanned the final line. "She is sending supplies to Atlantis to help them rebuild as we speak, and she has proposed a treaty with us too. A *real* one. She has requested that we allow her to send in a delegation with provisions to express regret for the actions of her brother."

The messenger looked astounded.

"*Surely*, it's a trick, Your Grace," he replied, shaking his head, and I was obliged to agree. But I remembered what Matt had told me: Melody had left Coral unharmed in the Sea of Souls. What would make Melody dismiss such an opportunity to murder the Reigning Queen?

322

"I will... consider her offer for provisions," I said finally. "But let's wait a few days and see how events unfold first."

The messenger nodded and headed off to find a fish small enough to slip through the cavern and deliver the message.

The rest of the afternoon was spent rebuilding the watch-tower Eugene's army had destroyed. We spent hours heaving stone and sticky mud to restore the foundation of the structure. The water darkened as night fell, every muscle in my body aching as I wiped lingering mud off of me and returned to the palace. I ate quickly in the dining hall to fill my empty stomach, then I dragged myself up the stairs, thinking of how much I longed for a glass of liquor before bed.

When I reached my quarters, I was surprised to find Kendra lounging on my bed, her head buried in a book, tail flicking lazily behind her. I clicked the door shut behind me, and she looked up, meeting my gaze.

"Kendra," I greeted softly, my stomach fluttering at the sight of her. She was a welcome surprise.

"You're finally back," she replied, pushing up into a seated position and closing her book. "I wanted to see you and thought I'd wait for you. But if you're too tired—"

I crossed the room, sweeping her up off the bed and holding her close as I kissed her deeply. She let out a soft noise, hands tangling in my hair. I'd been wanting this... for *days* now, craving her kiss, her touch.

"I've missed you," she whispered against my lips, looking up at me through thick lashes as she traced my cheek with her fingers. Her touch made me shiver in anticipation. She pressed closer to me until our bodies were touching, and I forgot about my aching muscles as the tension left my shoulders. My hand

323

snaked around her waist, holding her there, and I kissed her again—this time deliberately slow, teasing. I relished the way she moaned into my mouth... and then I kissed her properly. *Harder*.

Her tail fin curved around my ankle as I gripped the back of her neck. I pushed gently, guiding her back onto the bed, deepening the kiss as I explored her alluring body with my hands. I traced every soft inch and curve before meeting her gaze again. The way she looked at me, her eyes full of longing and desire... didn't she know what she was doing to me? Even now, I felt an ache building between my legs.

We'd barely spoken for days, and now all of this... it occurred to me that things were moving quickly.

"We should stop..." I warned her, but disappointment flickered in her eyes.

"I don't want to," she whispered, reaching up to cradle my neck. "I *want* you, Lysander. I've waited so long already."

I groaned and sucked in a low breath as I surveyed her near-naked body. Between the silk wrap around her tail and her bralette, there wasn't much left to the imagination, but I still wanted her clothes on my bedroom floor. *Now*.

I leaned over her, my wavy black hair drifting to tickle her cheek.

"Well then, I want to see all of you," I murmured, my fingers drifting upward, skimming her stomach, and she gasped as I brushed my hands over her chest. She shuddered, and I felt some of the tension leave her body. "May I?"

She nodded, and I made quick work of untying her bralette and discarding it. She helped with the silk wrap, and then she was bare before me. I leaned down to kiss her stomach, making my way up to her breasts, and she relaxed beneath me, tilting her head back a little.

For someone who had shown constant resistance and stubbornness to my requests, I loved seeing her come so easily undone in front of me. *For me*, specifically.

When I glanced up at her again, her cheeks were flushed, and her lips were slightly parted. Every single reaction filled me with satisfaction, and I couldn't help the smug pride that rose in my chest.

"Look at you," I murmured, watching her as I went back to stroking her breasts, lazily drawing circles there. Her eyes fluttered closed, and I traced my fingers back down her stomach. "The way you give in to me... so *easily*..."

A noise escaped the back of her throat, and my fingers rested along the navel of her stomach—teasing and taunting. I could feel her tail twitch as I grazed where her smooth scales began. Crawling up her body, I leaned down and grazed her ear lightly, eliciting another gasp from her.

"If only I'd known *this* was all I had to do to make you mine."

She whimpered, and that snapped something in me. My playful banter simmered, and something more primal took over—because I *knew* she would react exactly as I wanted her to.

"Do you want me to touch you?"

She made a noise, but it wasn't an answer—it wasn't good enough.

"Hmm?" I pressed, letting my fingers drift back down to her abdomen but never quite going lower. She wriggled beneath me, but I trapped her tail between my legs and held her there. She was panting now.

"Yes," she managed finally.

"Where should I touch you, my love?"

She made another noise, then met my gaze with burning eyes.

"You know where," she hissed back, and I let out a chuckle at her indignation.

"You're going to have to say it," I taunted lowly, a thrill going through me as her face burned. She squirmed needily, and I hummed at her, relishing it. It was written all over her face—she was debating whether to yield herself completely to me, to speak the deepest, dirtiest parts of her mind out loud. Something about it made her flush with embarrassment, and she wasn't so far gone yet that she'd succumb to begging me for what she wanted. After all, Kendra didn't beg for anything.

I decided to make it easier for her as I let my fingers slip lower, to the well-conceived slit just a few inches down. The scales were smooth and slick, and as I brushed the sensitive spot, her lips parted again. I didn't give her what she wanted— not yet—and the noise that escaped her throat was almost strangled.

"Please," she breathed finally.

"You want me to touch you here?" I asked, and she nodded.

I let my thumb press inward. Her hand found my shoulder, gripping it—and she let out something between a gasp and a moan. I slipped another finger inside, and she arched her back, her chest rising towards me. I relished her closeness, wanting to touch all of her, wanting to *taste* her, wanting to ravish her—

She began to move on me, and I let out a low hiss. I leaned down to kiss her neck, her shoulders, grazing at her ear again. She moaned again, this one louder, and that thrill ran through me again as I smirked.

"That's my girl," I whispered against her. "You're *mine*, Kendra."

She tilted her head back into the sheets.

"Harder," she breathed, her voice laced with pleasure. She was *finally* yielding, finally letting herself go for me.

"Like this?" I rasped, plunging my fingers deeper, and she cried out in response. I groaned as I watched her—she was *mine*.

I felt her tighten around me, and moments later, she came—her gasps sweeter than any siren song as she gripped the sheets under me. I thrusted my fingers until she rode out her high, and then she fell limp beneath me, breathless and distant eyed.

I moved back up her body, and she grabbed my shirt, crashing her lips to mine. Her hands went to my shirt, fumbling with the buttons in her desperation. I helped her undo them, and she practically ripped the shirt off of me, hands flying to my pants. We made quick work of those too, and then my lips were back on hers, tongue sweeping into her mouth as I lined myself up with her. Just for a moment, my mind unclouded, and it took all of my restraint to pause.

"You're sure?" I asked, every muscle taut and tense from holding back, and she let out a frustrated groan.

327

"*Lysander*," she begged, bucking her hips. I took the hint.

The first thrust was pure bliss, and she buried her face in the crook of my neck. Bubbles tickled my neck at the sound of her gasp. My hands entwined with hers, bringing them up on either side of her as I set a steady pace.

"Tell me you're mine," I breathed, as pleasure coursed through me.

"*I'm yours*," she moaned. "I'm yours. All of me is yours, Lysander—my heart, my soul, *everything.*"

As I exhaled, something pulsed through my chest. Warm and anchoring. I felt it ripple from my heart outward through the entire Undersea, felt it caress every being in my kingdom. I slowed my pace for just a moment, staring at her with wide eyes, barely able to breathe.

Her eyes locked on mine, and I knew she'd felt it too. Overcome with emotion, my lips devoured hers—*claiming* her—as I increased pace. She was lost beneath me as the pressure built like a tidal wave, and she finally came. It was my undoing, and I followed moments after.

Breathless, our foreheads touched, and her fingers drifted up to trace my cheek.

"What... was that?" she panted, her other hand moving to her chest. I circled my hand around hers, a knowing smile growing on my lips.

She was mine.

"You gave me your heart," I explained softly, warmth spreading through my chest. "You *switched* it with Coral's, effectively undoing her binding and replacing it with your own."

Her eyes widened with shock.

"Wait, *really*?" she breathed. "I didn't know I could do that!"

"Me neither," I replied earnestly, squeezing her hand, and she let out a soft giggle.

"But wait... that means..."

I nodded, leaning back and gauging her reaction with caution. I hadn't wanted to say anything when I first felt the bond snap into place in case she panicked. But instead, her eyes sparkled with excitement, and relief swept through me.

"Yes," I replied. "You are bound to me, Kendra. And I am bound to you."

"I'm... bound to you," she repeated, her voice a whisper. "And I'm bound to rule Veranis with you." She sat up, observing me thoughtfully. "You're okay with that?"

What a silly question, I thought, claiming her lips with mine again. Since the moment she'd gotten here, she had done nothing but think of Veranis first—transforming into mer-form to ensure the kingdom could be protected, fighting for its people when it was attacked.

And I loved her... if there was anyone I wanted ruling at my side, it was her. All of this rang through my mind as I told her, "I can think of no one better to be our kingdom's queen."

CHAPTER THIRTY-FOUR

Coral

Days passed, and I found myself sitting in Matt's workshop shed, where he kept his surfboards and paint. Maya sat perched on a wooden benchtop covered in sawdust and tools, swinging her legs as Matt worked at his table, and I leaned against the bench beside her. It was the first time I'd seen them since we arrived back on the island, as I'd wanted to give Maya the time she needed to reunite with her parents, her grandmother, and to be with Matt again. But I was curious as to how it had gone.

"How did your parents react the other day?" I asked her, and she smiled.

"They were shocked," she admitted with a soft smile. "And they had a *lot* of questions... but they mostly cried. I have to sleep with the door open because they keep coming in to check that it isn't all a dream."

I was glad they had her back and that she was back with them.

"Her grandma nearly had a heart attack though," Matt replied, looking up from his work and ceasing the long, broad strokes he was painting, and Maya nodded gravely. I could only imagine the shock on Ms. Mugo's face; despite being well aware of Melody's siren heritage and the Undersea, she'd said herself that she believed Maya had passed on.

"So... are you guys going back to school?" I asked, raising an eyebrow curiously.

330

"We *are* still minors," Matt reminded me, though we were all so close to turning eighteen that it seemed like an insignificant detail. Matt would be graduating soon, and Maya would have been too if she hadn't been assumed "dead" for the past year.

"I'll admit, school seems... irrelevant after everything we've been through," Matt continued. "But my parents are already furious with me for disappearing for weeks. I had to spin a story about Maya getting in touch and needing help with her rescue."

"And I have to repeat last year," Maya added, grimacing. "I don't think there's any way for us to escape it."

Well, that made things difficult for sure. I'd been wanting to ask them for help breaking my bond with Lysander, but if they were already under their parents' watchful gazes, then it could wait.

"Why do you ask?" Maya asked, glancing my way, and I pushed off the bench.

"Well, Leif and I are going back to the Undersea soon... but I'll be back every now and again," I told them, deciding to keep the details short. "So, I guess I just wondered if you were staying here and for how long. But you guys have a life up here to get back to, and I want to respect that."

"You're going *back*?" Matt demanded, rising from the table. "But you traded your tail... I thought you would turn to sea-foam if you went back to the Undersea!"

"Yeah... about that..." I huffed with a sheepish smile. "We found a loophole, so technically, I'm part undine now."

Matt's gaze bore into mine like stone.

"*What*?"

331

"Why didn't you say anything?" Maya intervened, throwing Matt a puzzled expression as she placed a hand on my shoulder.

I shook my head.

"It just... didn't seem relevant..."

"You *can't* go back there, Coral," Matt insisted, rounding the table now. "You escaped that place. You got away from Lysander—and look, I don't know what's going on with you and Leif, but you have an opportunity to start fresh."

If only it was that easy.

"Matt, you know I can't do that," I replied gently. "I'm still bound to rule with Lysander, and my *sister* is down there. She'll never see me again if I don't return."

He faltered, like he'd forgotten, and dropped his gaze.

"I didn't think about your sister," he admitted, his voice small now. There was a pained look in his eyes. I still had a *lot* to take care of really—I needed to speak to Melody about the mermaids, and we needed to figure out how to dethrone Eugene before he attacked Veranis. If one thing was certain, it was that my life on land would be limited and short lived in comparison to my duties in the Undersea... but I was thankful I could cross between realms now.

"I'll come back," I promised them both with a determined smile. "For surfing, remember?"

Maya's eyes lit up, and Matt's shouldered relaxed a little.

"I can't wait," Maya replied, beaming, and my heart soared in response.

Before heading back to the house, I made one more stop—
parking in a spot next to the boardwalk and stepping out into
the humid day. Palm trees rustled overhead, and the sun shone
so bright, it was blinding as I walked across the creaking
wooden beams toward Snack Shack.

The bell tinkled as I stepped inside, and I spotted Beverly
behind the counter. She was caught up in a midday rush of
customers ordering smoothies and cones, so I waited patiently
behind a group of tourists while she served them. When they
finally left, it was just me, and her eyes met mine and widened.

"Oh my goodness, Coral!" she gushed, dropping her scoop
and flying around the counter. She collided with me, wrapping
me into a tight hug. "Where have you *been?* What's this I hear
about your dad and Melody eloping all of a sudden?"

I stepped back from her.

"I'm really sorry," I said, and I meant it—I'd vanished on
her for weeks, dropping all my shifts. "Things happened, and I
got caught up in some family drama. I would have called, but I
wasn't able to, and I know that's a terrible excuse, but it's the
truth."

I waited for her to start yelling. After all, who couldn't find
just a *minute* of time to call their boss and explain where they
were, unless they were stuck underwater where phones didn't
work?

But she hugged me again.

"Coral, I was so *worried* about you!" she exclaimed, flicking her brown ponytail over her shoulder. "Weeks ago, your
stepmother was acting crazy. And then you *disappeared*, and I
thought she'd bloody murdered you or something!"

333

I nearly snorted—she had *no idea* how close to the truth she was. But her concern was touching—Beverly had always felt like the mother I'd never had. She'd looked out for me, and she'd *listened* to my rants about Melody without judgment when everyone else had assumed I was acting out.

"Things have changed, and I'm not going to be around much anymore," I told her. "So, I've come to officially resign. I know I should be giving you notice... but I can't, and I'm sorry again."

She let out a huff.

"Well, I kind of *assumed* you wouldn't be back," she admitted finally, wiping her sticky hands on her apron. "And I've actually already started training someone new. So this works out for both of us... though I will say, I'm going to miss you, Coral."

"I'll miss you too," I replied, and meant it. This time, I was the one who hugged her, and it felt like the last piece of my old life had been laid to rest for good.

CHAPTER THIRTY-FIVE

Coral

It was just after midday when I finally returned, kicking my shoes off in the doorway and dumping my bag on the side table. Leif had been sleeping on the couch, and I glanced into the living room as I crossed the foyer, expecting to see him lounging or watching TV. But to my surprise, he wasn't anywhere to be seen.

I continued on to the kitchen and found him there instead, drinking a glass of water. The sight made me freeze in the doorway—he was shirtless, and my gaze trailed from his broad shoulders to his throat, watching his muscles flex with every mouthful he swallowed.

Holy hell...

I wasn't usually one to get so flustered around men—I'd seen *plenty* of shirtless men over the years as a surfer. But with Leif, it was different. I couldn't bring myself to look away from him.

He turned to place the glass down on the island counter, and that's when he spotted me in the doorway. I felt my cheeks heat and quickly ducked my head, pretending to have just walked in.

"Hey," I said, trying to sound casual, and mentally cursed the unnaturally high pitch in my voice.

"You're back," he replied, his gaze following me as I crossed to the fridge, reaching up toward the freezer compartment. I heard the glass clink on the countertop as he placed it down. "Sorry... I hope you don't mind me using your stuff."

I grabbed a bag of frozen mango and banana, as well as the ice tray, and turned to dump the items on the counter.

"Please, everything here is yours," I said, giving him a soft smile. They'd given me the same courtesy in Veranis, so it was only fair.

"I didn't expect it to be this humid... and I was craving *water*," he added with a frown, like the concept was foreign— and then it hit me that it was. Leif got his hydration from *being* underwater.

He rubbed his neck with discomfort. His hand came away glistening with sweat, and my thoughts narrowed in on the hollow of his neck. A small part of me wanted to lick up the column of his throat, to taste the sweat there... and I shook the thoughts from my mind. *What the hell is wrong with me?*

I turned away to distract myself. "I'm making a smoothie. You should try some—it'll cool you down," I managed to say, and sidestepped to the pantry to check for shelf-stable milk. Thankfully, I spotted a carton of almond milk nestled at the back and grabbed it.

I hadn't bothered stocking many fresh groceries because I knew we wouldn't be here very long, so I didn't have any fresh spinach or kale. But as I pulled out my blender from under the island and plugged it in, I remembered all the weeks I'd gone eating nothing but sea berries, and I was *more* than thankful to have fresh fruit for my smoothie.

I looked over at Leif again, hyperaware of our proximity as he leaned against the counter and watched me from mere inches away. His gaze was distracting, and my heart thundered in my chest. I couldn't get over how much I wanted to kiss him—the way we'd been kissing nonstop these past few days, from morning to night. But I could sense things were getting more and more heated between us each time... and the thought of taking that next step was as thrilling as much as it was daunting.

As I began loading the blender, I gestured to the ingredients.

"Do you want a glass?"

"Sure," he replied, his voice low and soft. I clicked the lid in place and flicked the switch, and the roar of the blender sliced through the tension between us. Leif winced from the high-pitched noise, and when I flicked the switch off again, the silence between us was deafening. Wordlessly, I turned to grab two glasses from an overhead cupboard, but that's when a gentle hand snaked around my waist and held me from behind.

My hands fell away from the overhead cupboard, but I didn't stop him as he slowly pulled my hair aside, exposing my neck and shoulder, and pressed a feather soft kiss to the skin.

He was so gentle, but he lit a fire inside of me. I couldn't help tilting my head to give him more access, and he pressed warm kisses along my neck and down my shoulder. My lips parted at the sensation, a gasp catching in my throat, and then I turned in his arms. His eyes were dark with need as his lips claimed mine, slow and demanding, and I pressed my body to

337

his, my hands slipping around his neck. He let out a groan, hands moving to my waist as he lifted me onto the counter. Instinctively, my legs wrapped around him, pulling him as close as possible. His kisses were coaxing, and his tongue swept into my mouth as I opened for him.

After a moment, my arms began to stick against his bare chest, and we paused, breathless.

"Wow... you really *are* sticky," I breathed, observing the sweat coating my arms. "I guess you're just not used to the heat."

"It's *extremely* uncomfortable," he confirmed, his eyes seductive and his tone laced with amusement as he traced his fingertips down my arms to my wrists. "And wanting to kiss you was *not* helping."

An idea came to me—one that I was almost too afraid to voice aloud from pure nerves. But I kept my voice steady as I said, "I suppose you've never taken a shower before?"

Leif leaned in to pepper kisses along my jawline and murmured just below my ear.

"No, I haven't."

"Well, what if I told you that it would help with the heat? That you'd feel a lot better afterward?"

He met my gaze again, curiosity twinkling in his eyes as he breathed, "I guess you'll have to show me."

Every nerve in my body was alight and frenzied, and I slipped off the counter and took his hand. If he noticed the tremble in my fingers, he didn't comment as I guided him upstairs and into the main bathroom. I wasn't sure how far this would go... how far I wanted it to go... but I knew I wanted more. Over the past few days, I hadn't been able to shake the thoughts from my mind.

There was a wide, spacious shower on one wall, with a tub beside it and a sink across from that. The showerhead was modern and black, like the rest of the bathroom hardware, and everything else was made of white marble or stone. Even the cold tiles beneath my feet seemed to warm instantly from my heated body as I stepped aside to let Leif view the shower.

Nerves flittered through me, and I hesitated, not knowing what to do or say next, so I pathetically blurted out, "You turn the handle and stand under the water."

Really, Coral? I felt like such a *fucking* idiot.

But Leif didn't seem bothered as he took a step toward me, the hint of a smile on his lips.

"Will you be demonstrating?" he asked slowly, his gaze skittering over every inch of me. "Or shall I do the honors?"

My mouth went dry at the thought, and I couldn't help drinking in the head-to-toe view of him. I realized how easy it would be to command him to lose his pants and show me all of him. To just sit back and soak up the view as steaming, hot water ran down his naked torso. But something was stopping me.

It had felt easier to take the lead around Lysander—like there had been less to judge, less to lose, when he'd been driven by nothing but a curse. With Leif... I didn't want to mess it up, and I was afraid of acting foolish around him. I didn't have much experience... I didn't even really know what I liked or *wanted*...

He came to stand in front of me and ever so gently cupped my face in his hands.

339

"If you want to stop, say so," he said softly, not a hint of judgment in his eyes. "But you should know... I think you're beautiful and sexy as *hell*, and I want nothing more than to see where you were going with this."

His words fueled my courage, and I swallowed. Slowly, my fingers grasped the hem of my white T-shirt and pulled it over my head. His eyes darkened with approval as I unclasped my bra and let it fall to the ground. He let out a sound of appreciation, and before I could protest, he kneeled before me, his hands tracing up my exposed thighs, and once again, I was *so* thankful that I had my legs back because, *holy God*, the effect he was having on me was...

He reached up to grip the waistband of my denim shorts, his eyes meeting mine in silent question. Biting my lip, I nodded, and he dragged them down my legs, so I stood only in my underwear. His eyes seemed to glaze over as he pressed warm kisses to my inner thighs and removed the final layer.

I felt entirely exposed and vulnerable before him, but in a swift moment, he stood and gripped my thighs, lifting me so that my legs circled his waist and my arms circled his neck. He kissed me hungrily, needily, which elicited a moan from my lips. Then he moved, and I realized he was heading for the shower.

"Wait," I breathed, a giggle bubbling in my throat. "You're not naked yet."

"Do you want me to be?"

"You're *supposed* to be, it's a shower."

"I wear clothes underwater all the time," he replied with a faint smirk, but there was a hint of obliviousness in his tone. I couldn't help but laugh, and the momentary stall in tension grounded me in a place of comfort and trust in his arms.

"You sound like Lysander before his curse broke."

His gaze turned possessive—a look I'd never seen before, reserved just for me.

"Well, I hope I fuck better than Lysander," he growled, nipping my ear playfully, and I gasped. Heat pooled between my legs as he pressed me against the cool shower wall, a shiver of pleasure going through my body as his body pinned me there.

"Now, walk me through it again," he murmured into my ear, his lips barely grazing the sensitive skin of my neck. "I turn what, exactly?"

My mind was a haze, and I struggled to think clearly.

"The handle," I managed finally. "Turn it toward us."

He did, and warm water rained down on us both.

"And then?"

"You... wash yourself..." I breathed back, and he let out a low chuckle.

"You mean to say I should rub my body? *Touch it* all over?" I immediately got his drift and simply moaned in response, unable to form words. He grazed the sensitive spot under my ear as he shifted his weight, guiding my left leg down to the ground and keeping the other hooked around his waist. His fingers slid to the space between my legs, and my focus narrowed to that one spot.

"Should I do it like this?" he murmured as two fingers slipped inside of me, and pure pleasure coursed through me. My head fell back against the shower wall. His movements were tantalizingly slow at first, like he wanted to watch every

341

reaction, to study and memorize every movement he made that caused me to moan. Then he increased pace, and I couldn't think, couldn't *breathe*, just desperately wanted more of him, *all* of him.

I fumbled, one hand gripping his upper arm, the other sliding down his stomach toward his pants—*God damn it, why were his pants still on?*

"Not yet," he said, claiming my lips again in a chaste kiss before adding, "I want you to come for me first."

He was *intoxicating* as he coaxed me closer and closer to the edge of release, his warm mouth on mine. And then he bit my bottom lip, and I shattered, a string of breathy moans following course.

He didn't stop working me until I was limp in his arms, and only then did he slowly drag his fingers out of me. My cheeks heated like wildfire as he held them between us, and I wondered if I should be embarrassed. But then he locked eyes with me and slowly sucked each finger clean. My throat constricted—a strangled "*oh*" escaping me—and I was captivated by the way he looked at me. It was clear as day that he wanted me, *all* of me.

I placed a hand against his chest, walked him three steps back into the shower glass, crashed my lips against his, and traced the waistband of his shower-soaked pants. I gripped his belt buckle and hastily undid it, and in moments, the rest of his clothes lay in a heap on the ground. Heart pounding, my hand closed around the length of him, feeling his soft, velvety skin. He closed his eyes for a moment, letting out a soft hiss which lit a fire in my abdomen. I only got three stokes in when a cleaving pain hurled through me, from head to toe, and Leif's eyes snapped open as a choked a gasp. My hand flew to my chest, and his eyes locked onto me.

"What is it?" he asked, grabbing my shoulders as I doubled over. Staggering on the slippery shower floor, I tried to breathe through the rippling agony, and he guided me into a seated position against the shower glass. I closed my eyes, leaning my head against the glass as I took steadying breaths.

"Something just... snapped..." I gasped, waving toward my chest. The pain was fading now, each throb hurting less and less. He ran a hand through my hair, and if he was frustrated with the interruption, he didn't let it show. I felt terrible, but my whole body was shaking—I was going to need a few minutes.

"Something snapped in your chest?" he asked, his gaze serious. "Like a binding? Because I could have *sworn* I just felt something as well."

My brow furrowed.

"What do you mean?" I asked, my voice breathy as my heart beat furiously.

"It was similar to when you became Queen of the Undersea... We *all* felt it. That's how we all knew. Whatever just happened... I felt it too. But it felt more like a power shift."

"You don't think... you and I are bound somehow?" I asked, and he shook his head.

"No. It wasn't like that. But I *do* wonder if your bond with Lysander just broke... because that would explain why I felt it, as an undine."

But... wouldn't that mean he was heartless again? *Crap!* We shouldn't have been doing this. Instant regret washed over me for every kiss, every touch... we should have *waited*...

343

There was a sudden crash from downstairs—something had broken. I tensed, but before I could jump up to investigate, Leif put a hand on my shoulder and squeezed.

"Stay here. I'll go," he said firmly, with a steady gaze. He got to his feet and pulled his drenched pants back on. It was fascinating how he didn't mind wet clothes one bit after living his entire life underwater. I would have told him just to wrap a towel around himself, but I was straining to hear what was happening downstairs, which was especially difficult with the shower running.

Giving me a tender, reassuring look, Leif slipped past and out the door. I waited, trying to listen, but I couldn't even hear his footsteps on the staircase. Just the pounding water on the tiles. Curiosity and anxiety bubbled within like a dangerous concoction, and I tested my strength by pushing up from the ground. My legs were still shaky, but I managed to cease the shower by hitting the handle. Then, on wobbly legs, I crossed the bathroom and grabbed my pink silk robe from the cupboard. Kendra's was hanging inside as well, except hers was blue.

I tied the sash and took another moment to steady myself, waiting for my legs to recover. As moments passed, I tried not to overthink the strange disturbance. Perhaps Matt or Maya had come by and accidently knocked something over. Or one of the resort staff had come by looking for somebody. Rational thoughts continued to pop up as I left the bathroom and crept along the hallway toward the stairs, but with every passing minute, I couldn't shake the thought that something was wrong. And what *had* that strange cleaving sensation been in my chest?

I snuck down the stairs, and as a precaution, I grabbed my phone from my handbag, which I'd dumped on the side table earlier. As I scanned the foyer, I noticed the source of disturbance—a vase lay broken across the room.

"Leif?" I called, my voice wavering as it echoed through the house. I tiptoed to the kitchen and gasped when I spotted him lying on the ground. "*Leif*!"

I sprinted to him and dropped my phone with a clatter as I fell to my knees beside him. He groaned with pain, one hand holding a bloody knife, the other covering his leg. And then I saw the blood seeping through his pants, barely visible in the already-soaked fabric.

No... no, no, *no*!

"What happened?" I demanded, as I gently coaxed his hand away. One look at the wound and I knew it needed medical attention. *Shit*. Panic rose up inside of me. "I... I don't have my magic! I can't heal you!" I stammered, as tears sprung to my eyes.

"Coral," Leif rasped urgently, gripping my wrist with his hand. "*Run!*"

My breath quickened, and a low chuckle sounded. Wild eyed, I spun around and spotted Eugene lingering in the archway closest to the back door.

"*You*," I seethed, getting to my feet. Leif let out a grunt of protest behind me.

"Hello, Coral," Eugene purred, striding forward with a smug smile. "I see you've been busy... in more ways than one."

His gaze drifted down to my bare legs, then up to observe the robe. I gritted my teeth, fists clenched.

345

"Get the hell out of my house."

"Oh? But I'm afraid I have nowhere left to go," he pouted, his voice light and teasing as he flicked his blond hair back. He was so much like Melody, it was uncanny. "Since you insist on breaking every good curse and binding in the Undersea—*including* the one on my sister—I'm afraid I had to come here."

"I won't bind Melody's magic again," I growled. My mind was racing, trying to think of the fastest way to disarm Eugene so I could help Leif before he bled out.

"Oh no, you won't," he agreed. "*I will*. If my sister taught me anything, it's not to sit around and let others do your dirty work—as much as we sirens love handing off those kinds of tasks. But no, if I am to *truly* ensure she has no power over me, I must take it for myself and bind her with my own hands."

"Well, good luck with that," I replied promptly, hands sweating as desperation clawed through me. The only spell he had over Melody was his siren song, and it wouldn't bind her magic permanently without consistent use on her.

"It's precisely why I'm here," he continued, taking another step forward. Leif made a noise from behind me. "You see, my sister took back her throne and kingdom from me when she returned from her little *quest* with you. So now, I seek a higher power—one that not even she can overthrow." His eyes glimmered with greed, and my stomach turned as he said, "I aim to become *Reigning King*."

I shook my head, but I couldn't back up any farther. And I refused to leave Leif exposed to Eugene. "You've come to the wrong place... I'm not Reigning Queen anymore," I replied. My heart pounded as he came closer and closer.

"No," he agreed, a hint of song in his voice. "But my sister never would have left you alive unless she had good reason. So I'm here for leverage—if Melody wants you to live, she'll have to agree to my terms."

It was a fool's assumption, *surely*. Melody and I might be on... tolerable terms. But that didn't mean she was going to come running if Eugene held me hostage again.

"And what makes you think I'm going anywhere with you?" I seethed back, but I knew his siren song could sway me. I thought of turning to grab a weapon—another knife perhaps—but Eugene's song would be instantaneous to stop me.

"Because if you don't, *he* dies," he smiled savagely, and I recognized the low hum in his voice. Turning back to Leif, I watched in horror as he forced himself into a seated position, pain splintering over his face as he did. Shaking from effort, he brought the gleaming, razor-sharp knife to his own throat. His gaze burned as it met mine—burned with pure defiance, even though he couldn't act on it.

My stomach twisted, and my eyes burned with fresh tears at the sight of Leif struggling against Eugene's song. At the delicate edge already pressing lightly into his throat, promising bloodshed. Heaving a breath, I slowly turned back to Eugene. My blood thrummed with abhorrence, especially as his eyes gleamed with satisfaction.

I knew there was no other way. One subtle tone shift in Eugene's voice, and Leif would be dead at my feet. I wasn't about to let that happen.

Blinking back tears, I let my tense shoulders drop.

"What do you want me to do?" I asked finally, and he let out a low hum of approval. The worst part was that he didn't even have to use siren song on me, and he *knew* it. Using it on Leif was enough to get me to obey, and either way, he was going to walk out of here with what he wanted.

"Get on your knees," he ordered, and I let out a shaky breath. I thought of Leif behind me, watching me as I sank to my knees before Eugene, knowing his life hung in the balance of my actions. Eugene's gaze was predatory, filled with malicious intent as he reached into his jacket pocket.

"Give me your hands," he said slowly, and I refused to meet his gaze, glaring at the ground as I raised my clenched fists. I thought he might wrench my fingers free of the stone-like grip I had them in, but instead, I felt two cold shackles close around my wrists.

Startled, I looked up to see they were made of iron. *But I didn't have magic anymore...*

He noted the confusion in my eyes and let out a cold laugh.

"You stupid mermaid," he sang, his voice airy, and suddenly, I couldn't breathe. "I can feel your magic from here. But you were too distraught to even feel it, let alone *summon* it."

My heart plummeted. *No...*

I could have healed Leif this entire time? But how was that possible? I thought back to what the First Sea Witch had said when I made the trade; *soul of a human, body of an undine, heart of a mermaid.*

I'd traded my title for safe passage out of the Sea of Souls... and my *tail* for safe passage between land and sea...

But not my heart, I realized with a start. *Where magic had laid dormant since* before *I transformed into mer-form.* I'd just assumed it was gone with my tail! How could I have been so *stupid*?

Grabbing the chain connecting the shackles, Eugene yanked me to my feet, eliciting a cry from me. He twisted me around to look at Leif, who was still watching with anguish, and held my chin firm between his fingers to lock me in place.

"Take one last look, Coral," he breathed in my ear, and I shuddered with revulsion. "Because you're never going to see your precious undine again. Not when I plan to carve out your heart when I'm done with you."

He let out another laugh, and I knew he was saying this to taunt Leif more than me, who looked murderous as he sweated, straining to keep the knife at bay and remain upright with his injured leg. My heart thundered in my ears. At that moment, I wanted to kill him—more than I'd wanted to kill Melody, more than *anything*.

Eugene grabbed a fistful of my hair, and fresh tears sprang to my eyes as he steered me toward the door. But then he paused and turned leisurely toward Leif.

"You know what? Just in case—we can't have you following us, can we?" he mused, and I noticed the tone of his voice change. My heart rate spiked, and my breathing hitched.

"*No!*" I shrieked, yanking hard against him.

Leif moved, and I watched as he brought the knife down into his other leg. A howl of pain echoed through the room. I screamed at Eugene, angry tears streaming down my face, but he held me tightly with his claws as I thrashed and fought. I

349

could still hear the echo of Leif's howling as Eugene dragged me from the house.

PART FOUR

CHAPTER THIRTY-SIX

Leif

It was blinding, white-hot *agony.*

The moment the siren spell washed away, I slumped to the ground, knife clattering uselessly against the cool tile, my legs throbbing with pain. I knew Coral and Eugene were long gone.

Clenching my teeth, my fists, and inhaling shaky breaths, I looked toward the door. I tried to drag myself across the floor, but Eugene's orders to stab my own thighs had ensured I wouldn't get far. I'd already lost a lot of blood, and there was *no* way I could walk.

I breathed heavily, sweating, scanning the room for something to help me. My eyes landed on Coral's phone—she'd dropped it when she found me. My teeth nearly broke as I clenched them and strained my hand toward the phone. It was too far.

Inhaling a steady breath, I gripped the tiles and dragged myself forward, screaming through my teeth against the pain as my wounded legs pulled against the floor. I did it again and again until my fingers grasped the phone, and I was able to pull it forward. The screen was cracked, and it wasn't like the house phone—it was missing all the buttons. I tapped it everywhere—the front, the back, the sides. It finally flickered to life, and there was a bubble on the screen with Matt's name on it. I kept tapping desperately, panting from effort, and two more words appeared underneath the button. One of them read *call*.

A wave of dizziness hit. I tapped again, and a new screen appeared, with a red and green circle. Confused, I strained to study it, feeling my strength sapping, my focus fading. I didn't know what to do next, but it was already making a ringing sound. And then someone answered.

"Coral, what's up?"

"*Matt*!" I grunted, relief crashing through me.

"Leif?" Matt asked uncertainly, and I tried to talk through heavy breaths.

"Eugene has Coral," I managed to say. The pain was over-whelming, and my vision was spinning.

"*What*? Where are you?"

"Don't worry... about me," I breathed, and the phone slipped from my fingers. "Just... find her..."

It was the last thing I remembered before I blacked out.

"Maya, he needs a fucking *doctor*!"

"*Just trust me*!"

Voices swirled just beyond consciousness, but I was trapped in the dark, struggling to stay afloat, to climb my way out. The louder the voices grew, the more pain I felt, and I willed those voices to leave again.

They did, and silence enveloped me once more.

I didn't know how much time had passed once I came to, in some dark place that smelled of gardenia. A fringing antique lamp glowed dully in the corner, providing the only light that revealed dark wooden walls and weathered floorboards. I tried to sit up, but someone shifted beside me, pressing a damp cloth to my forehead.

"Don't move," she said, and my head lulled sideways to see Maya sitting there. She was reaching for something on the nightstand, and a glass of dark-green liquid came into view. "Drink this—it's crushed herbs that my grandma enchanted. It will speed up the healing process," she offered. With clammy hands, I reached for the glass and brought the strange drink to my lips. It tasted like dirt, and I wanted to spit it out, but I forced myself to drink the whole thing.

"Coral?" I croaked once I'd finished, passing the glass back. Maya shushed me again.

"You need to rest," she insisted. "You lost a lot of blood, and you're not fully healed yet."

I didn't care. I tried to push up from the bed, but my arms shook violently with the effort. Maya leaned back to watch me struggle for a moment, raising an eyebrow to give me a pointed look, and I realized she was right.

Sagging back against the pillows, I panted. My whole body ached, but not nearly as badly as my legs did. I couldn't even muster the energy to pull back the sheets and examine the damage.

I must have lain there for some time because darkness took over again, and I slept until morning. When I opened my eyes, light was streaming in through the windows, the sound of waves sloshed gently from somewhere outside, and birds chirped in the early morning breeze. This time, it was Matt at my side, his hair undone from its usual ponytail. He was sitting back in his chair as he watched but leaned forward as soon as he saw me moving.

"You scared the *shit* out of us," he said, his voice low. "What the hell happened?"

I felt less achy now. More alert. Peering under the sheets, I saw that my legs had been bandaged in cloth.

"Eugene came to the house," I replied slowly, as everything came back to me. "He used siren spell to stop me coming after him as he took Coral. He said he was going to use her to get something from Melody..."

Matt's expression was like stone as he listened.

"He said... he wants to be Reigning King," I continued, before turning to Matt. "He's going to kill Coral—as soon as Melody gives him what he wants. We need to find him."

I stared at Matt. I was grateful to him, but I wished he hadn't wasted time trying to save me. Coral could already be dead, for all I knew. Just the thought made my gut twist.

Matt's expression finally cracked, and something like guilt flashed across his eyes.

"I need to tell you something," he said finally, and suddenly I couldn't breathe. *No...*

It was already too late, wasn't it? I was going to be sick—

"When I went back for Maya... Eugene was on his way to attack Veranis," he confessed, and it took me a moment to pivot from one thought to the next and process his words. "By the time we got out, they'd already begun the siege. I don't know what happened to Lysander or Kendra... or anyone else

355

from your kingdom. But if Eugene came here, seeking *more* power..."

My heart was racing, and I shot up into a seated position. My sisters... my *mother*...

"Why didn't you say anything?" I demanded, my voice a near shout that caused footsteps to come running from somewhere in the house. Matt was eerily calm.

"I was trying to protect Coral. I didn't want her to go running back there, to Lysander, when she'd *just* gotten back to land. I thought... she might stay here with us and return to her old life again."

This was worse than I ever thought it could be. I had an obligation to defend Veranis, and I'd failed them. I'd *promised* my sisters I'd be there to protect them, and I hadn't been.

Maya and an older woman—who was short and frail with white hair—appeared in the doorway as I threw off the blankets and attempted to stand. All three of them leaped forward, crying out in protest.

"You *can't*!" Maya insisted, grabbing my arms. "If you want to walk again, you need to let the medicine do its work!"

"There's no time!" I snapped back, but between the three of them, they had me back in the bed in a matter of minutes. My legs were like jelly, throbbing angrily again from my sudden movement.

"How much longer?" I relented finally, and Maya turned to the older woman with an inquiring look. She sighed.

"Well... given that your undine body is accelerating the healing process, perhaps another day or two," she responded, giving me a once over. "I can see that your energy has improved, which is good. And we can probably remove the stitches tomorrow..."

"But that doesn't mean you can just go rushing straight into a battle," Matt added, with a firm look. "Let us help you. We'll come with you back to Veranis."

"If we do that, our parents are going to *freak*," Maya countered to Matt, but he shrugged.

"Let them. I didn't spend weeks in the Undersea trying to find *you* just to lose Coral immediately after."

The older woman placed a hand on Maya's shoulder and said, "Let me speak to both of your parents."

Matt and Maya frowned at her.

"What are you going to tell them?" Matt asked, and the woman pulled her lips together thinly.

"The truth," she said finally, her voice severe. "They, much like everyone else, have been wondering about those mysterious three weeks where Melody had everyone under her control. Those chunks of memory are missing, and the longer we wait, the more they will dismiss those weeks as a strange dream-like occurrence that never really happened. We should tell them now, while they already suspect something and desire answers."

"They're going to dismiss *you*," Maya protested. "My parents don't even believe in our lineage of witchcraft, let alone a whole *Undersea* of sirens and mermaids!"

"You cannot lie to your parents forever," the woman implored softly. "They will find out the truth eventually, one way or another. And besides... your cover story has holes in it. You think they won't investigate it further if they suspect that you're keeping something from them? If your parents don't pick your story apart, someone with more authority will, landing you in more trouble eventually."

She stroked Maya's cheek with a reassuring smile.

"Everything will be fine. Go with Leif when he is well enough. In the meantime, I'll make another herbal remedy."

She set off back down the hall, leaving Maya and Matt alone with me. Matt turned to me and spoke.

"So, back to Veranis first, then?" he proposed, and I shook my head.

"No. I'll send word to Lysander through fish and have him come meet us," I replied. That was, assuming he'd survived and that he was in a position to leave his kingdom. But as much as I wanted to see my sisters, my mother... we didn't have time to waste venturing all the way back to Veranis. "We're going straight to Melody."

CHAPTER THIRTY-SEVEN

Melody

It had been a long day of meetings and court obligations, hearing out requests from the people, and directing delegations to various relations. I sat in my study on a sturdy red kelp chair with sheer black curtains drifting in the evening current, and I focused on drawing up new documents for alliances.

If someone had told me I'd be doing this days ago, I would have laughed at them. But I'd promised Lorraine I'd take care of her daughters... that I'd make all of this right... and that meant no more war. No more bloodshed that either of them could get caught in the crossfire of.

My new court was full of sirens that Sloane had personally sourced from her small rebellion—all females who had been unhappy with Eugene's rule. But in a society where all one had to do was prove themselves stronger than the monarch, I couldn't understand why they'd so willingly backed me instead of challenging Eugene themselves.

A knock sounded at the door before it cracked open, and Sloane peered inside—she was dressed in a dark-red dress with a revealing slit up the side of her leg. I raised an eyebrow at her.

"No picking locks this time?" I mused, lips curving into a smile. She shut the door behind her and crossed the room. A dagger was strapped to her exposed thigh, and her boots clunked on the onyx floor.

"Well, there's no need to sneak around when you have the queen's favor." She winked and delicately perched herself on the table beside my paperwork. The curve of her bottom covered half of my treaty documents, but instead of annoyance, I found my gaze lingering for a moment. "No word from Veranis yet?"

"None." I shook my head, tapping my quill against the desk. Thankfully, the enchanted ink didn't seep into the water. "I guess everyone still sees me as a monster."

I leaned back in my chair, staring up at the ceiling. I let my thoughts wander for a moment before tilting my head toward her. "I want to know something... why did you seek me out all those weeks ago?"

Sloane watched me with an expression I couldn't quite place.

"Because I knew you were the most *direct* path to getting Eugene off the throne," she replied finally. I shook my head, grimacing.

"And yet, every single one in your rebellion—including yourself—could have gone after Coral, then challenged Eugene for the throne."

A sad smile appeared on her lips.

"Maybe we're tired of fighting the hierarchy for power," she replied, and I couldn't help frowning in response. She shuffled a fraction closer. "Look, it's not a secret that the higher up we females are in our society, the more oppressed we become. Our freedom is a lie—we have to claim a male to confirm our strength instead of marrying for true love. We're expected to prioritize wealth and power over our own well-be-

ing and happiness. The power we higher clans hold is an illusion—because we're not respected, nor taken seriously, unless
we can *prove* our worth through the males at our side."

I nodded—I knew this. It was the realization that Eugene
had helped me come to many years ago as he observed how
power and greed drove our mother to control us.

Sloane shrugged.

"You were the first female to challenge the norm... to show
us what was *really* possible in our society. You took your
power back and ruled independently for *twenty years*, Melody."

I shook my head.

"It wasn't like that... it wasn't intentional..." I protested.
Yes, I'd escaped my fate... but Nikolai's death had been luck,
and my mother's death had been pure desperation. I'd gone on
to lose myself to a curse when Lorraine fled, and I'd spent the
past twenty years focused on an intricate revenge plan to tear
her family apart. If I hadn't been so focused on that... *would* I
have taken a siren husband?

"When your brother stepped into power, things were different again... but your brother is not you, Melody. You are
one of the *only* sirens to have ever experienced true power."

"What are you talking about?" I asked, my brow furrow-
ing, and she smiled softly.

"Love," she said simply. "The most powerful magic of all.
You loved the Atlantis princess, and she loved you. How
many sirens go their *entire* lives without ever experiencing it?
Marrying for strategy instead of love? Ruining their family
ties out of power and greed, like your mother did?"

361

"So... you wanted me on the throne because you think I'm more powerful for having loved?" I asked carefully, and Sloane let out a sound of frustration, jumping off the table.

"But you didn't just *love*, Melody—you helped us see that things could be different. That we could create a society where true happiness is possible within its people. The problem is the lower clans would never understand. They have more options, more freedom... they don't understand what it's like to be in our shoes until they're so high up, they can never come back down without dishonoring themselves and their entire family. We'll never end the cycle without someone like you at the helm—someone with firsthand experience understanding love and *happiness*—who can change our society from the top down."

Ah.

I finally understood. It wasn't that they hadn't been strong enough to go up against Eugene. They saw me as the key to real, *long-term* change.

"Well, I appreciate that you trust me with such a task," I replied slowly. "But this is far easier said than done. To change the years of conditioning on our people... it will take time, and I expect there will be pushback from the lower clans."

"Yes, that's true," Sloane replied. "But we are all prepared to help you—you have advocates from the highest clans in Coronis backing you inside your very own court now. We all desire the same kind of change... we want the chance to know love for ourselves. To take back our own power, to experience total freedom and independence *without* the requirement of claiming a male to be seen as worthy."

I shook my head as I thought about all the things we would need to do, the changes we would have to implement.

"When Eugene first took the throne... we had riots in the streets over it," I muttered lowly. "People refused to come to court and make their requests. If we start making all these uncomfortable changes... how are we going to make them see and *trust* in the kind of society we're trying to build for them?"

"Well," Sloane said, her voice low and quiet, placing a hand on my upper arm. I glanced from her manicured claws to her brown eyes. "You could start by allowing yourself to have something you've always wanted. You could marry a *female*... for love."

My eyes widened at her bold statement, yet she continued.

"Can you imagine how many sirens have been sitting in the shadows, wanting to be with female partners and choosing not to out of pressure from their parents to claim a male and raise their status?" She continued quietly. "You giving in to what your heart *truly* desires is the perfect way you can lead by example. You can show us what a society filled with happiness looks like by *being* happy, Melody."

My heart beat with possibilities. But mostly, I found myself fixated on her—on the way she was looking at me as she spoke of all this marriage and love.

"I'm open to it," I replied finally, my voice strangely husky. "But the question is, whom would that female be?"

Her gaze softened, and she walked around my chair to face me head on.

"Well, I already bought *you* a drink. From memory, you still owe me one—even after all the times I scaled the palace to your window," she reminded me, leaning forward to press her palms against the sides of my chair as her lips quirked upward.

I raised an eyebrow coyly at her.

"Shall I make you a drink then, Sloane?" I asked, my tone soft as my lips curved into a smile. I leaned back in my chair, letting my gaze roam up and down—just once. Enough for the appreciation I had for her to show on my face, which caused her eyes to darken. She stepped forward and straddled my lap, her dress riding up her thigh to expose more of her skin. My heart began to beat faster as she wrapped her arms around my neck.

"You can make me one later," she whispered, and then brushed her lips against mine.

I woke the next morning to rapping on my bedroom door. My head had a subtle ache, and I groaned as I sat up.

"Enter," I commanded, checking that I was decent and pressing the heel of my palm to my forehead to steady the pain. The door opened, and one of the palace guards stood there, gaze focused ahead.

"Your Majesty, I must inform you that we've been stolen from."

I glanced at the guard, frowning.

"What has been stolen?" I asked carefully.

"The Atlantis crown, Your Majesty. There was a note left with it."

I crawled out of bed and crossed the room, taking the note and scanning it. My gut rolled by the time my eyes reached the bottom.

"Clear my schedule, and call an emergency council in the throne room," I said, grabbing a long sheer robe from near the door and tying it around my nightclothes before marching out.

Ten minutes later, I was sitting on my throne, already pondering the note and what my next move should be. My *insufferable* brother. Not only had he taken the Atlantis crown, but he had Coral and was demanding that I hand *my* crown over to him if she was to live.

On one hand, I had a duty to Coral's care, as per my promise to Lorraine. But on the other... I *finally* had my power back and a new purpose for my kingdom. Last night with Sloane had been... the most *amazing* night of my life in a very long time, and I wanted to bring the kingdom we both wanted into reality. That wouldn't be possible if I traded my crown for Coral.

And besides... I had already guessed Eugene's game. He had one crown already, perhaps two depending on what had happened in Veranis. One more, and he'd be physically stronger than me—strong enough to kill the Klassan twins before I could sing a single word to stop him. And then the entire Undersea would be at his mercy.

Sloane finally turned up, with heavy circles under her eyes—no doubt from the lack of sleep. We'd spent almost the entire night drinking and kissing and... touching, though things hadn't gone further than that.

"What has happened?" she asked, her voice rough from sleep as she came to stand beside the throne. I silently passed her the note, my gaze still trained to the floor. I hated to admit it... but I didn't know what to do next.

"Oh... Melody..." she breathed, as she finished reading. "You're not going to do as he says, are you?"

"I do not *desire* to hand him back power," I clarified, finally meeting her gaze. "But he has Coral. And he will kill her..."

Sloane shook her head, planting a hand on her hip.

"He'll kill her anyway," she pointed out. "As soon as he gets your power."

It was an impossible situation. I could create a binding to grant Coral's temporary safety... but it would be easily undone once Eugene had my crown. His siren song would overpower mine in every single way.

"Is there no other way to overpower Eugene?" Sloane pressed tensely, and I thought of everything I knew about ancient Undersea magic. Unlike the hierarchy systems and associated magic tied to each individual kingdom, becoming a Reigning Queen or King was much different. There were multiple ways to claim that power, but none of them easy. But if I was going to overpower Eugene... the only way would be to become Reigning Queen myself, which was something I'd already failed to do by brute force.

If I took the relationship route, I would need a tie to Veranis, Atlantis, *and* land, and my only ties were the Klassan twins. But it wouldn't be enough—our relationships lay in pieces that still needed mending.

The only person who had a better chance of overthrowing Eugene was Coral herself... and she was currently his prisoner.

Lorraine, tell me what to do, I thought, leaning back in the throne and staring up at our newly repaired glass dome ceiling. But Lorraine was gone forever—it was up to me to protect her girls now.

There was commotion from the foyer as voices began to echo, and I straightened once more. I thought I'd told the guards to clear my schedule, and a bitterness came over me. But then, three familiar figures entered the throne room, and my shoulders relaxed slightly.

"Well, well," I mused, eyeing the Veranis king's commander, the sea witch—who looked more vibrant and alive than ever—and Coral's human friend. "I suppose I should have expected you three."

CHAPTER THIRTY-EIGHT

Coral

My wrists and legs ached from where Eugene had strung me up, bound by thick, strong strands of kelp. My magic remained snuffed by the iron shackles around my wrists, the chain hanging limply between my arms.

Eugene had only used his siren song on me once so far, with one order: *don't talk*. And so, I'd remained hanging, my stomach gnawing with hunger, my limbs weak and taut. I didn't know if he was letting me starve on purpose or if he'd forgotten I needed to eat, but I couldn't utter a single word to ask.

Somewhere deep inside of me, I longed to scream and sob. All I could think about was Leif, how I'd left him bleeding, and the sound of his screams still echoing in my ears. My mind kept reminding me of the inevitable: *he was dead*.

I wanted to believe otherwise, to hope otherwise... but it was too painful. Too unlikely. I couldn't even let myself go there, only to be slapped by an unbearable reality at some point.

Silent tears had blurred my vision for days until I'd shed so many tears, they would no longer form. Eugene had paid no mind; not long after he'd strung me up, he'd busied himself, coming and going from whatever cave he'd dragged me to. The water was almost as cold as the Sea of Souls, and it was nearly as dark too.

Eugene had not long returned to the cave, placing two familiar crowns on a flat surface of rock across from me. I watched him and tried to distinguish the crowns from one another.

The first was bronze... so it must represent Atlantis. The second was bornite, so Veranis then. But I couldn't make sense of why they were here, how he'd come to be in possession of them.

He caught sight of me staring, and a smile tugged at the corner of his lips.

"Finally stopped crying?" he asked, striding over to me. My heart rate instantly spiked, but the kelp restraints stopped me from retreating, from putting any distance between us. He came to stand in front of me, drawing his dagger slowly. I eyed it with disdain, trying to calm my racing heart.

"Worry not, dear Coral—your misery will end soon," he promised, bringing the dagger up and trailing the sharp edge against my cheek. I stiffened, muscles locking, hyperaware of that deadly edge. My cheek stung, and I was sure he'd grazed me. "But unfortunately, I must keep you alive just a *little* while longer."

He stepped back, admiring the tinge of blood that drifted from the blade into the water, and I let out a steadying breath.

"Once I gain back the Coronis crown from Melody... I can finally take what I need from you."

He turned his back on me, drifting back to examine the crowns seated on the stone slab. If Eugene was desiring to take Melody's crown by force... then that meant these weren't the same crowns from the Sea of Souls. They *looked* the same, but perhaps the crowns I'd found there had been purely symbolic, more likely the root of the ancient bindings that connected each crown to its territory.

These crowns glinted rock solid, meaning he'd physically taken them from their territories. *From Lysander's very head*, I realized, and horror washed over me like a tidal wave.

Eugene wanted to be Reigning King... just as Melody had sought to be Reigning Queen. But Melody's strategy had been brute force—domination of kingdoms and strategic power plays. Neither of them had relationship-based ties to all four territories, meaning that Eugene would have to do what Melody had once done and take the power rather than inherit it.

Atlantis had been in ruins for years now. If Eugene had attacked Veranis while we were gone and taken Lysander's crown... then once he got Melody's crown, only one thing would remain—

To snuff out the last living heirs to land and rule over all four territories.

He would carve out my heart, then Kendra would be next... and just like that, he would be Reigning King. *The most powerful being in all of the Undersea.*

I *couldn't* let that happen. But I didn't know how I was going to get out of here.

I'd been so caught up in my thoughts that I didn't register his approach until he was right in front of me again. He grabbed my chin between his fingers and pulled me hard against the restraints toward him.

"Now," he sang slowly, his song washing over me. "I hate to do this... but I must meet with Melody for negotiations. And I can't have you escaping and ruining my plans while I'm gone. So I'm going to need you to go to sleep for a little while."

I wriggled, trying to break free of his grip. I was relieved that siren song had its limits; you couldn't command instantaneous results without an accompanying action, such as ordering someone to drop dead on the spot or fall asleep on command. But when Eugene's gaze narrowed into something cruel, I knew what he had in mind was far, *far* worse.

"Stop breathing until you pass out," he ordered with a vicious smile.

The lyrical command sunk into my skin, my lungs, and I couldn't inhale. Panic seized me as Eugene let me go. Crashing agony rippled through my chest. I couldn't scream—half because of his order not to speak and half because there was no air in my lungs anyway. I gasped helplessly, wrenching against the restraints as blackness dotted my vision. As water slowly filled my lungs. As a sluggishness took hold of my already aching muscles, lulling me into a dreamless unconsciousness.

CHAPTER THIRTY-NINE

Leif

"Take me through it again," I said, looking at Melody from the opposite end of a strategy table. Under normal circumstances, I doubted any of us would be allowed in here—where defense strategies and maps were openly displayed. So much vital intel and knowledge that I could memorize or swipe and use against Coronis.

But Melody hadn't once protested, insisting that we use the table to map out a plan of attack. She'd marked a spot on the map between Coronis and Atlantis—the meeting location Eugene had given her in his note. It wasn't where Coral was being kept, but we could only assume she would be somewhere nearby.

"I have until midnight to meet him here," she repeated, tapping the spot on the map. "If I don't show, he will kill Coral regardless of whether I deliver my crown. Except then, I expect he'll try a more offensive strategy or target someone else important to me."

Her eyes flicked to Sloane, but I was still trying to comprehend how Coral would ever be considered important to Melody.

"So, we need to trap him," I insisted. "And make him tell us where Coral is."

Melody shook her head in response.

"Absolutely not—my brother is not dumb," she replied slowly, folding her arms. "He will turn around immediately if he catches sight of any of you or senses that there is something amiss. Our *best* chance of getting Coral is for me to go in alone."

"You can't," Sloane protested, stepping forward from the corner of the room. "You're queen of Coronis, Melody—you're too important."

"I can guarantee he will suspect *anybody* else who delivers my crown," Melody replied shortly. "He will already suspect me, but at least he'll feel that he knows me well enough to overcome any of my tricks."

"He does know you—and it's very likely that he *will* overcome them," Sloane shot back. "That's *exactly* why we're in this position right now!"

"Stop fighting," Matt cut in, ignoring the scalding glare Sloane threw him. "I'm trying to understand something here—the crowns you keep speaking of. I thought they disintegrated with Coral?"

"They were symbolic," Melody explained, eyes trained on Matt now. "Based in magic and hidden away to maintain the bindings that the real crowns are tied to. The *real* crowns always reside with the True Ruler of each territory; hence Eugene needs me to hand mine over as it cannot be taken from my head without a power play of some kind. That is how Coronis hierarchy is structured."

Matt muttered something about how confusing that was, but his words gave me an idea.

"When we were in Atlantis, King Malvin wore a crown," I said to Melody. "Obviously, it wasn't the real one; it was a stand-in crown because you had the real one here."

Melody narrowed her gaze as she listened, nodding.

"What if we create a replica for you to bring to Eugene?" She paused for a moment.

"It's a good idea, but it has a flaw," she replied finally. "Eugene already knows how the crown is supposed to feel—the magic that flows through it. He'll know as soon as he touches it that it's fake."

"So, you don't give it to him until we can find Coral," I pressed, rounding the table to tap the meeting point. "We will hide ourselves somewhere around the meeting point, and you will go with Eugene, withholding the crown until you can get to Coral. We will follow you, and we can take him down together once we have her whereabouts."

Melody considered my words, nodding slowly.

"He will be persistent... but yes, I believe I can hold off until I reach Coral. You will need to act quickly once we reach her—as soon as he realizes he's been tricked, he'll turn on us all."

I was raring to go right this moment. But the journey to the meeting point would take at least a few hours... and we'd agreed to wait until nightfall in case Lysander showed up. I didn't know if he would be coming or not—I'd been able to send word to him through fish, but I didn't have the ability to hear them and receive their responses.

"I am going to go rest and prepare. I suggest you all do the same," Melody said, turning to the door. She gestured to Matt and indicated for him to follow. "Come. I have had rooms prepared, and I will show you how to find them."

Matt seemed hesitant, but after a moment, he followed Melody out of the room. Sloane brought up the rear, leaving Maya and I in the strategy room. I was inclined to follow

Matt, but my eyes raked over the map a few more times, wanting to memorize every single detail. Tension swirled in my gut—this couldn't go wrong. I *couldn't* lose Coral.

Maya came up to stand beside me.

"Leif... I know you don't want to hear this, but you should stay behind." I opened my mouth to argue, but she gave me a pointed look. "Your legs are *barely* healed. Let Melody and the rest of us deal with this."

I shook my head, backing into a seat behind me and burying my head in my hands. "I'm not going to sit around here just *waiting*," I said finally, meeting her gaze again.

Maya kneeled at my side, placing a comforting hand over mine.

"It's clear to me that you care about Coral a great deal," she said softly. "And I appreciate that—she's my best friend. But that's why we can't leave *anything* to chance. If you want to ensure the best possible outcome, you'll leave this to us."

I glanced at her hand and felt a strange shift of power pass through her fingers. *A binding.*

"What are you doing?" I snapped, yanking my hand back, and she gave me an apologetic look.

"Calling in my favor," she replied, getting to her feet again. "Until the mission is over, you and Matt will stay here, in the Cora Palace, and recover."

Damn it—the blasted manta ray! We *never* should have used it to rescue Coral the first time.

The door opened again, and I glanced over scathingly. But the anger ceased the moment I saw who stood there.

"Lysander!" I exclaimed, leaping to my feet and wincing as a dull ache went through my thighs. He was with Kendra and Nerissa, and all three of them met me halfway across the room. Without thinking, I pulled Lysander into a hug, slapping him once on the back. He returned the gesture.

"Glad to see you're alive," he replied with a smile, and guilt crashed through me again.

"I wasn't there when Eugene attacked—what *happened?* Is my family okay? Is the kingdom—"

He held up a hand to stop me from rambling.

"Everything is fine," he promised, and there wasn't a hint of anger in his gaze. "Your family was safe in the Vera Palace the entire time. And we've already started rebuilding the kingdom."

"How did you survive the attack?" I pressed, and he turned to Kendra. Only then did I notice that she seemed to radiate more power than before, wearing a mauve bralette adorned with amethysts and sapphires, and a chalcopyrite crown that would have complemented Lysander's bornite one.

"Kendra sealed the kingdom with crystal, putting an end to the siege," he explained, and there was a look of pride in his eyes. I glanced between the two of them.

"You're queen of Veranis," I stated finally, locking eyes with Kendra as it sank in. *That's* what I'd felt ripple through my chest few days ago—Lysander's binding hadn't broken; it had just shifted. "How did this happen?" I felt like I'd missed so much since leaving for the Sea of Souls.

Her cheeks flushed. She glanced at Lysander as their hands brushed, and I found myself regretting the question.

"You know what? Never mind—I'm happy for you both," I said quickly, and it was true. It seemed that they'd *finally* admitted how they felt about one another. I'd been growing weary of the constant sneaking around and dancing around one another's feelings, especially while Coral had been caught up in the middle of it. But now... we needed to focus on her and how to get her back.

"I ran into to Melody on my way over here," Lysander said. "She explained the plan and said she only wants a small party to accompany her to the meeting location. We've both agreed that only myself, Kendra, and Maya should go. After all, the less beings, the less chance of being spotted—and three of us will have magic at the very least."

"Last I checked, I was commander—" I protested, but Maya stepped in.

"Smart thinking," she advised, though her tone was carefully guarded around Lysander. She eyed him with disdain as she added, "I have already bound Leif and Matt, who will stay here until someone returns."

Lysander observed Maya for a moment, like he was seeing her for the very first time. I realized this was the first time since her death that Maya had her soul around him again.

"Well then, we should waste no more time," Lysander concluded with a firm nod. He glanced at me and added, "I'll bring her back. I promise."

I gritted my teeth, a lump in my throat as everyone began to file out of the room again. But as Maya passed, I found myself reaching for her arm.

"Wait," I said, catching her, and she glanced back at me. "Take this—give it to Melody."

I fished out the stone that the First Sea Witch had given Coral in the Sea of Souls and placed it in Maya's hand. "The only one who can use it is Coral—but don't let Eugene get his hands on it."

Maya nodded, her hand curling around the stone.

"Also, if something happens... tell Coral that I..."

I swallowed hard, the words getting stuck in my throat.

"Tell her that I love her," I said finally, my voice cracking, and Maya's eyes softened.

"Tell her yourself—when we bring her back to you," she replied with a smile.

CHAPTER FORTY

Kendra

The four of us rode our seahorses to a secluded valley of seamounts just before the meeting point. Melody stopped and encouraged us to make camp, saying she would ride on ahead and wait for Eugene.

We'd left in the late afternoon, and now, it was near midnight. Lysander guided the seahorses over to tether them on a rock, then found a place for us to rest in the shelter of the seamount, away from the rippling currents.

Maya was the first to slump down against a boulder. I tucked my tail underneath my bottom and sat opposite her, and Lysander joined me moments after.

"We have some time before they're supposed to meet," he told us. "But one of us should find a vantage point soon and keep an eye on the meeting spot."

"I'll go," Maya offered, getting to her feet again.

"You can rest first if you need to," Lysander offered, but she shook her head.

"I'm okay. I'll call out if I notice anything strange," she said, striding off around the seamount. I watched her go and didn't blame her for wanting to leave. It must have been so uncomfortable to be in the presence of the male who had pulled her from her regular life, drowned her, and sparked her transformation into the sea witch.

Lysander kept fidgeting like he too was uncomfortable, and I placed my hand in his to steady him.

379

"Don't stress about it," I told him gently. "The worst is in the past now."

He met my gaze, and his hand traced the side of my face, all the way down to my jaw.

"She's still our sea witch. I want to make amends with her rather than risk another curse."

"I'm sure time will heal the wounds it can heal... and everything else will fall into place the way it's meant to," I replied, and he gazed at me with appreciation. Leaning forward, he pressed a soft kiss to my lips.

"It's funny you say that because speaking of things falling into place... I have a working theory about our binding," he said suddenly, and I raised an eyebrow at him.

"Do tell."

"Well, as you know, I used to be heartless... and the terms of my curse were simple: one must give me their heart, unconditionally, in order for me to gain a moral compass and my humanity."

I nodded—this was common knowledge to me at this point.

"And what would eventually *break* the curse was a mortal being—an irregularity in our world, because for thousands of years before the last Sea Witch passed, none of us were able to go to land. I thought Coral was different—thought she was the *one*—because from the first moment I saw her, my soul recognized that she was part human, part mermaid. She was the irregularity."

He held my hand in his, drawing slow, lazy circles over the top with his thumb.

"But I had no emotions, no humanity, no compass to guide me back then... and my theory is that it was always supposed to be *you* who broke my curse, not Coral. Except I didn't know you existed until *after* I met Coral. And by then, my heart had already recognized an irregularity, and I'd grown obsessed, unable to see that you held the power as well."

"So, us being identical twins deceived your own curse?" I smirked, and he nodded with a sheepish smile.

"It probably didn't help that Coral was always the one surfing within sight, and you likely had your nose buried in a book up in your house—so I just didn't know there was any-body else capable of breaking it. And then you spent weeks trapped in a crystal coffin while I dragged Coral down to the Undersea... and I wasted so much time trying to convince and woo her, thinking that *she* was the key. In reality, you *both* held the power to break my curse... but I can't sit here and pre-tend like there aren't clear signs it was supposed to be you."

"And what signs do you speak of?"

"For one, the fish," he stated, gesturing to the flock of dwarf fish that now followed me everywhere I went—trilling contentedly. "It's *not* normal that you can talk to them—it's a power exclusively reserved for undine royals. It's almost like the Undersea knew you were meant to be queen of Veranis and gifted you the power to nudge us in the right direction."

"That makes a lot of sense," I mused, and I found myself lost in his sea-green eyes as he talked.

"And the way everything unfolded," he continued, leaning closer like he couldn't help himself. "You *immediately* felt at home in Veranis, were content to stay, and loved having ac-cess to the marine life and gardens. Coral spent the entire time fighting to escape, like she would never be comfortable. Plus, we have far more in common—we love to dance, we love marine life... we're a perfect match."

It was true, and I loved hearing how perfectly aligned we seemed to be.

"I wonder how different things might have been if you'd spotted me first," I said, leaning my head on Lysander's shoulder and nuzzling close to him. "But then again... if Coral hadn't been down here first, determined to find a way to save our father, then we would still have so many unresolved problems with Melody and Maya. Perhaps things played out *exactly* the way they were supposed to, even if it doesn't make sense looking back."

"Perhaps you're right," he agreed, and kissed the top of my head. "But what I do know to be undoubtedly true, Kendra, is that you and I are meant for each other. And my heart is wholly and unconditionally yours until the end of time."

I echoed the sentiment by reaching up and bringing his head down to meet mine, kissing him deeply. We were so lost in each other that we didn't hear the approaching footsteps until Maya cleared her throat. Jolting, my gaze whipped to where she stood a few feet away.

"Eugene has arrived," Maya said gravely. "We should send the fish now."

It was our stealth plan—to send the fish to track Eugene and Melody, then have them report back their location so we could pursue without being spotted and disarmed. We would have a narrow opportunity to pull this off, and we needed to proceed carefully.

"You know what to do," I told the fish flittering above our heads, and they chirped their agreement. The seven fish that always followed me most closely scattered, all taking an individual route as they headed off toward Melody and Eugene.

Then, the rest of us got to our feet and prepared to follow pursuit.

CHAPTER FORTY-ONE

Coral

My lungs felt as if they were filled with water—heavy and aching—as I slowly came to. My limbs were more sluggish than before, screaming for relief against the restraints.

I was starting to hope Eugene had been serious about death. Starting to wish he'd hurry up and get it over with. Too exhausted to care about much else, I closed my eyes and tried to drift off again. But it wasn't long before I heard voices, and my breathing stilled.

"She had better be here, Eugene," a female seethed, and Eugene's response was light and airy.

"Of *course* she is, Sister, have I ever lied to you?"

Footsteps echoed in the cave, and I pretended to be asleep. I didn't have the energy to face either one of them—though I couldn't believe Melody had actually shown up. I could sense their approach, and the logical part of my brain was screaming at me to open my eyes and pay attention. But every other part of me had given up.

Let them do their worst, I thought warily. Because even if Melody had come, I knew she wouldn't be strong enough to go up against Eugene alone.

A hand grazed gently over my arms, brushing the cuffs along my wrists. I almost flinched at the soft touch.

"I see that you took no chances," Melody said curtly, her voice laced with distaste. It appeared to be a casual, harmless touch—but I felt her hand press against mine, and something was pebbled there.

I stiffened, fingers carefully closing around the small lump. It was smooth, and I tried to figure out what it was...

The stone.

It took everything in me not to react, not to snap my eyes open. How had Melody gotten this? It had been on Leif... did that mean Leif was—

"Let her go, and I'll hand over the crown," Melody said, and I sensed a shift as she stepped away from me. "Her friends are waiting for her safe return—*all* of them."

She said it with emphasis, like she was trying to tell me *Leif was alive.*

I slowly opened my eyes, feigning as if I'd just woken. Melody blocked me from view, her back to me—perhaps she was trying to give me a chance to use the stone? But I was still bound by Eugene's siren song, unable to speak the words required to use the stone. If only I could request my freedom somehow...

No, I realized. Even if I got free, Eugene was too powerful. And even if Melody and I escaped this place, he would come after us again and again. He would never *ever* stop coming until he got what he wanted—and if it wasn't me he murdered first, it would be Kendra, my precious sister.

I couldn't use this stone to get free. I had to use it to stop Eugene once and for all. But how could I do that?

"Place your crown on the slab, and *then* I'll free her," Eugene replied coolly, with folded arms, as he eyed his sister. Melody didn't move, and I tried to speak—tried to, but

385

couldn't. I needed to break his siren spell first... but the only thing powerful enough to break it was love.

"What's the matter, Sister?" Eugene drawled savagely. "I do hope you're not trying to trick me when I've been so *openly* cooperative with you."

Melody let out a small noise. Slowly, she reached up to her head, to the golden crown glimmering there, and removed it. She crossed the room and placed it on the slab with the other three. Now they all sat together—a trio promising destructive power.

Eugene's eyes gleamed hungrily at the sight. He tilted his head at his sister.

"I knew I could count on you," he drawled, crossing to the crowns. Picking up the Veranis and Atlantis crown, he merged them—the same way I'd done in the Sea of Souls. Melody spared me a glance—her eyes wide with urgency as her gaze flicked up to the stone concealed in my palm. I shook my head, trying to convey that I was mute, and Melody restored her cool, masked expression as her gaze flew back to Eugene. His hand now hovered above the Coronis crown.

"Enough, Eugene," Melody mused, brushing his hand away firmly. "You promised to free Coral first—the crown will still be there when you're finished."

Eugene's eyes glittered darkly at his sister, and he straightened his stance, placing the first two combined crowns on his head.

"Very well," he purred. "But I won't have you getting in my way."

His song was so sudden, so overwhelmingly powerful.

"Back up against the wall, Melody."

She complied, looking furious as her legs betrayed her. Eugene followed her until she hit the cave wall, surrounded by strands of kelp, and he quickly tied her wrists so that she couldn't move. Then he finally looked to me.

"Now then—if you want Coral to be free, then I shall free her... of her *misery*."

My heart began to pound. *No...*

I'd thought Leif was dead. But he was alive, Melody had come for me, and I had the stone—*I couldn't die now*!

Eugene drew his dagger, the blade glinting dangerously, and I wrenched my wrists against the kelp frantically. Closer and closer he came, and the words I yearned to say burned on my tongue, but no amount of internal screaming caused them to manifest aloud. Melody cried out in protest, trying to angle her hand, her claws, but she was as trapped as I was.

Eugene came to stand before me, dagger angled at my heart, and he gave me a pitying look.

"I'd ask you if you had any last words, but..."

His smile was savage and knowing, and I closed my eyes, reality setting in.

I thought of Kendra—my precious sister—who I hoped would escape Eugene's vicious plans. I thought of my dad and my mother, whom I was moments away from joining. I thought of Leif... charming, kind, and wonderful Leif, whom I hadn't had enough time with. I'd never told him how I felt about him, deep down, and it pained me.

A tear escaped my eye, and sound choked from my throat as his name ran through my mind over and over like a prayer.

"*Leif*," I gasped, stunning both Eugene and myself as my eyes snapped open again. Eugene frowned, then snarled.

"How touching," he sneered, clearly not amused. But I'd realized my way out just as Eugene drew the dagger back, ready to plunge.

Love is more powerful than any siren song.

Heart pounding in a frenzied panic, I focused on Leif in my mind's eye—all the moments I'd shared with him, every physical feature, every detail—and felt into it as I tried to speak the words one more time. And like a rush of water, they spilled from me as Eugene's dagger shot forward.

"*I wish to trade my voice for Eugene's siren song!*" I cried, and the stone felt hot in my hand as the binding snapped into place—tearing through my throat and causing me to rasp. Eugene recoiled, stumbling back and snarling, his hand flying to his throat. The combined crown on his head broke into pieces, crumbling down around him as a ripple of power blasted through the Undersea.

"*No!*" he spoke, but his voice was normal. Not a single edge of harmony to it. His eyes widened, nostrils flaring as he stared at me. "What have you *done*?"

Snarling, he lunged at me again with the dagger.

"Stop," I ordered calmly, and my voice flowed with song, washing over him and causing him to freeze and drop the dagger. It clattered to the cave floor. A spark of excitement ignited—I'd never felt so powerful before.

Voice of a siren.

I was the embodiment of *four* beings now—mermaid, undine, human, and siren. I had each of their most powerful gifts. "Untie me," I added firmly, a slow smile spreading over my lips.

Eugene seethed and marched forward. Unable to help himself, he first bent down to free my ankles, then reached up and loosened the strands of kelp holding me up. My exposed wrists and cuffs slipped through the restraints, and I opened my mouth to speak my next order.

His clawed hand immediately seized my neck, squeezing as hard as possible. Pain erupted, and I let out a choked sound, hands flying to pry his fingers away but failing. He lifted me so I was inches from the ground, eyes blazing.

"Try to order me now, little mermaid," he taunted, narrowing his gaze. I was kicking, choking, desperate for air. Not a single sound escaped my throat from the pressure of his choke hold. I still couldn't use magic—he had freed me from the kelp but not the cuffs. I couldn't rip his hand away from my throat, so my palms flew to his chest, trying to push back. But he was too physically strong for me to fight.

"Eugene!" Melody pleaded. "*Stop!*"

Dark spots were appearing again in my vision, and I knew this time, I wouldn't wake up from it. He would carve out my heart the moment I fell unconscious. I'd been so close to freedom. *So close...*

A heaving cry erupted from behind us, and I heard a sickening squelch, fast as a whip. Eugene gasped, and his grip loosened. I managed to wrestle free, dropping to the floor and coughing violently. Bubbles blew past from my mouth, and I inhaled a deep breath of sweet, sweet air.

A moment later, Eugene slumped to the ground with me, and that's when I saw the blood tingeing the water. A clatter followed as Melody dropped Eugene's dagger to the floor and stared down at her brother.

One look at the side of the cave, and I saw that she'd ripped herself free of the kelp with her claws. When I looked back at her face, it had crumpled, tears shining in her eyes. She fell to her knees beside her brother, who lay between both of us now, rasping his last breaths.

"Eugene," Melody whimpered, hands trembling as they cupped her brother's face. "I'm so sorry... I'm *sorry*..."

Eugene just stared at her, like he couldn't quite process it. His own sister had stabbed him to save *me*. Melody clung to her brother as a choked sob escaped her, and they stayed like that for a few minutes as Eugene struggled to breathe.

"You didn't react to my siren song... I *had* to..." Melody said between heaving sobs.

Eugene's hand went up to grasp Melody's arm.

"Sister..." he breathed. "That's because I love you. I have always loved you."

Love was more powerful than siren song... even a song as powerful as Eugene's... and Melody and Eugene had loved each other the same way my dad had loved Kendra and me and protected us at the very last moment of his life.

Melody wept harder after that, and another moment passed before his hand fell to his chest, and he was still. I felt numb, overcome with shock and emotion. Melody's endless sobs were the only sound in the room as she held her brother's body and buried her face in his chest. Blood clung to the water around us.

After a moment, I managed to get to my feet and tentatively circled his body to reach Melody's side. She could have let me die. She didn't have to kill her brother.

But she had. She'd chosen *me*.

I kneeled down beside her, unsure how to console her. I settled for placing a hand on her back. She looked to me, eyes red with tears and lips trembling. I didn't have words—I only knew that she had taken someone from me, and now, I had taken someone from her.

It was a strange kind of realization that only we understood.

She leaned forward, and without thinking, I wrapped my arms around her, holding her as she mourned. I never expected to be in this position with Melody... but it felt like a new stone had been turned.

Footsteps echoed in the cave, and after a moment, three people burst in. I glanced over my shoulder and saw Lysander, Maya, and Kendra gathered in the cave entrance, led by a cluster of fish. My eyes widened, and Kendra let out a sob of relief as she swam over to me. She wrapped her arms around me, not bothering to inquire about Melody in my arms. Lysander and Maya observed Eugene's dead body, and relieved expressions crossed their faces.

"We thought..." Lysander trailed off, gaze trailing from Eugene to me, and I frowned.

"That I died?" I raised an eyebrow. What would cause them to think that? Other than Melody's crying—except I very much doubted she would cry this way over me.

"Well, yeah," Maya replied with a look of uncertainty. "Because we all felt it again."

I slowly shook my head.

"Felt what?"

Lysander's sea-green eyes met mine with a touch of sparkle.

391

"Coral... you're Reigning Queen again."

CHAPTER FORTY-TWO

Coral

Melody refused to leave her brother's body, so Lysander detailed what had happened in a note and sent it to Coronis with the dwarf fish.

"Should we go back to Coronis with them?" Kendra asked as her, Lysander, Maya, and I gathered outside the mouth of the cave. Once the shock of recent events had passed, I'd noticed her crown, and she'd filled me in on her becoming queen of Veranis. The moment she'd told me I was no longer bound to Lysander, relief had swept through me.

"We could," Lysander said, glancing toward Melody, who was still huddled over her brother's body. "But we're rather close to Atlantis... and we could return this crown to King Malvin now that the mermaids are free."

He held the fragments of the Atlantis crown in his hands. His own crown had restored itself the moment Lysander touched it, and now it rested on his head.

I realized it wasn't such a bad idea. The journey to Atlantis from Veranis was long, and we would only have to come back at some point.

"Technically, our alliance is fulfilled," I added, remembering our first trip to Atlantis. "The mermaids are free, and Kendra has stepped in as a direct tie to Veranis. We should probably touch base with the king to let him know what changes have taken place and even draw up new alliances for the future."

Lysander nodded in agreement.

"Well then, we should go on ahead and have the others meet us in Atlantis," he insisted. "Someone will be coming to collect Melody and assist with her brother."

I felt bad leaving her all alone, and I couldn't stop myself from crossing back through the cave to kneel beside her again. She stared blankly ahead, her face red and blotchy—the most vulnerable I'd ever seen her.

"Melody, we're leaving now. I think Sloane is coming to help you," I told her softly. She barely nodded back, and I swallowed hard. I didn't know what else to say to her... thanking her didn't seem right, in light of what it had cost. And we weren't close enough that I wanted to hug her again.

"Take care, Melody," I offered finally, and got to my feet. I left her with her brother, exiting the cave to see that the others had mounted their seahorses. I left the last one for Melody and climbed on the back of my sister's horse instead. We set off for Atlantis.

"So, you think *that's* what happened?" I asked, after we'd been riding for some time. I could already see the caves, which Atlantis was concealed in, in the murky distance. Daybreak was not far off now, the water growing lighter and lighter with every moment that passed.

"Well, it makes sense," Lysander concluded, riding on our left side, Maya on our right. "You already had a physical tie to each territory—soul of a human, heart of a mermaid, body of an undine. Taking Eugene's song was the final piece, and it must have tipped the scales in your favor again."

Nobody had seemed to know that it was possible to become Reigning Queen this way... but then again, nobody had ever gone to the extent that I had. When my mother traded her tail for legs, it had been the *most* extensive transformation the Undersea had ever known—and so scandalous that no one else had ever attempted it. Trading *four* aspects of my body to become a hybrid of every Undersea being was... new, to say the least.

Voice of a siren, I thought, letting out a soft hum. The music tingled over my skin, and every time I used it, it was like unbridled power washing over me. I didn't know whether I liked it or hated it... and I knew I would never use it unless absolutely necessary. And *never* against the people I loved.

We pulled up in a field of seagrass, and I looked up at the familiar wall of caves and coral towering above us and all around the kingdom. The first time we'd been here, we'd passed through a tunnel, and Lysander once again led us to it.

A thrill went through me as I remembered what was in this tunnel—*sun coral*. Kendra's favorite marine organism.

It wasn't long before the dark tunnel began to glow golden, and Kendra's eyes lit up. The roof and walls were crawling with it—thousands of tiny suns illuminating in soft shades of orange and yellow.

"Wow," she breathed, her smile wide as we passed through. "This is my first time seeing it in person!"

Soon, we reached the core of the kingdom, stepping out onto sandy ground and into the ruins that made up the kingdom. This time, the sunken structure and ancient Greek temples were brimming with life. Schools of colorful fish passed overhead, zigzagging through streams of light that poured through the cavern crevices, and mermaids glided around the kingdom, carrying supplies and tools as they worked together to rebuild.

"This way." Lysander guided us, and we headed down one of the paths toward the Alta Palace. We passed temples and stone columns that stood tall and proud. Some structures were entwined in the caves surrounding the kingdom, but stringing it all together were threads and nets of algae with shells and starfish dotting the edges of the winding paths.

Kendra's gaze was drawn to all the lush algae and seagrass that grew among the purple acropora gardens. We passed the rotting shipwreck that sat nestled a few paces away from the Alta Palace, and for the first time, I was able to see it when it wasn't encased in crystal. Before, it had glowed green like an emerald, but now, it sparkled opalescent.

The doors were wide open, guarded by mermen with their crossbows slack but ready. They regarded us with a nod, letting us pass through, and we crossed the threshold, our feet hitting polished marble. It was the only echo of thudding in a palace full of swishing tails.

A mermaid dressed in gold breastplate armor came to greet us.

"Your business?" she asked, and Lysander gestured to Kendra and me.

"The Atlantis heir and her sister have returned to speak with their grandfather, the king," he explained, and the mermaid's eyes widened.

"Of course—my apologies," she gushed, bowing, and I waved her off quickly. I still wasn't used to formalities. "This way."

The mermaid led us upstairs to a private study, lit by jellyfish bobbing along the ceiling. The doors and wall panels were gold, but the rest of the space was made of marble and mother-of-pearl. Seated at a desk was a familiar figure, with thinning salt-and-pepper hair, upturned eyes, and a triangular face like my mother's. He looked up from his work when the mermaid knocked and presented us, and then rose.

"My granddaughters," he greeted. Last time I'd spoken to my grandfather, we'd left things tense. I'd forced his hand, forced him to agree to an alliance, to give us whatever power they could to assist in defeating Melody. My grandfather glanced to Maya. "The sea witch," he added, earning a head tilt from Maya, and then he finally looked at Lysander." And the undine king." He scowled, his lips pulled thin with disapproval.

Lysander returned the look—he hadn't been impressed by the king's unwillingness to help his people the first time we'd been here.

"We come bearing a gift," Lysander replied stiffly, pulling the fragments of the Atlantis crown from his pocket and walking forward to hand them to the king, whose eyes widened with surprise. The moment the fragments touched his palm, the crown restored itself, shimmering under the jellyfish lights.

"I never thought I'd see this again," he murmured thoughtfully, then looked up at Kendra and me. "But then again, I

397

didn't think I'd see our people freed from Coronis either. How did you convince Melody to let them go?"

"I made a vow," I replied simply, folding my arms. "It's not so hard when you're Reigning Queen. I think we can agree that our agreement has been fulfilled. You have your people back... and a kingdom to rule again."

King Malvin had the decency to look ashamed, placing the crown on his desk before glancing to me.

"I must admit, I am impressed," he said finally. "And perhaps I let fear get the best of me all of these years. I owe you a great debt, my granddaughter—for your persistence and your belief in our kingdom."

His gaze then drifted to Kendra, and he swam towards her.

"We have not had the pleasure of meeting yet," he said to her, and she offered him a kind smile.

"Hello, Grandfather."

"It is nice to meet you, dear Kendra," he replied softly. "I am sorry I could not be there for you all these years before. For either of you."

He turned back to his desk and began shuffling his papers.

"Of course, you are welcome to stay until you journey back—though we are quite short on provisions at the moment. Everything is going toward our rebuilding efforts."

"We understand. We don't plan to stay long," Lysander stated, his tone carefully neutral. "Kendra and I must return to our duties ruling Veranis."

The king glanced at Kendra in surprise, then to me, and I inclined my head.

"Some things changed over the past couple of weeks," I confirmed. "Other than my title as Reigning Queen, I don't have a territory to rule anymore."

"I see," he replied. "Well then, I will have Poppy show you to your rooms. But I must ask, Coral, if you will stay a moment longer."

I nodded, and the mermaid lingering in the doorway led Maya, Lysander, and Kendra away, shutting the door behind them. I was now alone with my grandfather, who crossed to one of the plush golden couches and gestured for me to sit.

"I want to apologize for how things unfolded between us last time," he began, as I settled into the chair opposite him. "It's true that I was afraid of Melody... clinging to what we had left of our kingdom. You see, when I lost Lorraine to Melody, I realized just how much she was truly capable of taking from me.

"But you must understand... I was also hesitant to help you because Lorraine was so headstrong and impulsive. She left us so fast, without warning, and I feared it might happen again if I put my trust in you. *Especially* since you were a prisoner in the Undersea and used to a life on land."

Understanding washed over me.

"You were right to be wary," I replied carefully, my toes twitching. "I tried to trade my tail for legs and return to land, the way my mother had done. But we found a loophole. I didn't intend to let anyone down, but I still ultimately cared more about myself than anyone else."

It was a difficult thing to admit out loud—and saying it out loud was all the more rattling.

The king inclined his head.

399

"However, your efforts have proven your loyalty to me. You did not abandon your people. You risked great dangers to free them on multiple occasions. And you did more than your mother did... and I must honor that."

I didn't quite follow what he was saying, and he rose from the chair again, plucking the crown from his desk. He crossed the room and handed it to me.

"Coral, would you consider ascending to the throne as queen of Atlantis?"

I stared, wide eyed, at the crown. I'd always known it was a possibility, but *so soon*?

He noticed my hesitancy and lowered the crown.

"Alas, it seems you still have some hesitations."

I shook my head, trying to find the words.

"It's not that... I just... I'm still trying to figure some things out," I replied carefully. "I expected to be ruling alongside Lysander until hours ago, when I found out my sister was queen of Veranis. And I wanted to maintain a life both on land and sea... so I'm just wondering if that's still going to be possible."

And Leif, I thought. He would return to Veranis, as the commander. Could I stay apart from him for so long?

"Why don't you take some time to think it over?" he suggested, waving to the door. "There's no rush, after all. But I would feel confident handing my kingdom's duties over to you, and there are some immediate positions we need to fill."

I frowned at him.

"What sort of positions?" I asked, and he let out a huff as he headed back over to the scrolls he'd been sifting through.

"Well," he said, sliding some of the documents around. "We're in need of chamberlains, a constable... and though I'd prefer to remain a peaceful kingdom, you've shown me the importance of having a strong army and solid military strategy. Thus, I will be seeking to appoint an experienced commander too."

My heart skipped a beat, and his gaze flicked to me knowingly.

"Unless you have a personal recommendation in mind?"

A smile spread across my lips.

"Yes. I believe I do have someone," I replied.

Leif and the others would not be here for some time, and a part of me yearned to stay awake and wait for him. But as I was shown to a room, I found myself crawling into the soft clamshell bed filled with kelp and spent twelve hours sleeping—my muscles sore from being stung up by Eugene and my mind foggy from days of stress and exhaustion. By the time I woke, it was late evening, and someone had left me dinner on a bedside table.

Noting that I was still alone, I sat up, ate the bowl of kelp and berries that had been left for me, and scanned the room. It was similar to the room I'd been in last time—with pearlescent furniture and gold detailing on the walls. But the bed in here was larger, and there were more tall standing vases and pots with seagrass and anubias flowers.

Stretching my limbs, I decided to go for a walk and left the room.

I'd not long reached the end of the hallway when someone called to me, and I glanced over my shoulder to see Lysander approaching. He came to a pause in front of me, the top button of his loose shirt undone like he'd been lounging minutes before. Or perhaps doing things with my sister that I *really* didn't want to think about.

"You're finally awake," he noted. "Do you have a moment to talk?"

I nodded, finding that I was able to meet his gaze, that things no longer felt tense and weird between us.

"I just wanted to make sure that you are okay with Kendra and me. That... there are no hard feelings between us."

I shook my head, offering him a small smile.

"You clearly make my sister very happy," I said, remembering how enthralled she appeared in his presence. "I am glad you both found one another... and I'm sorry that I hurt you, Lysander."

I meant it. Things had not ended well between us, and we'd never had a chance to revisit the conversation before I left. I was glad for the opportunity to air things out now.

"It's okay. I'm sorry too," he said, and his eyes shone with remorse. "I wanted to ask you another thing as well—you mentioned on the journey that you were able to break free of Eugene's siren spell because you focused on Leif." There was a moment of hesitation in his eyes before he added, "On *love*."

I knew he was implying with his words, not stating—I hadn't even admitted it aloud yet, not even to Leif. But he knew—my actions had proved as much—and his gaze softened when I blushed and didn't reply.

"He didn't tell me much in the brief moment we talked in Coronis... but I did get a sense that you and he were... something more now. You love him, don't you?"

I found myself nodding, my heart warming at the very thought of him, and replied, "Yes. I love him."

The admission seemed to echo ever so gently in the air, and Lysander smiled warmly, his gaze flicking between me and something behind me. *Or someone.*

My eyes had barely widened when someone said, "I love you too."

I whirled around, and he was standing at the end of the corridor—one hand on the wall for balance, his hair wild and unruly like he'd ridden as fast as he could. His eyes shone at the sight of me, and a noise escaped my throat.

I ran down the corridor, and he did too, his arms circling me as he swept me off my feet and spun me around just once. Then his lips were on mine, conveying everything we both felt as he held me tight in his arms.

CHAPTER FORTY-THREE

Leif

I was never going to let go of her hand.

We walked through the near-empty streets of Atlantis, the water dull with the late hour. Purple acropora coral swayed gently in the currents around us, and Coral leaned her head against my shoulder, content.

As soon as word had reached Coronis from Lysander, Maya's binding had broken. So Matt, Nerissa, and I had ridden straight to Atlantis. We'd only stopped to rest once and only because Matt had demanded it after hours of riding, complaining of a sore bottom.

But it still hadn't been fast enough. I'd been going out of my mind needing to see her, to kiss her, to *tell* her that I loved her.

And hearing that she loved me too...

I smiled down at her, and she sensed it, her bright eyes meeting mine. Unable to help myself, I stopped in my tracks and tilted my head to brush my lips against hers.

We'd already spoken about what had happened after Eugene took her. It was brief, and it had only come up because both of us wanted to make sure that the other was okay. Now, it was over, and I never wanted to think about it—about what he'd done to her—ever again.

"I need to tell you something," she said, after we'd been walking for a while. Her eyes seemed hesitant, and I threaded

404

my fingers through hers reassuringly and showed her I was listening. She studied me for a moment before speaking.

"The king has offered me the Atlantis crown. He wants me to stay here and rule the kingdom." Her eyes were full of apprehension as she gauged my reaction. I tried not to let anything show, but I had a sinking feeling in my gut.

"That's great news," I replied with a smile. But I understood why she seemed hesitant—I was still Lysander's commander. If she accepted, it would mean the two of us would be apart more often than not. I wasn't against traveling... but I didn't think I could ever be apart from this devastatingly beautiful, stubborn, *fiercely* brave mermaid ever again.

"Will you take it?" I asked, after a moment. She traced from my wrist to my elbow, eliciting goosebumps as she gave me a pleading look.

"Only if you consider doing something for me," she replied carefully, and I blinked back. "King Malvin said that he is in need of a new commander, to strengthen Atlantis's army and create defense strategies. I told him that I would offer it to you... if you're interested in taking it."

My world slowed for a moment. I hadn't seen this coming.

"It comes with a pay raise," she added with a playful smirk, and I couldn't help smiling back. But it was a lot to take in... it would mean leaving my sisters and mother. Leaving Lysander, whom I'd spent years serving. He was my best friend, someone I'd grown up with.

But it was also... the perfect solution. It would allow me to stay here with her. I could still be commander—still continue my career. The challenge of rebuilding and leading an entire

405

army, of creating defensive strategies from scratch, was exciting compared to my previous line of work in Veranis. And it wasn't like I would never visit Veranis. We *both* would— Coral's sister was queen of Veranis now, after all.

I traced my thumb along her jawline.

"Let me speak to Lysander about it first," I said—not because I didn't want to take it, but because I owed him the conversation first—and she nodded.

"That's all I ask," she replied, her voice laced with deep gratitude, and then she pushed up onto her tiptoes to kiss me again. I smirked, deepening the kiss, and my tongue swept into her mouth. She moaned softly, and it stirred something in me.

I was only *very* aware that we'd never gotten to finish what we'd started before Eugene had intervened. And now that I wasn't stressing over her safety, it was something I'd had to keep pushing to the back of my mind. She'd been through a lot, and my thighs still had a dull ache to them. And yet... I still wanted her. *All* of her.

She pressed her body against mine, like she was thinking it too, wrapping her arms around my neck to pull me even closer. I groaned, and my hands slid down the side of her body, trailing the flowy green dress she wore. Her hands slid down my shirt, feeling every groove of my muscles, and when our kiss broke, her eyes were dark and full of silent question.

My instincts took over, and I scooped her up into my arms, eliciting a surprised giggle from her as I marched determinedly back to the palace so that we could be *properly* alone. I barely noticed any of the Alta Palace staff as I carried her up the stairs, and she murmured directions to her room in my ear.

As soon as the door clicked shut behind us, she was planting kisses from my jaw, down my neck, to my shoulder. My skin felt on fire with every kiss, every touch. I crossed to the bed and lowered her gently before climbing over her and claiming her lips once more. She arched her body into mine, and I huffed a laugh as her fingers gripped my hair. I was thinking of all the things I wanted to do first when she suddenly flipped me, pinning me beneath her instead. I'd barely caught my breath when her hands clasped mine, gripping them against the woven sheets as she leaned down to graze my ear.

"We were disrupted last time—let me make it up to you."

A shiver went through me. I wanted to argue that *she'd* been the one who got kidnapped and nearly had her heart ripped out, but the look in her eyes gave me pause as she slowly, tantalizingly undid the buttons of my shirt. I watched her every movement, her legs trapping me under her as she began to pepper feather-light kisses along my chest, my stomach, and worked her way down to my navel.

Her fingers grazed my belt buckle, and the sound of it unclasping had me almost wild with anticipation, my mind racing. I watched her intently as she dragged my pants down my legs, discarding them without second thought, but then she paused. Her gaze had landed on my thighs, where thin red scars were still visible. My throat felt tighter.

Her brown eyes turned almost black as they hardened. Slowly, tenderly, she leaned down and kissed each scar, tracing the lines there with her fingertips. I felt a soft tingle as the scars healed over, as the pain left my muscles, and she met my gaze again.

407

"If anyone ever hurts you like that again—" she said darkly, but with a swift movement, I brought her back toward me and kissed her hard. I couldn't take it. The intensity of her so close to where I needed her, the way she treated me with such gentleness... *I loved her*, and I needed her now.

I ground my hips against her as she straddled my waist, and she bit my bottom lip before whispering.

"Tell me what you want."

I could barely think straight.

"You," I managed, my voice hoarse. "Just you—anything—"

She bent down to remove the rest of my clothes, my hips lifting to help her, and then I felt her tongue sweeping up my length. I groaned, eyes nearly rolling into the back of my head, as I felt her mouth around me, and she set a steady pace. *Fuck...*

She drove me almost to the brink, and only then did I coax her back up to me. Wildly, I reached for the hem of her dress and dragged it off of her, tossing it to the floor with my clothes. I loved how she looked on top of me—every curve exposed for me to admire—and for the first time since beginning, she looked shy. But I pressed kisses to her stomach, between her breasts, up to her mouth and devoured it, and her doubts seemed to melt away quickly.

The place between her legs brushed against me, ever so lightly, as she lined herself up with me. I hissed from the sensitivity—I wanted her so badly.

"I love you," she whispered against my lips, hands braced on my shoulders. And then she sank down on me, and we were both groaning. It took everything in me to still myself, to give her a moment to adjust, and she kissed me so deeply, I thought I might burst.

Once again, she took control, pushing me back against the bed as she moved her hips achingly slow. But her pace picked up quickly, one hand pressed on my chest. After a while, my hands instinctively found her waist, and she let me take over, guiding her by the hips exactly how I needed her. Her head tipped back—the sight of her almost too much to handle.

I shifted, lifting her swiftly as I sat back on my heels and held her close, thrusting into her quickly. She moaned louder, fingers clawing my back as she gripped me, and I felt her pulsing. Finally, she came, crying out as she did, and I buried my face in the nook of her neck as I slammed into her one last time and came with her.

Both of us were panting hard, limbs weak with exhaustion as I lowered her back down to the bed. She lay down on her side, and I followed, pulling her close. I stoked her hair and kissed her cheek as she recovered. Then I pulled the blankets up over us both and nestled down beside her.

"So... Atlantis, huh?" I said finally, and her eyes opened to gaze up at me.

"What about it?" she replied, and I traced lines lazily up and down her bare back.

"You asked me about staying here with you... but is staying here, as queen of Atlantis, what *you* want?"

She was free from Lysander now, free to go between sea and land... and though our original plan had entailed her residing in the Undersea to be close to me and her sister, we'd never imagined she would get a whole kingdom to herself.

She let out a soft *hmm* and pulled me closer.

"It's warmer here than it is in Veranis," she replied. "And it's where my mother grew up. I feel closer to her here than anywhere else."

"Okay, but what about ruling?"

There was a moment of pause.

"Well... to tell you the truth, it makes me nervous, and I know I have a lot to learn. But Grandfather wouldn't have offered this to me if he wasn't certain I could do it, and I'm sure he'll be willing to offer his advice and wisdom along the way."

"I'll help too," I promised, placing another kiss to her forehead. I didn't have firsthand experience ruling, but I *had* spent more time around royals than Coral had. I could probably offer some advice of my own if she needed it. My mind skimmed through everything I'd ever learned about the royal hierarchy of Atlantis, and a thought occurred to me. She felt me tense up.

"What's wrong?"

"If we... ever get married..." I began carefully, meeting her gaze again. "You do realize that would make me *king* of Atlantis?"

"Oh... I know," she said quickly, pushing up onto her elbows. "I asked my grandfather about this when we discussed your position as commander. It's true that all royals are expected to marry eventually... but he also said that trying to force Lorraine into marriage early contributed to why she ran away. He doesn't wish for events to repeat themselves, so he's happy for us to wait as long as we need... and you can keep your position as commander until that time."

410

I nodded slowly. It made sense... and it was a fair trade. By the time Coral and I were ready to settle down... I would probably be more open to the concept of ruling a kingdom.

She smirked, waggling her eyebrows as she added, "And then, when you and Lysander are both kings, you can throw each other fancy dinner parties or whatever it is you two do when I'm not around."

I cocked my head at her as my lips quirked.

"You *wish* you were invited to our fancy dinner parties," I teased smoothly, and she practically cackled—except the sound was like bells, probably enhanced by her new siren song power.

"Well, if you're willing to wait to get married, then so am I," I told her softly. "But just so you know, I'd do it in a heartbeat if the circumstances were different."

Her gaze softened, and she replied.

"I don't mind waiting. Besides, I don't need a fancy ring just to know that you're mine."

And you're mine, I thought with a gentle smile. She lay back down and buried her head into my chest, and my arm slung around her waist to pull her close. After a while, her breathing became slower, steadier, and we both drifted off into a contented sleep.

CHAPTER FORTY-FOUR

Coral

Six Months Later

The distant sound of cheers was barely audible over the roaring wave wrapping around me. Salty ocean spray hit my cheek, and I couldn't stop smiling, couldn't stifle my pounding heart.

The white surf of the wave was on my heels as it chased me all the way to the shoreline, where a roaring chorus greeted me from the gathered crowd. Moments later, Maya stepped in line with me, dressed in a long-sleeved bodysuit and drenched from head to toe in ocean water. She clutched a custom-made surfboard to her side—hand-painted by Matt in gorgeous sunset-inspired colors.

Dylan O'Connell had resumed his position as commentator again for this weekend's fundraising competition—where locals were surfing to raise funds for a range of important causes. I'd already given a sizable donation from the funds our dad had left behind.

"Everybody, that was Coral and Maya, delivering one of the *best* performances we've seen today!" he boomed into a microphone, and the cheers seemed to heighten. By now, everyone had come to learn that Maya Rivers was, in fact, alive—and this had been our first time surfing together in public since the incident almost two years ago.

We beamed at the crowd for a moment before heading off toward a roped area, where Matt was waiting for us. He was shaking his head at both of us but grinning.

"You know, you *both* have an unfair advantage," he scolded halfheartedly, as we began to climb the sandy bank of the beach toward the parking lot.

"Don't go spilling our secrets, Matt," Maya teased, wrapping an arm around his shoulder and planting a kiss on his cheek.

"Yeah, Matt, just because we can predict the waves doesn't mean you can't win against us. You just need to train harder," I replied smugly, and he rolled his eyes.

"I'm half tempted to go seek out the First Sea Witch and become an undine myself—then we'll see who's *really* the best surfer."

Maya pouted at Matt.

"At least wait until after the wedding," she teased, then added, "Will it cheer you up if I buy you some ice cream before we leave?"

Matt pretended to consider, but I saw the way his lips tugged upward.

"Fine," he relented, and they pecked each other on the lips before glancing over at me. But I shook my head.

"Go on, I'll meet you down there," I told them, waving them off. The two of them headed for the boardwalk while I crossed to my car and slid my surfboard onto the rack atop my car. There was a space for Maya's as well.

Once my surfboard was secured, I walked along the sandy beach, around the cheering crowd who were watching the competition, and climbed up onto the granite outcrops fringing the shoreline. The sun had heated the rocks, and I moved fast to avoid burning my feet, following the rocks around the sloping hillside until I was out of sight.

Finally, I'd gone as far as I could and was looking down at the sloshing crystal-clear water. I smiled a knowing smile as I slipped off the edge of the rocks and into the cool turquoise water, and I submerged my head.

Matt and Maya would take a few days to follow, due to Matt's human body needing to adjust to the Undersea, but I knew they wouldn't be far behind. With a powerful kick, I began the descent to Veranis.

I couldn't tear my eyes away from Kendra as she emerged from the fitting room—Rue bringing up the rear as she held her train. She wore a translucent crystal wedding dress with long sleeves. The long flowing skirts were transparent, showing off her lithe figure, and they were detachable too—leaving a sparkling corset-style bustier top for the reception. I already knew the dress was going to drive Lysander wild, and I was tempted to make a bet with Leif as to whether he and Kendra would make it through their first dance before he hauled her upstairs.

"You look *amazing*, Ken," I breathed with a wide smile, and she beamed back at me. Her hair was pulled back into a loose bun so as not to get caught up in the currents, and her hair was done up in matching crystals. She also had a scattering of starfish and shells woven around the bun.

414

I pushed off the ottoman I'd been sitting on and approached her as Rue fussed over her dress, plucking and tucking to ensure everything was perfect.

"I'm so nervous," Kendra whispered, staring at herself in the mirror, and I shook my head.

"What are you nervous about? You're both head over heels in love with one another." I scoffed. It was only *painstakingly* obvious, especially when Lysander had delivered a scroll through fish to Leif and me last week—which could only be the equivalent of a drunk, late-night text. When unrolled, it revealed five pages of him panicking over the possibility of Kendra leaving him at the altar and wondering how he'd ever get over her.

Needless to say, the fish had not been amused.

"That's the thing—what if something goes wrong today?" she replied, and I let out a sigh.

"Oh my God, you're *both* being ridiculous. Nothing is going to go wrong. You're going to get married, go on your honeymoon, and live happily ever after."

At the mention of the honeymoon, Kendra's shouldered seemed to relax. I knew she'd been dying for the opportunity to escape palace duties for a while and have some private time with Lysander. It was a trip they'd both discussed in depth— they would be traveling to a faraway place that not even I had known existed, a place that could only be accessed between the spring equinox and summer solstice.

"Your Grace, you must get going—you'll be late to the ceremony," Rue said finally, patting her shoulders as if to say she was ready. Kendra inhaled a deep breath, then nodded.

I went on ahead to give them some space, heading down the stairs and out into the courtyard, where a small and private space had been set up for a ceremony. Four rows of chairs were placed on either side of an aisle, which had been lined with kelp and decorated with starfish. I spotted Matt and Maya in the second row, as well as Nerissa. There were a few court connections and palace staff that both Lysander and Kendra had invited taking up the back rows. I didn't see Melody though, and I knew Kendra still hadn't forgiven her for our dad. It had been a slow and difficult process, but I'd managed to establish some pleasant, neutral terms with Melody through our kingdoms' alliances—including an annual ball in Atlantis that the entire Undersea was welcome to attend, so long as all weapons were left at the door.

Looking farther ahead, I saw a romantic dome wedding arch—made entirely of stone and coral, with sheer kelp curtains drifting on either side of it. Standing underneath, in a black and gold baroque suit, was Lysander. He wore a matching vest and cuff links to complete the look, and he kept looking eagerly toward the doors where Kendra would appear soon. Giving Lysander a knowing smile, I nodded to him, and I walked quickly around the chairs to the front row. Spotting Leif, I slipped into the chair beside him. He turned as his eyes lit up at the sight of me. He brushed his fingers against mine in greeting. I leaned closer to him.

"Seeing Kendra in her wedding dress makes me want to get married sooner," I murmured in his ear, and he chuckled lowly.

"Patience. I promise I'll make our wedding worth the wait," he replied, pressing a light kiss under my earlobe. I had to shift away as my face heated—this was *not* the time to get all hot and bothered—and he chuckled again at my reaction.

The crowd's chatter died down, and a band of mermaids to the far right began playing delicate music on harps. We all turned to see Kendra at the end of the aisle. She didn't have anyone to walk her down the aisle—instead, seven dwarf fish clung to her train, extending it out behind her. She swam slowly down the aisle, her dress glittering as she moved, and every single gaze in the room followed her. Finally, she came to a pause at Lysander's side, and they joined hands. He looked close to tears at the sight of her, and she bit her lip as her smile grew.

The fish let her train down carefully, before circling around her playfully—as if wishing her luck—and perching on the coral arch above to watch the ceremony.

The ceremony began, and as I watched on, something white and bubbly drifting in the water overhead caught my attention. I looked up, and when I recognized what it was, a smile grew on my lips.

Sea-foam.

EPILOGUE

Something cool was sloshing against my feet.

My eyes fluttered open, but I had to squint in the blinding sunlight. It took a moment for my eyes to adjust, so I focused on the slow, rhythmic sound of waves in my ears and the salty breeze that caressed my bare arms.

When my eyes had stopped stinging, I dug my fingers into the matted, wet sand beneath me and pushed upright. Crawling into a kneeling position, I looked up to see a familiar sight.

Odyssey Bay... *before* it was Odyssey Bay.

The untouched beauty of the tropical jungle greeted me. Towering palm trees, tangled vines and shrubs, tropical flowers, and large boulders stretched from one side of the curved beach to the other, as far as the eye could see. No buildings, no marina, no boardwalk... just paradise.

"Beautiful, isn't it?"

My head whipped to my left, and a man in khaki slacks and a loose white button-up shirt stood there watching me. His charming smile lit up his entire face, his blond hair tussled by the breeze, and his kind blue eyes crinkled with adoration. He looked twenty years younger... as handsome as the day I'd first met him.

I stared at him, my hands beginning to shake, unable to breathe. It had been so long... *so long...*

Christopher offered me his hand as another wave sloshed against my ankles, soaking my white dress and threatening to sweep me back out to sea.

"Lorraine, my love."

At the sound of his voice, I burst into tears and leaped to my feet. In seconds, he had enveloped me in his strong arms and swept me off my feet, spinning me round and round. A rumble of joy rolled through his body as he squeezed me tighter. When my feet finally touched the sand again, he moved his hands to my cheeks and wiped my tears with his thumbs. The tears didn't stop as joy and grief swept over me at once.

"I'm so sorry," I wept, clinging to his shirt, which I was starting to stain with my tears and snot. "I tried to protect you... and I failed... and you had to leave the girls—"

He pressed a finger to my lips and tucked my windswept hair out of my eyes.

"You have *nothing* to apologize for, Lorraine. You freed us all."

I blinked slowly and swallowed hard as the words sank in. "I did?"

He nodded slowly, and that easy smile I'd fallen in love with so long ago appeared again. "Melody would have killed me regardless. But thanks to your sacrifice, I was able to save Kendra before she did. And now, Melody's heart has been restored, the girls are surrounded by people who care about them, and nobody is tied to any harmful song or curse anymore. *All because of you.*"

Tears threatened to spill again, but I managed to hold it together. It was all I'd ever wanted. My precious daughters, my beloved husband, and Melody... the one I'd cared so deeply for... I'd just wanted everyone to be safe and happy.

Christopher's eyes shone with pride as he gave me a moment to process, and when a smile finally broke out on my lips, he mirrored it.

"Now come on," he said, threading his hand with mine and tugging gently. He led me toward a small boat anchored off the crystal-clear shore. I didn't know if it had appeared suddenly or if I simply hadn't noticed it earlier. I glanced at him with surprise, and he grinned, his eyes lighting up the way they always did when we used to sail together around the islands, enamored in each other's company.

"Where are we going?" I asked, a thrill of excitement washing through me now as we waded through the cool water to reach the vessel. He climbed up first, then offered me his hand to help me. As my fingers met his again, he brought my hand up and planted a soft kiss on my knuckles. And then he said, "On to our next adventure."

ACKNOWLEDGEMENTS

After 6 years of authorship, fifteen manuscripts and ten published books... I can finally say that I've finished a complete series.

WOW.

What an amazing feeling! And like always, it's not something I could have done alone.

Firstly, I want to thank my amazing PBK community. When I started my first business, I didn't realize what an incredible community that would lead to and how powerful and supportive it would be to have amazing, genuine people follow me, root for me, and watch my journey. I am so thankful for all of you and especially the ones that came with me on my secret pen name journey, and become loyal fans of this particular series.

Secondly, I want to thank those who contributed to this book: Sam, for beta reading, Susan, for proofreading, Rebecca, for formatting, and Bianca, for cover design.

And finally, if you read this series through to the end, if you shared it or recommended it or left a review, if you helped beta read it, or if you merely enjoyed it in any way, I am so thankful for you. I write books for myself, but I *choose* to share them for you, so that you might enjoy the stories as well, and this particular project was so special to me because for the first time in all my writing years, I really felt like people were engaged in the characters, had opinions about them, and it was so much fun to deliver a story that I knew most of you would enjoy. So thank you for being here!

ABOUT THE AUTHOR

Pagan Alexandria is a fairy tale retelling author best known for her dual retelling of Snow White and The Little Mermaid, KINGDOM OF SIRENS AND MONSTERS.

She grew up in Proserpine, Queensland— a small, Australian country town on the edge of the Great Barrier Reef— when she gained the inspiration for her debut contemporary novel, STUCK ON VACATION WITH RYAN RUPERT (published under P.S.Malcolm).

Pagan quickly realised she had a love of blending contemporary worlds with fantasy, and went on to write a seven book fantasy series, THE STARLIGHT CHRONICLES (signed by Lycaon Press in 2015 and The Parliament House Press in 2017) before walking away from traditional publishing to go completely independent.

Today, Pagan writes dual retellings of beloved fairy tales— filled with star-crossed romance, morally grey characters, supernatural twists and a sprinkle of spice. When isn't writing, she's making charcuterie boards, playing cosy video games, and recording her podcast, Bestseller Energy.

Follow Pagan on Instagram for updates: @PaganAlexandriaCreative

A NEW SERIES IS COMING...

BLOOD MAGIC

The Salvharks and Guildwoods have just one rule in common: all vampires must die. Which is why Fleur Fontaine never expected to discover her vampire hunting rival, Percy Renaud, on her doorstep one night—covered in blood, and baring fangs at her.

But when he compels her, she is forced to keep his secret from everyone she knows, all while trying to sate his blood-thirsty cravings against her human roommate.

Unable to defend herself, and irresistibly drawn to his charm, Fleur realises her only other option is to go against her deceased father's wishes to find a vampire cure. But as their undeniable attraction to one another grows, she starts to unravel a darker, more sinister secret of her own—one that leaves her wondering which of the two of them is truly the deadliest to the other.

An enemies-to-lovers, Rapunzel meets Sleeping Beauty dual retelling.

Continue to the next pages for a free preview...

ONE

Fleur

Seven years before

As the four of us sat around the table, textbooks and papers scattered in front of us, I was reminded of why I hated group assignments so much. I kept my head down and focused on taking notes from my textbook. Together, we had to deliver a presentation on the Great Depression—which was due tomorrow, and we'd made absolutely zero progress over the past two weeks. We were supposed to be writing a speech and designing slides for it. But so far, I seemed to be the only one interested in doing the work, because the remaining three members of my group wouldn't stop gossiping during lessons.

I should have expected as much from a bunch of rich, popular kids.

Sparing a quick glance up, I listened in on their conversation, hoping to politely request some help without coming off like I was a loser.

"...yeah, she'll probably invite a lot of boys to the party," Victoria said casually, playing with the cap of her pen. She had long, brown hair that she usually wore in a ponytail and manicured nails with French tips. "But her boyfriend will be there too."

"Have they... you know, *done it?*" Blair asked, in a low voice, and Victoria raised an eyebrow at her. Blair had a strikingly different look to Victoria—with sparkly eyeshadow and choppy black hair that made her look edgy.

"What? Had *sex?* Yeah, she's done it loads of times, with loads of guys."

I frowned, taken aback by their conversation topic, and paused my note taking.

"With who?" Blair insisted, shuffling closer with wide eyes, and Victoria shrugged coolly.

"I don't know—she moves around a lot. She's had a few boyfriends."

"It doesn't count unless it's all the way," Percy scoffed from my right side, his lips curving up almost knowingly, and my stomach fluttered at the sound of his voice. He leaned back in his chair and I noticed how his broad shoulders flexed under his sleeved, white school shirt. He wore his brown hair with a side fringe. "I heard she's only done hand stuff."

"That's all I've done," Blair sighed longingly, twirling a strand of hair around her index finger.

I felt extremely out of place in this conversation. This was *not* the kind of thing I talked about with my one and only friend, Darcy—who, unfortunately, didn't take this class. Otherwise, I might have been more fortunate to have been paired with her instead of these three people.

Victoria's gaze landed on me—on the way I kept sneaking glances—and she smirked.

"What about you, Fleur? Have *you* done anything with anyone?"

I must have turned as red as a beetroot because I felt my cheeks heat, ducking my gaze back to my notebooks to gather my thoughts. I didn't know how to respond... but after a moment, I decided to be honest.

"I haven't even kissed anybody yet," I admitted finally, with a sheepish smile, and the two girls exchanged a glance like this was astounding.

"What do you mean?" Blair asked, shaking her head. I guess it was easy for her to say if she was doing *hand stuff* on a regular basis—finding boys to kiss must seem like a piece of cake compared to going that far. Blair glanced over at Percy, who was now watching me as well, and pointed between us while adding, "You two should just kiss right now. And then you *will* have kissed someone. Boom—*done!*"

She grinned, clearly proud of her idea, but my eyes widened with shock at her bold suggestion. I hesitantly turned my head and met Percy's gaze for a moment. He met mine too, reading the reaction in my eyes, and I wondered what he was thinking as his gaze flicked to my lips for a moment. *Would he actually kiss me?* My heart raced at the thought.

They must have thought their suggestion was so innocent. But none of them knew I'd been harboring a secret crush on Percy for almost a year now—they didn't realize kissing him was one of my biggest, hidden desires. And I *certainly* didn't want it to mean nothing, or to happen in History class, of all places. My gaze landed on our teacher, who was busy speaking to another student at his desk across the room, and my stomach knotted at the very thought of doing something so disruptive during class. *I couldn't kiss Percy here—or at all, for that matter!*

Finally, I let out a breathy laugh, hoping to brush it off as a joke, and returned my gaze to my notebook. My cheeks were still burning, and I couldn't bring myself to face any of them. They carried on with their conversation like nothing had happened, but I found myself distracted for the remainder of the lesson, wondering what it would have been like if Percy had closed the distance between us.

"Nice and easy, *Cherie*," Margot instructed from where we were crouched in the bushes, as I tracked the rabbit hopping among fallen logs and melting snow with my crossbow. I barely dared to breathe, and years of training kept me from trembling despite the icy, winter air.

Quiet as a mouse, I nudged my booted foot into the stirrup at the front of my crossbow, and pulled the crossbow string back evenly against both sides of the barrel until it was taut and cocked. I'd done this a thousand times ever since I was a little girl and was old enough to manage the weight of a bow.

I waited for Margot's next instruction. Her snowy, white hair fell around her face in a bob and though she was in her late fifties, she looked younger thanks to her rigorous skincare routine. The rabbit hopped a few paces closer to us, and I tensed, holding my breath. Margot lifted three fingers, and I moved quickly but silently, grabbing an arrow from my back and placing it in the barrel of the crossbow. I swiftly aligned the cock vane of the arrow in the barrel channel made sure it was aligned correctly. Then, I tipped the crossbow just above the bushes, and peered through the scope, aiming for the rabbit's head.

Then I pulled the trigger.

A pop sounded as the bow fired off. I watched the arrow travel at the speed of light towards the rabbit's skull—

It hopped away before the arrow landed it's mark, and I gritted my teeth. Margot let out a shushing sound.

"It's okay—this is why we're training," she insisted, noting my frustration. "You're improving every day, *Cherie*. Soon, you will be ready to tackle the real thing."

A rustle sounded from behind us, and Margot whirled around. Before either of us could react, something tackled her to the ground, and I gasped. A vampire had snuck up on us, no doubt tipped off by the sound of my bow firing. It bared it's sharp teeth at Margot as she grappled for her knife, but it had her pinned to the ground with it's strong hands. I scrambled to reload my crossbow, heart pounding, fingers trembling. The vampire lunged forward to bite her neck but I fired, an arrow lodging into the vampire's shoulder. It's red eyed gazed snapped to me, angry and depraved with hunger as it snarled in protest. It looked young—maybe seventeen or eighteen, and it's eyes were bright red, indicating that it was a newborn vampire.

My distraction had been enough, as Margot freed her dagger from her sheath and stabbed it clean into the vampire's heart, effectively staking it. The vampire let out a choked sound, it's gaze glassing over, and I watched as it slumped and began to disintegrate. Letting out a mumbled cursed, Margot shoved the crumbling body off of her as it turned to ash and dust around her.

"Are there more?" I asked, my voice unsteady as I re-loaded again and glanced around the dark woods. Margot brushed the ashes from her black coat as she got to her feet.

"Very likely," she replied, her voice low as she scanned the area. "The vampire who turned him is likely still here. We should go."

She met my gaze and added,

"You did well, *Cherie.* I'm so proud of you."

A relieved smile appeared on my lips, but then another crunch made me gasp and glance over my shoulder. This time, Margot placed a hand on my arm and said,

"Don't move—I'll take care of it."

She stalked off towards the sound of the noise, disappearing into the trees, and I swallowed hard, trying to keep my wits about me. I'd encountered vampires before, and I'd been trained in these woods plenty of times. But very few times had we been caught off guard, and I felt unnerved. My gaze kept trailing back to the space where I'd seen Margot disappear, the dark woods only allowing for so much visibility. Minutes ticked by, and I grew anxious.

"Hey, you!"

Eyes wide, I spun around and fired off towards the sound. The male behind me jumped aside as the arrow flew past him, then whipped his head to me. My throat went dry, and I felt like I couldn't breathe.

None other than *Percy* stood there—his brown eyes wide with shock and hands raised uncertainly. I couldn't seem to find the right words. What was he doing here? What was he thinking, seeing me out here with a *crossbow* of all things? Oh God, I'd just shot it at his *forehead—*

"Are you trying to *kill* me?" he growled finally, and my mouth slackened. "What are you *doing* with that thing?"

I began to shake my head, trying to come up with an explanation, an excuse... very few people knew about vampires, and the hunters that killed them.

In that moment, another figure stepped into view at his side—taller, older and with a striking resemblance to Percy. It didn't take me long to figure out that it must have been his dad, though I did wonder what the two of them were doing in the woods so late at night.

I suppose they wondered the same about me in that moment.

The man raised an eyebrow at me, looking at my crossbow.

"Are you a hunter?" he asked finally. "I don't recognize you."

"I..." I stammered, then managed to pull myself together. "Yes—I'm a hunter. A Guildwood hunter."

The man wrinkled his nose.

"Well, that explains the poor coordination and reflexes," he replied. "I thought I told you Guildwood hunters to stay out of our woods."

It finally clicked. *These people were from Salvhark.*

"We always train here," I countered, feeling my confidence build by the minute. "It's never been a problem until now."

"Well, I'm telling you now that it's a problem," he sniped back, folding his arms. "There's a newborn vampire loose in here—and given the fact that you nearly shot my son between the eyes, I highly doubt you're trained enough to hunt it.

We've been on it's tail for the past half hour and thanks to you, we've lost it."

Percy lifted his chin haughtily in agreement, and I felt all the feelings I'd harbored for him start to dislodge, swirling in a mass of confusion. Percy was from *Salvhark*—our enemy guild. I didn't want to believe it, but here he was.

"You can stop looking, because we've already dealt with that problem," Margot's voice called from behind me, and I heard snow crunching as she made her way back over to us. When I looked at her, I noticed a red heart, dripping with blood, in her gloved hand. She held it up for the man to see and added, "*and* the cause of the trouble. Perhaps you ought to re-evaluate who's fit to be leading vampire patrols in these woods."

The man scoffed, and gestured to me.

"Well, if *this* is your next generation of hunters, you're screwed," he jeered. "The poor girl nearly shot a fellow hunter in her panic. Monsec will be much safer in the hands of hunters like my son."

He slapped Percy on the back, eyes shining with pride, and bitterness clawed through me as Percy smiled, soaking up the praise. Just like that, all the fantasies I'd build up around Percy revealed themselves to be nothing more than just that—*fantasies*. Ideas of who I wanted him to be, not who he really was. Because I *knew* who Percy really was. Weeks of being stuck in in a group project with him had made it crystal clear that he didn't put effort into *anything*, didn't *care* about anything—let alone keeping this town safe.

I'd been blinded by his suave voice, his charming smiles, the delusional hopes that he might actually talk to me one day and realize that he wanted to take me out on a date. That was *never* going to happen—I'd been such an idiot, stuck in my daydreams.

Furthermore, I wouldn't trust Percy to hunt down a *single* vampire—and there was no doubt he'd only gotten into Salvhark because he'd been born into the right family, not because he actually valued the job. Resolve settled in me as I glared at him, and it must have thrown him because he frowned in response. From torturing their victims to experimenting on vampires, everything Margot had told me about the Salvhark Guild was horrible. And not only was Percy training to become a member, but he looked downright proud to be a part of it.

I felt sick to my stomach.

"That is why she's in training," Margot replied coolly, and I wished she would stop talking. I didn't want Percy to know I still needed vampire training—I wanted to be *better* than him, because I actually cared about fighting vampires and keeping people from dying.

I didn't want innocent people to meet the same fate my father had.

Percy's father exchanged a few more bitter words with Margot, before the pair of them left, and Margot turned to me with a serious expression, still clutching the vampire heart at her side. She forced my chin up with her free hand to meet her gaze.

"Fleur, don't let anything they said get to you," she told me. "You are a strong, capable young woman, and I have no doubt that you will be a wonderful hunter one day. And if one thing's for certain, it's the fact that you worked hard to *earn* your spot in Guildwood. Not like that pretty boy back there."

She winked and offered me a small smile, and I stepped forward to wrap my arms around her. I clung to the woman who was singlehandedly raising me, even though she never had an obligation to. She'd given me a home and carried on teaching me what my father had taught me before he died. She was all I had left in this world, and I would do anything to avoid losing her.

The next day, I arrived at the history classroom a couple of minutes early. I was still fuming over Percy from the night before, unable to shake my feelings about him. I couldn't believe I'd been crushing on his conceited ass for a whole year, or that I'd been so flustered over the thought of kissing him yesterday. It felt like I'd woken up from a dream and entered a harsh reality.

To add to my frustration, I'd stayed up most of the night completing the project that *none* of my group members had bothered to help me with. It was thanks to me that they had a project to present at all.

I knocked on the door of the classroom, and Mr. Gauthier welcomed me inside. He was a bald man who wore rounded glasses on his nose. Crossing over to his desk, I let my emotions drive me as I confessed the truth to him: that I'd been the only one to work on the project. I aired my concerns about failing the grade because of the lack of help I'd received, and I made it clear that I wasn't happy with how things had played out.

"Don't worry, Fleur—I know they haven't helped," he reassured me, shuffling his papers on his desk. "I've been watching your groups every lesson, and I saw you working hard. Leave it to me."

Shortly after, the rest of the class arrived. We spent an hour going through presentations, and I was the only one in my group who didn't read the speech straight from the notecards because I'd bothered to memorize and rehearse it. Percy avoided my gaze for the entire lesson, scowling at the floor instead, and I was thankful—Guildwood and Salvhark had been competitors for centuries, and learning that he was my enemy had created a clear tension between us. I wanted to forget about him, forget the entire interaction we'd had last night.

As soon as we finished our presentation and sat down, the teacher walked up to the front of the class to address our group.

"Guys, that was terrible," he scolded, but I knew it wasn't directed at me because I was the only person he didn't look at. "You were all reading straight from the notecards, and it's clear you didn't research your topic very well."

He walked around the room and handed each of us a sheet of paper with our grade, which he'd marked while we were presenting. On my page, a large A+ was visible in the top right-hand corner. I looked up Blair, who was sitting in the row in front of me, and I spotted a red D- on her page.

Instant guilt plunged through me, recalling the words I'd had with Mr. Gauthier before the lesson began. I'd been angry before, but now my grade felt completely undeserved. I hadn't meant to *fail* them... I'd just been worried that my own grade might suffer because of them. It was a group project, and we hadn't succeeded in working together as a group... I would have accepted a lower pass.

There was one more presentation after ours, and I noticed the teacher making his way to over to Percy, then Blair, then Victoria, and having quiet words with each of them. He didn't come speak to me, and I watched how Percy's eyes trailed the teacher, fuming. When I was skipped, Percy narrowed his gaze at me, and I felt my stomach turn. I focused my attention back to the current presentation hastily.

Finally, the bell rang, and I got up slowly as everyone else leapt to their feet, eager to head to the next period. Blair looked over at me and said,

"Sorry we failed you, Fleur."

She looked genuine, and I realized they thought I'd suffered the same grade as them. I ducked my head and stuffed my graded paper into my bag, unable to meet her gaze, as Victoria chimed in with her own apology. I awkwardly shuffled out from my desk and trailed behind them as we all left the classroom. My thoughts were focused on getting to English as quickly as possible, but as soon as we were outside, Percy rounded on me and grabbed my arm. He ignored my shocked gasp as he dragged me around the corner and backed me into the column of an arched walkway.

"What the hell is this?" he growled, thrusting his grade against my chest. I grappled with the page and stared down at his failed mark. The gnawing feeling in my gut grew worse. "I saw Mr. Gauthier speak to all of us, *except* you. Did you have something to do with this?"

I swallowed hard, and forced myself to meet his eyes.

"I only stated the truth," I replied carefully. "And I was just expressing my concerns that I might not pass this assignment—"

He let out a huffed breath, stepping away from me as he snatched the paper back and scrunched it up in his hand.

"I *cannot* be failing my classes," he stated finally, speaking so plainly you'd think he was lecturing me. "Everything would have been fine if you'd kept your mouth shut. We *all* would have passed with a simple C+."

I pursed my lips angrily.

"Well, maybe you should have done your share of the work—"

"—you know what your problem is? Why nobody's *kissed* you yet, Fleur?" he interrupted finally, shoulders squared as he stepped forward again. He stood so close I caught a whiff of spice and wood. His voice dropped lower, *taunting,* as he added, "Because you're a goody two shoes, a stickler for the rules—and nobody likes a *snitch.*"

He looked me over one final time, eyes blazing, before storming off. I was left standing there, staring at the ground. Tears blurred in my eyes as my mind raced.

A goody two shoes? Was *that* how people saw me?

I couldn't get the thoughts out of my head as I dragged myself off to my next class, wiping my eyes angrily. The *last* thing I wanted to do in that moment was go to class, but like Percy had said... I was a stickler for rules, and I wasn't about to skip a period and hide out in the bathroom just because I was crying. I couldn't bear the thought of getting in trouble over something so small and insignificant—I was supposed to be stronger than that.

I hate him, I thought as I walked, clenching my fists as I blinked away the last of my tears. I did exactly as he said I'd do— entering my English class and claiming a seat next to my best friend, Darcy. She greeted me vibrantly, but I couldn't bring myself to smile back. Deep down, emotions swirled.

Percy Renaud was a proper, Salvhark vampire hunter. He thought I was a conformist, stick-in-the-mud, Guildwood *wannabe* hunter. I hated him, I hated him, *I hated him*...

But I felt ten times worse when I realized I was actually hating myself—the person I was, and the person I was too afraid to change. I'd always followed the rules because they kept me grounded, and I felt like my world would fall apart again if I ever broke a single one. I'd already lost my entire world once... I couldn't risk it again. Couldn't repay Margot's kindness in taking me in by making trouble for her. I didn't think I'd survive on my own in this world if she turned me away.

The school day dragged on forever, and I was relieved when the final bell rang. I couldn't get out of the school gates fast enough, making a beeline down the cobblestone streets to Margot's cottage home—*my* home. The moment I stepped through the front door, I went straight to my room and came to a stop in front of the mirror on the wall beside my bed. My light brown, almond shaped eyes blinked back at me, framed by two wavy locks of hair that parted my fringe. I observed my full, pink lips, my narrow nose, my olive skin... and grimaced.

When I woke up that morning, I hadn't thought anything of my appearance. I wore my school uniform perfectly—no creases, no tucks, and the skirt wasn't even an inch above my knees. My makeup was light and minimal as per school rules. I'd even stuck cheap, flower earrings in my ears, thinking they looked cute. Now, they seemed cheap and childish.

Tears welled in my eyes, and I couldn't help hating how I looked. I stormed to the wardrobe and began tearing my clothes out of my closet—all the pieces I'd once loved now felt too immature, too girly, too *stupid*—

"*Cherie?* What are you doing?" Margot asked, appearing in the doorway with a shocked expression. She noted the tears and frowned, before crossing the room and wrapping her arms around me. I leaned against her and began ugly crying, and she guided me over to the bed to sit.

"Tell me what's wrong," she insisted, tucking my hair behind my ear, and I blurted out all the feelings that had built up over the course of the day. I didn't want to be some goodie two shoes. I didn't want people to see me that way, to look at me and think *"wow, Fleur's not the kind of girl I'd kiss or hang out with. She's so boring and she ruins all the fun."*

"*Cherie,* rules exist for a reason," Margot reassured me, stroking my hair comfortingly as she held me in her arms. "You're not wrong for abiding them, and I promise you nobody thinks less of you for it. Nobody worth your time, that is."

She pulled back and looked me firmly in the eyes.

"However... I understand wanting to fit in. And you're growing up. Maybe it's time to update your wardrobe, if it will make you feel better. A more mature look, hmm?"

A kind smile appeared on her lips, and she gently wiped my tears away with her thumb.

"There, now—don't worry, we can fix this. I can show you how to do makeup, and how to style your hair. We'll find you some clothes that help your wonderful personality shine. How about it?"

I'd never had anyone to show me how to do those things... and my heart warmed at the thought. After a moment, I nodded, and her gaze softened.

"Well, come on then. By the time we're done, you'll feel like a brand-new person," she promised, with a smile that filled me with excitement. She waved me up off the bed, and instructed me to gather the clothes I didn't want anymore into a bag while she fetched her purse.

I took one last look in the mirror—at the girl Percy thought I was—and in that moment, I vowed to become a better version of me. Someone who would turn heads. Someone who didn't need to snitch on people to get what she wanted. And somebody who wouldn't miss next time she fired an arrow between someone's eyes.

Want to know when BLOOD MAGIC releases?

Follow Pagan at @PaganAlexandriaCreative
on Instagram for updates.